The HOLIDAY HATE-OFF

ANGELA CASELLA

Welcome to
HIDEAWAY HARBOR

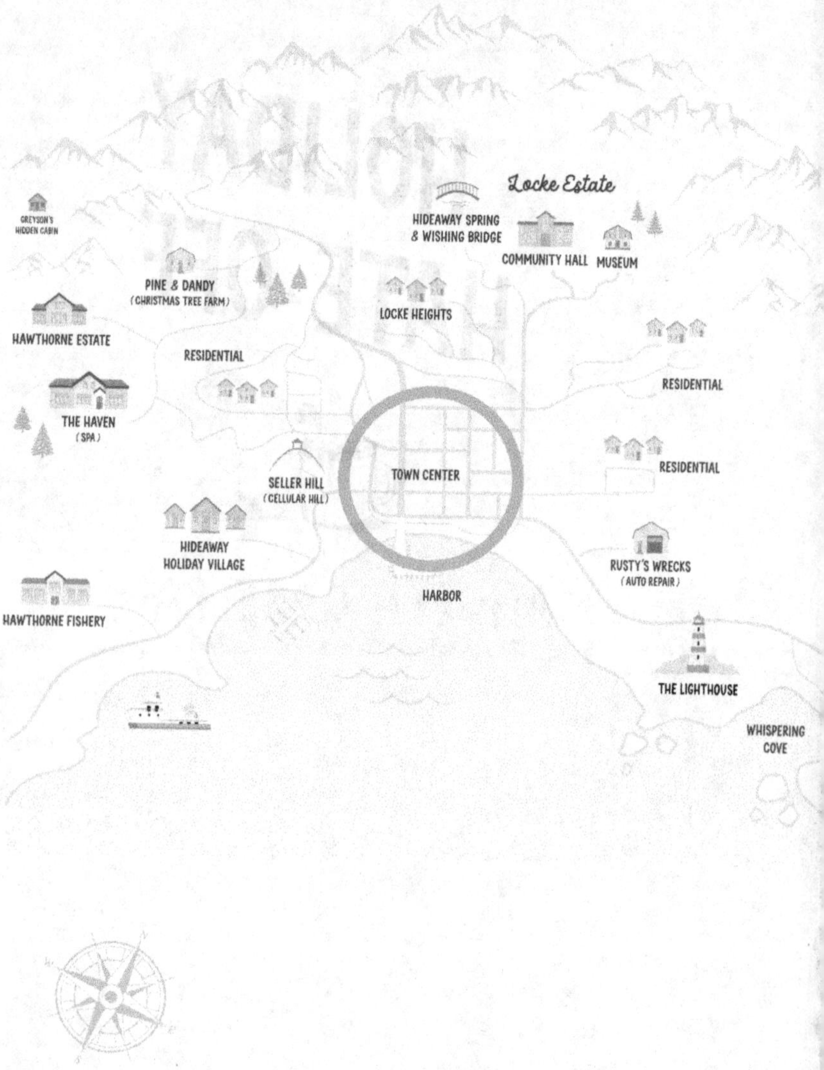

GREYSON'S
HIDDEN CABIN

Locke Estate

HIDEAWAY SPRING
& WISHING BRIDGE

COMMUNITY HALL   MUSEUM

PINE & DANDY
(CHRISTMAS TREE FARM)

LOCKE HEIGHTS

HAWTHORNE ESTATE

RESIDENTIAL

RESIDENTIAL

THE HAVEN
(SPA)

RESIDENTIAL

SELLER HILL
(CELLULAR HILL)

TOWN CENTER

HIDEAWAY
HOLIDAY VILLAGE

RUSTY'S WRECKS
(AUTO REPAIR)

HARBOR

HAWTHORNE FISHERY

THE LIGHTHOUSE

WHISPERING
COVE

The town center

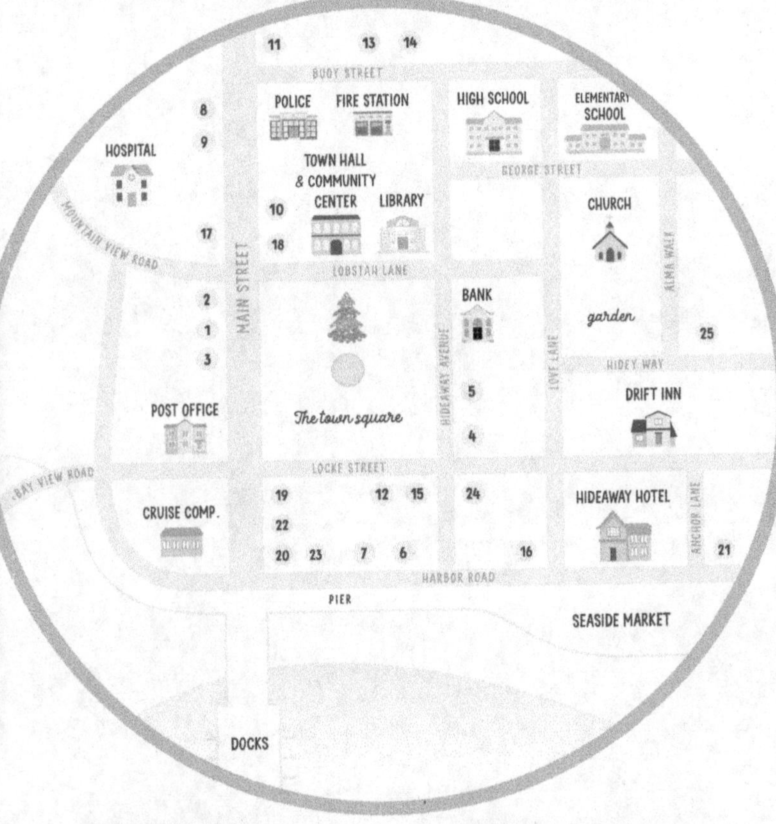

1	LOVE AT FIRST SIP (CAFE)	14	HIDEAWAY CLINIC
2	HIDDEN ITALY (RESTAURANT)	15	HIDEAWAY TREASURES (GIFT SHOP)
3	MAKING WHOOPIE (BAKERY)	16	THE CHOWDER HOUSE RULES (RESTAURANT)
4	HARD TO FIND (BOOKSTORE)	17	ALMANAC (TOWN PAPER)
5	CHRISTMAS WONDERLAND (POP-UP STORE)	18	KIPPIS (SMALL BAR)
6	HOOK, WINE AND SINKER (RESTAURANT)	19	THE SWEETEST THING (CANDY STORE)
7	THE SHORE THING (BAR/RESTAURANT)	20	BEAUTY PARLOR
8	THE PERFECT PACKAGE (ADULT TOY STORE)	21	SALT & EMBER (RESTAURANT)
9	SCENTS AND SENSIBILITY (PERFUME SHOP)	22	HOUSE OF PEARL (CLOTHING BOUTIQUE)
10	THE WILDE KETTLE (TEA SHOP)	23	THE MASTER BAITERS (BAIT & TACKLE SHOP)
11	HIDEAWAY GROCER (GENERAL STORE)	24	HAMMERTIME HARDWARE
12	PAPER MOON (OFFICE SUPPLIES)	25	OFF THE BEATEN PATH (ADVENTURE COMPANY)
13	LOBSTAH LIFTS (GYM)		

ALSO BY ANGELA CASELLA

Babes of Brewing

Best Served Cold

Worst Nanny Ever

Best Kind of Trouble (January 2026)

Worst Faking Idea (Spring/Summer 2026)

Unlucky in Love

The Love Fixers

The Love Bandits

The Love Losers

The Love Destroyers

Spin-off Standalone

The Thief Who Saved Christmas

Finding You

You're so Extra

You're so Bad

You're so Basic

You're so Vain

You're so Phony (coming soon!)

Fairy Godmother Agency

A Borrowed Boyfriend

A Stolen Suit

A Brooding Bodyguard

A Reluctant Roommate

Bringing Down the House (Nicole and Damien's story)

Highland Hills
(co-written with Denise Grover Swank)
Matchmaking a Billionaire
Matchmaking a Single Dad
Matchmaking a Grump
Matchmaking a Roommate
Matchmaking a Player (novella) by Angela Casella

Bad Luck Club
(co-written with Denise Grover Swank)
Love at First Hate
Jingle Bell Hell
Fraudulently Ever After
Matchmaking Mischief

Asheville Brewing
(co-written with Denise Grover Swank)
Any Luck at All
Better Luck Next Time
Getting Lucky
Bad Luck Club
Luck of the Draw (novella)
All the Luck You Need (prequel novella) by Angela Casella

*This one's for my grandmother,
the OG Nonna Francesca.*

*No one told a dirty joke quite as well as my grandmother. No one can
make tomato sauce like her either.*

CHAPTER 1

LUCY

NOVEMBER 26

"I can't *believe* you're getting married," I tell Charlie, smiling so hard my face hurts. Crap. Does she know it's a fake smile? I make it larger, feeling a vein pop in my forehead. My mouth droops slightly, the muscles confused.

"I know!" my friend squeals, pulling me into a hug. Her reddish hair is partially contained by a knit cap, but it brushes against my face with the force of her embrace. "And it's all because of you and Eileen."

Eileen beams at us from the other side of the counter and adds a splash of peppermint schnapps to Charlie's hot chocolate.

It's after closing at Love at First Sip, the coffee shop where my best friend Charlie and I work, run by the delightful Eileen Burrows, a former Hideaway Harbor beauty queen turned coffee shop owner. Her roots in Hideaway run so deep it feels like they span the whole town, down to the harbor. Or possibly the entire state of Maine. Every time I leave the Sip with her, at least a dozen people greet her by name. It's like working for one of the celebrities who like to vacation here. She looks like a celebrity too, with her barely wrinkled skin, which has never been touched by the slightest prick of Botox, her big blue eyes, and her long, perfectly curled white hair, which never seems to suffer the horrors of hat head. She does occasionally wear oversized reading glasses, but somehow she manages to make even those look elegant.

I look longingly at the bottle of schnapps in Eileen's hand, and she winks at me and adds an extra-large splash to my cup. She knows as well as I do that good news can be bittersweet. I'm thrilled for my friend, obviously, but I'm also sad my big adventure with her is ending.

Charlie has lived in Hideaway Harbor for a year and a half, ever since she answered an ad posted by an eccentric rich woman seeking a portrait artist for her cat. Painting animals is Charlie's specialty. The woman offered to pay for her travel expenses from our hometown of Asheville to Hideaway Harbor, along with a rental car and an Airbnb in town. It was exactly the sort of adventure I'd longed to go on myself—and would have if my mother's terminal illness weren't so far advanced at that point—so I'd urged Charlie to go. She'd fallen in love with Hideaway Harbor, and after her host introduced her to Eileen, she'd decided to stay. The part-time hours at the coffee shop fit perfectly with her commissioned work as an artist.

Then my mother died last fall. The house filled with an echoing emptiness that broke my heart again every morning. I was desperate to escape it. So I visited Charlie in Hideaway Harbor this past spring, on an unseasonably hot weekend, when everyone was walking around in shorts and summer dresses. We spent the day on the water, ate takeout with sand still in our toes, and then got cheap red mani-pedis while speculating about the wellness treatments offered at The Haven, Hideaway's fancy spa we couldn't afford.

It was the perfect visit, idyllic. So when she'd begged me to move here so we could live together again, just like we'd been able to do for that ever-too-brief semester my freshman year of college, it had felt like *fate*. Especially since Eileen had offered to hire me part time too—and said it would be "no problem at all" to mold my schedule around some online continuing education classes I was taking.

Eileen herself is an inspiration. Despite having lost Murray, her husband of thirty-two years, two years ago, she's in love with love and sees it everywhere. She can always look up at the sky and point out the one cloud that looks like a heart. Every drink at the café is named after a famous poet or romantic hero in literature. We have the Heathcliff, the Romeo, the Byron, and the Fabio—because he'd been on the covers of half of her favorite books for the better part of a decade—among others. Every latte and cup of tea comes with a heart-shaped macaron.

Even though I've never been in love with a man, I adore the idea of finding home in another person, and I fell in love with the café. I wanted to move to Hideaway and spend my days surrounded by the café's pink mugs, high-pile rugs, and expansive view of the quaint downtown area.

It felt like a world of possibility was waiting for me in Hideaway Harbor.

At the end of my perfect vacation, Charlie squeezed my hand and said, "Please come. We'll do all of it together, Lucy. All of the things left in your magic ball."

The "magic ball" was a gift from my mother—a spherical, mosaic glass container with a wooden lid. Before the last stretch of her illness, she'd secretly filled it with…prompts, I guess you'd call them. Her attorney had given the colorful container to me after she passed away.

The prompts were simple but beautiful in their simplicity.

> Bite into a ripe strawberry and think of that time we went strawberry picking and that man with the mullet tried to juggle with them.

> Take a walk along the water and listen to the sound it makes.

> Go to a psychic with a friend. I've always wanted to do that, but I wasn't brave enough.

She'd left me a prompt for each day after she died, for a full year, to help get me through my grief. True to her word, Charlie had completed many of the prompts with me, even after moving in with her fiancé Lars last month, but I'd decided to do the last one alone. Just Mom and me.

I pulled the final paper last night:

> Listen to your favorite song and dance like no one's watching.

I did just as it said, blasting my favorite song on Spotify, and I wept, which is probably the first time anyone's ever sobbed to Britney Spears' "Toxic." I figure it's definitely the first time anyone did it while dancing around a Christmas tree.

Eileen pushes the hot chocolate across the counter to me, pulling me out of the memory. "Drink it up, dear. You've earned it."

After I take it from her, she emerges from behind the

counter and wraps her arms around Charlie, who sets her hot chocolate down and hugs her back. I know from experience that Eileen's hugs are warm and smell like chocolate and cinnamon.

"If you hadn't set me up with Lars, this never would have happened," my friend says, beaming.

A sigh seeps out of me, escaping past the too-large smile. We *did* set them up. In fact, it happened on that warm, sun-filled spring trip, when love had seemed as obtainable as the popsicles sold by the beach. He'd come into the café, Charlie had taken notice of him, and we'd all but pushed her at him.

I'm happy for both of them—Lars is lovely and sweet and looks like a lost Skarsgård brother—but I have to admit I'm a little sad for myself. Because I've never experienced love for myself. Only through other people and in my books. I'm hungry for it. For *life*.

I've never had a pet, even though I long for one.

I've never gone to Europe, something else I long for.

And, up until last month, I'd never lived alone.

"Drink up," Eileen says, pointing to my cup, and I realize she and Charlie have stopped their happy dance and my friend is watching me with concern.

I take a sip and try to fix my wavering smile, probably overcorrecting. "So, are you going to wait until after Christmas to do the engagement party? Can we have it here? Or maybe—"

"Your smile is scaring me," Charlie says.

"It's scaring me a bit too," I say with a sigh, taking a bigger sip of the hot chocolate. "Have you told your mother?"

Charlie's not close to her parents, both of whom are stern corporate types who aren't pleased their only child is a bohemian artist whose environmentalist boyfriend makes a living following birds around.

"Yes, and she's *thrilled*," Charlie jokes with sparkling eyes.

"Come, sit." Eileen gestures to the pink armchairs assembled in the corner of the room by the front window.

A visiting businessman once fell asleep in one of those armchairs. Of course, Eileen being Eileen, she'd sent over a single local woman to wake him up, hoping it might be their meet-cute. It might have worked if he hadn't jolted and accidentally spilled the cold coffee he was still holding all over her blouse.

We lower into the chairs, and Charlie sets her hot chocolate on the coffee table and takes my hand.

"Sorry," I mutter. "It's just, I pulled the last prompt from the magic ball last night. It's hard to believe it's over."

Her eyes widen and she swears. "It was last night? Oh shit. I'm such a selfish bi—"

"No," I say, squeezing her hand. "You're happy. You should be happy! You and Lars are getting married, and you're going to have lots of enormous children together, and probably way too many pets for two people to take care of."

Eileen chuckles.

"Very funny," Charlie says, pulling off her cap. A few hairs dance above her head, static-charged. "And what an obvious deflection. I should have been there, Lucy. We should have done it together. What was this one?"

"Dancing to Britney Spears. It was cathartic until I realized the blinds were open and someone was watching me from the street."

"Was it a man?" Eileen asks excitedly.

"Oh, here it comes," I groan. "You've got one of your assistants engaged, and you've already moved on to the next."

"As if you weren't always on her matchmaking docket," Charlie says. "She's got half a dozen schemes running. You've seen her list."

I have. Eileen keeps a Google doc of the town's single people and is constantly trying to match them up. I know several of the people on her list, of course, and most of them aren't aware they're on there. I know for a fact that Audrey, the fantastically talented chef/owner of Making Whoopie, the bakery just next door to us, has no idea that Eileen has an ebbing and flowing list of candidates for her.

"Charlie's right," Eileen confirms. "But you're my number one priority this Christmas. I already have a short list of candidates for you, which is shorter now that Charlie crossed off two of them."

"You'll thank me later," she says with a grimace. "They were serious duds. One of them is that guy who's so terrified of Skippy he leapt into traffic and got hit by a car going five miles an hour."

Skippy is the town dog, a sweet Saint Bernard who has as many owners as there are people in Hideaway Harbor. He sleeps wherever he wants but never lacks for a warm bed.

Eileen grimaces. "Yes, I'd forgotten about that." Glancing at me, she says, "I'd love to see you with one of those Hawthorne brothers. There's a fortune on the line with that massive fishery of theirs, you know."

I make a face. "I get seasick."

"Or one of the handsome Cafiero boys next door." Her face lights up with the idea, but then she purses her lips. "It's too bad Francesca is still cross with us."

"That's one way of putting it," I murmur.

The Cafieros run Hidden Italy, the Italian delicatessen, catering service, and gourmet grocery next door, accessible only by a curving stone stairway leading down to the Hellmouth...or so Charlie and I like to joke. The two of us went there for lunch three times the week of my spring visit—there is no better eggplant parmesan sub in the continental United States—but our love affair with it was short-lived. We've been...well...banned.

There are a couple of reasons behind our ban. For one,

Francesca's granddaughter, Aria Cafiero, dated Lars before Charlie "got her claws into him," and even though Aria has moved on, her grandmother holds a grudge. Especially since Aria accepted a job at a resort in Greece and now lives halfway around the world.

But I have to be totally honest: I'm the main reason we were banned.

On my first week at Love at First Sip, a gorgeous blonde woman ran into the café sobbing. I was alone. Eileen was on a store run to pick up more oat milk, and no one else had come in, so I flipped the sign to CLOSED, made the woman a Byron, and sat down across from her. She told me all about her problems with her boyfriend Lorenzo, who constantly prioritized work and family over her. I patted her hand and assured her that she had every right to feel important in her own relationship.

Turns out she'd been talking about Enzo Cafiero, the Cafiero golden child and eldest son.

Apparently Enzo moved to New York City years ago to work as some kind of consultant. But that particular weekend, right after I'd moved here, he and his girlfriend were visiting his family here in town. According to her, he'd ignored her the whole time. He sounded like a total jerk and a terrible boyfriend, and I let her know it.

Within an hour of her conversation with me in the café, she'd dumped him and reserved a weekend spot at The Haven.

I know this because Enzo stormed in with a red face later that day and asked who'd given his girlfriend such stupid advice. I knew it was him because of the leading question, and also because he looked a lot like his two younger brothers—tall and broad with olive-toned skin, black hair, and thick, arching eyebrows over dark eyes surrounded by long lashes. Charlie describes the Cafiero eyes as brooding. Brooding eyes are her favorite to paint, even on the dogs she does portraits for.

It was not as fun to stare into a pair of brooding eyes on a six-foot-one man, especially one with a frown that instantly made me feel smaller. He was gorgeous, he obviously knew it, and he was even more intimidating because of it.

I gulped in air, choked on it, and then raised a hand like a middle schooler who knew they had the wrong answer.

He gave me a withering look and asked, "Do you know who I am?"

"No," I lied, because anyone who asks that question should be given exactly that answer.

"I'm Lorenzo Cafiero."

I didn't give him the reaction he was obviously searching for; I just tilted my head slightly.

"I'm the man you screwed over. What qualifies you to give relationship advice to a stranger? You're what, twenty-one, twenty-two?"

Honestly. I'm perfectly capable of being confrontational when the situation calls for it—I had to stand up to medical professionals while taking care of my mother—and I wasn't about to take BS from some gorgeous alpha jerk.

"I'm twenty-eight," I told him, standing up straighter.

"And you still haven't answered my first question."

"Seriously?" I said, exasperated. "Fine. Nothing qualifies me. But I'm not the one who made your ex cry, or the one who broke up with you. And the fact that you're here complaining and not kneeling at her feet says a lot."

He stared me down for a solid twenty seconds. And I stared back, full of anger but frozen in place, like I'd been turned into a mannequin. Then he shook his head, swore in Italian, and said, "I don't kneel at anyone's feet."

The way he'd said it unnerved me, but I found myself replying, "Then we both know why she wasn't satisfied."

It was a dumb thing for me to say, considering how little experience I've had with real-life dating, but I've read hundreds of books, maybe thousands. I know what men do to satisfy their women, even if I've mostly been left cold.

Someone in the café started giggling, but Enzo darted a furious glance at them, and they stopped immediately. He shifted his gaze back to me. "I *never* leave a woman unsatisfied."

The intensity of his tone, paired with that dark glower, was very...intimidating. It made my knees feel like jelly. But I stood tall and lifted my chin, saying, "Then I guess it must have been your sparkling personality she found lacking."

Enzo glared at me for a moment, his jaw clenched. Then he just stormed off...

The next day the Cafieros posted a flyer announcing our banishment from their deli, right where we were sure to see it, on the door by the stairs leading down to Hidden Italy. Not just a written notice either, but a flyer with actual photos of me, Charlie, and Eileen—stolen from our Facebook accounts— with big Xs printed over our faces.

People came in and asked us about it all day long, and each time, it generated a fresh wave of embarrassment. Especially since the whole town of Hideaway Harbor is always playing a game of telephone, where stories become embellished with each telling until they only slightly resemble what actually happened.

For a whole week, that flyer stayed up. Until finally a torrential rainstorm took care of it. I suppose it could've been one of the other Cafiero boys who actually took it down. They're big and handsome like Enzo, but they aren't outwardly hostile. Then again, they did allow their family's anti-us flyer to stay up for a whole week.

That was nearly four months ago, but even now, Eileen's offhand comment about Francesca Cafiero still being "cross" with us brings all the humiliation rushing back. Until those damn Cafieros, I'd never been banned from anywhere.

"The Cafieros are all jerks," I say, feeling my cheeks heat with remembered embarrassment. "Hot jerks, but still jerks."

"Well, I'm not so sure about that," Eileen says. "Though I haven't forgotten that Enzo *did* behave abominably toward you that day."

"Exactly. He's not at all the kind of man I'd want to be set up with. So let's move on. Mom said I need a man with a soft heart." In addition to the magic ball, my mom also left me a heartfelt letter I've read at least a hundred times. In it, she wrote that she was sorry she wouldn't be able to make it to my wedding and listed all the qualities she thought I should look for in a man.

Charlie grins and waggles her eyebrows. "Softhearted, maybe, but not soft—"

"Very funny," I say. "But yes, obviously." I pause. "Look, you know how much I want a family. I'm not resistant to trying this matchmaking thing, but I don't know how to date anymore. I'm totally out of practice."

I dated a normal amount in high school and in my one semester of college, but for the last eight years, I focused on taking care of my mom. I finished my undergrad math degree online and got a tutoring job that allowed me the flexibility I needed. I still went on dates—Mom insisted on it—but it turns out telling twenty-something guys you're a caretaker for your dying mom is a buzzkill.

I told Charlie as much back then, but she refused to see my situation as hopeless. Her solution? I should try being someone else for a night. A stunt pilot. An actress on the lam from Hollywood. Anything I wanted…

But I wanted to find a man who wanted *me*, and none of them did. I was too stubborn to pretend to be someone else for their benefit.

Now, I have no reason to lie about what I'm doing. I'm working here at the café and taking some programming classes to help me develop an idea I have for an app. But I've only gone out with four men since moving here, and they were *very* unremarkable.

One of the guys clearly only wanted to talk about himself, and he wasn't interesting enough for me to tolerate it.

Another ordered dinner for me while I was in the restroom. He'd chosen poorly.

The other two had immediately disqualified themselves for future dates with their reaction to learning about my virginity on Date Number Three. But while it's proven to be an effective litmus test for men, I've kept my virginity a secret from Eileen and even Charlie. I know they'd offer advice, and it would be excruciatingly embarrassing.

"You don't have to be a rocket scientist to go on dates," Charlie says, rolling her eyes. "There's no manual."

"Actually, there are a million manuals about dating, and they all offer conflicting advice. That's the problem. If there were only one manual, it would be easier to navigate."

Eileen taps her lips. "What if you could practice dating with very low stakes?"

"Like by dating the two dudes I crossed off your list?" Charlie asks, laughing. "Those *would* be low stakes."

"No," she says slowly. "What if we have an event at the café? Santa Speed Dating."

My jaw drops. "Like...all of the men will be dressed up like Santa?" My mind conjures a roomful of Santas drinking hot chocolate from pink mugs, their fake white beards stained with it, and laughter tries to spill out.

"Actually, that's not a bad idea," Charlie says with a grin. "Would you be less nervous if the guys are in costume?"

I consider this. "Maybe. I've never had a daddy kink. Will I have to wear a costume?"

"Only Christmas colors, dear," Eileen says. "Let's make the men work for it. Oh, this *is* an idea. I'll have to get it added to the town calendar. We can do it on the day we host the Advent calendar. We're December second this year." Her mouth flattens slightly, the closest to a disapproving frown it gets. "Hidden Italy has the first."

"They didn't even put up any twinkle lights last year," Charlie says, full of indignant rage.

"That's because they live in the Hellmouth," I joke.

"Well, they do have something planned this year," Eileen says, "and I'm truly happy for them. They've had some business troubles lately, something to do with the accounts. So they could stand to have a little holiday magic in their lives. Still, I'll confess I was a little miffed we didn't get the first day."

The Advent calendar is a Hideaway Harbor tradition. Each day in December, the calendar is carted to a different Hideaway location, which hosts the unveiling of the day's number in the countdown to Christmas. The business that hosts the big reveal usually holds some big event in honor of it. The bigger the event, the better the publicity. Sometimes local celebrities reveal the countdown number. Other times it's someone dressed up like Larry the Lobstah, the town's mascot, or one of Santa's elves. On one memorable occasion, one of the owners of Hook, Wine, and Sinker dressed up as the clown from *It*. Or so Eileen told me. This will be my first Hideaway Harbor Christmas.

It's a big deal here, I'm told. Which is a relief, because I've decided to reclaim Christmas.

Last Christmas was awful, the first without my mom, but I'm determined this one will be full of holiday magic.

Eyes gleaming, Eileen adds, "Perhaps we'll make a signature drink for it too. I've been experimenting with crème brûlée lattes."

"And a signature sweet," Charlie says, getting into the spirit of the thing. "What if it's a gelatin dessert called the bowlful of jelly?"

I laugh, but there's an uneasy edge to it. The truth is, I'd rather work at holiday speed dating event than participate in it. An hour of five-minute dates with men dressed in Santa suits sounds stressful.

Maybe they're right, though: if I practice with softballs, I might someday be able to play baseball.

"That wouldn't give us much time to prepare," I point out. "It's already November twenty-sixth."

"Oh, what's to prepare?" Charlie says offhandedly. "All we need to do is buy some discount Santa suits in bulk, and we're good to go. You know, I bet the tourists will actually love this."

"It could become a yearly tradition," Eileen says brightly. "But why stop there? Why limit our attempts to find Lucy a man?"

"Why indeed?" Charlie says with a snort. "Why ever stop anywhere?"

Eileen turns to me. "I'll have an event every night in December if it helps us find you a fine young man. We're going to get this sorted before a jolly *old* man makes his way down the chimneys of every house in Hideaway Harbor."

"That sounds way more disturbing than I think you intended it to," Charlie says with a grin.

"Oh, it was intended." She smiles at us both. "I love you girls. My purpose is to see all of you beautiful young people happily settled."

Charlie seems to agree with Eileen's declaration, offering her a reassuring pat on the hand. Then she turns to me with a hopeful expression. "I have to get going for now, but I'm in complete agreement with Eileen. I want you to fall madly in love, get engaged, and then we're going to have a joint wedding. It's written in the stars."

"Only if we exclusively play Britney Spears at the reception."

"Yes, Lars will be totally on board with that." Charlie blows us kisses, then carries her hot chocolate mug to the sink and rinses it before leaving, letting in a waft of freezing air.

Eileen gives me a tender look over the rim of her mug. "It's going to be okay, Lucy."

"I know," I say thickly, but we both know I don't mean it.

She takes my hand and squeezes. "I hope you don't think I overstepped, but I made an Advent calendar for you." She wrings her hands together. "Each day offers a different suggestion for how you can enjoy the season. I thought you might miss having—"

Before she can get all the words out, I'm already hugging her, feeling the press of tears behind my eyes. Oh, dear, sweet Eileen. Here she goes again, giving people what they didn't know they needed. "Thank you. *Thank you.*"

CHAPTER 2

ENZO

DECEMBER 1

$\mathcal{I}$'d promised myself I'd never have anything to do with Hidden Italy. It was my grandfather's business and then my dad's (in name), but anyone who knows my family knows the truth—Nonna Francesca has always run the show. She still does, at eighty-three, long after Dad retired to Charleston, but as she always says, eighty-three is different for a Sicilian woman. *It's only made me tougher, caro, like a piece of dry salume.*

"I don't want to be here," I complain over the phone to my sister, Aria, as I straighten my tie in Aria's mirror. I'm using the landline because Hideaway Harbor is so remote, so inconvenient, that most cell phone conversations tend to be cut short by bad service.

I'm staying in Aria's old apartment because when she left town she still had five months on her lease. Her landlord was a real dick about it, so I offered to take over the lease and stay here during my visits to Hideaway Harbor. At the time, I didn't expect to end up living here, but no one with even half an ego ever expects their world to implode.

But here I am in Hideaway Harbor, where it's five and has been dark for almost an hour, and Aria's halfway across the world, up past midnight, because that's what twenty-five-year-olds do when they're living the good life.

I've been here a week, and it already feels like too long.

"I know you don't want to be there," Aria says softly.

My sister is the only one in the family I'd ever admit that to. My brothers, Nico and Giovanni, would never leave this town. It's in their blood. They constantly bitch about Dad's choice to spend most of his retirement in a fishing boat off the coast of South Carolina, not that Dad had bothered much with the deli or any family matters even when he was here.

All of the Cafiero kids worked at Hidden Italy as teenagers, either the catering business or the store, and my brothers still do. Nico makes the food and Giovanni manages the stocking and the kids and seasonal employees who man the register. Nonna oversees the entire operation and keeps the books. Which is what's caused this colossal fucking problem.

When I told my brothers they shouldn't have been allowing an eighty-three-year-old woman to be in charge of the math, they'd acted shocked.

She's always done the books, Nico had said.

Yes, but she used to be able to see.

She's got glasses.

And doesn't wear them, whether out of vanity or pure stubbornness I couldn't say. It doesn't help that she's still using a real paper book to do the accounting. One that looks as old as she is, although I know better than to say so.

The result? Hidden Italy is in the hole, and someone has to pull it out.

Hello, I'm Enzo Cafiero, and I'm "someone."

It was my idea to petition for the first day of the Advent

calendar unveiling to be held at Hidden Italy. Someone had to. Nonna would never have appealed to the mayor for a favor, no matter how badly the family business might need it. The woman can hold grudges for decades, and she'd held one against Mayor Locke for ages, having famously declared the man was dead to her after he said Nico had made him a dry sandwich.

It *was* dry. Nico had been nursing the hangover from hell, and he'd forgotten to use the oil and vinegar. Nonna knows this. But never let the truth get in the way of making a point when a Cafiero is involved.

I was not about to let Nonna's pettiness get in the way of fixing things. So I took the mayor out for lunch at Hideaway Café well over a month ago, back when I still had my own life in New York City, and insisted that he wouldn't regret it if he advocated for scheduling Hidden Italy for the advent calendar's first day this year.

"But you never decorate for the holiday," he objected. There was mayo streaked across his face, but I wasn't about to tell him and risk the possibility of inflaming old grudges about condiments.

"We will this year," I promised. "And my best friend is willing to be the guest of honor. You saw Will's book hit the bestseller list, right?"

I was stretching, and I knew it. Sure, my high school buddy Will was a bestselling author now, but he'd written a book about finance that was so boring I'd only managed to skim it. He probably wouldn't appreciate me offering his services, but desperate times…

"No. No need for Will to make the trip on a weekday. I want your grandmother to be the one who unveils the number," Mayor Locke insisted stubbornly, pushing his plate away. And I knew this was his revenge for the dry sandwich.

He wanted to be the man who made Francesca Cafiero

swallow her pride and act grateful to the man who'd dared question her family.

I made him that impossible promise, because I was supposed to be the man who made miracles happen. The man who'd taken a company that had been in the red and given them their best year ever.

If I could do it for a huge, multinational corporation, I could surely do it for an old mom-and-pop shop like Hidden Italy. Even if I privately thought we'd be better off if we just gave it up.

But that was probably the one thing that would put Nonna in her grave, and no one wanted to be the Cafiero responsible for that.

"Of course you don't want to be there, dipshit," Aria says with her usual grace. "But you just lost your job, and the family needs help, so you got to swoop in like Superman."

"I didn't lose it," I say, scowling at my reflection. "I decided to step away. It was getting stale."

"And there's definitely nothing else to that story," she says wryly. "But you'd obviously like to change the subject, so I'll play along. Nico showed me the decorations at the shop. They're classy. You do it yourself?"

"What do you take me for?"

"A person capable of stringing lights?"

I laugh, rearranging my collar so it's perfectly centered. "I paid a couple of high school kids. Look at me supporting the locals. But I did get Nico to make panettone."

Everyone in the family knows panettone is Nico's nemesis. It all tastes the same to me, which is why I was never the chef in the family, but he's never happy with his efforts.

"Already making waves. Enzo to the rescue."

"Giovanni's into it too. He made us all wear suits."

"You sure it was Giovanni and not you?"

"I know, I'm proud of him too. We look like Frankie Valli

and the Four Seasons. We're going to sing a Christmas carol while Nonna tears off the number."

She snorts. "Does Nico have a suit?"

"He does now," I say, smiling at the memory of suit shopping with my brother, who only owned a single button-up shirt.

"I wish I were there to see that," she says with a sigh. "What else are you guys planning?"

"Samples from the deli and the good stuff we import." I roll my eyes at my reflection. "Lots of samples of that damn Italian sub, because Nonna's determined to prove, once and for all, that it's not dry."

"She does enjoy making a point," my sister muses. "But she's not wrong to want to prove we can make a good Italian sub. What kind of Italian deli can't make an Italian sub? It's a bad look. How about entertainment?"

"Didn't I say we'd be singing?"

"Yeah, but you know how it goes. Everyone likes to pull out all the stops for these things."

"We make and sell food," I point out. "Tonight we're giving it away. I offered to have Will come up, but the mayor didn't seem interested. Though I have to be honest: when Will starts talking about finance law, my eyes cross, and I *like* finance law."

"Oh God," Aria says in disgust. "Will was your big idea? I'm with the mayor on that one. Couldn't you do a Secret Santa thing or hire someone to dance to the Nutcracker or something?"

"Those would have been useful suggestions a few days ago."

She laughs. "Fine. Don't worry. It's going to be awesome. Lots of single ladies who come in to ogle you and eat Nico's food. Take photos. That goes for the whole holiday season. Especially of the lobster trap tree. That's my favorite."

It's a Hideaway Harbor tradition—an enormous tree made entirely of lobster traps with a glowing lobster at the top. Every year they make a big show of having one of the antique Hawthorne Fisheries boats ferry a costumed Larry the Lobstah to light the hideous tree, with plenty of pomp and circumstance and as little production value as an elementary school play. But you've got to keep the tourists, and my little sister, happy.

"Ooh, and definitely get photos of Amanda Willis if you can," she says, referring to the movie star who oversaw the tree-lighting in town square last weekend.

"I'm sure that's exactly why she came here. Because she wants us hiding behind telephone poles to snap photos of her."

"She probably wouldn't mind. She seems really nice. I've heard she's going to be around for a while."

"You're not coming home for Christmas?" I ask, turning from the mirror. The tie is straight enough.

"No," she says with a snort. "Lars just got engaged, and I don't need to hear Nonna flipping out every five minutes about my biological clock and her need for great-grandchildren. As if I don't have three older brothers who are perfectly capable of impregnating women."

"Should I go around offering that tonight?" I ask. "Would you like a sample of the lobster ravioli, or maybe some semen? It would definitely be a new spin on holiday entertaining."

She snort-laughs, and I feel a pang of missing her.

The last time I saw her, she'd been crying inconsolably over that blond asshole Lars. What she'd seen in a guy who spent his whole life chasing after birds, I'll never know. What I *do* know is that he wasn't good enough for my sister. Then again, no man could be.

I'd told her so once before, and she'd asked, *What about a girlfriend? Would you do the whole pompous, chest-beating thing if I had a girlfriend?*

I'd considered her question for a second before shrugging and admitting I probably wouldn't. She'd retorted that I was a chauvinist grandma's boy, I'd agreed, and we'd both had a laugh.

God, I miss laughing with her.

It was that asshole's fault she left, even if he hadn't accepted the job in Greece for her or driven her to the airport.

No, I was the one who'd brought her there.

Four months ago, Rachelle and I had come to Hideaway for a weekend visit with my family. She'd made plenty of "quaint" plans, but I'd put them on hold so I could help my sister with her spontaneous move to Greece. I'd helped her pack, then driven her to the airport. Rachelle had elected not to come. Apparently, she'd pitched a fit about what a terrible boyfriend I was as soon as the car disappeared from view, first to Nonna, who'd been less than sympathetic, and then to a stranger in the café next door.

I still don't know exactly what the barista said to her, but when I came back, Rachelle was already packing her bags for a weekend at The Haven spa. She acted like the death of our relationship was old news. The only thing she wanted to talk about was the spa's wellness treatments, and did I think her skin looked "old"?

Naturally, I had questions about what the fuck had happened in the couple of hours I'd been gone. So I went over to Love at First Sip—*stomped*, I can hear my sister saying—and asked.

The woman behind the front counter had looked so innocent I could hardly believe she was the one who'd screwed me over. She had one of those faces that made me think of the ceiling frescoes in Rome—long curly hair and sweet rounded cheeks.

A new soul, my grandmother would probably have said. Then again, my grandmother can be superstitious and has strange beliefs ingrained so deeply into her personality it would be impossible to change or update them.

But this girl didn't talk like an innocent. I can still hear her telling me that if I didn't like getting down on my knees, I couldn't possibly have satisfied Rachelle.

The absolute nerve.

Also completely untrue. Rachelle's problem with me was that I'd prioritized my sister over her, which I was totally unwilling to apologize for. Family is everything to me. Rachelle's inability to accept that meant we would never have worked out long term.

"Enzo?" my sister says. "Earth to Enzo. Are you still there?"

"Yeah," I say, leaving the bedroom. "The event doesn't start for a couple of hours, but I'm going to head over to the shop to remind Nonna to get along with everyone. Don't be surprised if you never hear from me again."

She laughs. "The worst that'll happen to you is a swat from a wooden spoon. That woman worships the ground you boys walk on. Always has."

"She feels the same way about you," I tell her. "She banned three people from the deli on your behalf."

She makes a sound of disbelief. "It was all because of you and that awful woman you were dating."

"Is this where you tell me no one's good enough for me?"

"Oh, there are plenty of women who are good enough for you. You just have awful taste. But I love you anyway. I'll drink some ouzo in your honor."

Greek ouzo isn't the same as the Italian stuff, but I don't say so.

I also don't tell her that I haven't dated at all since Rachelle and I broke up four months ago. After our break up, I went back to New York City, and I barely had any downtime before I stepped right into another crisis, this one at work. The situation was more complicated than I'd let on, but I had, technically, quit my consulting job. By then, I already knew things weren't going so hot in Hideaway Harbor. So I did what any good grandson would.

I came home to help fix them.

When you're going through back-to-back crises, getting laid is the last thing on your mind. But the dominoes have all stopped falling—I'm not going to look for a new job until Hidden Italy starts turning a healthy profit—which means I've started noticing my months-long dry spell. It's gotten bad enough that a *Victoria's Secret* catalogue can make my blood heat.

I know better than to screw around in my home town, though. I've made that mistake before. Won't be doing it again.

"You do that. *Saluti.*"

"Down the hatch," Aria replies, and I can tell she's smiling. "Don't be too much of a grinch."

I make no promises as I end the call and then put on my outdoor things.

Here goes nothing.

I step out of the apartment, lock the door, and then glance down the hall at the door of the unit with the street-facing window. I know a woman lives there—the other night I was walking home and looked up from the street and saw her silhouette dancing. Her apartment was dark other than the glow of a Christmas tree, so I'd only seen her shadow, pirouetting gracefully and without any self-consciousness.

Until she looked down and spotted me on the street. She'd shut her curtains like I was some pervert, which had made me feel like one. But that wasn't why I'd been watching her.

It was one of those stolen moments when you get a glimpse into a stranger's life—not the polished version they show the world, but them, through and through.

I'm curious about her now.

I'd like to know why she was dancing at midnight, her body gliding in concentric circles.

Acting on impulse, I head back into the apartment and scrawl a quick note into a blank notecard. I fold it and then prop it against her door on my way out.

It's cold as a witch's tit tonight, colder than it should be for early December, but instead of heading straight to Hidden Italy, I make my way to the stone bridge spanning the spring that supplies the town with water. It's the famous Wishing Bridge. Locals, known as Hidies, and tourists have been coming here for years to whisper their wishes and express their love for their significant other or a secret crush by attaching a lock to one of the detachable metal spokes supporting the railing. They're always covered with them, practically from top to bottom, even though the town removes them regularly.

It's a place for desperate people, and I feel stupid as soon as I get there. I'm not a man who believes in wishes. Action is the only thing that matters.

But this place reminds me of the innocence of childhood. Of when I was young enough to think a jolly old man in a fancy red suit, trespassing, could solve my problems—or that a wish, made on a bridge, could change a life.

I'm not that person anymore. Still, I'm here, so I stand at the edge, looking down at the water—freezing my ass off, if I'm being truthful—and say, "I want a miracle."

Then, louder, "I can make a miracle happen."

Because I'm Enzo Cafiero, damn it. The man who makes miracles happen. I may have been humbled professionally, but my name still has to mean something. I need it to.

"Someone's watching us," I hear a voice hiss in an undertone nearby. "Put on your pants."

I sigh, remembering this is also a make-out spot—and

sometimes a public sex spot. I came here often enough when I was younger and looking for a place I could get some action without getting caught.

I turn to leave, and nearly collide with a woman.

It takes me only three seconds to register *which* woman. It's the barista from Love at First Sip. The woman who took a hammer to my relationship and then questioned my virility in front of my neighbors.

She's in a thick coat, mittens, and boots, but there's nothing concealing her hair. It's long and curly and lush, surrounding her face and covering her shoulders. Her hair's what makes her look like one of Michaelangelo's or Raphael's angels. From the dim glow of the lights at either end of the bridge, I can see her eyes are a deep mossy green, a color that makes me think of being lost in the woods.

For a second, I'm speechless. Was she this beautiful four months ago? Surely I would have noticed. A man notices when a fist pounds him in the face, and that's what her beauty is, a fist to the face, or maybe the gut.

Then again, the low lighting does something for her, along with the setting of the stone bridge. She looks unreal. As if she's a Christmas angel sent in response to my wish…

The thought instantly pisses me off, because I should know better. Nobody cares about mortal wishes, neither the ones we keep silent, nor the ones we shout to the skies. And the only person who can solve my family's problems is me. It's always been that way, from the day my mother left. Or maybe the day we realized she was never coming back.

The woman gives me a baffled look. "What are you doing here?"

The way she says it makes me bristle. The magic of the bridge fades away, and I'm so angry at myself for having momentarily believed in it that I snap. "This is my hometown. What are *you* doing here?"

There's a hurt look on her face, and for a moment I feel guilty, until her features harden and she says, "You willingly left. I moved to Hideaway Harbor because I love it."

"Do you also enjoy watching strangers have sex?"

Her eyes widen and she steps back, nearly colliding with the stone railing of the Wishing Bridge. It's too low, and if she's not careful, she could careen right off it.

Alarm sets my heart hammering within my ribs, and I grab her hand to pull her away from it. She bounces against me, her body molded to mine for half a second—long enough for me to smell her hair. Spicy and sweet, like one of those candles my sister left all around the apartment. I breathe it in deeply, the cold air stinging my nose.

The woman jerks away from me, her eyes ablaze.

"You nearly fell," I say quickly.

"I did no such thing." She crosses her arms over her chest. "Are you some kind of..." Her gaze darts around before she whispers, "*pervert?*"

For a second, I'm rendered speechless, both by the question and the way it was delivered. Then the injustice of the accusation registers. "First I don't know how to please a woman, and now I'm a pervert? I can't keep up."

"The two things aren't mutually exclusive."

I wave toward the edge of the bridge. "There's a couple down there having some fun. I was trying to save you from a peep show. Then again, maybe that's why *you're* here. You and your boss obviously get off on messing with people's love lives."

It's not a fair thing to say, but I wasn't raised to fight fair. I was raised to win.

From the way she's looking at me, though, she doesn't see me as a winner, just as an asshole. Then her eyes focus on something behind me. I glance back to see a couple of twenty-somethings, now fully clothed, creeping up the other side of the bank, almost level with the bridge. The man's smoking a cigarette.

She sneezes as the smoke reaches us and then starts coughing. She wheezes out "allergic" before asking in an undertone, "They were really doing *that*?" There's a hint of innocence in her response, which makes me feel a softness toward her I stifle.

"I tried to warn you," I say. "It's a known hookup spot."

She arches her brow. "So what are *you* doing here? As a Hidie, you should have known."

I shrug. I'd prefer for her to write me off as a pervert than to guess the truth—that I'm scared I'm going to fail my family, and I'm superstitious enough to have found myself here tonight.

"Maybe you were right, and I just wanted to take in the view," I lie.

She shakes her head and looks at me like I'm an idiot. I'm familiar with that look: I'm on the receiving end often enough from Nonna.

"You expect me to explain myself to you," I say, "and I don't even know your name. Maybe we should start there."

"I'm not telling you my name."

I lift my eyebrows. "That hardly seems fair. You know my name."

"Because you marched into the coffee shop like an arrogant jerk and announced it like it was supposed to mean something. I'd forget it if I could."

I smile at her, somewhat enjoying myself. "But you can't, can you? You clearly haven't forgotten me at all, if you've been carrying around a grudge all these months."

Her cheeks turn a pretty pink. She points a gloved finger at me. "You're the one who had his grandmother ban me from her store. That's low."

"I don't tell her what to do," I say with a snort. It's true enough. Nonna Francesca doesn't ask for permission, never has. By the time she issued her "ban," I'd already returned to New York following my disastrous weekend visit in Hideaway. I didn't even learn about it until Giovanni called to tell me he'd torn down the flyer our grandmother had posted outside of Hidden Italy. Apparently he'd done it while Nonna was getting her hair curled. But this woman doesn't need to know all of that. "You really won't tell me your name?"

"No."

"Okay, fine. I'll call you Devil Woman. It suits you."

Her lips pinch together. "You know, the Sip may only be hosting the second day of the Advent calendar, but it's going to be the one everyone talks about. You're not going to get much of a crowd tonight."

There's a smug look on her face, like she knows something I don't.

"Are you talking about Santa Speed Dating?" I ask archly, laughter bubbling up. "You think *that's* going to blow a classy cocktail party out of the water?"

I've seen the flyers, along with everyone else in town. They must have ordered them by the truckload, because they're everywhere I look. It feels like the shirtless Santa on them is stalking me. I stopped by Hard to Find Bookstore yesterday because Will wanted to know if they had his book in stock, and there was a thick stack of them by the cash register.

On the poster, Santa's velvet coat is open to show his abs, and beneath his dancing feet it reads:

Santa Speed Dating, December 2 at 7 p.m.
Dress festive!
Santa found Mrs. Claus, and you could find your soulmate too!
(beards, hats, and coats available)

I shook my head in amusement, because the scheme had

Eileen all over it. Although I hadn't spent much time in Hideaway since she lost her husband, Murray, I heard all about her matchmaking schemes from my grandmother and my two single brothers. Especially after Lars got with Charlie.

Devil Woman is still looking at me with victory all over her face, so I say, "I saw those ridiculous flyers."

She stiffens, and laughter bursts out of me before I can stop it. It's the complete affront in her expression.

"You made them, didn't you?" I ask. "Who posed for you?"

"It's a stock image," she snaps. "Eileen and I designed it together."

"Are you going?" I ask. "Or is there a Mr. Claus at home who didn't make the cut to be a model?"

"I'm going. *You're* definitely not."

"You've got that right. You couldn't pay me to go," I retort. "And I'm sure most of the guys around town would say the same."

She gives an aggrieved sniff, looking down at the gently flowing water beneath us. "Shows how much you know. We sold out within hours of distributing the flyers. We're thinking about doing a second round so we don't leave anyone disappointed."

"You'll leave people disappointed, all right. You ever been speed dating?"

"Have you?" she asks pointedly, her eyes full of fire when they meet mine again. A breeze brushes one of those impossible curls across her face, and I have the unhinged urge to brush it behind her ear.

"No," I have to admit. "But I can't imagine you get past useless pleasantries if you only have five minutes."

"Sounds like it would be your ideal form of dating."

I laugh, because damn, I obviously got off on the wrong foot with her. And then I stepped that wrong foot straight into a pile of shit.

"I'm sure it'll be great," I say. "Really…festive."

Her scowl deepens. "You say that like it's a dirty word."

I shrug. "You know this town loves their celebrations. Anything to please the tourists."

"The tourists are why we get to have all of this." She throws one arm wide, almost like she's going to burst into song. "A little place like this wouldn't have this much entertainment without them. Or so many great restaurants and bars."

"Yeah, lucky us," I say wryly. "Some of them might even choose to stay forever, like you. The newest residents always shout the loudest about what a great place this is. But they don't have much to say about the cold winters or the gossips. Not a word about the pageantry and showboating."

She stares at me mutinously, her lips parting. No doubt preparing some really pointed barbs.

I hold up a hand to ward off her inevitable outrage. "Listen. Your enthusiasm is admirable. It's just a little misplaced."

She plants a hand on her hip, the rounded curve visible even through her coat. "I see you're still mansplaining. Rachelle told me all about that."

"Who?" I ask, distracted momentarily by the sight of her hand firmly gripping her hip, though her self-righteous fury quickly tugs me back to awareness.

"You don't even remember her name?" she asks incredulously.

"Of course I do. But I try not to dwell on the past. And don't you think that's a low blow?"

"Yeah, well, you've earned it. Wouldn't you be bitter if I'd shown up at your office to yell at you?"

"Not really. I would have enjoyed watching security escort you out."

I watch, fascinated, as her posture straightens. "Just like I'm going to enjoy watching your event crash and burn," she snaps. "People around this town want festive. They want fun! That's why they're going to be bummed out by your party. If anyone even shows up at your place tonight."

"Why wouldn't they?" I ask, suspicious.

She lifts one shoulder. "I haven't seen any flyers for it. Just the town calendar and the notice near your store's sign."

"Word of mouth," I say, but my heart's beating faster. Shit, I should have thought about flyers. I'm not operating at one hundred percent, and it's showing. This was a thoughtless screwup.

"I heard you don't even usually decorate your store for Christmas."

"How would you know?" I ask. "The flyer may have come down, but I'm guessing you're still banned."

Her mouth firms into a line, her lips soft and pink and full even like this.

It seems unfair for such a difficult woman to look like she does.

She huffs, then says, "As if I'd want to go to a place that serves dry sandwiches."

Fuck me, I actually laugh. "You know, that's my little brother's cooking you're insulting."

If I'd wanted contrition, it's clear I'm going to be disappointed.

She looks me straight in the eye. "I was hoping it was yours."

Another laugh tries to escape, but I swallow it down. "I'm not a cook. I'm a…" I trail off, because I don't know what I am anymore, and I certainly don't owe her any explanations. "I moved back about a week ago. Temporarily. To help my family."

"Lucky us," she says dryly.

I grin in response, which seems to be the exact opposite of the reaction she was hoping for.

"Oh, just go away and leave me in peace," she says.

"Ah," I say knowingly. "I see now."

She came to the bridge with a goal, one she has yet to meet. There was no concealing the scandalized expression on her face earlier, so I'm guessing it wasn't a rendezvous for sex beneath the stars.

She's here to make a wish.

"Don't let me get in your way," I say pointedly. "Go ahead and make your wish." I lean casually against the railing, making it clear I have zero intention of leaving.

From her flustered expression, she obviously wants privacy, but I'm not going to leave a woman out here alone in the dark. My grandmother raised me to look after other people. It's been my role for so long, I don't know how to stop.

"Go on then," I say with a shooing motion. "*Wish.*"

"You're a jerk," she says, her cheeks pink in the spare light.

"You wouldn't be the first person to think so."

"I need to be alone."

"And I'd be a real asshole to leave you here by yourself, knowing there could be weirdos and flashers hiding underneath the bridge. Can't do it."

"That's not why you're staying," she says fiercely. "You just want to get the last word. Rachelle told me all about that too."

I shake my head, smiling tightly. Feeling the burn just like I'm supposed to. This time, I have to admit they both have a point. And since I *do* like getting the last word, I say, "Rachelle's not your friend. She probably forgot your name within five minutes of meeting you."

"Oh, so she's like you?"

I laugh. "We already established that you never told me your name."

"You could have asked someone."

I raise my eyebrows. "People were already whispering about you calling me a bad lover in front of half a dozen people. You think I wanted to encourage the rumor mill?"

She has the grace to look embarrassed. "I didn't say you were a bad lover. I said if you didn't—"

"Oh, I remember exactly what you said. My brother emailed me the following week's Lady Lovewatch column, which featured a direct quote. So thank you for that."

Lady Lovewatch is the anonymous gossip columnist for our local paper. It's all very good-natured and civilized, until it's about *you*.

Devil Woman balls her gloved hands into fists. "Since you want to discuss the past, I remember *exactly* what Rachelle said. That you only care about yourself."

I straighten up to my full height. "Hardly. She didn't like that I cared so much about my family, but blood runs thicker than water."

She flinches as if I'd hit her. "Not always."

There's something sharp about the way she says it. Still, my need for the last word pulses inside of me. "When you're Italian American, always."

"No wonder she broke up with you," she says, lifting her chin like a prizefighter.

A tired sigh escapes me. "Look, let's cut this conversation short. You don't know me. You don't know this town. You're an outsider, a tourist who decided not to go home. You'll always be an outsider."

"At least I'm not an asshole." She whips away from me, one long curl brushing across my arm, and runs off the bridge.

A feeling of remorse settles into my chest. I was in the wrong, but I wasn't wrong. A person can't get the lay of the land that quickly when it comes to something as intimate, as intertwined, as a small town. She may think I'm arrogant, but isn't it arrogant to assume you know what's best for a bunch of people you don't even know?

At the same time, I've stayed away from Hideaway Harbor for years. What right do I have to still call it mine?

I wait a few minutes to make sure she's long gone before I set off. She must have come on foot, because I don't hear an engine turn over.

I'm about to leave the bridge when I notice a folded piece of pink paper on the ground. It's dry and unmarred, freshly dropped. Devil Woman must have lost it as she fled.

Curious, I stoop to pick it up and open it.

Make a wish on the Wishing Bridge.

Beneath it, in neat, tiny writing, I see:

Lose my virginity to a rando so I can be ready for Mr. Perfect.

Holy shit.
I drop the note as if it had burned me.

CHAPTER 3

LUCY

"*H*e's horrible," I complain into my cell phone to Charlie as I stride across town to my apartment building. Thank goodness the call went through, because I absolutely need to vent. "Can you *believe* he said that?"

"Which part?" she asks distractedly, and I can tell without asking that she's working on one of her Etsy portraits. I feel a pull of longing for the short time we'd lived together, our shoes next to each other on the rack, her paint brushes constantly drying by the sink—an annoyance then, a fond memory now. Living by myself feels strange. There's no one to take care of, no one to cook for, only the empty press of space without bodies in it.

"All of it," I say with vitriol. "He said I'm an outsider, and I'll always be one. He obviously meant it. My only comfort is that he obviously didn't know about the big event they're holding at Hook, Wine, and Sinker tonight. Of course I didn't tell him. I'd like to see his face when he finds out after the fact."

Maybe it would help banish the memory of the way he looked at me when he told me I didn't belong. His conviction practically radiated from those intense, brooding eyes.

As I near home, I reach into my coat pocket for my keys. They're there, but the crackle of paper I'd felt earlier is notably absent. I fish around for the pink slip of paper. Nothing. With increasing alarm, I turn my pockets inside out. Empty except for my keys, wallet, and a gum wrapper that falls onto a pile of dirty snow.

"Oh no," I say with dawning horror as I stoop to pick up the wrapper. "Oh no, oh no."

"What's wrong?" Charlie asks, her voice more alert.

"I think…"

Oh, it's too awful to say out loud.

This morning, I had a wonderful feeling of anticipation as I opened the first door of the Advent calendar Eileen lovingly constructed for me, having decorated each of the little doors with gorgeous, thick holiday paper. I've always loved Advent calendars, so much so that I've been known to buy them off season so other months can feel special too. The one Eileen made for me is even more special, because she made it out of love. I felt that love when I opened the first door earlier, the same way I had every time I picked one of the prompts out of my mother's magic ball. Optimism had thrummed through me as I removed the little pink paper, scrawled down my plan, and tucked it into my pocket. That optimism had been buoying me up all day, but now that wonderful feeling has been tainted by *him*.

I imagine Enzo Cafiero finding that deeply personal note. Unfolding it. He would read it with an intense expression, but then his face would transform with laughter.

He'd be laughing at *me*. The dumb little girl who thought she could choose a new home without it choosing her back. The naïve virgin who doesn't understand relationships or sex but still gives advice to others.

The lonely woman who wants a home so badly she fools herself into thinking she's found one.

The lost woman who followed her friend into her new life like one of the puppies she paints.

I swallow the bitter thoughts, then say, "I think I may have dropped Eileen's prompt from the Advent calendar on or around the bridge. This is *very* bad."

"Why?" Charlie asks. "No one will know... *Oh.* You're worried Enzo will find it."

"I have to go back and get it," I say, already dreading the cold walk. What if he's still there? What if he's waiting with the note so he can shove it in my face and laugh, his perfect handsome eyes crinkling with mirth?

"Well, that's okay," she says. "It just told you to make a wish, right? Nothing weird about that. He must have been there to make a wish too. Lots of people go to the bridge to make wishes."

I'd told her about it earlier, but I'd kept quiet about the line I'd penned beneath the prompt.

Swallowing against my dry mouth, I ask, "What do you think *he* wished for, an alliance with Satan?" It's hard to imagine a man like him having a wish. He probably has everything he needs or wants, and if he doesn't, I'd bet he'd find a way to take it.

And now, maybe he has my wish.

She laughs. "Let's hope not. Last week, I went there to wish for an engagement ring—"

"That was quick work."

"I know, right? So if he wanted an alliance with Satan, he probably got it. Then again, he might have gone to the bridge to watch people messing around beneath it."

I release an exasperated breath. "Am I the only person who didn't know about that?"

"Probably," she says, and I can practically feel her smile. "You can take one of the Santas down there tomorrow night."

"Right," I repeat woodenly, my mind glued on that paper.

I can't explain how perfectly awful it would be for Enzo to have found that paper, because I haven't told my best friend the real reason why I no longer know how to date.

A twenty-one-year-old virgin isn't all that surprising. Most people would assume she hasn't found the right guy yet, or that she's holding onto it for someone special.

But a twenty-eight-year-old virgin?

That requires an explanation, pretty early on in a relationship too, especially if you're not religious, which I'm not.

So yeah, as a virgin closing in on thirty, dating hasn't been much fun. It's no wonder I latched on to Eileen's idea about practice dating. But then I got to thinking, if I could practice dating, why not also practice sex?

I want to meet someone wonderful, someone *remarkable*, someone my mother would have approved of wholeheartedly, but I can't imagine that happening if I still have my virginity hanging over my head. It could ruin everything with my perfect man before our love story even got started.

I'm sure if I told Eileen and Charlie, they'd say something like, *A real man will understand.* Or, *He'll totally be into that.* But I know differently...

Like I said, I've dated a little over the years, and guys always get weird as soon as I tell them. They either become obsessed with being *the one*, which is awkward and uncomfortable and a total buzzkill, or they back off and break up with me for "my own good."

But if I could find someone to have no-strings practice sex with? I could go from being a twenty-eight-year-old virgin to being sexually inexperienced.

Sexually inexperienced, you don't need to make explanations for.

So, yes, I've decided that what I want for Christmas is to get rid of my virginity and practice sex. Not with the right guy, but with someone who's perfectly okay, so I'll be prepared when the real thing comes along.

Practice.

Softballs.

"I need to go back for that note," I murmur into the phone, already turning back. "I'll talk to you later."

"Call me when you get home, and I'll come over. We have to figure out what you're wearing for Santa Speed Dating."

I don't tell her no, because I've already concluded that Santa Speed Dating might be the best place for me to find my anonymous Mr. Perfectly Okay.

Eileen decided to keep the coffee shop closed until the event tomorrow, so we can spend all day preparing and make it truly epic. We figured out how to make seating for twenty couples with an efficiency that would probably impress a wedding organizer. The Santas will stay put in their assigned seats, and the women will move from station to station. But if a woman finds her perfect Santa, she'll put on his Santa hat, and they'll officially withdraw from the running.

It's a ticketed event, and even though we only officially announced it a few days ago, we've already sold out.

"*Twenty* five-minute first dates," Charlie had gushed, with an enthusiastic thump on my back. "You have to admit. You said you needed practice, and Eileen *dee*-livered."

She truly did.

Surely, one of those twenty men will be Mr. Perfectly Okay.

He doesn't need to be brilliant or super-hot or funny. All I need is for him to be single, discreet, and capable of having an erection. And willing, obviously. All the better if he's also a tourist, only in town for the weekend. Because he won't be the one I'm going to have a relationship with.

Heck, I can get this taken care of before I work my morning shift on Saturday. Maybe I'll have a postcoital glow, and everyone will remark on my rosy cheeks. I can say something like, *Santa has already been generous this year, and*—

You know what? Maybe I'll have sex with a few tourists before the end of the month, and by the time the new year begins, I'll be ready to meet the love of my life—no awkwardness required.

As I get closer to the bridge, my thoughts shift to Enzo. He's probably still pissed at me for bringing up Rachelle.

Admittedly, it was a little unpleasant of me to do so, but I was only meeting his unpleasantness with my own. My mother always used to tell me I should meet people where they are.

But if I'm being honest, I was also annoyed by how my pheromones were responding to his closeness. My poor body has only received affection from silicone toys lately, and it's just so different to be pressed against a man like that, so... carnal. For all his personal failings, there isn't a single offensive thing about his face or body, or that sexy rumble of his deep, manly voice. My senses overloaded in the face of that, and it's unnerving to have your body react so acutely to someone you dislike.

What if Enzo is still at the bridge and he looms over me again, spreading his spicy scent all around him like a pheromone cloud, arching those perfectly slanted eyebrows?

Worse, what if he pulls me toward him, and I find my body plastered against him the way it was for half a second on the bridge? I could feel his hard chest. I could feel him *breathing*. For a moment, our personal bubbles merged into one, and I experienced him in a visceral way.

This is why I need to find Mr. Perfectly Okay now. So I can prevent my body from overloading every time it's around a nice-looking, nice-smelling man.

I slink toward the bridge, then release a breath I very much realized I was holding. No sign of him, thank God.

But there's no sign of the note either.

I comb over the area in front of the bridge before scanning the length of the stone bridge itself. No sign of the pink note, but a hulking, shaggy body rises unsteadily from a balled-up heap of fur on the bridge and wags its tail.

"Hi, Skippy," I say.

The dog lumbers toward me, and then I see it: he has a shred of pink paper adhered to the drool on the side of his face.

Oh, thank God. Enzo doesn't know my secret. It's working its way through Skippy's digestive system.

I give the Saint Bernard a good rubdown. "Do you want to come home with me, buddy?"

His long, furry tail starts wagging, but he licks my outstretched hand and then plops back down and curls up. I'm not worried about him—he has dozens of warm sleeping options and knows it. But it feels a bit like a rejection, after what Enzo said earlier.

You're an outsider...you'll always be an outsider.

I shake off the thought, give Skippy a final pet, and turn toward home.

I will not let that asshole hijack my mood or my plan. I will not let that asshole hijack my mood or my plan...

No. In fact, I'm going to spend the rest of the night working my butt off like Buddy the Elf so I can make Santa Speed Dating the most special, most memorable, and most Christmassy event in all of Hideaway Harbor.

Let's see him best that.

Then I'll choose a not-so-memorable Santa to resolve my virginity problem for me.

I'm still feeling a righteous high when I reach the door of my apartment and see the little note propped up against it on a thick, creamy notecard. I pick it up and unfold it.

Sorry if this is a strange thing to do, but

*I noticed you dancing in your window last week.
It made me smile, and not a lot of things do
that lately. You're a beautiful dancer. So
thank you for the smile.*

Gasping, I glance around, but whoever left the note is long gone.

I step inside, shut the door, and head straight for my landline phone and dial Charlie's number. "The man who watched me dancing in front of my window a few days ago left a note in front of my apartment. Is that scary or romantic? I've been spending so much time with Eileen I can't tell."

"Holy crap," she remarks. "She would have a fit. What does it say?"

I tell her, and she mulls it over for a second before saying, "He could live in the building. It's definitely less weird if he lives in the building."

"How can I tell?"

"Write him back and ask. Also, I'm coming over."

"Good, because I feel my competitive streak coming out. I plan on going full Buddy the Elf over this advent calendar reveal. Are you with me? We can plaster the café with so much Christmas people won't know what to do with themselves."

"Always," she says adamantly.

Near bursting with holiday spirit now, I hang up and go sit by the Christmas tree to write a response to my secret admirer. I'm feeling so festive, I scrawl it into a Christmas card.

CHAPTER 4

ENZO

She's a virgin.
She's looking for a random man to deflower her.
She wants it to happen soon.

The note had fluttered from my stiff fingers and blown away on a cold breeze too fast for me to catch it.

I don't know why it bothers me. I don't even know this woman's name, and I'm positive she's a pain in my ass. The situation is also none of my business. If she loses her virginity to a random person she doesn't intend to see again, she'll be no different from most people.

For me, it was Edie Wheeler at sleepaway summer camp when I was sixteen. We fucked on the ground behind a tree. It lasted for four minutes, and we got covered in poison ivy, so it wasn't a magical experience I'll take to my grave. The memory of the poison ivy rash lasted longer.

It's just...

I don't like Devil Woman's plan.

Maybe it's because I was raised to feel protective of women, and I know there are plenty of predators out there who'd take advantage of an innocent woman's offer.

Or, maybe, like Aria would say, I have an impulse to control everyone.

I like the situation even less because every single person here in the crowd at Hidden Italy—which is much sparser than I'd hoped—has been whispering about Santa Speed Dating, and whether the women will be asked to wear costumes too.

Have I been imagining what Devil Woman would look like dressed up in a little red outfit fringed with white?

God, I can't seem to stop.

Like I said, my blood's been running hot, in more ways than one.

I've been asked five times what else we have planned for tonight, as if what we're offering isn't exciting enough given what's been advertised next door. While I need to focus on amping up the party, I can't stop thinking about tomorrow's event at the café either. Something tells me Devil Woman is the reason for the Santa Speed Dating plan. Like maybe the whole event was organized so she could have a roomful of men to choose from.

None of my business.

Except...she made it my business. Because this was supposed to be a big night for Hidden Italy, dammit. The people here shouldn't be gossiping about what Love at First Sip is planning for tomorrow. They shouldn't be gossiping about who's going and what they're going to wear. But they are. They're standing in little clusters, eating our food, drinking our drinks, and talking about *them*.

"What's up with you?" Giovanni asks, nudging my shoulder. "You look even more dissatisfied than usual."

I grunt in response, watching as Nico holds out a plate to Mayor Locke, offering him what must be his fifth sample of our "famous" Italian sandwich. Or at least that's what it says on the placard on the tray. My grandmother is standing right next to him, watching.

"Uh, no, thank you," Mayor Locke says as he shifts uncomfortably on his feet. He's several feet away from me, standing by the wall and surveying the lukewarm crowd.

"You don't like it?" Nonna asks, her tone hostile. She's been downing grappa all evening, but she's still salty. She dressed all in black tonight—not unusual for her, but she told me she's mourning my manhood, which I gave up to the mayor by begging to host this event.

So be it.

She agreed to tear off the number for the Advent calendar countdown. So she can give me as much shit about it as she wants.

"You think there's something wrong with my grandson's cooking?" she asks the mayor.

He sighs wearily, probably wishing he'd asked for Will after all. "It's perfect, Francesca." He glances around, taking in the Christmas tree, the huge bowl of roasted chestnuts, and all of the hired students circulating with trays of samples.

"But is it *moist*?" Giovanni asks, just to cause trouble.

That's Giovanni for you. He's the shit stirrer of our family. Aria even gave him a "Chief Shit Stirrer" plaque for his place a couple of Christmases ago.

"Just the man I need," I say, stepping forward and putting an arm around the mayor's shoulders. "Will you excuse us for a moment?"

My grandmother makes an annoyed grunt. The mayor looks like he's liable to kiss me, however, and I lead him away to a mostly quiet corner.

"This event was on the town calendar, wasn't it?" I ask, gesturing to the thinner-than-expected crowd. "Have the people of Hideaway Harbor stopped caring about Christmas?"

He sighs, glancing over at his pretty blonde wife, Erica, who's on her second limoncello cocktail. She's whispering to a woman I don't recognize, and I'd bet the contents of my bank account it has something to do with Love at First Sip, especially since Eileen and Erica are close friends. "Well," he glances back to me, "I'm not happy about it either, to tell you the truth. There's another big event tonight, a bachelor auction at Hook, Wine, and Sinker, and it's drawn people away."

My stomach sinks. "You've got to be kidding me. You didn't think to mention this when I asked about December 1st?"

He gives me a glare that suggests he remembers what I looked like in the suspenders Nonna made me wear to Easter mass when I was a kid. "I didn't know about it when we had lunch."

My mind shifts to Devil Woman. *She* knows about this. She was baiting me about it earlier. Well played.

But the game's not over…

I return my focus to the mayor.

"If you'd known about it then, you would have wanted to do the calendar reveal at Hook, Wine, and Sinker," I infer.

The mayor shifts uncomfortably again.

My grandmother whispers something to an awkward kid holding yet another sample tray, and he beelines toward us with a forced smile. "Sir, would you like another sample of the Italian sub?"

Mayor Locke gives me a long, pointed stare before declining the sample.

"I'm going to turn this around," I tell him. "You wait."

"It's a very pleasant party," he tells me easily, waving around.

But I notice none of his several children came, and more than half the people here would qualify for a senior citizen discount at the local restaurants.

"And more people will probably wander in off the street if they hear the music," the mayor continues. "You don't need to do anything."

It's like he's never met me.

"It's no problem," I say, my mind scrambling, because I'm a

fixer. I see a problem, and I come up with a solution, even if I have to use a bulldozer to make it happen. I'm going to turn this thing around, whatever it takes. "Excuse me, sir. We're about to turn it up."

I step away and hunt down Giovanni, pulling him away for a private talk.

"Are you thinking what I'm thinking?" I ask.

He grins at me. "That it would be nice to be in Greece or South Carolina right about now?"

I laugh, because that was, undeniably, a good one. "What else…?"

"This party is a bit…" He teeters his hand from side to side.

"No shit. Apparently there's a bachelor auction event at Hook, Wine, and Sinker." I gesture in the direction of the Sip. "And then there's the Santa Speed Dating thing at the Sip tomorrow night. That's why we've barely got anyone under fifty. They all want this dating shit. I ran into that woman who works for Eileen earlier, and she definitely knew about the Hook, Wine, and Sinker auction."

"You mean the hot barista who ripped you a new asshole?"

I give him a look I'm really hoping will shut him up. "She knew," I say, "and she didn't warn me."

"Why would she?" he replies with a laugh. "She hates you."

"And she just started a war."

He rolls his eyes. "Ah, here we go. Don't we have enough Cafiero grudges?"

"We're going to make this a night people are talking about for months, Giovanni. You mark my words. It's not over yet. We're going to pull something big out of our pockets tonight. Something to compete with that auction and Santa Speed Dating."

He shakes his head, his lip curling with amusement. "Good luck. That's not gonna happen unless you've got Amanda Willis hiding in your pocket."

Ah yes, Amanda Willis. The celebrity my sister is obsessed with, who is reportedly spending the holiday season tucked away in Hideaway Harbor. Probably because she's been all over the tabloids recently after coming out as gay. I figure it's nobody's business who she wants to date. Her romantic life is hardly a matter for public scrutiny or a cause for heightened notoriety. But there's no denying her star power, whatever the reason for it. If she were here, people would come in just to meet her. She's a no-show, though, just like most of the town.

Maybe she figures there's no point searching out Italian food in a town known for its lobster and Finnish roots. Maybe that's the real reason so few people bothered to come tonight.

"Initial thoughts?" I ask.

He shrugs. "I say we don't bother trying to charm people. We'll have Nonna unveil the number, bring out the panettone, and send everyone packing. No need to debase ourselves any more than we already have. We'll call it a wash and try something else."

But a thought clicks into place, and I snap my fingers, grinning at him. "You absolute genius."

He grins, his eyes the same warm, liquid brown my nonno's were. "While I enjoy being called a genius, I'm not sure I can lay claim to it this time."

"That's it." I give his arm a shove. "We're going to debase ourselves. We'll do our own bachelor auction here. You, me, and Nico. But it won't be some stodgy, black-tie event. We'll pour more drinks and turn up the music. It'll be *fun*. We can donate the money to Toys for Tots. The publicity will be great for the shop."

He gives me a long look. "You want me to strip my shirt off and hold a big log of salami up against my pants so you can take photos for a calendar while you're at it?"

"Stop giving me good ideas. We don't have time for all of them."

He huffs a laugh, shaking his head, but his response barely registers now that I'm sinking deep into planning mode. This is how we can turn the tide and save Hidden Italy.

"Nico's gonna want no part of this," he says, gesturing toward our brother, who has moved on with his tray of samples and is talking up a pretty redheaded tourist.

"You sure about that?" I ask. "We'll sell it so he thinks that pretty tourist will bid on him."

"The woman who wins him would probably be an old lady," he says thoughtfully. "You were right about the people who showed up tonight."

"Most likely," I agree, clapping him on the back. "But you're a man who likes to play the lottery, aren't you?

"Not really, no, but I don't mind who gets me. I can talk to anyone."

He's not exaggerating.

Rubbing my hands together, I nod in agreement with myself. This is happening. We're doing it.

"Shouldn't we, like, come up with different date plans for the women who win us?" he asks, gesturing to the people around us. "That's what people do on the shows."

"You watch dating shows?" I ask in disbelief.

He laughs. "I lived at home with Aria longer than you did."

I nod, my mind moving rapidly again. "Nico can make dinner for his date. Something special. Four courses."

"Can he also make dinner for our dates?" He smirks.

"Nah, we'll play to the Hideaway Harbor hits. I can bring my date to the parade, and you can take yours to the Christmas market."

"That would take all of five minutes," he protests.

I laugh. "Consider yourself lucky, then, presuming your winning bidder may be an old grandma."

He pauses, eyeing me with an amused smile. "You're serious

about this," he says thoughtfully. "You think women will really pay to date us?"

"We *are* wearing sharp suits."

He snorts. "You are so full of yourself, Enzo, God love you."

"We'll throw in a basket of delicacies from the shop for each of the winners. Come on, this is a good plan."

"Sure. I'm game. You just need to convince Nico to play ball."

No problem. If I can sweet-talk CEOs, I can sure as hell talk my little brother into compliance. "You get the baskets ready on the down-low, and make them good. I'll talk to Nico."

He gives me a salute, and I head off to cockblock our little brother.

I tell Nico there's a culinary emergency and guide him away from the redheaded woman, who looks disappointed for half a second before striking up a conversation with some silver-haired guy I don't recognize, dressed in a suit more expensive than Nico's. My interruption puts my brother in a real mood, I can tell, but desperate times and all that.

"What's this about, Enzo?" he asks, giving the redhead a wistful glance. "Better be good."

I tell him, and he starts shaking his head before I'm halfway through. "No way. We'll make fools of ourselves. I'll never live it down. The guys at the gym will be talking about it all year."

I could point out that they work out at a place called Lobstah Lifts and have no right to make fun of anyone, but then again, my apartment building has a gym. His doesn't. "Come on, man, it's going to be a huge success. Do you want to be a part of that success?" I nod in the direction of the redhead. "What if she buys your date?"

"It's looking unlikely."

I wave a hand at Silver Hair, not caring if he notices. "He could be her father. Maybe her grandfather. You're Nico

Fucking Cafiero. You look sharp in that suit. *And* you can cook. I'm told women love a man who can cook."

He shakes his head, but his mouth is inching into a smile. "How the hell would you know?"

"From all the women who didn't love it that I can't cook."

"I don't like the thought of a woman paying for me."

I lift my hands. "Aria would say you're acting like a caveman. Besides, you'll technically be paying for dinner. She'll be giving the money to charity. Win-win."

He considers this for a long moment, then says, "You have to help me make the rest of the panettone until Christmas. You're better at kneading."

I still remember the way our nonna taught us—

If you grab a woman like that, you pazzo, it's the last time she'd ever let you touch her. You knead it softly.

Despite what the devil woman thinks of me, I'm a man who's capable of compromise. I hold out my hand for a shake. "You've got it, brother. You won't regret this."

"Pfft. I regretted it the moment I let you and Giovanni talk me into wearing a suit."

"But hey, the ladies like it, am I right?"

He groans. "Classic Enzo, wheeling and dealing."

"You bet."

I stride back toward my grandmother and the mayor, feeling more of a bounce in my step. Halfway there, I stop to talk up a cluster of people who are whispering about Santa Speed Dating.

"Hey," I say, "we've got something special for you tonight, just you wait. I think you're going to like it." I wink at them, feeling the high of knowing I've done it. I've cracked the code.

These people want drama. They want the illusion of romance. Well, they don't need to go next door to the matchmaker of Hideaway Harbor and her assistant to get it. We'll give it to them here.

I sidle up to the mayor and my grandmother, who are in the middle of a fraught conversation about oil and vinegar.

I drape an arm around her shoulder. She pinches me. "Why do you look like *il capo*?"

"Can I have a word with you, Nonna?" I ask.

She might be the harder nut to crack, but if I tell her it'll save our asses, there's a chance she'll only raise the usual objections—a sour face and barbed comments for the next six months.

I get her to a mostly deserted corner of the store, which is good, because she immediately gestures toward the mayor. "That man doesn't know a good sandwich from a Happy Meal. Our Nico could make a sandwich so delicious it would make the angels weep, and still he'd say it was dry."

"Nonna," I say, deciding to circumvent the dry sandwich argument altogether, and quickly explain my plan for the auction.

I expect her first response to be no. Possibly even *no, you idioto, why don't you have the brains God gave a slug?*

But she listens and then shrugs. "We'll do it. It's a good plan."

"Really?" I ask, wondering if the wishing bridge made good on my miracle after all.

Devil Woman flits through my head, looking more like an angel with her hair blowing in the breeze.

"Really," my grandmother says sternly. "It's time for you boys to settle down. Especially you, *Madonne!* Thirty-three and no wife." She makes the sign of the cross on her chest. "Your father was married at twenty-one, bless him, and he gave me four beautiful grandchildren. If selling yourselves gets you closer to the altar, then so be it. Our Lord God works in mysterious ways."

Damn straight.

Because if I weren't locked into a weird back-and-forth with Devil Woman, I never would have thought of this.

Your play, Devil Woman.

CHAPTER 5

LUCY

To my stalker,

Okay, maybe you're not a stalker. But you WERE peeping into my window, and then you left a note at my door. They make documentaries about these kinds of things.

Do you live in the building? My friend tells me your stalking is less creepy if you live in the building.

Also, thank you. I lost my mother last year. We used to dance together, before she got really sick, and the other night it felt like she was dancing with me. I got to pretend for a few minutes.

This was her favorite time of year, and she died just before last Christmas, so I'm trying to find ways to enjoy this season for her, even though it's hard. You know what I mean? Luckily, there's a lot to enjoy about Christmas in Hideaway Harbor.

I realize I'm probably talking into the void, but maybe that's why it's so easy.

Best—

Dancing Queen

I prop the Christmas card against my door before leaving on Friday morning, feeling like an idiot, because whoever wrote to me last night is probably long gone. But it feels kind of nice to commune with a stranger—and maybe a little like kismet, considering my Advent calendar prompt from Eileen this morning was:

Reach out to someone unexpected.

Writing the message also helped me shake a dream I had about Enzo finding the pink note. It was a nightmare, let me be clear. He showed up at my door, holding the half-eaten note, and said in a low, deep voice, "What are we going to do about this, Devil Woman?"

Then he advanced toward me, and—

Needless to say, I woke up feeling disturbed.

And, yes, a little turned on, but that was not my fault. It was simply the natural reaction of a sexually stunted woman to a man with a beautiful body and face. I do not like Enzo. I *dislike* him. But my Freudian *id* has taken notice.

I just have to hope my hyper-reactiveness goes away once my body is less of a sexual desert.

Before I head to the café, I walk downtown to The Sweetest Thing, our local candy shop, to pick up some special treats for tonight. The exterior bricks are painted in colorful stripes that unfailingly attract tourists, especially tourists with children. The owner, Portia, is only my age and already a huge success. She makes these gorgeous candy canes in all kinds of special Hideaway Harbor-inspired flavors, like lingonberry and even lobster. She says she only makes the lobster ones because she enjoys watching the faces of the people who're brave—or foolish—enough to try them.

I make my selection of mini candy canes for the event and take them to the register to check out. Portia, who's manning the counter today, greets me. We're friendly acquaintances, if not friends yet. I came by last week to interview her for the final project in one of my classes—an interactive app that catalogs information about Hideaway Harbor's various businesses. The town already has an official app, but the user interface for mine is more intuitive.

Portia grins at me as she rings up my purchases, all while keeping up friendly conversation. She's so inspirational and cool it's frankly a bit intimidating. She has black hair and routinely wears colorful hair extensions. They're sparkling green today, and she's wearing green eyeshadow and knee-high socks to match. Sometimes her appearance gets stares, but she doesn't give a flying you-know-what what other people think of her. It's refreshing.

"Did you hear about the auction last night?" she asks, smacking her gum.

"The one at Hook, Wine, and Sinker?" I reply, handing over my credit card. "It sounded really swanky. I'm sure Eileen will have lots of gossip about it."

She takes my card but doesn't run it, instead tapping the

edge against the striped counter. "No, I was talking about what happened at Hidden Italy."

It's like she just tossed a cup of sugar into my blood. I'm suddenly buzzing from the inside out.

"What did he do?" I ask without thinking.

From the way her eyes gleam, my question was more of a tell than I intended to give.

People in town aren't unaware of the tension between Enzo and me. There were witnesses, of course, and that Lady Love-watch piece, followed by the BANNED flyer outside of Hidden Italy.

"Have you seen Enzo since he got back to town?" she asks.

"Unfortunately," I murmur. "He's just as unpleasant now as he was four months ago. But what happened yesterday? Last I heard, the Cafieros were going to have some boring cocktail party for their advent calendar event."

"That might have been the plan, but that's not what happened," she says with a wide grin. "The brothers found out what was happening at Hook, Wine, and Sinker and up and decided to auction themselves off for charity too."

My heart is pounding faster now, as if a second cup of sugar were tossed in with the first. Enzo acted like I was a feeble-minded idiot for helping Eileen set up Santa Speed Dating, and a couple of hours later, he pulled off a stunt like that?

"Was it impromptu?"

"Yeah," she says, smiling. "But I have to admit, it was a hell of a good time. The party started out a bit boring, but by the time they announced the auction, we'd all had a few limoncello cocktails. They put together a few baskets filled with goods from the store to sweeten the deal, then each of them got up on a table to show off their own goods, if you know what I mean."

"Enzo did that?" I ask in choked disbelief.

"Gio's the one who got on the table first. But Enzo won't let anyone best him."

"Well, that certainly sounds like him," I mutter.

"So the next thing we know, he's on a table too. Of course, Nico, the youngest brother, doesn't like to get left behind, so he was the third one to climb up. Their grandmother looked like she was about to have a stroke, so I got her some limoncello. Which she definitely needed once the guys started dancing."

"Dancing?" I'm basically echoing everything she's saying now, but I can't help myself.

"It's too bad Eileen wasn't there. She would have thought it was a total hoot, but her friend Erica was in the front row. She threw a bunch of crumpled dollar bills at them, and then the money started flying. Someone even threw a bra, and Enzo caught it in his teeth. No one admitted it was theirs, but we all knew whose it was, because her girls were hanging low. You know, I think the Cafiero boys were inspired by *you* too. They're donating the profits from their auction to the same charity you're donating to for Santa Speed Dating."

Anger ripples through me, and it takes me a moment to get a grip on myself. I remind myself that I *want* money to go to Toys for Tots.

Still, I mutter, "He's a copycat."

I can practically see the way he'd look at me if he heard me say that—eyes narrowed, mouth curled slightly up.

Naïve little girl.

Portia smiles at me. "They call it the highest form of flattery. But those boys might be regretting it soon enough. All three of them, I'm guessing."

"Why?" I ask, leaning in slightly.

She casts a glance at the tourists milling around the shop, then leans over the counter. "They said the woman who won the date gets to plan it. Each of the brothers had a pitch for possible activities, but I figure all of us winners have our own plans. I won Giovanni, and I'm going to make him pull taffy in my shop. I think I can get every woman in Hideaway Harbor in to watch. He'll be doing it shirtless."

I laugh, surprised and delighted. "What'd he do to you?"

"Not a damn thing. Giovanni's my buddy, but I like to give him shit, and we're all protective of Eileen. That's why Enzo should be worried. Erica got into a bidding war with a tourist and won him."

"I'm not sure what she intends for him," Portia continues with a sparkle in her eyes, "but I'm sure it won't be easy. Maybe she and Mayor Locke will ask him to be a walking sandwich board advertising Love at First Sip. Or she might have him dress up like Larry the Lobstah and do the tree lighting this year instead of what's-his-face."

The thought of arrogant Enzo with his suits and ties and luxurious cashmere jackets being forced to dress as a giant lobster with a Santa hat makes me feel absolutely effervescent.

"What about the youngest brother?" I ask.

"Nico was won by a local too. A pretty girl named Resa, and he was looking smug about it too until she said she wanted him to pose for an ice sculpture. They're having a competition at the Locke Reserve in a couple of weeks. She said it would take at least an hour and a half to carve."

"Oh, you've made my day, Portia. That is freaking amazing."

"I thought you'd be glad to hear it," she says with a wink. "Now, how's that app coming along?"

A couple of women form a line behind me, and Portia finally runs my card, then hands it back.

"Slowly," I admit. "Have you checked the board at *The Almanac* today?"

This is one of Hideaway Harbor's little quirks. There's a huge bulletin board in the lobby of *The Almanac*, the town paper, and each day they share the weather report and the projected state of the Wi-Fi. They do it with little smiley or frowny faces.

She scrunches her nose. "The Wi-Fi was the *meh* face. I sent a text to my mother half an hour ago, and it still hasn't gone through, but my shop's always had the worst signal and Wi-Fi in town. I think there's a hellmouth buried beneath it."

"No, that's beneath Hidden Italy," I say before I can contain myself.

She smirks. "Enzo better watch out for you."

"He'd better."

Because her words go a long way toward erasing the accusation Enzo made last night.

Always an outsider.

"Say hello to that friend of yours," she says, grinning at me. "Charlie made me that, you know." She points to a framed painting of a snarling little dog.

"Oh," I say, caught off guard. Charlie's paintings are usually of sweet moments. Pets with their hearts in their eyes.

"I asked her to paint him like that because he was a little shit. Always snarling at people and causing them trouble, but he was *my* little shit, and I liked him just the way he was." She shakes her head, smiling at the memory. "Love's a funny thing."

There's a sad look on her face for half a second, and I make a mental note to ask Eileen if she thinks Portia's lonely. Then she bags the candy canes and hands them over. "You go get yourself a sexy Santa Claus. I'll let you know when to come by for the taffy pulling. You won't want to miss it. No one will."

No, I don't want to miss it. But I *especially* don't want to miss whatever Erica has in store for Enzo.

WHEN I GET to the café, Eileen is in the small kitchen in the back, frowning down at a tin tray of Bowlful of Jellies. She has her red, scalloped apron on, and she looks positively adorable. The Bowlful of Jellies do not. She used circular molds to make the lingonberry and cream jellies. The unfortunate end product is a pile of jiggling pink balls.

To be perfectly honest, they look like testicles.

Yes, I *have* seen testicles. I've been to third base enough times to know my way around a dick. I've just never rounded the bases to home.

"Would you eat one of these?" Eileen asks, jolting me from my thoughts.

I glance down at the jiggling "treats." "I don't think so? But I also don't like Jello. They always put it on Mom's hospital trays, and sometimes I ate it out of pure desperation, but yeah, not good."

She glances up and meets my eyes. "They had panettone favors for every guest at Hidden Italy. Handmade."

I hear her. I want to respond. But my mind is elsewhere entirely.

"What is Erica going to do with Enzo?" I blurt.

Damn it. That sounded much too eager. I try again. "Uh, I mean, I talked to Portia earlier, when I went in to pick up the treats, and she told me *all* about the Cafieros' copycat auction. Enzo obviously did it because he knew our Advent calendar unveiling would be way more memorable, so it serves him right if she makes him do something embarrassing. He's going to have to wear a Larry costume, isn't he? Or, wait, is he going to be one of the mayor's elves?"

Mayor Locke always dresses up as the town's Santa Claus. God help me, it would be *amazing* to see Enzo dressed as an elf, in some ridiculous curling shoes, hopefully with fake pointy ears. Maybe I can even offer to help Erica source the outfit for ultimate embarrassment.

A strange look passes over Eileen's face. "So you've heard about the auction. Let's sit down for a moment."

We enter the main part of the café, then slide into the big corner booth with its plush, pink, faux-fur seat. Last night, we moved the tables in preparation for the big event, but we haven't set out the decorations yet. The café looks like it normally does, white and pink, pretty, and full of love.

"Santa Speed Dating is going to be so much cooler than their auction," I say, feeling my cheeks heat. "I'll bet they didn't even dress up."

"They were wearing very fine suits, Erica said. But there wasn't a single Santa hat in the place. A missed opportunity, if you ask me, but let me get to the point..." She pauses, having undoubtedly honed her flair for dramatic timing in her beauty queen years. "I have to confess...Erica participated in the auction on my behalf. When she called me last night and told me the Cafiero boys were setting up an impromptu auction, I thought it might be a nice opportunity for us, because of what we discussed *the other night*."

My pulse quickens. "What do you mean?"

"I asked her to bid on one of Enzo's younger brothers for *you*. Now, I know what you're going to say, but they're fine-looking boys, and going on a date with one of them would be excellent practice for you. Plus, Erica was already at their event, and she was happy to help." Her lips pucker. "Unfortunately, she drank too many limoncello samples and got a little carried away by the spirit of the evening. She forgot which boy was which and bid on the one she found most attractive."

My heart pounds faster, harder. "You mean..."

"She won the date with Enzo for *you*, Lucy."

A memory of his hard chest flashes through my mind, and I cross my arms to steel myself against it. *My id will not win. My id will not win.* "There's no way I'm having dinner with him."

Eileen nods as if this is no more than she expected. "I'll dine with the young man myself. Maybe I can find him a new girlfriend, and then—"

"*No.*"

She raises her eyebrows. "Why not? Men are *so* much more agreeable when they're in love."

"Not him," I insist, my heart pounding hard. "He doesn't deserve it. Can we *please* just make him dress up like a Christmas elf or lobster and call it a day?"

"Leave this to me," she says in a placating tone I've heard a dozen times. I know what that means. She still one hundred percent intends to find a girlfriend for Enzo. Maybe she's right, and he'd be a different man if he were getting laid. And yet…

"I don't like him."

"I know, dear," she says with a soft smile. "You know, I'd hoped to have a different friend bid on someone for you at the auction at Hook, Wine, and Sinker, but the competition was fierce. I'm afraid I don't have that much money in my reserves."

"At least Enzo was cheap."

She laughs. "I didn't say he was cheap."

Less expensive would still gall him, I'm sure.

"I don't want you to help him, Eileen. I mean it. He was an awful boyfriend to Rachelle."

She sighs softly. "Indeed, but I heard from Wren, that lovely young woman who runs The Haven with her father, that Rachelle was a bit of a nightmare as a guest. She snuck her phone into yoga class and kept complaining about the poor reception."

"I'm sure she was upset about Enzo. He *is* upsetting."

"Very possible. But I've also heard that she asked her massage therapist to do something that made the young man very uncomfortable, and then she left The Haven a one-star review and didn't tip anyone."

"Seriously?" I ask, appalled.

"Oh, yes. Wren was very upset. She'd gone out of her way to be kind to her."

"Okay, fine," I concede. "Rachelle does sound terrible. But that doesn't mean Enzo doesn't suck, too, Eileen. He's not a nice man. Actually, it makes sense that two awful people would find each other."

"I understand why you think so, of course."

Still, she doesn't promise she won't help him, and the thought of her finding him a nice, sweet girlfriend to love him and inflate his huge ego creates a sore spot in my chest, one that no amount of rubbing will subdue.

The door at the front of the café opens, and Charlie enters. "Lucy, why are you rubbing your tits?"

"I'm not." I drop my hand and open the box of decorations we'd organized. "I have a psychological ailment that has physical manifestations."

"The bowlfuls of jelly didn't work out, I'm afraid," Eileen tells her. "They look a little like testicles."

I swallow a laugh, then snap my fingers. "Audrey can save us."

Making Whoopie is right next door. The owner, Audrey, makes whoopie pies that are to-die-for. Charlie and I took a cake decorating class with her a few months ago, and we've gone out for drinks a few times. Of course Eileen is *dying* to set her up with someone.

Oh, dear God, I can't let her set up poor Audrey with Enzo. What if she gets tricked into liking him, and then he gets to eat her delicious whoopie pies every night? He doesn't deserve her whoopie pies!

I'll have to convince Eileen not to have dinner with him, but now's not the time. We need to pull off a Christmas coup first.

"We can decorate the whoopie pies to look like elves," I add, feeling inspired. "This is going to work. Everything is going to be awesome. So much better than last night at Hidden Italy."

Eileen grins in response. "That's the spirit."

So why do I feel like I just jinxed us?

CHAPTER 6

ENZO

"*R*emember that guy? He's a total douchebag," I grumble, watching across the town square as the douchebag in question accepts a Santa hat and beard at the door of Love at First Sip.

It's Friday evening, December 2nd. My brother and I just watched the enormous Advent calendar get wheeled away from the café by the ancient woman who's in charge of it, signaling the end of the Advent calendar portion of the evening. She was followed out by Charlie and Lars, their arms wrapped around each other.

Now, the time has come for Devil Woman's big moment: Santa Speed Dating.

Did I temporarily lose my mind last night at Hidden Italy?

Yes, but I have a competitive streak that doesn't quit, and Devil Woman challenged me by claiming her event would be better than ours. Then the mayor inadvertently threw down the gauntlet when he told me about the auction at Hook, Wine, and Sinker. To carry on with our evening as planned would have been unthinkable. I couldn't let the evening be a forgettable dud, a hiccup in Hideaway Harbor's jam-packed holiday calendar.

So I pivoted, the way I've trained people to do throughout my consulting career.

And look what happened—I danced on a table and caught a bra in my teeth, all while my grandmother was watching, probably saying the rosary for me the whole time.

In some ways, the evening backfired. My brothers are pissed at me, because we all got purchased by women who planned to torment us as payback for my grandmother banning Eileen and her "girls." But at least we raised money for charity, and we definitely made a splash.

The party only got wilder after the auction, with limoncello and champagne flowing freely. People really did come in from off the street, attracted by the chaos.

We sold out of a few of our artisanal pasta and olive oil imported from the hills of Sicily and handed out dozens of cards for catering orders.

So I'm calling it a success, if only because I need a win.

Of course, Giovanni, Chief Shit Stirrer, recruited a friend to capture video footage of me table dancing. He sent it to Aria, so she's been laughing at me all day, sending memes of dancing men.

I'd be more pissed at my brother, but when I told him we needed to do some surveillance on the Sip to make sure Santa Speed Dating didn't out-do our event, he agreed with an eyeroll. Which is why we're sitting across the street by the front window of Kippis, the Finnish bar that has karaoke on Thursdays and is thus a good place for a pint on any night but Thursday. It gives us a distant view of the comings and goings of the coffee shop, although we have to peer past a whole host of tourists milling around Town Square to see it. Still, I used to go bird watching with my grandfather when I was a kid. I learned how to spot Maine's rare birds from a distance. I can sure as shit spot a douchebag, like the one who just walked into Love at First Sip.

Call it a stakeout, if you will, but I like to think of it as vigilance. I want to know who's in the running for Devil Woman's virginity. Someone has to look out for her.

"Do you want a pair of binoculars?" Giovanni asks with an amused twist of his mouth.

"Do you have any?"

He gives me a sidelong glance. "Want me to ask around? I can let everyone know why you need them too."

I shake my head dismissively, then gesture to the window. "The guy who just went in there….he's the weirdo who got caught jerking off into our English teacher's handbag."

Giovanni laughs. "And guess what? Now he folds women's underwear at the lingerie store."

"No shit."

"Sometimes God works in mysterious ways."

I snort, my gaze still glued across the street. "You sound like Nonna. God, *all* these guys are douchebags."

My brother lifts his beer for a drink. "Yeah, that's probably why they decided they had nothing better to do on Friday night than go to Santa Speed Dating. I'd sooner give up my left nut. I'll bet no one's ever washed those beards they're handing out. But you know what? At least those guys have a choice in the matter. I bet they didn't have their big brother whispering in their ear."

"You're still pissed about the taffy thing," I reflect, my gaze locked on the small storefront across the way. I watch as another douchebag struts up. Sure, he's a stranger to me, so it's possible I've got him all wrong, but I don't think so. He's wearing a black coat that has the brand emblazoned across the back. Only douchebags choose to be walking advertisements. If you're going to advertise for someone, you make *them* pay for the pleasure.

My brother groans. "Yes, I'm still pissed about the taffy thing. So be prepared to hear about it at least a dozen times tonight."

"That's fair, I guess." I can feel him staring at me, so I look over. "What?"

"Why do you care so much about who's coming and going over there? Is this about that Lucy woman?"

"Lucy?"

He lifts his eyebrows. "Bro, if a woman told me I was a bad lover in front of my neighbors, you can bet your ass I'd find out her name. And I'd volunteer to show her how wrong she was so she could write a Yelp review and let everyone else know."

"Her name's Lucy?" I ask in an undertone, watching as a few women enter the shop.

"Lucy Taylor."

I frown as another guy lines up at the café's door. "Brandon Fucking Wright is going to this thing?"

Everyone around town knows he hooks up with a different tourist every weekend, because he enjoys bragging about his conquests.

My hand tightens around my pint glass.

If she sleeps with him, he'll tell everyone. He'll…

"I have to go," I say, setting the beer down.

He turns on his high stool to give me an incredulous look. "Are you going to sabotage Santa Speed Dating?" He pauses. "There's a sentence I never thought I'd say."

"I don't know," I tell him, which is true. But I feel sick over the thought of Lucy going home with that guy. I can't let it happen. I just can't.

"Don't you think this feud with Love at First Sip has gone on long enough? Literally everyone is on Eileen's side. Hell, I think even Aria is on Team Eileen."

"Sounds like Aria," I murmur.

"*I* might even be on Eileen's side. You should leave it alone."

I clench my jaw and watch as the door across the street opens from within. Lucy stands in the doorway and ushers in the guests. Even though I can barely see a crescent of her face, I know it's her.

I watch the line of people shuttle in, frowning when Brandon pauses to whisper something to her.

"Aria's happier than she's ever been, so there's no point in holding a grudge on her account," Giovanni continues. "And let's be honest, Rachelle was going to break up with you anyway. She was also kind of...I don't call women bitches, so I'm going to say she was an asshole. Everyone thought so. Did you hear what she pulled at The Haven?"

"Do you honestly think it's possible that I haven't?" I ask, rolling my eyes. "At least five different people have told me. Another two sent me the review she left them. I would have ordered Wren an apology bouquet, but if anyone found out, it would probably be considered a marriage proposal."

He chuckles. "Gotta love this town."

"Do we, though?"

"It's that or go mad."

Maybe I *am* going mad. Because I can't keep my eyes off that door. I have to get over there. The need to intervene is pounding through me, buzzing in my blood. But it's a ticketed event, and I don't have a ticket. I'm pretty sure no one would have sold me one, either, all things considered. "I'm not trying to mess with them. I swear on Nonno's grave. I just want to make sure Brandon Wright doesn't cause trouble. You know what he's like."

The look of disbelief he gives me does not flatter my ego, but I can't tell him about that pink slip of paper I found. Or that Lucy is a virgin looking to get laid by one of these jerks. Telling him would make me like Brandon Wright. A douchebag.

Maybe I shouldn't care what she does. She's made it very

clear what she thinks of me, and there's no denying she's an aggravating pain in my ass. But she doesn't know what it's like here yet. She thinks she does, but she hasn't dealt with the underside of Hideaway Harbor—the way the gossip can grind a person down to an old stump. I don't want her to find out the hard way.

He watches me for several seconds, then nods. "Okay. But don't just barge in there. They'll throw you out. Worse, they'll get a guy like Brandon to do it. Sure, you could beat the shit out of him, but you don't want to get thrown into jail for hitting a guy in a Santa suit. Wait until one of the guys comes out, and then you can bribe him to let you take his place." He points at the coffee shop. "The creep who jacked off into the handbag is a chain-smoker. No way he's not going to come out in another ten minutes for a smoke."

"Right, yeah, that makes sense," I mumble, drumming the table with my fingers.

Am I really going to do this?

Yes, I'm going to do this.

"Are you coming with me? Maybe we can pick off two of them."

He smirks. "No, man. I'm going to sit here and drink while I watch my big brother make a fool of himself."

"I'd do the same in your place," I say with a small smile, surprised to realize I'm enjoying myself.

"Now, the question is how you're going to linger outside for the ten minutes or so it takes for the perv to need a smoke without looking like a stalker."

"The problem has occurred to me," I admit.

"So I'm going to do my final good deed of the night and tell you I may have a way to help. Nonna made a batch of cinnamon brooms late last night while she was muttering about her idiot grandchildren, and she made me carry them into the shop this morning. I've smelled like cinnamon all day."

It was Giovanni's turn to stay with Nonna last night. She's getting on in years but refuses to leave her home to live more permanently with any of us, so instead we take turns sleeping at her house. Before I came back, Aria was in the mix. Now, it's me, Giovanni, and Nico. We always pretend it's unplanned—that it's easier to crash in one of the spare bedrooms or on the couch than to return home to our comfortable beds. We do it for her, out of love. Because she may be a piece of *salume*, but she's everything to us.

"You can take one of the brooms and go hang it under our storefront sign now. Take your time doing it so you have an excuse to linger outside the café without looking like a total stalker," he continues. "You know Nonna's proud of her brooms. She might forgive you for the chaos you caused last night."

I snort. "She was happy enough to auction us off. She just figured we'd be bought by women who wanted to date us."

He laughs and claps me on the back. "So do her proud by hitting on a bunch of women while you're dressed like an old man with a potbelly."

I get up to leave, but Giovanni grabs my arm before I can pull on my coat.

"I want to know what happened in New York," he says, his expression uncharacteristically intense.

I pull free and tug on my coat. "My job no longer interested me, so I quit. I'll find something else when the store's doing well. No big deal."

"And your apartment there?"

I rub my chest. "I haven't decided what to do about that."

I'm paying thousands a month for an apartment I'm not living in. If I stay here longer than another few weeks, I'll have to find someone to take over my lease. I have some money put aside, but there's no reason to blow through my savings just because I want the comfort of knowing the apartment's there. That I can go back to it when I'm ready to.

Even if aching to leave Hideaway Harbor makes me worry that I'm just like my father. Or, worse, my mother.

"I'm only a few years younger than you, Enzo. You don't have to treat me like I'm Nico. There's more to the story. You wouldn't just randomly quit your job like that."

"But I did. And you're four years younger."

"Three and a half."

I shrug. "Semantics."

He glares at me. "So you're not too embarrassed to tell me that you want to crash Santa Speed Dating, but you won't—"

"I'm not embarrassed of anything," I say tightly, feeling the hot pull of shame. "I didn't do anything wrong. I was just ready to move on, and the timing was good to come home and help out for a while. Win-fucking-win."

"You've been here all of a week, and you've already got me pulling taffy, you asshole." He sighs, telling me in his way that he'll let it go, but not forever. "I expect to hear all about New York at some point. You can't stay Island Enzo forever."

"Sure, we'll have a family meeting," I say, rolling my eyes. "Nico can make appetizers."

And then I'm out the door.

Hidden Italy's closed, but I use my key to unlock the door so I can grab one of the brooms from the storage closet. Nonna made them to sell, but she won't begrudge me hanging one outside.

Within minutes, I'm attaching the thing to the bracket just beneath the boot-shaped sign attached to the side of the brick building at eye level. Mom used to hang pretty dried-flower arrangements in baskets from this bracket, one for every season, but it's hung empty for years.

Except for this year.

It feels surprisingly good to attach the cinnamon broom to the sign, like I'm reclaiming something, but it takes all of five seconds. There's no sign of Handbag Guy. So I spend the next several minutes messing around with the broom, pretending I'm trying to get it to some precise, unknowable angle. I feel like a *pazzo*, to be honest, especially since I know Giovanni is watching me from across the street, having a laugh at my expense while he enjoys the warmth of the bar and drinks his beer.

What the fuck am I doing?

I don't even like Lucy, so why am I putting myself on the line for her? Sneaking into an event I think is ridiculous?

I guess I just don't know how to give up. Never have. Not since my mother abandoned us when I was ten, leaving my dad with four kids he didn't know what to do with. My brothers were six and five. My sister was only two.

Not long after that, my grandmother took me aside and said, "You're going to have to be the man of the house now, Enzo."

"What about Dad?" I asked, even though I already pretty much knew the answer. My mother had left for a reason, after all.

"He's my son, God forgive me, but he's only worth the grandchildren he gave me. And your mother…" She spat on the floor. "She's just shown us her worth."

Nonna was right. She's *usually* right. I learned how to be strong from her and my grandfather, who was a much better man than my father.

So I adjust that broom about two dozen times, swearing to myself under my breath and trying not to be too obvious about my interest in the goings-on at the Sip. I catch a couple of glimpses, though. There are tons of over-the-top decorations inside, from paper ornaments to garlands in various colors. Lots of men and women are dressed in red and green, and everyone seems to have a mug in front of them. It looks warm and comfortable, and I can hear the muted Christmas carols.

Finally, Handbag Guy comes out in his Santa suit and pulls a crinkled pack of smokes from his pocket.

"Hey, man," I say, leaving the perfectly straight broom alone and walking closer.

He inclines his chin slightly in acknowledgment.

"You having fun in there?" I ask.

He gives me an incredulous look. "What do you want, Enzo?"

So he remembers my name. That makes one of us.

"Well, I was wondering if I could convince you to let me spend the rest of the evening in there in your place."

He snorts as he pulls out one of the cigarettes. The guy's standing directly beneath a cutesy little sign that says, "No smoking on the patio, please!" and I remember the way Lucy started hacking on the bridge. My fake smile tightens.

Waving the cigarette at me, he says, "No way. We all know about your grandmother's vendetta against this place. If I let you in there, you'll probably pour Ex-Lax into the hot chocolate or something. I won't do that to those poor women."

I bristle. My grandmother is a difficult woman, no doubt, but she wouldn't stoop to something like that, and I sure as hell don't like my good name being besmirched either.

He pulls out his lighter. "Truth is, I've got designs on that hot little piece who works for Eileen."

If I was pissed five seconds ago, now I'm a man made of fire and brimstone. He shouldn't be talking about a woman like that. And he definitely shouldn't be the first man to put his hands on *any* woman.

Fists balled, I say, "If you don't hand over the Santa hat and beard, I'm going to remind everyone about that time you jerked off into Mrs. Sandis's handbag."

He blanches, his cigarette still unlit. "Hey, man, that's not cool. How would you like it if I pulled out something you did from—"

"I've never jerked off into a handbag in my life, and if you light that cigarette, you'll regret it."

"Are you threatening me?" he asks, his tone somewhere between wheedling and whining.

"Yes, I thought that was obvious."

He wipes his nose with the back of his hand, the unlit cigarette crumpling a little. I resist the urge to cringe, which becomes harder when the Christmas carol playing inside the café switches over to "Grandma Got Run Over by a Reindeer."

"My cousin works at *The Almanac*," he says. "She'd find it very interesting that you're threatening an upstanding citizen. I mean, do you even live here anymore, man? When was the last time you paid Maine taxes?"

I point to the no smoking sign. "Learn to read. The woman you're lusting over is allergic to cigarette smoke."

I might not like Lucy, but I don't want her to hack up a lung simply because he can't be bothered to follow simple instructions.

He swears at me but tosses me the Santa hat, then detaches the beard and hands that over too.

I grimace at the thought of putting it on. He looks like he hasn't showered since high school, but desperate times and all that.

He flashes both middle fingers at me as he walks away. "If something happens in there tonight, I'll know who did it. And I'll tell my cousin Mary, and—"

"We all know she's a volunteer," I say wearily. "You can stop acting like she's a top investigative reporter."

"Amanda Willis said she might give her an interview," he snaps. "The movie star. You know, the one with the good tits. She signed a headshot for me."

"Did you get to jizz in her handbag too?" It's a cheap shot, and it's very likely this whole thing will blow back on me, but I'm feeling worked up.

"You're an asshole."

I pull on the Santa hat and nod to him. "Merry Christmas to you, too, *buddy*. Be sure to give my regards to Mary. Maybe she can write another deep think piece about Skippy. Or convince Lady Lovewatch to write about you and that handbag."

He gives me the finger again as he walks away.

Ignoring him, because he did grant me the last spoken word, I strap on the beard, putting the loops over my ears. It smells like stale smoke and Cheetos, but I've been standing out here for at least fifteen minutes by now, freezing my ass off, and for all I know Lucy is already...

Yeah, I don't want my mind to go there.

I step inside, and thankfully the smoke and Cheetos smell is mostly overpowered by the sweet scents of hot chocolate and baked goods. I glance around the room and find a roomful of Santas and women in red and green staring at me.

"You're not Curtis," says one of the guys sitting at a two-top near the door. The name rings a bell, and I realize he's talking about handbag guy.

The card table next to Curtis's bud has a single empty seat opposite a nervous-looking woman in red.

"Thank God, I'm not," I murmur, lowering into the empty chair across from her.

Plenty of eyes are still glued to me as the song shifts to "Silver Bells." And that's when I see her, a few tables down.

Lucy Taylor, with her long, curly hair down around her shoulders, wearing a white sweater and a red miniskirt trimmed with white fake fur paired with black stockings. She's staring daggers at me.

My first thought is: *Good God. This woman's so new to Maine she's going to give herself hypothermia.*

Okay, fuck, I'll be honest. That definitely wasn't my first thought...

She looks fantastic. If she was an angel last night at the bridge, tonight she's a Christmas gift, all ready to be unwrapped. I let myself acknowledge what should have been obvious: I might not like this woman, but I am attracted to her. *Very* attracted to her.

She's still giving me the death glare, so I smirk back at her and lift two fingers to my forehead in a salute. Her eyes narrow, and I can't help but be amused. For half a second.

Because Brandon Wright is absolutely going to make a play for her. He'd be the biggest idiot on the planet not to, and even though he's a douchebag, he's not stupid.

Damn it.

I need to have a talk with her, preferably before she gets to him, and he's a few tables down from her.

I survey all of the tables, getting a feel for the seating, which is in a circular formation.

"Is this moving clockwise? Counterclockwise?" I ask the woman sitting across from me, who is staring at me in disbelief, probably waiting for some kind of explanation.

She signals to the left, which suggests Lucy's going to be on her date with the douchebag in another three rounds.

"You're *definitely* not Curtis," the woman says, echoing Curtis's slack-faced friend next to me.

I recognize her, I realize. Mabel, I think her name is. Or maybe Maple. She went to school with my little sister, which makes her much too young for me, not that I'm here to pick anyone up.

No, I'm here to stop a pickup from happening.

"What'd you do to him?" Curtis's buddy asks me.

I clear my throat. "Nothing. Curtis had a minor medical mishap. Too much hot chocolate." I give the guy a knowing look that suggests Curtis blew chunks in the street or shit his pants. "So I offered to sit in for him." I smile at Mabel/Maple. "He knew it wouldn't be right to leave these lovely ladies alone."

"That sure doesn't sound like something Curtis would say," the guy continues, completely ignoring the woman across from him, a pretty blonde who's scrolling on her phone while she picks at a whoopie pie decorated to look like an elf. (So far the elf has lost an eye and half a nose.) She's one of Mayor Locke's daughters, but I can't tell if she's Harper or Piper.

"Maybe it's a Christmas miracle," I say with a grin. "They say this time of year brings out the best in people, don't they?"

CHAPTER 7

LUCY

"Is something wrong?" asks the man across from me. "You seem…distracted." He's perfectly pleasant—*perfectly okay*—and if Enzo Cafiero hadn't interrupted the rhythm of our conversation, maybe he could have been the answer to the silent wish I made on the bridge last night.

I grit my teeth, feeling my heart thumping double time in my chest. "Nothing's wrong," I say, sounding very much like something is wrong.

"I'm a good listener," he says with a smile. It's hard to tell what he looks like behind the ridiculous fake beard—the beards were a flaw in Eileen's plan—but he has a nice enough smile. Nothing devious or calculating or wicked about *him*.

I beam back at him, willing myself to feel something, but I'll be totally honest: everything inside of me is focused on that absolute *asshole* sitting near the door. I knew it was him instantly. No Santa disguise could hide the depth or dark brown of his eyes, or those painfully perfect eyebrows. Poor Curtis doesn't really have any.

What did Enzo do to Curtis, anyway? Bang him over the

head and steal his beard? I know Curtis wouldn't have just handed over his things and left; he was having a *wonderful* time.

Surely Enzo would be brought to justice for something like that, even if he knows half the police force. At the very least, he'd get a slap on the wrist.

Why is he here anyway? Is he trying to destroy our event because his dumb bachelor auction had unintended consequences?

It's not our fault the people of Hideaway Harbor prefer Eileen to the Cafieros. Eileen goes out of her way to help others, always, and she doesn't hold super-long and unnecessary grudges.

Yes, I could have warned him about the event at Hook, Wine, and Sinker last night, but so could have dozens of other people. Heck, if he checked the bulletin board at *The Almanac* regularly, he would have known.

It's completely ludicrous for him to—

"You're *awfully* pretty," says the Santa across from me.

Honestly, I feel terrible, but I can't remember the man's name. It was something like Gary or possibly Harry.

It's because of Enzo. After he burst through the door, every other thought was instantly wiped from my mind.

Eileen jingles the bell signaling the end of our date. I give the man across the table a sympathetic smile, making a move to get up, but he pulls out a business card and hands it to me.

I glance at the name. *Mark Parks, Attorney at Law.* Huh, I wasn't even close.

"There aren't many attorneys here in Hideaway Harbor," I say. "There's not much need for them, I guess. There are few lawsuits, few divorces. In fact, Eileen tells me they have one of the lowest divorce rates in the country."

It's a point of pride. Hideaway Harbor is a place that believes in love.

He grins and nods. "It's practically an untapped market.

Don't you think that low divorce rate is partly from a lack of opportunity? I mean, there must be half a dozen old people who are so sick of each other that a misplaced sock could set them off. Same thing goes for the low rate of lawsuits."

"Uh, don't you think people could drive to the next big city to consult with a lawyer, or find someone online if they really wanted to?"

He purses his lips. "People need to be told what they want. If you get them at the right moment, while they're still steamed up about their neighbor putting up a fence a couple of millimeters in the wrong direction, you might find they're ready to do something about it. That's why I'm here. I'm going to help the people of this fine town, whether they like it or not."

Well, crap, that doesn't sound good. I glance at Eileen, who's beaming at me. She gives me a thumbs-up; I give a tiny shake of my head. In response, she tips her head slightly to the guy to my left. I can practically hear her silent message: *Move on to the next one, dear. Better luck next time!*

"Will you have dinner with me?" Mark asks, shifting my attention back to him.

Honestly, I *really* don't want to get dinner with this man. But I also don't want to insult him and then sit down a couple of feet away from him.

The situation is even more awkward because the next date he's supposed to charm—a pretty, dark-haired woman with a worried expression—is standing beside my chair. She clears her throat.

I understand why she's in a hurry. When I talked to the guy before Mark, he tried to sell me on using his company's carpet cleaning services even after I explained that I live in an uncarpeted rental. But I don't have high hopes for her and Mark.

"I'll text you," I lie to him, moving on to the next station.

"I hope you don't," says the Santa who's waiting for me. He has a beard under the Santa beard, which gives him an unsettling double-bearded look. "How can I convince you to have dinner with me instead, gorgeous?"

"Hey, man, that's not cool," Mark gripes. "You're voiding the social contract."

Double Beard snorts. "Neither is trying to get people to sue each other. You should have asked her out during your scheduled time with her. Now you're disrupting my date. Why don't you focus on your own?"

The dark-haired woman perks up as she slides into the seat I vacated. "I'm Daisy," she says. "I've been meaning—"

But Mark isn't done. "You shouldn't sabotage other people," he tells Double Beard. "That's not what the spirit of Christmas is about."

"And lawsuits are?"

My gaze flits back to Enzo's seat. He's still staring at me, even as he says something to his date.

The absolute nerve!

What if Curtis is that poor woman's soulmate, and now she'll never know?

Sure, I'd decided within two seconds of sitting down across from Curtis that he wasn't Mr. Perfectly Okay. There was a crumb sticking to his lips that had made the thought of kissing him abhorrent. He'd seemed pleasant enough, though, and he's probably taken care of the crumb problem by now. It's perfectly possible Enzo cut a beautiful romance short before it could even get started.

I have to get that jerk out of here before he ruins more potential love stories...

I glance at Eileen, whose attention is on a red-haired Santa who's having a lively conversation with a woman with wavy black hair. My heart swells when I see him remove his hat and offer it to her.

Oh, good! We haven't had any love matches yet, so this—

I crane my head in response to movement in my peripheral

vision. It takes a second for me to process what happened: Daisy just threw a whoopie pie at Mark's face. It bounced off his fake beard, leaving behind a dollop of whipped filling.

"You're an asshole," she says, then stomps off, leaving him staring after her with his mouth agape. Seconds later, the front door opens and then slams shuts, wafting chilly air into the room.

Enzo meets my eyes again, hiking up his eyebrows in an expression of innocence that is infuriating.

"But...but *he's* the asshole," Mark says, way too late for her to hear him. He's pointing at Double Beard, who's laughing so hard he's bent over, the end of his Santa beard dipping into his hot chocolate like a paintbrush.

Oh, this is a disaster. And it's all Enzo's fault. If he hadn't interrupted my mini-date with Mark, then Mark wouldn't have asked me out after the five-minute mark, and this unpleasantness could have been avoided.

I motion to Eileen to call a temporary halt to the proceedings. We're one woman short now, but on the plus side, we have one extraneous jerk who isn't supposed to be here. If we send our party crasher away, we'll be back on track.

Eileen walks into the middle of the room and clinks a mug with a spoon to get everyone's attention. "My wonderful guests," she says, "let's take a moment to consort with our friends and enjoy a wonderful Christmas treat. My dear assistant Lucy got you all some delectable candy canes from Portia's shop."

"Are they free?" Double Beard asks.

"Yes," I say, rubbing a tense spot between my eyebrows.

He stands up so abruptly his chair almost falls over. "Well, sign me up. I had to pay twenty bucks to get in here, and I haven't gotten a single number yet."

"They *did* guarantee love would be in the air," Mark reflects, as if he's considering whether he'd have a case to sue us.

"No one can guarantee that," I say morosely. "It was a heart-felt wish."

Like the one I made on the bridge yesterday.

I glance over at the red-haired Santa, hoping I'll see the woman across from him wearing his hat, but it's back on his head now, and there's an awkward tension between them that says she rejected him.

What was left of my optimism tanks.

I sigh as I get up, making my way through the crush of festively dressed people practically climbing over each other to access the free candy.

Enzo is standing placidly by his seat, watching me. *Waiting.* As I reach him, I press my teeth together, making an unintended clicking sound. "I need to speak with you. *Alone.*"

"I'm glad, Lucy," he says with an amused look on his face.

"So you figured out my name. Someone should give you a detective badge."

He shrugs. "Maybe it was a lucky guess. It was between Lucy and—"

"I don't care," I say. "I'm sure you were raised to think everything you have to say is very important and interesting, but it's not, not to me."

"Yes, you obviously couldn't care less what I think. I'm guessing that's why you need to speak to me." His eyebrows wing up. "Alone?"

My pulse pounds in my ears. This man is so smug. So arrogant.

I hear bickering in the background—something about lingonberry candy canes—but the sound is muddled, my peripheral vision blurred. My fury is so focused on Enzo, he's the only thing I can clearly perceive. He shrugged off his coat and scarf after arriving, revealing a black, long-sleeved shirt that clings to the outline of his muscled chest and biceps, making it very hard to look away from him. Which only makes me resent him more.

"You know why I need to speak with you," I say through gritted teeth. "You're here to sabotage us, and I won't let it happen."

He smiles at me, his lips surprisingly full beneath that fake beard. A shiver works through me.

You're too close to the door, that's all.

"Did you set up that scene back there so you could talk to me more quickly?" he asks.

Rage consumes me. "Let's go outside," I say tightly.

He shakes his head. "No. We'll stay inside unless you have pants to put on over those."

I glance down at my stockings. I *do* have a change of clothes, but I hadn't planned on wearing it. It's not overly cold outside tonight, and I've always run hot.

"Outside is fine."

"I was raised to be a gentleman."

I give him an incredulous look. "Whoever tried to teach you failed."

His lips press together, and I know I've displeased him. Good. He deserves to be displeased. But he's obviously as stubborn as his grandmother, because he doesn't take a single step toward the door.

"Fine," I snap. "We'll talk in the kitchen."

He extends his hand in a *lead on* gesture.

"You go first," I say, because I don't like the thought of him watching my butt. I thought it looked really good in this skirt earlier, when I used a hand mirror and my full-length bathroom mirror to check, but "really good" is probably barely passable for a man like Enzo. After all, I spent half an hour with Rachelle. I know what his type is. Tall and blonde and shaped like Jessica Rabbit.

"So you *do* like to watch," he says, his mouth lifting into a half-smile.

I can hardly let him take the lead now, so I stomp off toward the kitchen, nearly mowing down Mark Parks, who seems like he's actively seeking out a lawsuit now, because he's murmuring something about the slippery floor.

I can feel Enzo following me. He's like a dark shadow being cast over me, an apex predator on my trail.

The feeling is intensified when I hear the door swing shut behind him, sealing us in here together. I can still hear the hum of conversation from the adjoining room, but it's muted, making the rest of the world feel distant.

I need to get a grip on myself and reclaim control of the situation. I take a deep breath, taking in the scent of Eileen's cinnamon rolls proofing just feet from me. It smells delectable back here, like sugar, spice, and everything nice. Like *Christmas.* The scent is remarkably soothing.

My mom used to make cinnamon rolls on Christmas Eve before she got too sick. They'd rise overnight and she'd pop them in the oven on Christmas morning.

Enzo steps a little closer, shrinking the space between us to something more intimate. "Can I take off this beard now?" he asks. "It smells like Cheetos."

"What did you do to Curtis?" I hiss, glancing at the door. Then again, if we can't hear their words, they won't be able to hear ours.

"I didn't do anything to him," he says, tugging off the beard and exposing his strong jaw. He hasn't shaved today, and his dark stubble makes him look a little rougher around the edges than usual. So do the slight circles under his eyes. It's...

It's devastatingly attractive, and it makes me even angrier.

"Of course you did. He was having the time of his life. You should have heard him sing along to the Chipmunks' Christmas song."

He laughs under his breath, and I stomp my foot.

"Eileen and I are trying to make people happy," I say, my voice rising with every word. "Why would you want to get in the way of that? Do you really hate this town that much?"

Some dark emotion passes over his face. "You're not going to make any of these women happy if you're trying to set them up with sexual predators and predatory lawyers. Where'd you find these guys, anyway?"

I bite my lip, feeling called out. He isn't entirely wrong about the quality of the men out there. Then again, the quality of single men seeking partners on the internet isn't any better. "That's none of your business. You didn't buy a ticket, and you're not wanted here. It's time for you to leave."

He lifts his dark, commanding eyebrows and folds his arms over his chest. They fill out the sleeves of his long-sleeved shirt in a way that distracts me for half a second, but I snap my gaze back to his smug face. "I traded for a ticket, fair and square, and I've been a delight to my dates. What justification do you have for kicking me out?"

"I didn't crash *your* little copycat event," I say, barely holding back from poking him in the chest. "Although I have to commend you on your originality."

His smile infuriates me. "Humanity's been around for long enough that nothing in this world is truly original. It's all in the delivery."

"So then you must be doubly unhappy with the outcome. I heard the town showed up in defense of Eileen."

"Did you also hear we raised a couple thousand dollars for charity and sold out of some of our specialty foods? The event was a success by any metric."

I sense weakness and dig. "Does that mean your brother's looking forward to pulling taffy? I confess, I really look forward to seeing it. Portia said *everyone* is invited, so Eileen,

Charlie, and I will definitely be there. We haven't been banned from the candy shop."

"Give it time," he says in an annoyed undertone.

I prop a hand on my hip. "Portia is my friend. And you know what? Erica is Eileen's friend. I can't *wait* to see what she has planned for you."

Sure, Eileen plans on taking over the date and being nice to him, but he doesn't know that. Besides, there's still a chance I can convince her to take a different tack.

"I hope it's really wicked," he says with a smile that infuriates me.

"She's the mayor's wife."

"Then she shouldn't be bidding on bachelors. In front of her husband, no less. I wouldn't let my wife do that."

Oh, this man is infuriating. "As if you can *let* a woman do anything. I don't believe for one minute that poor Curtis gave up his place 'fair and square.' You must have forced him. What did you do to him?"

He shrugs. "I told him I'd remind everyone of the time he jizzed in our English teacher's handbag if he didn't let me take his place."

My mouth falls open in shock. "He really did that?"

His full lips tip up at the corners. "Would he have taken off at a run if he hadn't?"

"But *why*?"

"He's a pervert," he says with some heat. "Just like half the guys out there. Which is why you need to reconsider your foolish plan."

The air feels like it was sucked from my lungs. "*What* plan?"

His eyes bore into me. Surely it should be illegal for a man to look at a woman like that, like he can see past her clothes and undergarments. We stand there for a second, a strange energy arcing between us in the cinnamon-scented kitchen.

We're alone, so alone in here, even though there are dozens of people just beyond that door.

You hate him.

And I do, I really do. And yet...

He fills out that shirt so well, and part of me responds to his feral, commanding energy—wanting to bite back. And then strip his shirt off so I can see what's hidden beneath it.

He clears his throat, his Adam's apple bobbing, and the tension breaks. "I found the slip of paper you dropped on the bridge."

Oh no. Oh no, no, no. Skippy ate that note. He was supposed to have saved me from this awful moment.

My face hot with shame, I say, "You don't understand what you saw. It was about someone else."

"No," he says firmly, his intense dark eyes glued to mine. "We both know it wasn't. And you can't go through with this. You don't know what those men are like. *I* do. They'll talk. If you're going to go through with this crazy plan, you need to choose someone who's discreet."

My mouth goes dry. Surely he doesn't mean...

"I'll do it."

For half a second, molten, sensual heat floods my body, but it's chased out by pure, undiluted fury.

Enzo Cafiero just offered to take my virginity as if he were taking one for the team.

CHAPTER 8

ENZO

I didn't mean to say that. The words came spilling out of my mouth, and only once they'd been said did I realize what I'm really doing here tonight. I don't want Lucy to hook up with some other guy because *I* want her.

I might not like this woman, I definitely don't want to date her, but I *want* her, and the thought of anyone else getting to be the first man who sinks into her is driving me around-the-bend crazy.

Lucy reaches out, and for half a second, I'm convinced she's going to pull me in for a kiss. My entire body clenches with anticipation as I prepare to kiss her back.

She leans in close, so close, but then drills her pointer finger into my chest before snatching it away as if the contact had burned her.

It definitely burned me.

"How. *Dare*. You."

I throw up my palms and step back from her. She probably wouldn't believe it, but the last thing I want to do is make a woman uncomfortable. Ever. "It's an honest offer. You said you want it to be a random guy, someone who means nothing to you. What would mean less than sleeping with a man you hate?"

I barely even know what I'm saying. None of this is coming out right, it's just…

She smells so impossibly good—like the cinnamon candy we used to get in our stockings back when I actually enjoyed Christmas—and she's so pretty with her head tipped up slightly to look at me, that long hair curling down past the swell of her breasts. Standing here with her, even though she's insulted everything about me, from my manhood to my character, it's obvious what I want.

It seems like she might actually be considering my logic, but then she gasps, a new fire entering her gaze. "You're only offering because I said you were a bad lover."

"So you're admitting you said that," I comment, probably hammering a few nails into my own coffin.

"Do you seriously think I'm going to sleep with you just so you can prove your point?"

"I'm glad you think I can prove my point, because I am a good lover. A *generous* lover, I've been told. But no, that's not why I made the offer." I can tell I'm not forming a strong case for myself. I've been told I have a silver tongue and the ability to turn anything to gold just by touching it, but this woman isn't impressed with me and never has been.

"So why did you?" she asks, planting a hand on her perfectly rounded hip, pulling the fabric of her sweater taut.

I swallow against a dry throat, knowing already that I'm not going to get what I want, at least not tonight.

"I'm going to be in town for a while, at least until the shop is doing better. I know what dating is like around here. Everyone knows your business. It's a nightmare. But I also don't want to be celibate for months. If everyone thinks we hate each other, they'd never—"

"Know," she corrects firmly. "If they *know* we hate each other."

I tip my head in acknowledgment. "Yes. And I'm also trying to protect you from other men who wouldn't keep their mouths shut. I would never say a word about you. The last thing I want is to end up in that gossip column again."

"No one wants to end up in that column," she says pointedly.

I shake my head. "Not true. Some people consider it a badge of honor."

People like Brandon Wright.

I won't let her go home with that kind of guy, a known smooth talker who would broadcast everything that happened between them to the entire town. Maybe that makes me an overbearing asshole—hell, it certainly does—but there it is. I feel an insistent need to make sure she doesn't trust the wrong man.

"I'm trying to be a gent—"

"A gentleman?" she challenges, lifting her eyebrows and leaning in slightly, an antagonistic move that still gives me a whiff of her cinnamon scent. "Like I said, whoever tried to teach you failed. Your mother should have put you in finishing school."

This again. I could tell her what happened with my mother, but I don't. She'll find out soon enough, given that everyone in this place knows everyone else. I don't need pity.

"They refused to enroll me, sorry."

"Of course they did," she says, shaking her head, her hair moving with the motion. It's mesmerizing to watch, but I snap my gaze away to prove my self-control isn't completely nonexistent.

"Look. I'm not going to sleep with you," she continues. "That's a horrible idea, even if you have the whole thing planned out, and you're…you know." She waves a hand at me as if the answer should be obvious.

My body heats up as if she'd cast an invisible spell. "Even if I'm what?"

A tiny crease appears between her eyebrows. "You know what you look like. Your stunt yesterday made that perfectly obvious. You knew women would whip open their wallets."

I can't help but smile. "And do you know what *you* look like, Lucy Taylor?"

She blushes. "Twenty-one or maybe twenty-two?"

I did say that at the café, didn't I? I realize now that it's not her appearance that made me think she was that young. It's her new soul quality. Life hasn't stopped surprising Lucy yet. She's not jaded like I am. Life ceased to surprise me a long, long time ago. I lost joy in the little things even earlier than that.

I cross my arms. "It's not like I have a thing for younger women. I was trying to—"

"Be condescending?"

"Kind of like finishing someone else's sentences," I respond pointedly.

She shifts her weight from one foot to the other. "Are we done here? Because it feels an awful lot like we're done here. Eileen's probably worried about me. She definitely should be."

"If she were worried about you, she'd be in here. She may not be friendly with Nonna right now, but she knows us. She babysat for my sister. She was friendly with my mother." Someone should give me a medal, because I managed to say those last words without sounding bitter. "She knows you're safe with me."

She gasps, and then her lips flatten into a taut line. "You're trying to remind me again that I'm not from around here. That I don't get it. That I'll *never* be a Hidie."

I smile, shaking my head. "No, but it's not the curse you think it is. Consider yourself lucky. It's not so easy to get out of this place. It has a gravitational pull that should be studied by NASA. I'm convinced that's the real reason the Wi-Fi sucks."

"I *don't* consider myself lucky," she says fiercely. "It's not fair that you don't value this town but you get to have it."

"And it's not fair that I don't want this town but can't escape it. Life isn't fair, and it never will be. That's a certainty."

"And the other certainty we can count on is that you'll take any possible opportunity to be condescending."

I sigh, suddenly tired. It's this season. All the forced merriment wears me out. And it's also her, so tempting and infuriating and out of reach. "That's not what I meant. I just wanted you to know you'd be safe with me, and even if we don't see eye to eye personally, I find you very attractive. Stunning, actually."

Her lips part, and for a moment, I think she takes it as the very genuine compliment it is. I knew she was beautiful the first time I saw her, but Rachelle had just broken up with me, and I didn't fully register her beauty. My pride had been bruised, my ego fractured. But I'd felt the full force of her beauty like a smack with a wooden spoon last night.

Lucy quickly composes herself. "You'd say anything to get your way."

"There you go, making assumptions again."

She studies me, her gaze moving over me in a way I can feel. It's as if her hands are tracing me and trying to decide whether I'm worthy. Finally, she says, "You think you're the first man I've ever come across who's obsessed with the idea of being my first? That's why I'm going to sleep with someone who doesn't know. I'm sick of it being some big thing. It's *not* a big thing. It's just something that happened because I had too much going on in my life, and now every guy who finds out acts like it's a huge deal. Either he gets obsessed with being *the* guy, or he acts like I waited this long because I wanted to give it up to my soulmate. It's bullshit."

"I'm definitely not worried you'll think I'm your soulmate," I say wryly. "And I know better than to think physical attraction has nothing to do with emotional attraction."

She groans. "Of course you'd say that. Of course you'd *think* that. What I'm telling you is no. Just no. It needs to be—"

"I know some of those guys out there," I say, waving at the door. My blood is hot, pounding through my veins, in my ears. I'm upset. Angry, even, but not at her. "They'd talk about you. Spread rumors. I wouldn't stand for that."

"Why do you care?" She gives me an incredulous look. "The only reason people were talking about me before tonight was because of what happened at the coffee shop four months ago. And that was *your* fault."

"Not yours for questioning my sexual prowess in front of my neighbors?"

I already know I shouldn't have said it, but there's no taking it back now.

"We're done here," she seethes. "You're *definitely* done here. It's time for you to leave. And you know what?" Her hand, which had fallen to her side, returns to her hip. I watch it, wishing things had gone down differently.

"What's that, Lucia?" I say, not meaning to call her that, but it fits. She's too fiery to be a mere Lucy.

Her gaze burns into me. "You're banned from Love at First Sip, effective immediately. I'm sure Eileen will back me up."

Surprised laughter spills out of me. "Are you going to put up a flyer with my photo too? Maybe design it with Eileen?"

"You'd like that, wouldn't you? It would feed your enormous ego."

I smile at her. "Yeah, I would, actually. Make sure you choose a good shot of me. I'll have my brother bring over a selection in the morning. Feel free to use the rejects for dart practice."

"I don't need to practice. I have impeccable aim."

I'll just bet she does.

"Go," she says, pointing, and then her finger actually pokes into my chest again, lingering for half a second, the pad grazing up and down my shirt.

"Are you sure you want me to?"

"*Yes*," she says hotly. "The sooner you leave, the sooner I can enjoy this event."

"I wish for your sake that were the case. Goodbye, Lucia."

I leave the kitchen, letting the door swing shut behind me as I enter the dining area. I expect her to follow me, to make sure I heed her command, but she doesn't, not yet.

I let myself accept the disappointment funneling through my veins, but disappointment is not the same as defeat.

Lucy may not want to sleep with me. She may never want to sleep with me. But I will do everything in my power to make sure she doesn't go home with Brandon Wright tonight. That is unacceptable, and I do not allow unacceptable things to happen.

Which is why you're unemployed, you stubborn idiot.

Be that as it may, you can't change your basic personality just by wishing it so.

The guests are still milling around, some of the guys holding their Santa beards by the ear loops while they sip hot chocolate. A few of the women are sucking seductively on candy canes while they scope out the miserable selection available to them, like a Mother's Day buffet just before closing.

Eileen gestures me over from behind the front counter.

"Are you leaving, dear, or could I interest you in some hot chocolate? We have The Naughty List and The Nice List." Eyes twinkling, she cocks her head and asks, "And which one would you be on tonight?"

I laugh despite myself. "That's been made quite clear to me. I've been banned from the Sip, so I'm guessing I should hand in my Santa paraphernalia."

She tsks but nods. "Lucy has my complete support, so I'll stand by her decision. But will you say hello to your sister for me? And your grandmother. I don't like having bad blood between us, especially at this time of year. We never quite recovered our relationship after your mother left, but I was hoping we could overcome these recent hiccups."

"I'll tell her," I promise. "You know how she is. She'll be angry until she's not."

Nonna Francesca has gotten more mercurial lately, her anger lasting longer and for less of a reason. I'm worried age is catching up to her, confusing her and making past battles leak into the present.

I'm approaching my fears about her aging carefully, though, because I know my grandmother's pride is as ironclad as my own.

"I do, my dear," Eileen says. She hands me a little pink box, patting it softly with her hand. "I packed up some cookies for your grandmother while you were in the kitchen, and some of those delightful whoopie pies from next door."

"She'll assume they're poisoned," I say truthfully.

"I know," she replies without any sign of indignation. "So tell her they're from Audrey at Making Whoopie. A free sample."

"She doesn't believe anything in life is free."

Eileen pats my hand. "Kindness is, Enzo."

I feel a little hot behind the ears. Embarrassed, I realize. I came here to seduce her pretty barista, and here she is, being kind to me—like giving a plated meal to a fox that snuck into the henhouse.

I force a smile. "Isn't this a little dramatic, like we're the Montagues and the Capulets?"

"It *is* exciting, isn't it?" she says with a sweet return smile. "Now, off you go. I have some matchmaking to do, and I'm afraid we may be at cross-purposes."

"Brandon Wright is a player," I warn her. "He's no good for Lucy."

"I *have* heard stories," she says, clucking her tongue. "Then again, I've heard stories about every single young person in this town, including *you*."

Well, damn. I'm not sure I like the sound of that. I've only ended up in that column in the paper once, after the whole mess with Rachelle and Lucy, but once was enough. "I've never trifled with a woman. I'm always honest about my intentions."

"There are many different ways of trifling with a person," she says archly. "Including trifling with their hearts." She gives a dramatic pause, during which I'm supposed to feel like shit, and then continues, "I think you'd better leave now, dear. The Santas are getting restless."

I glance back at the kitchen door, still closed. Maybe Lucy is waiting behind it. Maybe her ear is pressed to the wood, and she'll only come out once I've left.

I don't like the thought.

I like it so little, I find myself rubbing my chest.

But at this point I've been kicked out by two different women, and even though Lucy would never believe it, I have some manners. When a woman says no, she means it. When someone tells you to leave, for the love of God, listen.

So I gather my coat and scarf and step out into the chilly night, but I'll be perfectly honest. I have no intention of going home.

CHAPTER 9

LUCY

I'm having a perfectly decent conversation with a Santa named Brandon, who seems to tick all of my Mr. Perfectly Okay boxes, but I have to admit my heart isn't in it.

I can't *believe* Enzo came in here and offered to deflower me.

The ego of that man!

The absolute nerve!

Did he really think I'd accept?

I'm almost angrier about that than the fact that he asked in the first place.

"Hey, where'd you go just now?" Brandon says, reaching across the table and touching my arm.

I'm hoping to feel something—a spark of awareness, at least—but it just feels like a strange man in a Santa suit is touching my arm. It's kind of unpleasant, to be perfectly honest.

Pulling away, I ask, "Do you know the Cafieros?"

"Yeah, sure," he says. "I went to school with Enzo." He hooks a thumb toward the door, indicating he's well aware that Enzo was the interloper Santa.

"Was he an asshole when he was a kid too?" I ask, then cover my mouth.

He barks a laugh, running a hand over his fake beard. "Sweetheart, that man was born with a stick up his ass. But don't worry. He won't bother you when I'm around. He's afraid of me."

"I seriously doubt that," I say, before I realize he's doing that posturing thing men do, measuring their dicks against each other. But I *know* Enzo wouldn't be afraid of him. I don't think Enzo is afraid of anyone.

Brandon pushes back in his chair. "You want me to prove it? I'm happy to prove it! I'll—"

"He already left," I say, exasperated. "And even if he hadn't, what would you do, randomly punch him? We'd have to call the cops."

His mouth gets pouty beneath the beard, and I'm suddenly disgusted with myself.

Did I seriously think I could find Mr. Perfectly Okay in five minutes? I mean, what would have happened if I'd talked to Brandon about something else, like the weather? I might have mistaken him for a reasonable person.

I mean, I'm not looking for my soulmate here. But I'd prefer it if Mr. Perfectly Okay weren't a psychopath or a whiny man-baby.

As much as I hate to admit it, Enzo might have been the tiniest bit right.

"You don't think a man has a right to be protective of his woman?" Brandon asks, scratching beneath his beard.

"Whoa," I say, extending my hands in what I hope he understands is a *hell no* gesture. "We met two minutes ago. I am *not* your woman. In fact, I think—"

I don't get to finish, because a high-pitched scream rises up from two tables down.

A man throws his fake beard into the air, shouting over

Bing Crosby singing about a white Christmas, "The beards have head lice! Take off your beards!"

Shouted swears travel across the room like wildfire, and more beards are thrown into the air. It looks like a graduation at a school for Santas, where they toss beards instead of hats. Brandon practically rips his ear off in his haste to get his off.

No, Enzo would *definitely* not be afraid of this guy.

Beard disposed of, Brandon leaps to his feet and starts stripping off his clothes.

"What are you *doing*?" I ask in shock.

He has his hat and sweater off already, and he reaches for the hem of his undershirt. "Getting rid of the head lice."

"But they'd be in your hair! They're *head* lice."

A couple of guys holding their coats march past us and head directly out the door, cold air wafting in again.

"You forgot your goody bags!" Eileen calls to them as Brandon continues disrobing. He's shirtless now, his pale chest beaming at me while he starts unfastening his belt. It's mesmerizing, but not in a good way.

"Stop that," I snap at him. But he doesn't, even when I clap my hands like a preschool teacher. "Stop. You're in a public space. You're embarrassing yourself."

More people are heading for the exit when the man who called *head lice* shouts, "Sorry! False alarm, it was just some poppy seeds."

Brandon's expression shifts from horror to horrified awareness that he's stripped down in front of a room full of people. It happens the exact moment before the overhead lights flicker off.

"What is even *happening*?" a woman shouts, panic filling her voice.

There's a rumble of footsteps as people try to leave the café en masse.

"One at a time," I shout, getting to my feet. "File out one at a time. But you don't need to rush out. Eileen has candles. It's probably just a power fluctuation."

An emergency lantern flickers to life at the front of the room, illuminating Eileen's startled face. "There were no head lice in the beards, to be clear," she says. "Zero head lice. They were all professionally laundered."

But it's clear the event is over. Everyone who hasn't already left starts preparing to do so, pulling on jackets and throwing away trash. Brandon takes the longest given that he'd stripped off nearly all of his clothes.

"Hey," he says as he pulls on his coat. "Now that you've had a preview, would you—"

"No," I snap.

None of the men who showed up tonight were what you'd call quality, but it wasn't *their* fault Santa Speed Dating was a catastrophic failure.

It's Enzo's fault. I'm sure of it. And, no question about it, I will one hundred percent get the scoundrel back.

I'm still steaming about it when Eileen and I lock the door after the last emotionally scarred speed-dater.

"We certainly put on a memorable event," Eileen says, chuckling as she slides behind the front counter and pours me some of The Nice List hot chocolate. She must sense my dark thoughts and want to blunt them.

"It was a disaster," I proclaim.

She nods, surprising me. "But every disaster can be learned from. And you *did* get some dating practice, didn't you, Lucy? Perhaps you're ready for a real date. I know Charlie wasn't overly impressed with the candidates on my list, but there are some very nice boys on it. Lots of eligible bachelors your age in Hideaway Harbor right now."

"I don't think I'm ready for that," I blurt.

"More practice then. Will you come to Crochet Club on Tuesday night?"

Crochet Club seems like an awfully strange place to meet a man, but I nod distractedly. Right now, Tuesday feels as distant as Charlie's spring wedding. My mind is locked on Enzo.

His smug smile.

His low, gravelly voice.

The way he looked at me as he said, *I wish for your sake that were the case...*

"Eileen, I think Enzo is out to get us," I murmur. "He purposefully ruined our event."

She studies me silently for a moment. "You believe he planted fake head lice in the beards and cut our power?"

"Well, it sounds insane when you say it out loud, but yes! All he'd need to do was pour some poppy seeds into the storage container for the beards, and as for the power...I'm guessing excessive use of power in their shop could possibly cause a blackout for the whole building. Or...I don't know. What I do know is that man has designs on me."

"Yes, he *does* seem quite taken with you," she says with a sprinkle of excitement. "But we need to make sure his heart is in the right place. He isn't known for being an open book."

"Oh, no," I say with horror. "I don't find him appealing in the least." The words have the sour mouthfeel of a lie. I don't like Enzo, but I'm far from immune to his charms. "He's good-looking, anyone could see that, but he's probably a psychopath. I'm not sure he even has a heart." I wave around at the dark interior of the café. "Look what he did to Santa Speed Dating." I'm about to say something about *poor Curtis*, but I remember Enzo's story about the handbag and shut my mouth.

"Now, we don't know that he had anything to do with that, Lucy. It's a windy night, and the power might have fallen victim to it." She releases a gusty sigh. "And Enzo definitely has a heart. I think that boy would do just about anything to protect his family."

"Maybe so," I concede, remembering what he said about

blood being thicker than water. It had chafed then, and it chafes more now. Because if family only means blood, then I've never had one and never will. "But that doesn't mean he's not trouble."

"There we can agree." She pauses for a sip of her hot chocolate. "I'll have a stern chat with him when he and I get dinner."

"You're seriously having dinner with him after all of this?" I ask incredulously. "We banned him from the shop!"

"Problems usually lose steam if you talk them through, don't you think?"

She's right, *of course* she's right, but I can't stand the thought of Eileen having dinner with Enzo and being nice to him. It would be like breaking bread with a war criminal. I know I'm being hysterical, but seriously, what man offers to sleep with a complete stranger simply because he knows she's a virgin? It's like something out of the Middle Ages! He can't, and shouldn't, get away with that scot-free. He needs to pay.

Having a pleasant dinner with sweet Eileen does not qualify as paying.

A wave of inspiration hits me, center mass.

"Tell Erica that *I'll* have dinner with him next week. Let him know. Tell him we'll talk it all out over food."

"You will?" she asks, giving me a surprised look.

"I will. And he's never going to forget it."

Her gaze lingers on me, her eyes filling with warm humor. "You're not planning on murdering him, are you? I'm too old to handle a shovel, and his grandmother is already upset with me. She'd ban me forever, and I do enjoy their eggplant parmesan."

"It's delicious," I say with a sad sigh, because I will surely never taste it again. "And no, I'm not planning on killing him, but there's no denying that man does things to me."

She nods slowly, meaningfully.

"Not like that," I insist. "I hate him."

"Yes, hatred *is* an interesting emotion, isn't it?"

I STOP at Charlie's house on the way home and unload about the horrors of Santa Speed Dating while Lars makes us mulled wine, good-naturedly participating in the conversation even though he spent all day tracking piping plovers in the cold. I tell her almost everything, leaving out only the part about the pink note Enzo found, and make it sound like he made me a more typical "enemies with benefits" offer.

"Wait," she says when I finally get to the end of my story. "You're seriously going to have dinner with Enzo?"

"No," I scoff. "I'm going to stand him up. See how he likes sitting alone at a restaurant, watching out the window for someone who's never going to come. That's *definitely* going to hurt his precious ego."

"Uh, I don't know about that," Charlie says. "One of his brothers has to pull taffy in front of an audience, the other is posing for an ice sculpture, and all Enzo has to do is have dinner by himself at a nice restaurant? I mean, boo-hoo, poor guy."

"What if I ask Erica to choose a bad restaurant?"

"Bite your tongue. There are no bad restaurants in Hideaway."

"That's not true," Lars says as he pours the wine into glasses for us. "One of my friends swears he got food poisoning at The Chowder House Rules, from the crab bisque. I think he just had a bad hangover, though."

"Even so. Bad food wouldn't be enough," she insists, then rubs her nails over her lips, an old habit that always suggests she's thinking extra hard.

"Uh-oh," Lars says, grinning at me. "Charlie's plotting."

I grin back, feeling a rush of affection for him. He makes Charlie happy, and he's accepted me as her family. He didn't have to, but he did.

Lars knows that family is more than matching DNA.

She points at him, her eyes lighting up. "You know Enzo. You dated Aria."

"I remember," he replies wryly.

"What can you tell us that will help us ruin his night?"

"I only met him once, when he said he'd destroy me if I upset his sister. I'd prefer not to remind him of that promise."

I make a mental note of this anecdote as further evidence of Enzo's psychopathy. I can use it to convince Eileen he's a problem.

Is it Eileen you want to convince or yourself?

Definitely Eileen, I decide.

He's a menace to all of us. And a pig, offering to take my virginity, like it would be some kind of favor.

I'm almost, maybe, completely positive his offer isn't appealing to me.

"What would be the worst thing that could happen to him on this date?" Charlie asks Lars. "Psychoanalyze him like you would one of your birds."

He laughs. "Lesson one of conservation work: don't anthropomorphize wildlife. But sure, I'll play. What would he hate? I think he'd probably be pissed off if I showed up to be his dinner date instead of Lucy. But I won't do it. Not even for you."

She reaches up and squeezes his chin. "Yes, I like your face exactly like it is. No Enzo for you."

He tilts his head in thought before glancing at me. "What if you stood him up, but still showed up for dinner at the same restaurant with another man?" He snaps his fingers. "That would probably do it."

"You're an evil genius," Charlie says lovingly.

"But who would I go with?" I ask.

"You work for the town matchmaker," Charlie says with a

grin. "Remember that list of men she wants to set you up with?"

"You're right," I say, feeling a swell of positivity. "This is going to be great. He won't know what hit him."

We spend a couple of hours chatting, and I help Charlie choose a few of her paintings to sell in the local Christmas market. It's on the edge of the town square next to the library, an adorable little assemblage of wooden booths selling Christmas gifts and treats. She's sharing a stall with a few other vendors, working around her painting schedule and hours at the shop.

The walkability of Hideaway Harbor is one of my favorite parts of this town, and my apartment building is a short jaunt from Charlie's house. She and Lars insist on escorting me home, though, and I don't put up a fuss. We take some mulled wine in to-go cups and stroll around for a while, checking out the holiday light displays. My heart fills with love for this place and for my friends as we soak everything in and greet people who poke their heads out to say hello.

The people of Hideaway Harbor get very competitive about their Christmas lights, especially after one Hidie got featured in a national TV competition. He didn't win, but Mayor Locke gave him a participation trophy shaped like Larry the Lobstah that he keeps on his lawn. People love to put accessories on him—hats, sunglasses, and the other day I walked by and saw him holding a blunt in his claw.

My friends give me hugs at the door of my building, and I watch them walk away together, hand in hand. Happiness swells inside of me, and then, as if my happiness balloon has a slow leak, it seeps away. It's replaced by a darker feeling as I open the door and head upstairs.

Just what the heck am I doing, anyway?

Christmas with my mom was always so warm and fun. Even after I realized the truth about Santa, we kept leaving out proof of him for each other. A mislaid hat, cookies with bite marks in them. One year, I even wrote her a love letter from Santa that she adored so much she framed it. I haven't unpacked it yet because it hurts too much to look at it, to remember that all the things I gave her are now once again mine.

Christmas was always about good feelings, not about pettiness or resentments. The whole month of December felt like a warm, cinnamon-scented hug.

What would Mom do about the Enzo situation?

She'd probably tell me to kill him with kindness. But it's not like I can make Christmas cookies for him and call it a wash. He did a few completely unacceptable things, and I will not accept the unacceptable. I shouldn't have to.

The thought reignites my inner fire as I pass the other apartments on my floor. I'm steamed up by the time I arrive at my apartment door, where I find a sealed note waiting for me, propped against it.

I'd completely forgotten about my friendly stalker. I bring the note inside, smiling, because this is what Christmas should be all about—making connections with strangers. Being kind.

I sit in my cozy chair by the tree and open it, feeling a surge of anticipation.

To Dancing Queen—

Whoa! Stalker?

I prefer the term neighbor. Yes, I live in this building, although I suppose you'll have to take my word for it. I was a Lobster Scout, if that adds to my credibility.

If you're not from around here originally, you may be wondering what a Lobster Scout is.

It's like regular Scouts, only you have to go for a swim in the harbor. In January. I'm not ashamed to admit I screamed like a baby the moment I jumped in, but it also felt good.

Are you going to do the polar bear plunge this year?

Needless to say, as a scout, I'm a perfect gentleman. It would be very ungentlemanly to stalk someone.

What do you think about the big to-do about Christmas around here? I'm guessing from your tree and lights that you have thoughts. I'm not a Christmas guy anymore, but I remember loving it when I was a little kid. It felt like anything could happen. My favorite was the lighting of the lobster trap tree near the docks. It's not much to look at until they turn on the lights, and suddenly it becomes something else entirely.

Speaking of which: what are your thoughts on Larry the Lobstah as the town mascot? I, personally, think the Christmas version of him with the Santa hat is a nice touch, even though most people would call me a grinch.

Also, should we keep this anonymous for now? There's something freeing about writing to someone anonymously, but I guess I'd feel like a real idiot if it turns out you're Lady Lovewatch.

With regards,
Your Stalker

I'm smiling as I read it.

I have no idea who this man is, and part of me doesn't want to know. This isn't a romantic connection, but it's a little capital-R Romantic. Two lost souls reaching out in the most old-fashioned way possible. Maybe he'll become my friend in real life. Or maybe we'll keep writing to each other, our lives touching but not overlapping.

Either way, he makes me feel less alone, as if the quietest, saddest thoughts I don't dare whisper out loud are heard and known.

CHAPTER 10

ENZO

"I'll bet Lucy's gonna choose the full-body photo for dart practice," Giovanni says as he rocks back in his desk chair. "Get you right in the dick. She looks like a broad who could make a bull's-eye."

While Nonna runs the register and Nico handles the food orders, Giovanni and I are sitting in the cramped back office in Hidden Italy, brainstorming about what else we can do to dig us out of the hole.

Naturally my brother is more interested in giving me shit than in getting down to business. It's one of his favorite pastimes. All of my siblings enjoy the *drive Enzo crazy* game. It comes from being the oldest, I guess, the one who used to chew them out for bad behavior after my dad checked out and stopped caring. But Giovanni tends to work the hardest at annoying me.

Part of me is grateful for it. His dedication to screwing around is a sign he's mostly unaffected by what happened to our family after our mother left. I'm even a little jealous, because I don't have the ability to relax.

Unfortunately, Giovanni is sometimes *too* relaxed. Which is a contributing factor in the current state of Hidden Italy, no doubt. My brother's a good face for the business, certainly better for that role than Nonna Francesca, but he's not serious enough about success.

Then again, right now I don't have much room to talk.

Stories about what happened at Santa Speed Dating have spread through town like wildfire, and despite what I said to Lucy, I'm guessing something about it will end up in the Lady Lovewatch column. That's what happens when a dating event implodes.

The first thing Giovanni asked me this morning was if I'd had anything to do with what went down at the Sip. My response was to hand him a few photos to give to Lucy so she could make my BANNED flyer. A man is only as good as his word, after all.

Giovanni took that as a, *Hell yes, I did.*

Apparently, when he delivered the photos this morning, Lucy looked him dead in the eye and told him she'd be keeping all of them since I'd volunteered them to be dart practice. Then she offered him one of the elf whoopie pies from last night.

He took it, too.

It's sitting on his desk right now, mocking me with its stupid little piped-on smile.

I'm tempted to tell him not to eat it, in case she tampered with it in some way, but he'd think I was crazy for considering the possibility. Maybe I am crazy. Lucy's outspoken, but she's obviously a sweetheart to most people. I bring out a darker side of her, though—just like she does for me.

"You think you'll feel it when she makes a bull's-eye?" he asks, rocking back in his chair again. I push the chair right back down and give him a level look.

"What are you, twelve?"

He snorts. "Says the man who short-circuited the Sip's

power supply because he couldn't convince a woman to give him the time of day."

"That's supposition," I say. "Besides, I don't want her to give me the time of day. I was just trying to look out for the new girl in town. She hasn't been here nearly long enough to know what she'd be getting into with Brandon."

His expression suggests he doesn't buy my bullshit, and that I shouldn't buy it either. "Sure, brother. That's why you snuck into Santa Speed Dating and then used the basement to access their power supply."

"I never said I did that."

He lifts his eyebrows and taps the side of his nose. "Plausible deniability. I got you."

I swear under my breath, then very deliberately change the subject. "Say, did you ever meet the woman who lives down the hall from Aria's old apartment? In the unit to the right with the window facing the street?"

She left me another note last night, written into a Christmas card with a smiling snowman on the front.

Dear Lobster Scout—

That is ADORABLE. But no, I will never do a polar bear plunge. Nothing could convince me. I might run hot, but I don't run THAT hot.

I'm excited for the lobster trap tree you mentioned in your note! But I have to be honest, I can't eat lobster. I'm not saying it doesn't smell delicious, but the way they're cooked makes my skin crawl.

Yes, I know. It's not very Hideaway

Harbor of me. But I was the kid who couldn't stand to swat flies.

If I had to choose my favorite part of Christmas in Hideaway Harbor, I'd say the town square. I LOVE the tree and the little huts they've set up for the Christmas market on one end. I've always wanted to go to one of those Christmas villages in Europe, where they have mulled wine and you can walk around getting drunk in a classy way while you soak in all the music and lights and happy vibes.

In case you can't tell, I'm not a Hidie born and bred, but I want to make my home here.

After losing my mother, I feel like a plant that has plenty of water and sun but no soil. So I'm trying to put down some roots here, even if a few people have made me feel like that's not possible.

—The Dancing Queen

P.S. Yes, let's stay anonymous! I would NEVER be able to look a Hidie in the face after admitting I don't like lobster.

It's kind of fucked up, but Dancing Queen has become the one person I've genuinely confided in since returning home to

Hideaway Harbor.

Part of me likes that I don't know who she is. Still, I can't help but wonder.

"Wow, you must be truly desperate to change the subject," my brother says, kicking back in his chair again.

"I'm curious about my neighbors. It's natural for a person to be curious."

He looks less than convinced, but he shrugs. "Sure, I ran into her once or twice. She looked like she was in her forties. I think she works in data entry or something else with computers, and she cooks a lot of cabbage. The only other thing I remember is that her favorite show is *The Golden Girls*. Her hearing's not too great, so she always pumped up the volume. It was loud enough that Aria could hear it down the hall."

"Cabbage?" I've never smelled it in the building, and it's a distinctive smell. I haven't heard *The Golden Girls* either. Which isn't to say none of that's happening, I suppose. I don't spend much time at home.

"It's disgusting," he says with a theatrical shudder.

I'm surprised by his description of Dancing Queen, and honestly a little disappointed. I wasn't romantically interested in my neighbor—a person can't be romantically interested in a shadow and a handful of letters—but it felt like we were making a personal connection, and my mental image of her wasn't of a shut-in, data entry clerk with a thing for old sitcoms. It's hard to imagine being friends with a person like that. But I still want to write her back. Partly because she opened up to me about something so personal—losing her mother.

Even though I lost my own mother in a different way, I lost her all the same. After she left, she used to call a few times a week. But she never asked for shared custody, and then she got remarried. All of us kids had gone to the wedding. And it was one of the last times we ever saw her.

Her husband didn't like kids, and it turned out she didn't like them much either. Every now and then a random birthday or holiday card will arrive, and that's the extent of our relationship with her.

I've tried to protect my siblings from the pain as much as possible, and God knows my grandparents stepped up, but fuck. That doesn't make it easy.

Losing someone to death isn't easy either. I've lost other people that way. My nonno. Friends. Work colleagues.

I push the thoughts down and try to shift back to the present.

My neighbor...cabbage...

"Well, she seems nice, anyway," I say with a sigh.

Giovanni looks surprised by this, probably since I just made it very clear I've never met her.

"We've exchanged a couple of notes," I explain.

"Notes?" He furrows his brow.

"Neighbor stuff."

"Okay, champ. I think you're just trying to shift the subject off a certain difficult woman."

"Devil Woman," I say.

"Sure. Speaking of devil women, Portia told me my taffy pulling debut will be next Saturday afternoon, before the lobster trap tree lighting. She figures she can gather a big crowd and then send them out to the harbor."

He looks amused, not pissed, so I know he doesn't mind too much.

"You got a thing for Portia?" I ask with interest. She's friendly with our sister, Aria, so she hung out at our house a few times when we were younger. Even though I've seen her at least a dozen times over the past few years, I still remember her as a skinny goth teen.

He shrugs. "Nah. We just like giving each other shit. Besides, I'm pretty sure she's into women. Both of us were checking out Amanda Willis at the tree lighting in town square."

"I mean, it's Amanda Willis," I say with a half-smile. "She's a movie star."

"*You* weren't checking her out," he says pointedly.

No, because I hadn't gone to the tree lighting. I'd just arrived back in town, and I'd spent that night in Aria's apartment, poring over Hidden Italy's books and trying to tap into the brilliance that seems to have seeped out of me.

"If I'd been there, I'm sure I would have been checking her out too," I hedge.

"Or checking out Lucy."

"She hates me," I huff.

"You know, I really think she does. I have to say, you have your work cut out for you."

"I'm not interested in dating anyone," I say flatly. "I don't even know how long I'm going to be here."

He gives me a quizzical look. "Taking off on us already, brother?

"No. We're gonna get the business right."

He nods, a dimple forming in his cheek. "Well, hallelujah. Then you're never going to leave. Anyway, if you want an in with that woman you're totally not interested in, maybe you should tell her that Portia wouldn't be opposed to some match-making from Eileen."

"You want to set up Portia with an international celebrity?" I ask with a skeptical laugh. "I guess you *do* like her."

He grins. "Hey, if I can't impress Amanda, I might as well make a play for my friend. Besides, maybe Portia will take it easy on me with the taffy crap if I can get her a sit-down with Amanda."

"Yeah, good luck with that," I mutter as my phone buzzes in my pocket. It buzzes again, and then again, texts coming through rapid-fire. It happens that way in Hideaway Harbor.

Your phone won't be able to find a single bar of service for hours, and suddenly the texts all arrive in a gush.

I've been spoiled in my apartment building, where the Wi-Fi seems to work better than in other places.

My brother picks up the whoopie pie and bites it, cream spurting onto his shirt.

"Damn," he says with a moan. "That's *good*."

My phone buzzes *again*.

I know my brother, and there's no way I'm getting his full attention until he's inhaled that whole whoopie pie, so I pull out my phone and find a screenful of texts from Erica that were sent half an hour ago. They're written in all caps, so it looks like my phone's screaming at me.

HELLO, BACHELOR #1!

THANK YOU SO MUCH FOR THAT BASKET OF TREATS. JOHN GOT HEARTBURN FROM THE SARDINES, BUT I DON'T BLAME YOU FOR THAT, OF COURSE. IT'S HIS OWN FAULT FOR EATING THEM ALL.

I MADE HIM SHARE THE PANETTONE!

HE SAID HE NEEDS TO GET INTO SHAPE TO PLAY SANTA CLAUS, BUT WE BOTH KNOW THAT IT WAS JUST THAT GOOD. :-X

NOW, I HOPE YOU WON'T MIND, BUT A CERTAIN YOUNG LADY WE BOTH KNOW WANTED MY PRIZE FOR HERSELF, AND I WAS *MORE* THAN HAPPY TO SHARE THE WEALTH.

YOU KNOW EILEEN AND I ARE ALWAYS THRILLED TO HELP YOU YOUNG PEOPLE. ;-)

> SHE ASKED ME NOT TO REVEAL WHO SHE
> IS UNTIL SHE SHOWS UP AT THE
> RESTAURANT. ISN'T THAT EXCITING? YOU
> CAN MEET HER AT HOOK, WINE, AND
> SINKER THIS THURSDAY AT 7:30 P.M.

> I'VE HEARD YOU'RE A BIG FAN OF THEIRS.

> THE RESERVATION IS UNDER YOUR NAME,
> DEAR.

I glance up sharply as Giovanni polishes off the rest of the whoopie pie, then dabs his shirt with a napkin.

"Damn," he says. "This is the first one of these things I've ever tried. They're from that place next door to the Sip. It's too bad Nico can't bake like this. If he could, we'd have people in and out that door all day."

The thought sparks something in my brain, an idea waiting to be born. It's related to whoopie pies and maybe even Portia, but I can't flesh it out yet. I'll have to coax it, feed it…and right now the front of my brain belongs solely to Lucy.

Something tells me this invitation to dinner is no olive branch. She's making her next move against me, but what is it?

And why the fuck do I feel so turned on by the thought?

"Check it out," I tell him, showing him the screen of my phone. "Erica's talking about Lucy. Has to be."

He moans. "No fair. You came up with this dumbass idea, and you get to go on a date with your dream girl, while Nico freezes his ass off and I have to pull taffy like a *pazzo*."

"Life isn't fair, Giovanni," I say with a shit-eating grin. "Besides, she's definitely up to something."

"You think she's going to poison you or slip Ex-Lax into your drink?" he asks with a laugh.

"Maybe," I say, half serious. Lucy did look pissed off enough last night to try something like that. "But I tell you what. I look forward to finding out."

CHAPTER 11

ENZO

By the time the parade starts that afternoon, Lucy has already put up a flyer next to the door of Love at First Sip with a giant X over my face.

It says:

> *This man has been banned from Love at First Sip. Turn away without service.*

There's a little frowny face sketched beside it.
After I read the flyer, I pull out a pen and add:

> *Am I allowed to order takeaway?*

That evening, there's an answer. Someone has painstakingly written out the dictionary definition of "banned" beneath my question.

The next morning, I get a special delivery at the shop—an electrical fuse, along with a handwritten note:

I know what you did.

Since we're sending each other gifts, I order her a delivery of a lobster candy cane from Portia's shop, hoping she hasn't heard about them yet and assumes it's a flavor people want to eat. The note suggests it's from a secret admirer.

We close at noon on Sundays, because Sundays are family days, so I leave before Lucy can make her rebuttal.

It snows that night, big thick snowflakes coming down, and I find myself wondering if it snows much where Lucy is from. Does she like it?

Will she dance around in it and try to catch the flakes on her tongue?

Yup, I'm officially losing my mind.

I walk to Hidden Italy early on Monday morning, finding the cold refreshing. Although I wouldn't care to admit it, I like the crisp crunch of the fresh snow drifts beneath my boots, and the sleepy way the town looks when it's covered in a fresh layer of snow with smoke curling up from the chimneys. Even the Christmas tree in the town square is covered in snow, so scenic it's as if someone came in and strategically placed the white drifts in the middle of the night.

This is the part of Hideaway Harbor I love, the town when it's at rest. Not performing. Not trying to impress. But covered in a snowy blanket and looking much the same as it probably did after George Locke and Alma Keye founded it all those years ago. Sleepy and sweet. Quiet.

When I get to the shop, I'm not surprised to find the lobster candy cane taped to the Hidden Italy sign with another note:

Is that the best you can do?

I'll be honest, it makes me smile.

The sidewalk in front of their café is covered with snow, so I shovel it after clearing our steps. Eileen's elderly, and if Lucy's working, she may not be used to shoveling snow.

No big deal. Just doing the gentlemanly thing.

Later that morning, Nonna comes into our shop, looking especially sour.

"Everything okay?" I ask.

I spend most of my time in the back office, but I also like hanging out in the front of the shop, seeing what people look at, what they order. It's supposed to help ideas germinate, but so far all it's done is keep me up to date on a bunch of town gossip I couldn't care less about.

She waves her hand toward the door. "Those women next door have a cappuccino special. *Che chazzo!* I'm the one who taught Eileen to make them years ago."

"I'm sure she doesn't mean it as an insult," I say, remembering what Eileen told me the other night. "She wants to get along."

"And this is how she tries?" my grandmother asks incredulously, waving a fist at the door as if she wants to break it.

I exchange a glance with my brother, Nico, behind the sandwich counter, and feel a grin tugging at my mouth. Shifting my attention back to my grandmother, I say, "So we'll show them how it's done, Nonna."

I don't have to look at Nico again to know he's shaking his head. Giovanni's off today, so at least I only have one brother giving me a hard time.

A few minutes later, I head outside with a sandwich board sign and a dry-erase marker. Sure enough, Love at First Sip has a cinnamon-stick cappuccino advertised on their own white-board sign as their daily special. So I offer one too, setting our little sandwich board sign next to the staircase leading down to

Hidden Italy. I make ours a quarter cheaper and add that it's an authentic Italian cappuccino, underlining "authentic."

At around noon, I go outside to hang up a wreath on the bracket under our sign—a wreath at least twice as big as the one hanging on the door of the Sip. Our cinnamon broom was nowhere to be seen when I arrived this morning. Either the snowstorm swept it away, or Lucy sent it to sleep with the fishes.

While I'm outside getting the wreath to hang straight, Lucy marches out of the café with a red dry-erase marker. I can only assume she's been watching for me to come out here.

She gives me the finger and then changes their sign to make their drink a quarter cheaper than ours.

I laugh as she adds,

The best cappuccino in Hideaway Harbor!

Then laugh harder when she underlines "best."

"You're really testing my grandmother," I caution. "I couldn't care less, but those are fighting words. Especially since she claims she taught Eileen how to make cappuccinos."

Lucy gives me a feral smile as she tucks a curl behind her ear. I notice her red lipstick and feel a lurching sensation. Is she wearing it to taunt me, or did she put it on for another man?

I shouldn't care—this woman really does seem to loathe me, and I enjoy arguing with her too much to try to change that. But I do care. Far more than I'd like.

"Speaking of really testing people, how's the power in your shop?" she snaps. "Funny how our building was the only one affected on the whole block, and the power was perfectly fine in the morning."

I rub the back of my neck, avoiding her gaze. I feel hot all of a sudden. Like I need to plunge my head in a snowbank.

"How are you adjusting to the snow?" I blurt.

"What? I—" Her brows knit. "How do you know I'm not from a place that has tons of snow?"

"The way you dress."

She scowls at me. "I run hot."

"I certainly believe that."

She wraps her arms around her body. "I like the snow."

Her gaze strays to the town square. The snow is still fresh other than a few track marks across it. No yellow spots yet.

"It's beautiful. Like it was plucked from the pages of a fairy tale." She pauses, looking thoughtful. "I take it there's some service that comes through and cleans the stoops?"

"Maybe it's the Hideaway Elf. Wouldn't be the first time it's happened. Word is, some mysterious altruist cleared your snow and ours in the middle of the night a couple of weeks ago. Just doing something good for humanity." I'm not totally making this up. I overheard a few people gossiping in the shop earlier about random acts of Christmas kindness.

"Sure. Whatever. Someone cleared the snow today. It wasn't me, it wasn't Charlie or Lars, and it *definitely* wasn't Eileen, thank God."

"Must be a really great person to have done something like that. Possibly a god among men. Or a goddess among women."

She narrows her gaze at me. "Did you—"

"Did you take our cinnamon broom?" I ask, not wanting to confirm or deny that I shoveled the snow.

"You think I stole your stupid broom?" she asks in a tone of disbelief.

I tsk-tsk. "My grandmother made that broom."

"I would never steal anything."

"You should have," I say. "They smell really good, and she already sold out of her latest batch. I'll talk to her about making some more."

From the expression on her face, I've confused her. Good. We might as well both be confused.

A moment of silence hangs between us. A breeze whips her hair into her face, and I watch eagerly as she tucks it behind her ear.

"You better not do anything to interrupt Crochet Club tomorrow." She glowers at me, wielding the dry-erase marker she's still holding as if it were a sword.

"Or else you'll beat me with that dry-erase marker?" I ask, raising my eyebrows. "Consider me intimidated."

A scowl creases her brows, but then she uncaps the marker and attacks the BANNED flyer with it, giving me a red mustache that makes me look like a cartoon villain.

"You know, I don't look half bad with a mustache," I muse, knowing I shouldn't needle her but enjoying it too much to stop. "Maybe I'll stop shaving. How about adding a kiss mark on my cheek? Red's the perfect color. You wouldn't even need to use the marker. You could—"

I start laughing, unable to finish the thought, because she just added a zit to my face on the flyer. She adds another before shooting me a smug look. "I recommend salicylic acid. It works wonders."

Laughing, I ask, "Are we still getting dinner on Thursday night? If so, can I request that you bring the dry-erase marker? Maybe I'll even let you draw on me. You can bring a green one too, if you'd like. Make it festive."

She nearly drops the marker before tucking it into the pocket of her coat. Giving me a holier-than-thou look, she says, "I have *no idea* what you're talking about, and I'd rather not find out."

"Of course not. By the way, I'd appreciate it if you didn't poison me. My grandmother and siblings are fond of me."

"God only knows why."

"I agree," I say, rocking on my heels. "Say…I have a hot tip for you and Eileen."

She plants a hand on her hip. "You'll excuse me if I don't fall all over myself in excitement."

"I think I'd like to see that."

She glares at me.

I lift my hands in surrender. "Okay, fine. But you'll want to hear this. My brother Giovanni told me he thinks Portia wouldn't be opposed to spending more time with Amanda Willis. I guess they had a moment at the Christmas tree lighting."

Interest sparks in her eyes, immediately extinguished by suspicion. "Why are you telling me? Does this have something to do with the lobster candy cane you sent? Are you going to bribe Portia to—"

I'm already shaking my head. "No, I just know Eileen likes her matchmaking. I figured I'd help out. The spirit of Christmas compelled me."

She snorts. "I'd be less surprised if I caught Santa eating my milk and cookies."

"Is that a euphemism about Santa Speed Dating?" I ask, cocking my head. "You got a thing for men who dress up like the big guy?"

Her expression turns pinched. "I wouldn't know, would I? Because I never got a chance to talk to half of them."

"I look forward to seeing what your next move is, Lucia."

Then I uncap my own marker and lower the price of our cappuccino on the sandwich board. She gasps and hurries inside, probably to ask Eileen for permission to continue our price war.

The competition with Lucy really heats up, and keeping up with our game requires nearly all my focus. By the end of the day, I'm sweating, Nico is calling me a dozen different swears in Italian, and we're giving away our cappuccinos for free.

Nonna Francesca, who has never met a grudge she didn't want to get behind, is all for it until we run out of milk.

Before I head out to get more, I text Erica to check whether the dinner date is still on. Cell service is decent today, and it only takes a few minutes for her all-caps reply to come through.

ABSOLUTELY!

I'M SO EXCITED TO HEAR HOW IT GOES.

NOW, REMEMBER, NO QUESTIONS ABOUT WHO SHE IS UNTIL THURSDAY NIGHT.

Of course not.

Lucy's *definitely* up to something, and I can't wait to see what it is. But we have a few days to go before Thursday, and the war is still in full effect.

That night, I give serious thought to what I could do to mess with the Crochet Club. Unleash a stray cat?

The thought amuses me, but Lucy would probably just crochet the cat a sweater and declare it the café cat, making it a win for her.

I could mess with the power again, but it would be unoriginal. If I'm going to pull something, it has to be unexpected and impressive.

Maybe I can hack into their music streaming system and play that ridiculous old Christmas song "Dominic the Donkey" over and over again? It would be enough to drive a person insane, that's for sure. But the phone service and internet in Hideaway aren't nearly reliable enough for me to depend on it working.

"What the fuck is wrong with you?" I mutter to myself. I should be scheming to save Hidden Italy, working hard to cultivate the nugget of an idea I brainstormed the other night. That's why I'm here. Instead, I'm staying up late thinking of ways to sabotage a crocheting club that's probably full of grandmas.

If I were smart, I'd go straight home after Hidden Italy closes tomorrow night. I know from some roundabout questions I asked my brothers that the club meets at seven.

But Lucy will be waiting for something to happen, expecting it…

I'd be an asshole to let her down, wouldn't I?

THE NEXT NIGHT, I go back to Kippis with Giovanni and Nico at around six forty-five so I can watch everyone arrive for Crochet Club. Nonna Francesca is closing up Hidden Italy with one of the high school kids who works for us part time.

"What exactly are we looking for?" Giovanni asks, tilting his head toward me. "Are you afraid this woman's going to attack you with knitting needles?"

"You only use a single hook for crocheting," says Nico, as if he's suddenly a crocheting expert.

"How do you know this?" I ask. Our mother used to knit, but I never paid much attention, to be honest. And after she left, I threw most of her knitting stuff away one night. No one ever called me on it.

"I go sometimes," Nico says with a shrug. "Or I did before you got banned from the Sip and Nonna Francesca said the rest of us had to stay away out of solidarity." He taps his temples. "It's good for the mind."

"There's no age limit for this club?" I ask.

"Nah," he says. "You'd be surprised by the people who show. Like that bookstore guy."

Well, I really don't like the fucking sound of that. The owner of the local bookstore, Fredrik, is my age, or close enough, and I overheard Aria calling him a fox once. He's a widower, too, and an occasional subject of speculation in the Lovewatch column.

"Seriously?" I mutter. "Don't tell me he crochets too."

My brothers exchange a look.

"Oh, sure," Nico says. "He goes all the time. He's a crocheting machine."

"But let's be honest." Giovanni lifts his beer, giving me a wicked glance. "He's probably there tonight because he wants to get lucky with Lucy. Everyone's saying Eileen's determined to set her up with someone, and that guy has the looks *and* a bookstore. You know how much women like bookstores."

I'm steamed up but trying not to look it. Lucy made a point of telling me not to interrupt her tonight; was it because she's interested in Fredrik?

Trying to look like I couldn't give a shit about what's going on across the street, I say, "Good luck to him. Maybe she'll draw a mustache on him instead."

"I heard she got someone to blow up that full-body picture of you and drew a bull's-eye right at your crotch," Giovanni says, his eyes dancing with glee. "You think it's true? Maybe Fredrik will hit the bull's-eye tonight. You think Lucy will give him a prize if he does?"

I wave my beer at him. "I'm going to go to the Wishing Bridge to wish some woman gets it into her head to drive *you* crazy."

"Portia's already doing that," Nico says, happy to pile on and give our brother some well-deserved grief. "I heard she got the taffy pulling added to the town calendar."

Giovanni rolls his eyes. "She's just hoping Amanda will show."

"What a coincidence," Nico says. "I'm also hoping she'll show."

"You know Amanda is only interested in ladies," Giovanni tells him.

"So she and I have something in common."

A few more minutes pass, during which a couple of other old ladies arrive across the street, as well as some surprisingly young ones.

"No sign of Fredrik," I murmur to myself, and my brothers exchange another look and burst out laughing this time.

"Oh, you assholes," I say, dismissing them with a wave of my hand. "You were messing with me."

"And you totally bought it," Giovanni says smugly. "You're losing that killer edge, Lorenzo. What would Nonna say?"

Probably nothing complimentary.

"Are you ready to admit you have a thing for this girl?" he presses. Nico nods in agreement.

"It's really not like that," I object. Although, in all honesty, I'm not entirely sure what it's like anymore. Lucy and I haven't had a single civil conversation, yet she's all I can think about.

"She always gives me a hard time," I add.

"You ever consider you're into her *because* she gives you a hard time?" Giovanni says.

"Rachelle gave me a hard time too."

Giovanni nearly spits out his beer because he started laughing mid-sip. Choking, he says, "She gave everyone a hard time."

"Did you hear what she did at The Haven?" Nico adds.

I sigh. "Yes, Giovanni and I discussed that the other night."

"Wren Wilde's hot," Nico declares, waggling his eyebrows. "Did you discuss *that?*"

"You think everyone's hot, dumbass," Giovanni says, cuffing him playfully.

"Well, she is. Anyone would think she's hot. It's factual—and a compliment."

"Not everyone seems to think that's a compliment," I interject without intending to, and my brothers exchange another of those significant looks.

"I think Enzo's obsessed with Lucy because she's the only woman who hasn't fallen all over herself to impress him," Giovanni says, looking pretty proud of himself.

"So we're back to me, huh? Can't we give Nico some more shit about his crush on the lady who runs The Haven?"

Nico waves this off. "Oh, she's got her hands full. I've heard she's dating all three Hawthorne brothers."

I laugh. "Sounds like a load of Lady Lovehearts bullshit."

"You mean Lovewatch," Giovanni says. "And yes, that it does. Welcome back to Hideaway Harbor, brother. Where you'll freeze your tits off and drown in gossip."

"Yeah, it's good to be home," I deadpan.

But the thing is, in this moment, sitting with my brothers, it *is* good to be home. The only thing missing is Aria—and the confidence, now lost, that our grandmother, despite being old, is going to live forever.

My brothers leave after half an hour of shooting the shit, but I stay by the window, nursing my one and only beer, watching until all of the guests leave Love at First Sip. Still no sign of Lucy. It's almost eight and dark other than the glowing Christmas lights strung up around town square, the glowing tree at its center, and the little stalls for the Christmas market.

The café looks empty, but I still haven't seen Lucy leave, so I remain stationed at the window, lost in thought.

"You must really enjoy this view of the tree," a woman says from behind me, her voice sultry. I turn to look at her. She's pretty, with long, blonde hair and bright blue eyes. I'd have known she was a tourist even if she weren't wearing a Larry the Lobstah hoodie sweatshirt that says, *Want to play hide the lobster?*

"Something like that," I mutter.

"There's an even better view from my bedroom." She laughs, pressing a hand to her chest. "I can't believe I said that.

But my friends and I are betting on who can come up with the worst pickup line, and I like to win."

"So do I," I say with a smile, my gaze traveling across the square again. It's overcast and snowing a little, enough to obstruct my view of the shop fronts across the street. But I'll know when Lucy leaves because the coat she usually wears is a bright lobster red. No way I'll miss that.

"So what do you say?"

It takes me a moment to remember I'm midconversation with someone. I turn back to the blonde woman, raising my eyebrows. "I haven't heard their pickup lines, so I'm afraid I can't judge."

"That's not the contest." She leans closer in a clear invitation. "The aim of the contest is to find a bad line that works."

It would be easy to go back to her room with her, and maybe it would lessen this horrible desire that's been eating away at me since that night on the bridge—a need that's only intensified with every trick Lucy pulls. Every time we catch a glimpse of each other. But I'm not even tempted.

And when I see a flash of red at the door of Love at First Sip, I practically lunge out of my chair.

"Sorry," I say over my shoulder. "But I have somewhere to be. Good luck with everything."

I hurry out, intending to walk Lucy home.

She'll say no, of course, but I'll insist on it. She can't deny a well-meant gesture like that, can she? But I stop halfway across the square, because two other figures have joined her—one tall, one short. Lars and Charlie. The three of them are laughing.

God, she looks so happy.

It freezes me in place, my boots planted in the snow.

I stand there as she links arms with Charlie and the three of them walk off. Watching them puts a twist in my chest like the bitter peel in a cocktail.

I infuriate Lucy, but her friends make her happy and—to quote my grandfather—*cara mia, what a sight.*

I've enjoyed our war, but part of me yearns to see her like this because of me.

I'm probably just lonely, I rationalize. It's natural to feel lonely sometimes. Especially here in Hideaway, where I always feel a little less like Lorenzo Cafiero, business consultant and badass, and a little more like a ten-year-old boy who watched his mother drive away and knew life was never going to be the same.

It doesn't help that Christmas is a time of year that's supposed to be the opposite of lonely. Everywhere I look there are people smiling and laughing, pointing toward the tree, feeling something special, when right now all I'm feeling is down.

I could go off and find my brothers. Call Will or my sister. Hell, I could take that tourist up on her offer...

But I still don't want to. Not any part of me.

Instead, I walk home, trying to shake off the heaviness, which only gets heavier as I soak in all of the showmanship of Hideaway. The fairy lights hanging everywhere, the heavy wreathes, all the trappings of Christmas feeling almost like a threat. *You will be merry, or else...*

By the time I get home, I'm lonely enough that I knock on the door down the hall, figuring I'll ask my neighbor if she'd like to have coffee. Or maybe share some cabbage.

Hell, I'd probably even watch *The Golden Girls.*

But she doesn't answer, possibly because we've agreed to anonymity, possibly because she's not home.

So I let myself into my apartment to write her a note. She might enjoy data entry and tasteless food, but she's a good pen pal. In some bizarre way, it's easier to talk to her than it is to share with my brothers. Definitely easier than talking to my grandmother these days.

Back when I was a kid, Nonna Francesca was my guiding light, but she's not what she once was. She never will be again, a thought that chafes.

My father should be here, taking care of her. But he's not the man I wish he were, or the kind of man I would like to be.

I pour myself a whiskey and sit down in my favorite chair to write.

To the Dancing Queen,

I'm sorry I didn't write back sooner. It's been a strange week.

You can tell whoever made you feel like you don't belong that your stalker thinks they're an asshole. They may be a bit confused, but don't offer an explanation. I'm guessing they don't deserve one.

You confided in me, so now there's something I want to tell you. Something no one else knows.

I got fired from my job a few weeks ago. Sort of.

I was good at it, really good, but I stopped liking it a long time ago. Because a big part of what I did was making other businesses more efficient, and a lot of the time, as you might imagine, that involved firing people. It didn't used to bother me, because I figured they'd land somewhere else, somewhere they fit better. Win-win for everyone, right? Only with this one particular job, they wanted to cut ten percent of the workforce the month before Christmas.

I've got to level with you. I don't care much about the holidays, but two of the employees who were the least productive had big families. One of them was a pregnant woman.

I told my boss I wasn't comfortable with it, we had words, and I wrote him a long document proposing another way of handling things without eliminating those positions. He didn't take too kindly to that, as you might imagine. He told me it was his job to make the final decisions based on our reports, and if I wasn't willing to do MY job, he'd find someone else who would—and I'd be the one who got fired.

Well, I knew he was all the way wrong, and I've never been so good at being told what to do.

I did a stupid, hotheaded thing, and I quit.

I'll bet you can guess what that means. If I'd been fired, I would have gotten severance pay. Benefits. Now, I've got nothing, and no one to blame for it but myself. I feel pretty stupid, if you want to know the truth. Those people will still lose their jobs, and I lost mine.

It's made me question my instincts. But I don't regret leaving. It was the right thing to do. The thing that would have made my family proud, even if I can't bring myself to tell them about it.

I don't want to sound like a hero when I wasn't. When I failed those people and myself.

So, there you have it.

—Your hotheaded Lobster Scout Stalker

I feel better when I leave the note at her door. I've been carrying this secret with me for too long, and now it's no longer mine alone.

CHAPTER 12

LUCY

"So, I didn't tell you earlier, because I was worried you'd challenge him to a duel," Charlie says as we settle into one of the cozy booths at The Shore Thing, Lars's favorite bar. "But I saw Enzo walking toward you across the square earlier."

"You did?" I ask, realizing too late that I sound eager. I'm *not* eager. But I *was* expecting him to try to pull something at the Crochet Club meeting tonight. I figured he'd crash it, the same way he'd crashed speed dating—and that it would come as an unpleasant surprise to him when he discovered we were crocheting vaginas.

Yes, really, and it's *very* amusing.

It would have been even more amusing if he'd barged in, looking for my supposed lover. The expression on his face would have been epic.

So I was understandably a bit disappointed when it didn't happen.

"It was definitely him," Charlie says. "The Cafieros all have those brooding eyes. But there's something extra broody about him, and he has that delicious five-o'clock shadow."

"I'm still here, you know," Lars says, his voice amused as he sets down a mountain of shopping bags he's been carrying beneath the table. Charlie started her Christmas shopping before they met up with me this evening. She always believes in starting early and finishing early, since she usually has dozens of commissioned paintings to finish later in the month. The only people I really have to shop for are Charlie, Lars, and Eileen, and I've already custom-ordered Eileen's gift: a sign that reads *The Town Matchmaker* to hang beside the front door of Love at First Sip.

Charlie wraps an arm around Lars's waist, leaning into him as she unzips her coat one-handed. "You have a terrible five-o'clock shadow," she teases. "Truly awful. Nothing worse than a blond beard."

"At least I'll never get an outsized ego," he replies as he reaches in and tickles her side.

"Not like Enzo," I mutter as Charlie squirms and then disarms him with a kiss.

I look away, frowning at the lone cactus positioned in the front window, completely out of place with the joyful holiday décor of pine garlands. I'm about to point it out when Charlie says thoughtfully, "Well, he didn't look very egotistical just now."

"I doubt that," I say. "He couldn't look humble if he tried."

"He didn't look humble," Charlie agrees. "He looked sad."

I feel a stab of sympathetic pain in my chest, which is ridiculous. I should *want* Enzo to be sad! His tears should be nectar for me. Okay, maybe not nectar, but they should be welcome.

Before I can think better of it, I ask, "Was he looking at me?"

"Now, that's egotistical," Charlie teases with a gleam in her eyes. "But yes. I got the impression he felt left out."

"Or maybe he was weighing whether he still needs to kill

me now that Aria has her dream job," Lars says drily, glancing at the drink menu.

"What do you two know about Enzo?" I ask.

"I know that he's terrifying," he says with an easy smile, looking up from the menu. "He told me he knows where to bury a body, which may or may not have been true."

"Why are you asking?" Charlie says, giving me a suspicious look.

"Know thy enemy," I quip.

She nods as she tugs the menu over for a look.

"I'm getting this round," she says, then gets up and places our order at the bar—hopefully for something warm and spicy. Returning, she continues the conversation as if it had never halted. "Okay, let's go over what we know about Enzo." She glances at Lars and lifts one finger. "He's terrifying." She puts out a second. "He used to live in New York City." A third finger juts out, her middle finger. "I know from Eileen that his mom left when he was little, but you'd probably be a jerk to use that against him."

I gasp in horror. I wouldn't wish that on…well, my worst enemy. "How old was he?"

"Nine or ten. Aria was just a couple of years old. We think that's why he's so protective of her."

It feels like my stomach just dropped to my feet. His mother left four children to fend for themselves. It's hard to imagine. Then again, my mother's husband left her when I was still too young to even remember him.

"That's *awful*." I feel guilt clogging my throat. This must be the reason Enzo hates this beautiful, sweet town.

It may look like a gingerbread house in the window of a master baker's shop, but it's haunted by the worst memories in his life, and everyone knows it. Worse, they talk about it. Not maliciously, I'm sure, but that wouldn't make a difference to him.

Oh, crap. We're *currently* talking about it.

"We really shouldn't gossip about this," I say.

Charlie shrugs dramatically. "I'm going to take the high road and not point out that you brought it up. Ooh, I think those are our drinks!"

Lars gets up to grab the mugs of mulled wine, delicious and exactly what I usually enjoy during the holidays. We drink them and talk about everything but Enzo. The Sip, my classes, Charlie's art, and Lars's birds. But the whole time, I'm thinking about Enzo as a little boy, watching his mother drive away.

It must have hurt so badly. It must *still* hurt.

My own pain and sense of loss flare to life again at the thought.

Which means it's time to put pause on Plan Revenge-zo on Enzo.

I'd asked Eileen if she could set me up with a fake date for Hook, Wine, and Sinker on Thursday so I could mess with Enzo, and she'd responded that she had an "inspired" idea. Apparently, Erica has two gorgeous sons, one of whom is a *very* single firefighter and already on the short list of men Eileen picked out for me. She'd promised me this hunky firefighter, Hudson Locke, would know it's just a fake date, because I didn't want to mess with anyone's feelings.

But what I'd once thought was a harmless prank no longer feels so harmless. Knowing what I now know, it would feel unethical to continue tormenting Enzo.

The thought is disappointing for reasons I can't put into words.

Charlie and Lars walk me home after we leave The Shore Thing, and I hug my friends goodnight and head upstairs. Trying to keep it together.

The only thing that lifts my mood is the note card slanted against my door, from my neighbor/friendly stalker.

I'd thought he'd stopped writing to me. I'd been sad about it —and felt silly for feeling sad.

I bring the note inside and curl up on my couch to read it.

My heart swells, because goodness, he was so real with me. So *open*. It makes me want to do something for him, so I write a quick reply into a Rudolph card and then leave it against my door with a tin of cookies I baked yesterday while doing schoolwork.

Dear Lobster Stalker,

Your secret's safe with me, and only partly because I have no idea who you are. And, for the record, you DID make the right choice with your job. Even if you should have totally forced them to pay you severance.

You know, I've always had a strain of pettiness, so if I were you, I'd send that report you wrote to your boss's boss. If your strategy is better and your former boss ignored it, they should know. Especially since it's VERY BAD policy to eliminate jobs right before the holidays. Even more so if one of the employees is pregnant.

Actually, now that I'm warming to the topic, I think that's exactly what you should do. Maybe you can still save their jobs, making your resignation far from pointless.

Okay, petty rant over. I pinky promise.

By the way, these cookies are for you. I think you need one tonight. I sure did.

I've struggled to feel the Christmas spirit this year. I'm so full of anger, and it doesn't take much to set me off. I'm angry because I lost my mother just before last Christmas. I knew it was going to happen, and I'd been preparing myself for years, but I wasn't ready to say goodbye. Not like that. Not in a room full of wires and beeping monitors. Not after she'd lost so much of herself.

I wanted to remember her the way she'd been when I was little. When we used to dance around the Christmas tree, the way you saw me doing.

I wanted to be able to keep her, because she was the only person who was ever really mine. But she was taken away from me anyway.

My friends keep asking what I'd like for Christmas, but the truth is that I want the one thing no one can give me. My family.

God, that sounds depressing. I'm sorry, really. I LOVE this time of year, and most of the time I can find joy in the little things, but it feels like everything that's heavy is heavier around the holidays—just like how all the good things are usually more joyful.

    —Dancing Queen

    p.s. What do you think of your new nickname?

After leaving out my offerings, I call Eileen. She and Charlie are the closest thing to family I have left, and right now, I need to feel like I'm not entirely alone in the world.

"Lucy, dear," she says, her voice sweet and bright. "Are you working on your vagina?"

I laugh. "No, I haven't touched it."

That feels a little too accurate.

"Oh, I've been crocheting away at mine all evening. It's surprisingly invigorating, isn't it?"

"The club was a lot of fun," I agree.

There's a lull in the conversation, the silence brimming with unsaid things. I want to ask her about Enzo, but I'm worried she'd read too much into it.

Finally, I say, "I think Portia has a thing for Amanda Willis. You know…the actress."

"Really?" she asks with interest. "I *did* notice them talking at the Christmas tree lighting, and Amanda is such a sweet girl. So down-to-earth. Have you spoken with her?"

"No." I swallow, bracing myself. "Enzo's the one who mentioned it."

"Oh, how interesting. Is he still banned from the Sip?"

"*Yes.* But I thought you might want to know. We can maybe add Portia and Amanda to your matchmaking list."

"Indeed," she says with a smile in her voice. "Portia's already on my list, of course. You know, I have just the thing to get them talking. Amanda mentioned to me the other day that she was interested in branding opportunities. What if I suggest that she and Portia develop a candy together?"

"It sounds perfect," I say, my heart warming. This is so like Eileen, always scheming so people can find their happily-ever-afters.

"Are you lonely tonight, my dear?" she asks, reading my uncomfortable thoughts without making me voice them.

Tears spring into my eyes. "Are you?"

This is something Eileen doesn't talk about much with anyone other than me, maybe because I'm still in the thick of my grief and can understand. She misses her husband desperately. He's been gone for two years, but his loss still casts a shadow on her life.

"Yes," she says with a sigh. "I miss Murray the most at Christmastime. We had our little traditions, and it's not the same now that he's gone."

"What would you be doing if he were here?"

She pauses. "We used to have competitions to see who could make the best hot chocolate, sometimes using the most unusual ingredients, especially after I opened the Sip. I'd put the strangest ones on the menu as specials."

"Would you like to do that now?" I ask. "I mean, if it's not too late and you're not busy."

"I would love it, dear. Come on over. And *do* bring your vagina. We can work on them together."

❄

I DIDN'T ASK Eileen about Enzo's mother last night. It would have felt...inappropriate.

Okay, I didn't say anything because she started talking about all the "wonderful young men" she wanted to set me up with. It had seemed like any sign of interest would be like blood in the water.

I don't work at the café on Wednesdays, and I have plenty of work to do for my classes, including finishing my final project, but the prompt in my Advent calendar this morning felt too on point to be ignored: *Are you at odds with someone? Make amends, dear. This is the season of forgiveness.*

The first couple of prompts were contemplative like today's. The others have been fun challenges—*eat a multicolored candy cane, pet a dog, buy a stranger hot chocolate, buy yourself a new ornament.* They've all been a delight. Hopefully, today's challenge will lighten the dark feelings I've been carrying.

I take the rest of the cookies I made and make my way to the town square, a woman on a mission.

I'm going to apologize to Nonna Francesca and Enzo and end this ridiculous feud. Have I enjoyed it? Admittedly yes. But I meant what I said in my letter to Lobster Stalker. I'm starting to suspect my hostility toward Enzo stems from my unresolved anger, and that doesn't say anything good about my character.

When I get to the stairway leading to Hidden Italy, though, I feel my resolve start to waver.

What am I going to say?

What is *he* going to say?

What on earth is Nonna Francesca going to say?

I suck in a deep breath through my mouth and release it through my nose. I can do this. I got through that awful last year with my mom. I can do anything.

So I march down the stairs with purpose, then slip on ice on the last step and face-plant into the door, my cheek ramming into the glass. The cookie tin tumbles from my hand, hits the landing hard, and bursts open. The cookies scatter, some of the little gingerbread men losing heads and arms.

It's a cookie massacre.

The door opens a second later, before I have a chance to right myself, and I stumble inside, graceless.

It's Nonna Francesca, wearing all black. She has a massive

bosom but surprisingly straight posture, and is wearing a rosary around her neck. She mutters under her breath, then gestures to the destroyed cookies.

"Now you come to litter on our doorstep? Is it not enough that you've defaced my beautiful grandson's picture?"

"I...that was kind of a joke. I actually came over to bring a peace offering."

Nonna Francesca gives me an unimpressed look. "And this is your peace offering, all over my doorstep?"

"Uh, yeah, sorry. I slipped on the ice."

I glance around, find no one to save me, and decide to just go for it. "Look, I heard about what happened with Enzo's mother, and I realized he has a legitimate reason for not wanting to stay in Hideaway Harbor."

"He doesn't want to stay?" she asks, reaching for her rosary.

Uh-oh. I need to turn this around. *Fast.*

"He wants to fix the store first, I'm sure. He did say that. So he'll be here for a while."

"And what is wrong with Hidden Italy?" she asks sharply.

I can feel sweat beading on my forehead.

"I don't know? Anyway. I really am sorry. I can take the flyer down."

She's still staring. "Why don't you like my grandson Enzo? *Everyone* likes my grandsons."

"I don't really know how to answer that question," I say, which is at least honest.

She grunts. And then closes the door in my face.

So I spend the next few minutes gathering broken cookies and returning them to the tin they spilled out of. I don't want to make the situation even worse by leaving behind a mess.

Of course, things get worse anyway. When I head over to the coffee shop to share my woes with Charlie, she pushes *The Almanac* into my face. "You need to read Lady Lovewatch today," she says, her eyes sparkling. "You're famous."

Dears,

We all think of the holiday season as a time of merriment and joy, but there's a holiday hate-off brewing at Love at First Sip. Discerning customers have noticed the BANNED flyer posted between the café and its next-door neighbor, Hidden Italy, as well as a bitter price war that gave all of us some very delicious drinks for cheap. Now, I don't know about you, but I've always thought the line between hate and love is the thinnest. Does anyone else sense love in the air?

CHAPTER 13

ENZO

Dear Dancing Queen,

I'm sorry for your loss. Now that I know the story behind your dance, I feel even more privileged to have witnessed it.

As for the anger you've been feeling, I understand completely.

Maybe we should normalize being angry during the holidays. We can suggest a new activity to the mayor: beating an unsuspecting pine tree with a baseball bat, or smashing old ornaments.

One of the things I struggle with most at this time of year is the pressure to be happy —as if you're failing everyone if you don't constantly have a smile on your face.

Sometimes, walking down the crowded streets or passing one of the events organized for the holidays, I half expect someone to scream, "Are you not entertained???" But it's only a week into December, and I'm afraid we have at least two weeks left of forced merriment.

That is not to say I don't value merriment or smiles, whatever prompts them, for their own sake. But I will always prefer a smile that comes from the heart.

Know that I smile that way whenever I receive a note from you. And if you should ever wish to watch The Golden Girls, you can count on your friend down the hall to watch it with you.

—Your friend, Lobster Stalker

P.S. I got a little drunk last night and did exactly what you advised. I sent the whole brief to my former boss's boss, letting him know exactly why I left the company. Screw it. Why not? You're right. It's worth it if he doesn't fire those people.

Giovanni would be merciless if he knew I was offering to hang out with the neighbor he'd written off as a middle-aged woman with a cabbage obsession. But there's something special about the friendship we're forming. It's changing me in ways I didn't expect.

When I sent that brief to Martin, I felt a weight lift from my shoulders. I was defending myself, but it was more than that. I was trying to salvage something that had been broken.

Honestly, my correspondence with Dancing Queen is one of the only parts of this holiday season that's made me feel festive, the other being my game with Lucy.

After propping the note against my neighbor's door—written into a *Golden Girls* card I'd purchased for the occasion —I head into Hidden Italy.

The walk is cold and brisk, but it feels good. Morning is my favorite time in Hideaway Harbor. So I'm in a good mood when I arrive, but the first thing Giovanni says to me is, "Thank God you're here. Nonna Francesca is in a state."

He doesn't seem annoyed or aggravated. He sounds almost...scared. Like my kid brother who used to ask me when our mother was coming home—and then if he could sleep beside me because he didn't want to be alone.

"Where is she?" I ask, nodding hello to Nico behind the deli counter. Mornings are slow, so there's no one else around to help out. No need.

Giovanni leads me back to the office and cracks the door open.

Our nonna is sitting in one of the chairs with her head cradled in her hands, murmuring to herself softly in a mixture of Italian and English.

My grandmother has always had a fiery temper—*her anger is as hot as her love*, my grandfather used to say—and I'm used to seeing her angry. This, I'm not used to.

Giovanni, who looks like he was up late and isn't emotionally prepared to do anything but drink coffee, steers me back into the hallway and says in an undertone, "She's been like that for fifteen minutes. Something your girl said to her."

"Lucy?" I ask in disbelief.

He shrugs. "Is there another woman you're obsessed with?"

I sigh, clap him on the back, and head into the office. After entering the room, I shut the door behind me.

"That girl from next door came to see me," Nonna says after a moment. "She made a mess on our bottom steps. Cookies everywhere. But she said she'd take that awful flyer of you down."

"She threw cookies at the door?" I ask, confused but not disbelieving. It's not a huge leap from the behavior we've both been engaging in all week.

"She tripped on the icy steps."

I clench my jaw. "Is she okay?"

My grandmother gives me the kind of look that knifes through flesh and bone. "You seem very concerned about this girl who sent Rachelle away."

"You hated Rachelle."

"*I* would have liked the pleasure of being the one who sent her away. Do you like Eileen's girl?"

"I'd rather not say. You taught me to be a gentleman," I hedge.

"We both know you only listen when it suits you."

"It suits me now." I crouch beside her chair. "What's wrong, Nonna?"

"You don't want to stay," she says, looking down at her gnarled hands clutched in her lap. She used to wear lots of silver rings, but she had to take them off several years ago because of arthritis. The change in her hands hits me hard. *She's getting older*, Giovanni told me a few months ago. *You see it more clearly when you're here and have a front-row seat.* He was right; I've seen evidence of it every day. "You're leaving me again, just like your father. Just like Aria. Just like your grandfather."

"I won't be leaving in a body bag unless you put me in one, Nonna. And I'm not going anywhere until I know you're all in a good place. You know how important the family is to me."

She looks up at me, tears streaking down her cheeks, and a bolt of pure fear strikes me. I've only seen her cry once, at my grandfather's funeral. It's like seeing a statue weep—it should be impossible.

"Nonna, what is it?"

"The books weren't unbalanced because of my eyesight. I'm losing myself, Lorenzo, and I don't know how to make it stop. My memory comes and goes. Things that happened twenty years ago feel more real than today."

I run my hand over her hair gently, feeling its texture, so soft and fine, almost like dandelion fluff that might float away on the wind. I'm not ready for her to leave me. I'm not ready to be the pillar of strength in this family. For so long it's been the two of us, working together. Keeping everyone else happy. Carrying the weight of it.

Even when I was in New York, I'd infused money into the store. I'd helped smooth things over when our father decided to sell his house in Hideaway Harbor rather than rent it to Giovanni, who'd been looking for a new place to live.

Another tear trails down her cheek, and I wipe it away, as if I could extinguish it from existence. "Nonna. We'll find a doctor to help you."

She laughed. "No doctor can save me from getting old."

"We'll never know if we don't try. You're going to live forever, Nonna. Think of all the people you won't be able to spite if you don't."

She smiles. "Thank you, Enzo. Thank you for coming home. Eileen's girl—"

"Lucy," I say.

Something knowing gleams in her eyes. "Lucy. She knows about your mother. It brought me back to that day, *caro,* when you came to me in tears. You were so little but such a man already. So good to your brothers and sister. I know it's not easy, but this is where you belong. *This* is where you are needed."

Anger pulses through me. If there's one rule the people in this town *do* follow when it comes to gossip, it's to never, ever mention my mother to Nonna Francesca. It always upsets her. Puts her in a state. Lucy mustn't have known that. Whoever had filled her in on the town gossip about *those poor Cafiero children whose mother abandoned them* obviously hadn't thought to mention it.

The fact that they're still gossiping about the past chafes. My grandmother shouldn't have to be subjected to that shit, and it makes me want to pack up for all of us—Nonna, Giovanni, Nico, and me—and leave this place. Abandon it without a backward glance, like a hermit crab that's found a better shell.

But my grandmother doesn't need my anger.

I smile and smooth her hair again. "Yes, Nonna. You're right, as always. Let me bring you home for the day. Giovanni and Nico have it covered here."

She agrees, which is evidence that something really is wrong. I'll call her doctor. Make an appointment. But in my heart, I know she's right about her health. She's slowed down, and at a certain point, a person no longer has the ability to speed back up. It would take a Christmas miracle to change that.

On the walk to her house, she talks nearly the whole way, telling me more about her interaction with Lucy. How Lucy had said she'd take the flyer down. How the broken cookies were a peace offering, and they did smell good.

When we get to her house, I kiss her forehead and make the impossible promise that everything will be all right.

My heart is raw in my chest by the time I get back to the shop, and when I see that the flyer with my face on it is still taped up by the door of Love at First Sip, I pause beside it. There are a few fresh blemishes drawn onto my face.

Did she do this after telling my grandmother she would take it down?

Doesn't matter. It's just a game. I'll be gone soon.

But I'm no longer sure that's true. How could I leave Nonna like this? Or my brothers?

I've been trying to find some genius solution to save Hidden Italy, but despite that nugget of an idea I had the other day, nothing has come to me other than the obvious—spend less on materials, charge more if the demand will hold, advertise better.

I go inside the shop and take off my coat. Try to sit down and think of a solution. But my mind keeps skipping back to Lucy.

Did she hurt herself when she fell down the steps?

Did she say anything else to my grandmother?

I don't like that she knows about my mother. I'd prefer it if no one knew. But I can't take the knowledge back from her.

Still, almost as if I'm in a dream, I find myself getting up and heading for the door. It's madness. I don't even know if she's working today—she can't possibly work every day—but she was over here earlier, and it's possible she's at the Sip now.

Besides, I'm being practical. I need to tell her not to talk to my grandmother about my mother.

I stalk out of the office and through the store, driven by the need to see her.

"Is it too much to hope you just had a genius brain stroke that's going to make us all rich?" Giovanni asks from the register.

"Strokes are bad, numbnuts." Nico smirks at him from the sandwich counter.

I ignore both of them and step out into the cold air. On my way up, I look for the slippery spot on the steps, then head back inside to get a shovel to take care of it.

I'm not doing it for Lucy; I just don't want anyone else falling down the steps.

I pass the flyer again and pause in the doorway, making a point to open it but stay outside.

My gaze only takes half a second to find her, not behind the counter but sitting at a table in the back with a latte and a book in her hands. She's staring down at it, her curls cascading toward the pages. Botticelli would have been pissed that he'd never had the privilege of immortalizing her in paint. Even though I haven't sketched in years, not since those days of bird watching with my nonno, I find myself wanting to sketch *her*.

"In or out, son," says a grizzled old man near the door.

"I don't want to get arrested."

A woman at the table next to him gasps. "Why, it's the handsome man from that flyer. I thought it was a joke."

"No joke, ma'am," I say. "I got banned for talking to one of the owner's assistants."

Charlie, who's standing behind the counter, throws a dish towel at me and laughs when I catch it. "Ignore everything he says, folks. He's a known menace." Then she calls out to Lucy—who must be reading something engrossing, because she appears to have missed our entire interaction—saying, "Your nemesis is here, Lucy."

She drops the book, then curses and frantically thumbs through it to find her place. I barely feel the cold as I watch her, taking in the slightly red blotch on her right cheek. That must be where she collided with the door.

"Can I speak with you in private for a moment, Lucia?" I ask as she marks her spot in the book with a receipt unearthed from her bag.

"You'd better go with him," Charlie says. "He's letting in the cold."

"Why don't you just come in?" Lucy asks, her eyes moving over me. "You're not wearing a coat."

"I've been banned," I say wryly. "Even though certain promises were made to my grandmother, the flyer's still out here, collecting new graffiti."

She puckers her lips and gets to her feet. "Let's take a look at it together. I take defacement of my property very seriously."

"Don't forget your coat," I say.

She gives me a look that accuses me of being half a dozen things, a hypocrite first and foremost, but I merely smile at her in return.

She puts on the coat, so I guess this once she'd prefer being warm to being right.

"I'm calling the cops if she's not returned safely within ten minutes," Charlie taunts.

Lucy rolls her eyes at her friend, then steps through the door I'm now holding for her. Her body passes a whisper away from mine, her coat brushing my shirt. Should the brush of fabric against fabric feel this erotic?

Probably not, but this woman is my kryptonite.

I follow her, letting the door shut behind us.

"Are you trying to get hypothermia?" she asks me, gesturing to the snow.

"Feeling hopeful?"

A smile flashes across her face for half a second, and then she tugs at her scarf. "Do you want this?"

It's covered in red flowers.

I hold back a laugh. "So your friend can take a photo and put up a new flyer? No, thank you."

"She's busy with customers." She arches an eyebrow,

smiling smugly, a dare in her eyes. "Are you not confident enough in your masculinity to wear flowers?"

"I have two Hawaiian shirts."

"No, you don't."

"I didn't say I bought them. But I'm still not putting the scarf on."

"My scarf is offended."

I'm about to banter back when my gaze catches on the flyer. Right. I'm not here to flirt with her. "*I'm* offended."

"I suppose you've heard about the paper," she says stiffly.

"What paper?"

Her mouth scrunches to one side. "There was something in Lady Lovewatch about us."

A groan escapes me, and I rub my temples. "No, I haven't seen it. I've been distracted by other news. I heard you threw cookies at my grandmother this morning."

Her eyes widen, and she adjusts the scarf nervously. "Did she say that? Because it was definitely an accident."

I lift my fingers to the red spot on her face, and she flinches. "Does it hurt?" I ask.

"No…you touched me."

As if I have a transmittable disease. My momentary good humor slips away, and suddenly all I see are the fresh blemishes sketched onto my face on the flyer.

I lower my fingers. "Does it hurt?" I repeat.

"No, it was just a silly accident. I wanted to apologize to your grandmother."

"But you mentioned my mother to her."

Both of her cheeks are red now, the little bruised spot barely darker. "I was trying to be nice."

"Lucia, everyone in Hideaway Harbor knows better than to mention my mother around my grandmother. Around anyone in my family."

She grimaces. "I'm sorry."

Despite the apology in her eyes, I can tell from her tone that I've offended her again.

I shift my weight, trying to find a way to explain myself to her, and also to control my mood, which is everywhere today. Up, down, and in the moon. "Something happened to our family over twenty years ago, and no one allows us to forget it. The busybodies are still talking about it. Talking about all kinds of things they have no business talking about. Telling strangers—"

"I'm not a stranger," she says tightly. Then she glances toward the Sip to make sure the door hasn't magically burst open before adding, "You *propositioned* me last week."

"I'm glad you remember," I say, smiling despite myself. "You know, I was worried someone might spread stories about you, but maybe I should have worried about *you* talking about *me*."

She gasps. "As if. No one needs to talk about you. Your ego is already the size of Maine."

"Only Maine?" I say. "Surely you can do better than that."

She's inched closer to me, seemingly without realizing it. We're so close only a foot separates us, maybe less, the air between us a billowy white from our warm breath.

She pokes my chest, and despite her reluctance to touch me earlier, I layer my hand over hers.

"You're freezing," she says softly.

"I'm fine. My blood runs hot too."

Our gazes lock in an intense stare-off.

Distantly, I register people passing us. People watching. But at this particular moment it's hard to care.

"I wasn't gossiping about you," she says quietly. "And I'll take down the flyer. I told your grandmother I would."

This is the moment where I can let it go. I *should* let it go. I don't hate this woman. I don't even dislike her anymore. Maybe I never did.

But I *do* like this game we've been playing. It's one of the only things that's made me feel alive since leaving New York a defeated man.

So I say, "Then you lied to her face. I want you to keep it up. And I'm going to put up one of my own."

Gasping again, she wrenches her hand from my grip. "You wouldn't."

"You've had so much fun with your little marker." I gesture to the marked-up flyer. "I feel left out."

Her chin tips up. "Don't you already have a little marker?"

I laugh. "Always building me up, Lucia. No, there's nothing little about me. And although I've been told my dick can work miracles, I still haven't figured out how to write with it unless I'm peeing on snow."

She gapes at me. "You're disgusting."

"Thank you."

"I'm leaving."

"Please do."

But we stand there for another long, loaded moment, our eyes locked, the air between us fraught. I'm tempted to close the distance between us, to lift her stubborn chin and kiss her.

Maybe she even wants me to.

But that would be as good as a declaration, and even though I'm desperate to touch Lucy, I don't want to walk hand in hand with her through the streets of Hideaway Harbor, the way her friend and my sister's ex-boyfriend do. And I definitely have no desire to see this moment recreated in the pages of *The Almanac*.

"My proposition stands," I finally say.

She scowls. "So does my refusal."

"Very well," I say. "We can discuss it over dinner tomorrow night."

"Like I said the other day, I don't have *any idea* what you're talking about," she says, her expression almost convincing. "But I've heard the only person who'll give you a pity date in Hideaway Harbor is a woman old enough to be your mother. That's got to burn."

I grin at her, because arguing with this woman is addictive. "For a moment, I was worried you'd gone soft on me."

"No, from what I've heard, *you're* the one who goes soft."

The look on her face says she's hoping I'll assume Rachelle told her something embarrassing. But there's nothing embarrassing to tell. Not like that, anyway.

I shake my head. "I thought you weren't a gossip, *cara mia*. Or a liar. But if you'd like, I'd be happy to prove *you* wrong. Anytime."

She's breathing rapidly, her chest rising and falling. My gaze takes it in hungrily.

"Have the day you deserve," she finally says, "and put on a damn coat." Then she stomps into the café.

I return to Hidden Italy, my teeth chattering, and pour myself a large coffee from the carafe by the deli counter.

"Who won this round?" Giovanni asks as he looks up from his phone.

"We both did," I say with a grin, and I head back into the office.

I sketch Lucia, the way I used to sketch the birds in my book. She's so beautiful the drawing can't be seen as anything but a compliment, so I add a hairy mole to the middle of her forehead with a marker.

That night, it's my turn to stay with Nonna Francesca. She insists on making me dinner, saying she's not worm food yet. Afterward we watch her favorite Christmas movie, *It's a Wonderful Life*, even though it always puts a saccharine taste in my mouth. I must be truly bored, because I find myself wondering what it would be like to watch it with Lucy. I'd keep up a running commentary about all the parts that were ridiculous and illogical, and she'd tear down my criticisms.

I'll bet she'd enjoy that.

I certainly would.

Damn. I'm looking forward to seeing what she has planned for me at dinner tomorrow night.

Despite her protests, I have no doubt she does have something planned, and it's almost certain to be awful.

CHAPTER 14

LUCY

TEXT CONVERSATION WITH CHARLIE

> Do you know any young guys who like the Golden Girls?

Uh…what?

> You know the guy who left that note at my door?

The stalker?

> Well, he lives in my building, and we've been exchanging notes, but he left the last one in a Golden Girls card and mentioned something about watching it together. Do you think he's elderly?

You're asking if I think hot, young guys watch Golden Girls? Say that out loud and listen to what it sounds like.

Oh, forget it. It doesn't matter. I'm not into this guy. We've just been exchanging friendly notes, but I guess I was envisioning someone younger.

You can't see me, but I'm laughing my ass off.

Have fun tonight.

HUDSON is young. And hot. Practice with him. Practice HARD.

Yeah, Enzo's going to be so pissed. (Message error, Redelivered.)

Forget Enzo.

Who?

Despite my casual dismissal of Enzo in my text conversation with Charlie earlier this morning, forgetting him is easier said than done.

I've been thinking about him constantly since that moment outside Love at First Sip yesterday.

It felt like the whole town, maybe even the whole state, had shrunk to just us, with a short stretch of sidewalk between us, dirty snow piled all around.

The air had felt charged with possibilities.

I'd thought he was about to dip in and kiss me, which had pissed me off and excited me in equal measure.

But he hadn't.

Instead, he'd chosen to revive our war.

I'd truly intended to make peace, but Enzo obviously doesn't want peace. At least not with me.

So I've decided I'm going through with my dinner date plan.

I just told Eileen as much via text message. She left the Sip early today to talk to Amanda, which went "very well," and then headed over to Erica's house to make cookies with her.

Five minutes after I sent my text, she replies with a clapping meme—the delay either a result of Hideaway Harbor's perpetually slow cell signals or because she and Erica are gabbing.

Probably the latter, because she starts sending me minute-by-minute updates, and each of them comes through immediately.

> Hudson just put on a dress shirt. Ooh, this is so exciting.

> He looks very handsome, Lucy.

> You know, this is just the kind of practice you need! I wish I'd thought of it sooner.

> I understand you said it's a "fake" date, but if there's chemistry, you should go for it! He is SUCH a nice boy.

> Erica and I already talked about what we'd do for the wedding.

> No pressure, though. ;-)

> Ooh, he just stepped out the door! You're in for a treat.

I mean, honestly.

I pace around my apartment, tempted to watch *The Golden Girls* with my probably elderly pen pal instead of going out, but Hudson arrives exactly on time.

I open the door to find him grinning at me. "Well, damn, I wasn't sure how I felt when I overheard my mother planning my wedding, but I don't have any objections after all."

I feel myself blushing all the way to the roots of my hair. So he's charming *and* good-looking. His mother is petite and blonde, but he's tall, dark, and very handsome with thick, muscular arms. Like, seriously thick. The man is as fit as a bodybuilder.

Truthfully speaking, he's much better than *perfectly okay*, and if he's as nice as Eileen says, he'd be a great candidate for Project: Lose The V, but I'd never sleep with him. For one thing, his mother and Eileen are already planning our wedding. For another...

Well, isn't that enough?

So, no, I will not be sleeping with him tonight, but I'll be totally honest: I want to convince Enzo that's my plan.

"Keep up the shameless flirting," I encourage him with a grin. "It'll drive Enzo crazy."

"Ah, yes," he says with a knowing smile. "I've heard all about the holiday hate-off."

"You've read Lady Lovewatch?" I moan as I follow him out of the apartment and lock the door behind me.

"Of course. But that's not the first time I've heard people mention your feud. You know, I've got my money on you."

"People are *betting* on it?" I ask in horror.

His grin widens as we head to the building's front entrance. "Not literally." He shrugs, pausing in front of the door. "At least not the people I know. But people like to talk, especially since some think Enzo's gotten too high-and-mighty after being in New York City so long."

He opens the door for me, letting in a whoosh of cold wind. I step through it, and he follows me out, linking our arms together as we walk toward the harbor.

"So...Enzo didn't used to be like this?" I ask, trying not to sound as curious as I feel.

"He's always been pretty sure of himself." He shrugs. "But he had to be. It wasn't easy, his mom leaving like she did."

"Are you friends?" I ask in horror.

He laughs and shakes his head. "No. I took Aria to the prom, and he told me where he'd bury my body if I tried to do anything more than kiss her. I haven't forgotten it."

"Now, that sounds like Enzo."

But it hits me that this is exactly the sort of thing Enzo doesn't like about Hideaway Harbor—that people are still talking about him, speculating, after so many years away.

I shake off the feeling as Hudson and I make our way toward Hook, Wine, and Sinker.

"Are you okay with me flirting a little?" I ask as we get closer. My heart is thumping harder now, because it's almost the moment of truth. I'm going to see Enzo sitting alone at his table, and he's going to see me walking in with Hudson.

The look on his face is going to be *epic*.

Hudson gives me a sidelong glance. "I wouldn't mind if you flirted a lot."

I nearly trip over a stone as I process his words. Looking back at him, I say, "I don't want you to feel used, Hudson. You seem awesome, but—"

"I'm not in the market for an arranged marriage either, Lucy," he says with a grin. "But I do look forward to getting to know you, and you can use me all you like. I don't object."

He doesn't totally sound like he understands it's a fake date, but I'm distracted by the sight of the restaurant up ahead. Even though it's freezing outside, I feel sweat bead on the back of my neck as we approach the entrance.

"There it is," I say, sounding like a hunter who's spotted her prey.

"Yes, the same place where it's always been," he says in a teasing voice, but I barely register it because we're passing the front window now, arm in arm, and I spot Enzo inside. He's sitting at one of two tables facing the sidewalk. I feel an almost feral joy at the sight of him. He's staring out of the window— waiting for me, no doubt. I see recognition on his face as he catches sight of me. Then his gaze shifts to Hudson, and I can see my dart has hit the bull's-eye. (Again. I've managed it before with his photo at the café.) He shakes his head slightly, one corner of his lips lifting as if he's pissed off but still amused.

Oh, if I could snap a photo of that look, I'd frame it and keep it forever.

Maybe it's a little strange that I want to preserve a photo of a man who drives me crazy, but Enzo is clearly not someone who's easily surprised or caught off guard. Who could blame me for feeling victorious?

I only realize I've completely stopped walking when I feel the tug of Hudson's arm, still looped through mine.

I hurry forward as he holds the door open for me. When I pass him, he says in an undertone, "If someone murders me, let the police chief know you can identify his number one suspect."

"Oh, Enzo's definitely angry at me, not you," I say, feeling a little giddy at the thought. "I tricked him, and he can't stand it. But he deserves it after what he did at Santa Speed Dating, not to mention half a dozen other things."

He laughs. "Yeah, my sister Harper was at your dating event last weekend. I got an earful. But, hey, at least there weren't really head lice in the beards."

The hostess smiles at us and leads us to the table directly next to Enzo's two-top. Our tables are the only ones in the alcove near the window, giving it an intimate feel.

My breath hitches as I take him in. He's wearing a dark gray suit that fits him perfectly, hugging the muscles in his arms. His tie is bright red, which is downright merry for him. I dislike him…and yet my pulse is thundering now. I shiver with a sense of excitement that was notably absent when Hudson met me at my apartment.

My gaze flits from Enzo to the glass of wine in front of him. Excellent, I've already driven him to drinking.

I give him a look of wide-eyed innocence. "What a coincidence to see you here, Enzo. Are you meeting someone?"

He smiles savagely at me. "I thought I was meeting *you*."

"Why would you think that?" I ask. "I've told you twice that I didn't have any idea what you were talking about."

"Uh-huh," he says skeptically, eyeing me with a knowing gaze. The corner of his mouth lifts in a grudging acknowledgment of my victory. "Well played."

The hostess's eyes widen. "Is there a problem with the location of your table? We could—"

"Oh no," I say with a dismissive wave. "I'm not afraid of the big, bad wolf."

"Good," Enzo says, giving a small, hard nod to Hudson. "Then you wouldn't mind if I join you?"

I tighten my grip on Hudson's arm. "Yes, we would actually. This is our first date."

"But hopefully not our last," Hudson says, his eyes sparkling like he's enjoying this game too.

"We'd prefer privacy," I demur.

"Of course," Enzo says in a low, gravelly voice. "I understand completely. I don't like to share either."

His words send a hot shiver through me—just like they're meant to. He wants me to think about that moment yesterday, when only inches separated us. And in the kitchen last weekend. He wants my mind to keep dipping back to his incredibly rude offer.

And that's exactly where my mind goes. To be perfectly honest, I've thought about it a lot. Every night. I've been desperate to take out my vibrator. But I haven't, because that would be like letting him win. And I'll be damned if I do that.

I feel Enzo watching us as Hudson pulls out my chair for me. The hostess hands us our menus and takes off, probably grateful for the chance to escape.

"A gentleman," Enzo comments. "Your mother raised you right."

I ignore him and smile at Hudson. "Would you like some wine? I'd love some wine."

"I recommend the malbec," Enzo says, lifting his glass in a toast.

It's then I realize the flaw in my plan. He's sitting on the same side of the table as I am, which puts him next to me. Barely two feet away. If I held my hand out, I could touch him.

A server arrives to take our drink orders. Damn it. I *do* want the malbec. It's my favorite red. But I pointedly place an order for a glass of merlot, even as Enzo gives me an *it's your funeral* look.

Hudson grins and orders the malbec for himself—"Sounds great," he says breezily with a nod to Enzo.

No, they will *not* be friends.

"Are you sure?" I ask. "I'm not confident I trust Enzo's taste buds. I've heard the sandwiches at Hidden Italy are *very* dry. Wasn't it your dad who thought so?"

Again, I feel Enzo staring at me, so I pick up my glass of water and sip it.

"Oh, we've fixed all that," Enzo says in a seductive voice. "If anything, they're too wet."

I fumble the glass of water, splashing cold liquid onto the tabletop.

"Oops," I say sunnily, setting the glass down. I will not look at Enzo or even acknowledge his existence. "What will you be having tonight, Hudson? Everything looks so good."

I haven't actually glanced at the menu, but I came by a few weeks ago to talk to the manager while I was working on my app project, and she let me taste-test some of the appetizer specials with the staff.

Hudson smiles sweetly at me. "The lobster roll's the best in

Hideaway Harbor, if you ask me—other than my mom's, of course."

I nod, not wanting to admit out loud that I don't eat lobster. If I did, Enzo would give me one of his withering looks, reminding me without words that I don't belong.

I check out the menu, finding a vegetarian entrée that looks good, then set it down.

"So, you've always lived here, Hudson?"

"Born and raised," he agrees. "Wouldn't want to live anywhere else. And you?"

I have to smile. "I'm sure you already know everything about me. Everyone in Hideaway Harbor seems to know everything about each other."

He shrugs. "You'd be surprised. The only thing I was told is that you're gorgeous and single. The first I could have seen with my own eyes, and I'm hoping the second is still true."

"It is," I say, not able to resist a slight, dagger-eyed glance at Enzo. "*Very* true."

Enzo chuckles. "Surprising you didn't meet your soulmate at Santa Speed Dating last weekend. Seemed like those five minutes should've led to something beautiful, huh?"

I turn in my seat to look at him more directly. "They probably would have if you hadn't messed with the power."

A satisfied smile spreads across his face, and I realize I gave him exactly what he wanted: my focus. "They call that an act of nature, Lucia. I'm not a god, believe it or not. You tell her, Hudson. Is it unusual for the power to cut out at this time of year?"

"It's happened before," he agrees politely. But he's not without mischief, because he adds, "And sometimes it has remarkable timing."

"You know," Enzo says, his eyes on mine, "if your soulmate had been at that event, he wouldn't have been scared off by a little darkness. They're a bunch of cowards if they ran because the lights went off. You deserve more than a coward."

The server sets a glass of wine in front of me, startling me as my eyes had been glued to Enzo's in a first-grade-level stare-off. I immediately take a sip.

Shit. It's not great.

Hudson, on the other hand, makes an appreciative hum as he tries his wine.

"Should've ordered the malbec, huh?" Enzo taunts me with a laugh, and I shoot him a dirty look.

"This is the best wine I've ever tasted," I lie, then pointedly turn toward my fake date, ready to escalate the war. "So, Hudson, I'm told you're a firefighter. Do you do one of those shirtless calendars with the kittens and puppies?"

He laughs, and an adorable *aw shucks* look passes over his face. "We do, actually. Except we pose with lobsters."

Genuine laughter spurts from me. "Do you really?"

"Nope, but maybe I should run it by my boss."

"Gosh, I would love to buy something like that," I say, fluttering my lashes at him. "Firefighters are so sexy. I've always been drawn to burly men. Men of action, none of that corporate nonsense."

Enzo coughs around his latest sip of the much more delicious wine he's drinking. Good. Another point for me.

Hudson looks amused, probably because I forewarned him that I might be flirtatious to get Enzo's goat.

"Were you at the parade last weekend?" he asks.

"I'm afraid I missed it," I say. "I was helping my friend Charlie pick what she's going to sell at the Christmas market. Was your fire truck part of it?"

"It was."

"Did you take out your hose?" I ask, eyeing Enzo.

"Uh…no," Hudson says with an incredulous look.

"What's Charlie selling at the Christmas market, anyway?"

Enzo asks me, acting as if he's an important part of our conversation—an invited guest.

"Her pet portraits. Would you like her to make one of you? She'd give you an extra-pretty collar."

He lets out an amused grunt. "I wouldn't want to cause a bidding war."

"Like you did at your knockoff bachelor auction?" I quip, my pulse racing. It's like my body thinks it's marching into battle, not verbally sparring with Enzo. I wave to the empty side of his table. "Impressive."

He barks a laugh before turning toward Hudson. "Good luck, man. She's a spark plug. Then again, you're trained to put out fires."

Oh no, he didn't.

"Not everyone can be middle management," I say tightly. "What is it you used to do, anyway?"

Enzo meets my gaze and holds it, his eyes dark and intense, a black hole threatening to suck me in. I focus on his nose, instead. There's a slight bump in the middle, but somehow that makes him more attractive instead of less—a touch of character in what would have otherwise been a too-perfect face. My gaze drifts downward, taking in his mouth, surrounded by a sea of sexy dark stubble. His smiles widens, as if he can hear my thoughts, before he responds, "I'm glad you asked. I like to be in control."

Heat flash-fries me before I school my features into an incredulous look. "Life must be a constant disappointment to you then."

"It is," he agrees, his expression playful. "My grandmother listens to me less than the CEOs I've worked with. But what can I do? Blood is thicker than water."

This again. I scowl at him. "Not always."

The server comes back, stopping at Enzo's table first. She looks at him as if he's made of chocolate cake.

"What would you like, handsome?" she asks. Her lipstick is the absolute perfect shade of red, and she's gorgeous. They'd probably have insanely good-looking children.

I'm surprised by how much this thought annoys me, but I tell myself it's only because the attention she's giving Enzo is feeding his ego.

He gives her a blinding smile. "I don't know, Nadine. What would *you* get? I need a woman's perspective."

I snort before I can catch myself. From the scandalized look on Nadine's face, I might as well have sworn loudly in a church.

"Lucy?" Hudson asks, and I realize he just asked me a question.

"I'm so sorry. I missed that," I say. "The acoustics in here are a bit wonky."

The server turns to us, her lips compressing into a tight line. "My brother worked on this building. I can assure you there's nothing wrong with the acoustics. Do you know what you'd like?"

I'm flushing as I order the vegetarian entrée.

"Are you sure?" she asks hesitantly.

"Is it bad?"

"No, of course not," she insists. "I didn't say that. I'd *never* insult the chef. It's just…this is a high-end *seafood* restaurant."

Which is all well and good, except I've never really liked seafood. But I remember trying their classy play on fish and chips and mostly liking it.

"I'll get the fish and chips," I say.

She takes Hudson's order and then walks away.

"Oh, this is funny," Enzo says, lifting up his phone, demanding we give him our attention.

I give him an incredulous look. "We're on a date, Enzo. We don't care if you found a hilarious YouTube video."

"Actually, it's a message from your mother, Hudson. She says my date was supposed to be with your sister, but she forgot to tell her." He lifts his hands in a *what can you do?* gesture. "If you want to know the truth, I thought she was sending Lucia to have dinner with me. She certainly made it sound like that, but she never mentioned her by name. Isn't that a funny coincidence?"

"Not really," Hudson says. "But if you'd like, I'd be happy to text Harper."

"No, no," he says. "I don't want to disturb her night. Besides, she's a little young for me." His eyes widen theatrically. "Oh, I've put my foot in it. I forgot that you're younger than Lucy. This is awkward."

"Younger by two years," I say, repressing the desire to throw a fork at him. Barely.

"I prefer to date older women," Hudson says with a grin.

"Wonderful," I say, beaming. "So do I."

Oh crap. That's not what I meant.

"I mean, I love older men," I say. Enzo laughs as I correct myself yet again—"*Younger* men. Older men think they know everything. They're controlling, and no one wants that."

I take a long sip of my shitty wine.

"Soooo," Hudson says, and then diplomatically changes the subject, "Eileen tells me you're making an app cataloging businesses for one of your classes. She says you've been talking to all of the shop owners in Hideaway Harbor."

"You haven't spoken with us," Enzo interjects.

"You're being rude," I say hotly, feeling a flush rise into my cheeks. He's right, though. I haven't spoken with anyone at Hidden Italy. I felt self-conscious about trying to go over there after Nonna Francesca's ban, but the real reason was that I hadn't wanted to run into him. "We're trying to have a private conversation."

He lifts his palms up. "Of course. I'll entertain myself."

And he actually does. He quietly studies his phone while

Hudson and I exchange small talk about Hideaway Harbor, my classes, his work at the fire department, and his family.

The server reappears to set Enzo's dish down in front of him, momentarily distracting me, and walks off to get ours. Then Hudson's phone issues a loud beep. He pulls it out of his pocket and checks the screen, instantly swearing under his breath. "I'm so sorry, Lucy. I almost never get called in when I'm not on shift. I've got to go. I'll settle up with the server, but can we do this again sometime?"

"Of course," I say, wondering if he means it or if it's part of the act. "I totally get it. I had a lot of fun tonight." I mean it. He's a nice guy with plenty to say, but if Eileen and Erica sensed even the slightest hint of flirtation between us, they'd probably send out wedding invitations.

Besides, there's no real chemistry, no click. I can't imagine him kissing me, let alone undressing me.

Not once did I feel like the restaurant had narrowed down to only the two of us.

Hudson and I both stand. I hug him, feeling nothing but a pleasant awareness of his very impressive strength, and he leaves after nodding to Enzo.

"Alone at last," Enzo says as soon as he's out of earshot. "You know, he wouldn't be half bad for your random sex plan. He's good-looking, nice enough, and he wouldn't tell anyone. Too bad Erica's his mother. She'd have you in a white dress before Christmas."

Is he a mind reader, too?

"How do you know I haven't already found someone for my devious plan?" I ask. "For all you know, I've already done it."

We have a stare-off for several seconds, his dark, heavily lashed eyes making me squirm.

Finally, he says, "You haven't."

"That's what you think."

He grins at me. "Is my next line 'I know you are, but what am I?'"

"You *do* act like a playground bully most of the time," I retort.

His grin stretches wider. "There we go, the perfect segue. I know you are, but what am I?"

Damn it, I'm half tempted to laugh, but I hold it in. He doesn't get to make me laugh. If using my vibrator while thinking of him would be a loss, then so would that.

"I'm getting my dinner to go," I say tightly, annoyance making my blood hot. Yes, totally just annoyance.

He gets up and sits in the other chair at his table, placing him across from me, where he can look directly at me. "You'd prefer eating at home alone? I thought you loved downtown Hideaway Harbor." He waves to the window and the view of the harbor stretched out in front of us. "This isn't doing it for you, Lucia?"

"You keep calling me that, but you know my name's Lucy."

"In Italian it would be Lucia. You look like more of a Lucia to me."

My body pulses with need, but I push it down, refusing to give in to that either. "You don't get to choose my name."

"You can give me a nickname, too, if you like."

"Will you answer to asshole?"

He grins at me, a devastating smile that lights up his usually serious, broody face and makes him look like the devil himself, fashioned to lure a woman into sin. "If you call me that, yes, I believe I'd answer."

His words travel through me like a shock wave, but I steel myself against them. "Why did you want to have dinner with me, anyway? We don't like each other."

"Who says I don't like you? Maybe I'm just sour that you're using my balls for target practice."

"You're the one who gave me the idea."

"See." He raises his eyebrows. "It's not so bad, letting me be in control."

"I am *not* sleeping with you," I say. "So you can stop asking."

Of course, that's when the server walks over to check on us. She looks at me like I'm a madwoman, and I clear my throat and ask for my food to go.

"Sorry, Nadine," Enzo says, taking out his thin leather wallet and removing his credit card. "Could I possibly have mine to go too? We'll both be leaving."

She looks a little put out, but she gives him a tight smile as she picks up his plate. "Of course. No trouble at all."

I wait until she's several feet away and then say, "I am *not* leaving with you."

"I'd like to help you with your app."

"You didn't even know about my app until a few minutes ago."

"But now I'm deeply invested. I'd like to earn a place for Hidden Italy on it. I hope you won't let your dislike of me cloud your opinion of our family business."

"Your grandmother's the one who originally banned me," I remind him. "Besides, the app is just a silly class assignment. It'll probably never amount to anything else. There's already a town app, anyway."

He shrugs. "It's shit."

I try not to laugh. "How do you know mine isn't?"

"I know. As for my grandmother…" He glances around, then leans across his table toward me, his smile fading into something more serious. "Between you and me, Lucia, Nonna Francesca shouldn't be working anymore. She's a Cafiero, though, and she's having a hard time giving it up. I'm not saying she's never banned anyone from the shop before now, but usually she'd be more reasonable about it."

Surprise radiates through me. It's obvious he's telling me something real, something that's been bothering him.

"I upset her yesterday," I say ruefully, feeling a stirring of guilt.

"Yes, but these days she's easily upset. A few days ago, she ranted for hours about a tourist who didn't realize there would be cheese on his chicken parmigiana sub."

"I'm sorry," I say, meaning it this time. "I know what it's like to watch someone decline. Your grandmother seems…"

He laughs darkly. "She's not a nice woman, no, not like your Eileen. But she's loyal and strong, and she makes the best parmigiana known to man."

I nod. "She does. I've missed it."

He grins smugly, but I don't mind. He can have this round.

"I wasn't going to keep Hidden Italy off the app," I add. "I just asked Eileen about your family business instead of your brothers and grandmother. Eileen knows a lot about this town, and she's always fair."

"She is. And thank you for being fair to us, too," he says. "I expected nothing less."

"You want something," I accuse, because he's being *much* too nice to me.

The way he looks at me in response has me squeezing my cloth napkin.

"You know what I want," he says, his voice husky.

I check all around me for listening ears before answering in an undertone, "You want to prove you're not bad in bed."

He shrugs one shoulder, his expression entirely smug. "If you'd like to look at it that way."

"It's never going to happen," I say, my heart thumping faster as vivid images begin assailing my head. Enzo dipping his head to kiss me. Enzo unzipping his pants. Enzo—

My mouth is suddenly as dry as the desert. I sip more bad wine, then frown at the bitter taste.

"Take mine if you like," he says, nodding to his glass. "Or your friend's. I doubt he'll be back."

"I like my wine," I lie. "But I think you're an arrogant jerk."

"I *am* an arrogant jerk. But let's set that aside for now. I'd like to give you a personal tour of Hidden Italy and answer any questions you might have. Can we have a temporary truce, for the sake of Hideaway Harbor?"

I hope I look as unimpressed as I am. "You've made it very clear how you feel about Hideaway Harbor."

"Nevertheless, my brothers and my grandmother live here, and my sister will come back someday. I care about Hidden Italy and Hideaway for their sake." He taps his forehead. "Something tells me this app of yours will be more than just a class assignment someday, and I want our deli to be part of it." A grin stretches across his face. "If they ever fix the problem with the internet."

It feels like a moment of truth.

If I walk away, maybe he'll leave me alone.

If I go with him, then…

I have no idea what will happen, and there's something thrilling about the not knowing.

Maybe that's why I roll my eyes but find myself nodding at the same time. "Okay. But I'm only doing it for Hideaway."

"Of course."

CHAPTER 15

ENZO

I hadn't known what to expect tonight, but Lucy got me good. If she'd seemed genuinely interested in Hudson, I would have left. But she spent more time looking at me than him.

And now…

Honestly, I don't know what I'm doing, but I'm not ready to stop.

"I can't walk there with you," Lucy hisses, her tone scandalized as we step out of the restaurant. "What if people see us together?"

The wind is bitter tonight, and she's not wearing a scarf. I'm tempted to unwind mine and tie it around her neck, but I know better. She'd never allow me that victory.

"You don't want anyone to know we're talking?" I ask, feigning innocence. "I was going to offer to carry your food for you too."

"No. I am very capable of carrying a plastic bag, thank you very much. And we are *not* talking. I'm interviewing you for the app. The same way I've interviewed everyone else."

"Exactly," I say. "Wouldn't it look more suspicious if we're seen sneaking in separately through the back door?"

"I'm beginning to think you just enjoy arguing for the sake of argument."

"Then you're beginning to know me, Lucia. Let's go."

She definitely wants to argue more, but a brisk wind comes in off the water, prompting her to start walking briskly in the direction of the town square, rubbing her gloved hands together.

She walks with purpose, but she's distractible, too, her attention drifting to the window displays and the holiday wreaths lining the streets. We pass tourists, some of them holding stuffed shopping bags from earlier purchases, as well as Hidies. Several people are clutching cups of hot chocolate that are probably already chilly enough to be a disgrace to the drink's name.

Lucy told me she loved this place, and it's evident on her face. Her green eyes are full of appreciation, with a hint of excitement. I'm surprised by how much I savor her joy. I wouldn't say it helps me see Hideaway through new eyes, but it strips away some of my resentment.

When we cross the town square, there are people clustered around the tree. A group of drunk-looking people dressed up like Santa's reindeer are playing some kind of game.

Lucy's gaze lingers on the drunken group of reindeer.

"You think Charlie would want to paint them?" I ask.

The smile I was hoping for flits across her face before vanishing. "Yeah, maybe."

"This class you're making the app for. It's a programming class?"

"Yeah," she says as we stroll toward the shop front, the giant Christmas tree looming to our left. "I'm taking some classes to gain skills for an app I want to make."

"The Hideaway Harbor one?"

"No."

We've reached the corner of our block, and I nod toward her BANNED flyer of me.

"I still think I should grow a mustache like that."

She smiles slyly at me, her hair whipping in the wind, and I think about wrapping her up in my scarf. I shouldn't want her to put on something that's mine, but there it is—an intrusive desire I can't shake. "I thought it was a nice touch," she says. "I considered adding some devil horns in green, but Charlie convinced me there's something to be said for subtlety."

"You should have gone for it." I nod to the flyer I put up beside it—Lucy, gorgeous as all get out, except for the hairy mole sprouting from her forehead, which has been joined by an oozing lesion on her cheek.

"What even is that?" she asks, groaning.

Then, no shit, she takes out her red marker and draws a Santa hat on her head.

"You really brought your red marker with you?" I remark. "That looks a lot like cheating, if you ask me."

She smiles at me. "We have rules now?"

"Oh, there are always rules."

"Do you know what they've been saying about us?"

It's like icy liquid is flooding my veins, taking away the fun buzz of being around her.

"What are you talking about?"

"I wasn't the one saying it," she clarifies.

"I'd guessed. Go on."

"It was in Lady Lovewatch."

I nod and rock on my heels. "Oh, that. Yes, I've seen it."

"Aren't you...upset?"

"Not really."

She frowns. "Seriously? According to Hudson, people are betting," she says, gesturing back and forth between us, "like on who's going to win the hate-off."

"Ah, bless the Hideaway Harbor gossip mill. Nothing can happen without thirty people you barely know remarking upon it. Which of us has better odds, out of curiosity?"

She points to the drawing of her, now wearing a hat. "It must be me."

"Can I borrow your marker?"

"Absolutely not," she says, sticking it in her purse.

"Fine, this round goes to you, Mrs. Claus. But I reserve the right to make a hat for myself too."

"Fair is fair." A smile flirts with her lips, and I feel a fresh awareness of her. The way little curls are constantly billowing around her face. The pinkness of her cheeks in the cold. The mischievous glint of her eyes whenever she looks at me.

I gesture for her to precede me down the stairs—*see, Lucy, I can be a gentleman*—and she narrows her eyes at me before descending the steps.

Even though I didn't ask her to go first so I could watch her go down, I find myself doing it. Taking in every sway of her body. She's covered by that big coat, but it's still doing it for me.

Sighing at my own folly, I follow her down the stairs and unlock the door, then flick on the lights. It's well past eight, so the deli's been closed for an hour and no one's here—thank God, because I would never hear the end of this if anyone were.

"Wow, I wasn't expecting you to have a tree," she says, glancing at the ornamented Douglas fir set up to the right of the door. "It's actually nice."

"Thanks for the commendation," I say with a laugh.

"You really decorated this?"

"Well, no," I admit. "I hired some high school kids."

She seems satisfied with this, as if it's further proof of my flawed character.

"They needed money for Christmas shopping," I say. There. Now I'm a Christmas hero.

"Of course that was what motivated you," she says, rolling her eyes. Then her stomach growls, and she gasps. Embarrassed, maybe.

"Would you like a wet sandwich?" I ask.

She shakes her head in a study of annoyance. "No, I have food. I guess…if we're going to do this interview, we should sit down somewhere."

"Feel free to eat your dinner. Don't stand on ceremony for me. I don't care if you get fish in your teeth."

"Gross." She scrunches her nose, which is cuter than it has any right to be, but eyes the takeout bag. Her stomach growls again. "I guess I am a little hungry. Are you sure you wouldn't mind?"

"Not at all," I insist, then signal to one of the tables in the back. "Let's sit down while you eat."

We sit down, and she shoots me a self-conscious glance before shedding her coat, revealing the tight black sweater dress underneath, shot through with gold thread. She wore it for another man, technically, but I tell myself she really wore it for me. To piss me off. It's enough.

When she pulls out her box of food, it hits me that she doesn't have a drink, so I grab a *pompelmo* Sanpellegrino for her from one of the refrigerators and set it in front of her. Sour and sweet for Lucy.

"Oh. Is that for me?" she asks, sounding so shocked I almost laugh again.

"Yes," I say, "and before you ask, it's sealed. I may be godlike, but even I can't poison a sealed drink."

She rolls her eyes and cracks the drink open. Then she takes a fry out of the box and waves it at me. "What about you? Didn't you bring your food back?"

"I'll eat it later, but if you're offering to share your fries, I won't say no."

She scoffs, "I might be a nearly thirty-year-old virgin, but I know what a double entendre is."

"It wasn't one," I say, struggling not to react to that. Or to the fact that french fries are a much more sensual food than I ever gave them credit for. I can't stop watching as she lifts one to her mouth, parts her lips, and then bites it in half.

Her cheeks flush slightly. "You can have a few. Would you mind if I record our conversation?"

"Not at all."

I watch with growing anticipation as she sets her phone face up on the tabletop.

"Tell me about this place," she says, her tone professional. "I know your grandparents opened it. What was their vision?"

"They wanted to open a family business. Something that could make a good life for us here but also bring Italian food to Hideaway. When they moved here, they were one of the only Italian families. They thought they had something different to offer, and the fact that Hidden Italy's still here says they were right." I shrug. "We've been flooded a few times, so the location isn't the best, but my grandfather won this unit in a poker match."

"He didn't," she gasps as she sets down a half-eaten fry.

"He did," I say, grinning. "My grandfather was a persuasive man. The guy he won it from was friends with the current mayor's grandfather. No one believed this man would actually hand over the deed, but he was honest if not sensible. You know, the two of them became good friends, and on his deathbed, my grandfather admitted he'd cheated. The guy who'd handed the deed over without argument said he'd always known but hadn't cared. He'd admired my grandfather's audacity."

Surprised laughter gushes from her, the sound like music. "That's *amazing*. I wish I could have met him. He sounds like a real character."

"My whole family's amazing," I say firmly. "They've thought about relocating the business over the years, but my grandmother is not a woman who embraces change. Whenever there was flooding, she'd clean up, restock, and start again, like nothing had happened. My grandfather was like that, too, but no one ever questioned who was in charge. He admired her leadership. We all did."

"I can see why you think so highly of your family," she says. "It's hard for me to imagine having so much history. It was always just my mom and me."

"You didn't know your grandparents?"

"No, they passed away young. I never met them, and my father left us when I was little."

"I'm sorry," I say, stroking her extended hand. "A man who doesn't take care of his family isn't much of a man at all. My grandmother taught me that." I pause, weighing how much to tell her, but there's a deep sadness on her face, an old grief that prompts me to be honest. "My own father wasn't a family man, either, which was an unpleasant surprise for Nonna. After my mother left, my father shut down. He'd never bothered with us much, but he stopped trying entirely."

She looks surprised, and fuck, she's right to be. I didn't mean to tell her all that.

"I took care of my mother," she says. "I dropped out of school to take care of her, but I finished my degree with online classes."

I feel an uncomfortable sensation in my chest, as if my heart is trying to assert its existence and soften. "I'm sorry. That's rough."

She gives a short nod. "Yes, but it's also the best thing I've ever done. I'm glad I got to advocate for her."

Her words drill in deep, tapping into something inside of me. It hits me that my grandmother needs an advocate. She has my brothers, of course, but she might need all of us.

I tamp down the thought as she finishes a french fry. Looking at me contemplatively, she asks, "Did your grandmother take care of you, since your father didn't?"

"Yes, but I took care of my brothers and sister a lot. We spent plenty of time here. Making sandwiches, stocking shelves, making orders for catering."

"That's a lot for a young person to shoulder."

I can see her putting the pieces together in her head, forming a new image of me, painted with sympathy and understanding, and for some reason it aggravates me. "Family is important to me."

"I know."

"And this business *is* my family, Lucy. Blood, sweat, and tears."

"So why don't you like it?"

Her words feel like a slap to the face. "I never said I didn't," I say, sitting back. Whatever strange spell had been weaving us together feels like it's unraveling. "I'd *never* say that. I didn't leave because of Hidden Italy."

"Sorry," she says. "It's just something I picked up on."

"Most people leave town after high school graduation. I'm hardly the only one who decided to move away. There are barely any jobs around here."

I'm being defensive, but I don't know how to stop. The thing is, I *do* hate Hidden Italy. It felt like a prison when I was younger. It still feels like one, its walls getting a little snugger with each passing day. I also love it and everything it represents.

"I'm sorry," she says again. She finishes her drink before continuing. "And I'm sorry for earlier. I was a little prickly."

I raise my eyebrows. "You mean you're sorry for standing me up?"

"It was Harper who stood you up, wasn't it?" she asks with a sly smile. "That's too bad. Her brother's really nice. I met her at

Santa Speed Dating, and she seemed really nice too. I'm sure it was an innocent mistake."

"I'll bet. But I'm not going to tell you it's too bad your date got interrupted. I was relieved."

"Ex-*cuse* me?"

"You heard me. I don't think you'd be a good match for someone who's so polite. You enjoy arguing with me too much."

She sniffs, getting to her feet. "Who says I enjoy it?"

"We both do." I stand too, and she steps slightly closer, invading my space. Her coat's still off, giving me a clear view of that pretty dress and the way it molds to her body. My blood heats instantly, every inch of my skin buzzing with awareness and need.

"You're full of yourself," she says, poking my chest.

"I don't know how I could be with you working next door, constantly pointing out all of my flaws. Why don't you take out that marker of yours so you can draw on me right now?"

She laughs and reaches down, pulling it out of her bag.

"Are you going to give me a mustache? Maybe a pustule or two?"

Her eyes are shining as she uncaps it and lifts it to my face, her fingers brushing my skin and sending sensation skating across it. But she frowns just before the marker makes contact. "I can't. It would be like defacing the Mona Lisa."

I laugh. "You think I look like a middle-aged Italian woman?"

"You know what I mean." She crosses her arms over her chest, the marker still clutched in her hand. "You're not going to force me to say it. Your ego is already overinflated."

"And you just made it bigger. Would you like to give me any other compliments?"

Her forehead creases. The next thing I know she's gliding

the marker across my face, the tip cold and wet against my skin.

She starts laughing midway through her artistic experiment, which makes the marker wiggle against my skin. I don't try to stop her. The other night it occurred to me that I'd like to make her smile—really smile—and it's happening, as magical as if I'd made a wish on that damn bridge.

She finishes with a flourish of the marker.

"Did you just give me a mustache curl?" I ask, grinning. I probably look like an idiot, but it's a dry-erase marker, so I can wash it off before I see anyone else.

"You look ridiculous," she says, laughing as she caps the marker and tucks it away.

"Do you consider it your duty to humble me, Lucia? You're doing a good job of it."

She meets my eyes, hers sparkling with mischief, and laughs harder. "You made me do it."

"Remind me never to take you to the Louvre. There are penalties for messing with the Mona Lisa, you know."

She takes the marker out again, then tucks it into my shirt pocket and gives it a tap. It's an expensive shirt, and red wouldn't wash out, but I don't have the slightest urge to stop her. The feeling of her hand against my chest is heaven. She lets it rest there, just over my pocket.

"I'll let you retaliate," she tells me, the moment taut and fall of promise.

"What if I draw something worse on your face?"

"You haven't looked in a mirror yet."

"Menacing," I respond, smiling. "But no. I won't retaliate yet. I want you to spend the next few days thinking about when it'll happen. What it'll be."

"Please," she scoffs, her eyes dancing with mirth. "I'm not going to lose any sleep over you."

"Why shouldn't you? I've lost lots of sleep over you."

Her eyes widen, but she doesn't step back. "Why?" she asks after a moment. "You're worried we'll start selling sub sandwiches just to spite you?"

"I wouldn't put it past you, but no. That's not why I haven't been sleeping, Lucia. You know it's not."

"I don't like you," she insists, her palm still splayed over my heart. Her fingers are moving slightly, caressing me. Her voice is low and sultry.

"So you've said. And you've made it one hell of an up-and-down night. One minute, you're standing me up, and the next you've got your hand all over my chest."

She drops it the instant I point it out, and regret fills me.

"Now, I didn't say I didn't enjoy it." I reach down and clasp her hand, lifting it back up to its previous spot. "I've always loved roller coasters."

She smiles at me ruefully, caressing my chest—the heat and press of her hand almost enough to make me hard. "You mean you remove the stick up your ass to go on coasters? I don't believe it. I—"

She cuts herself off as I tilt my head down to hers, our faces only inches apart now. Our breaths mingle as I stare into her eyes.

"You were saying, Lucia? What else is wrong with me?"

Her gaze holds mine for a long moment. "I'm not going to sleep with you."

"Who said anything about sleeping?" I reach up to weave my fingers through her soft curls, a sigh escaping me as their silkiness engulfs my fingers, even better than I'd imagined.

She lifts up a little on her feet, her lips so close to mine I can barely take the teasing. But still, I'm going to let her come to me. She has to be the one to close the final distance between us.

"Will you admit that you messed with the power in our building last weekend?" she asks.

I laugh. "I'll tell you the truth if you'll kiss me. Don't you wonder what it would feel like? I know I do. That's why I haven't been sleeping. All night long, all I can think about is your smart mouth."

Her response is to push up on her heels and press her pretty mouth to mine. Her lips are soft and luscious, and the moment she opens her mouth to me, I'm a goner.

Oh, who am I kidding? I've been a goner for days.

I grip her hair a little tighter, tilting her head to deepen the kiss as our tongues meet and do battle.

It's like I thought it would be.

It's also better.

I reach down without looking and sweep away the takeout container and empty drink can, which fall to the floor. I don't care. At this moment, I don't care about anything but having my mouth on her and her sweet body pressed against mine. Wrapping my hands around her hips, I back her up to the table and lift her onto it, my mouth still on hers.

She gasps into my mouth, and I swallow it. I nearly die when she opens her legs for me, inviting me to invade her space. Stepping in, I bend to her, kissing her harder, full of a deep, pulsing need that's stolen what's left of my sense.

I come undone when she wraps her legs around my waist. I'm already hard, so hard it hurts to feel the zipper of my dress pants pressing into my dick, and I roll my hips against her as I deepen our kiss. One of my hands finds her hair again and the other her hip, tugging her into me.

Oh, Christ, this feels good.

Then she pulls away panting, her lips dark pink from our kiss, her eyes full of surprise.

"It was good for you too." It's not a question. I fucking know it was.

She scrunches her face up in familiar annoyance, then presses a hand over her eyes. When she looks at me again, I can't quite read her expression.

"The power," she says. "Was it you?"

It takes me a second to register what she's saying. To remember that English is a language I speak too, and I'm normally pretty good at it.

"Are you going to stop kissing me if I say yes?"

"I don't know," she says, her legs still wrapped around my waist, keeping me close, my dick pressed against her, hard and needy. "But I want the truth."

"I did it," I admit. "I didn't want you leaving with any of those guys. I couldn't stand the thought. That guy Brandon's an asshole. He—"

"You couldn't stand thinking about it because Brandon's an asshole?" she asks, her face so close to mine. So pretty. So damn kissable.

"I was jealous," I confess.

It's apparently the right answer, or at least not the wrong one, thank God, because she kisses me again, sucking on my bottom lip. I grind against her as I kiss her back, my breath nearly knocked out of me when she starts rolling her hips into me.

Need spirals through me, coiling tighter and tighter, making me feel like a teenage boy sneaking around and making out in the stockroom. Been there, done that, got caught too. This time we're out on the main floor, but there's only a minimal chance that one of my brothers is going to show up this far past closing. My grandmother is hopefully asleep in her bed.

I break our kiss, panting, and say, "Can you push down your stockings? I want to feel you. I need—"

To feel how wet I know she is, but I don't want to call it out there.

Sucking on her bottom lip, she lifts up and pushes her stockings down, showing the creamy expanse of her rounded thighs.

I swear under my breath, then swear again as she parts her legs for me, inviting me in again.

I slide between them, then touch her, groaning when I feel the slickness of her need for me. "Oh, Lucia, you feel so good."

She gasps and lifts her hips into my fingers as I thrust them inside of her and rub a spot that has her arcing her head back, giving me the perfect opening to dip my head and kiss her there. Her skin is soft and smells like heaven, and right now, I don't have any objection to being in Hidden Italy. Right now, it's my favorite place in town, in Maine, *on the planet*.

I move my fingers, my dick hard as stone, because she's so tight and wet, and I want this. I want *her*. Fuck me, I can't remember ever wanting anyone like this. It must be this dance between us that's gotten under my skin. It's only gone on for a week, but it's been the best foreplay I've ever engaged in, making me desperate.

Her hips rise to meet my hand, and she makes a sweet moan. I capture her bottom lip in my teeth and nip on it, then suck as I continue to move my hand, wanting to give her pleasure. Needing to feel her come.

I lean back so I can watch her face: her eyes closed, her lips parted, her head tipped back so her hair sweeps the table.

"You are exquisite," I say, working my fingers. I lower my head so I can brush my mouth over her breasts through her dress, and even though there's fabric barring my way, I can feel the points of her nipples. I run my tongue over one and then the other, and she bucks on the table.

"Oh my God, that feels good. So good."

"And I haven't even gotten onto my knees yet," I say, giving her a wicked look, knowing she'll appreciate the reference.

I'll be damned if she doesn't instantly get wetter.

"But you said…"

"I know what I said," I say, moving my fingers frantically now, because I want that look on her face to stay there. I like being the man who put it there, just as much as that smile earlier.

With her next moan, I get to my knees. A plastic fork digs into me, but I don't bother to move it—I just angle her legs over my shoulders and bury my face in heaven.

I need the breathy, surprised sound she makes more than food. More than water.

I suck and lick as I push her closer to the brink, worshipping her body the way it deserves, and she buries her hands in my hair. She's tugging hard enough for it to hurt, and it hurts so good—too good—that I'm in danger of coming in my pants just from pleasuring her.

"I'm going to come," she says. Then: "*Enzo.*"

Hearing her say my name like that, her voice tight with pleasure, is a revelation. I instantly need to hear it again.

I suck harder as she bucks her hips, her body going taut before it relaxes, and I lay a soft kiss before I pull away and look up at her.

She's staring down at me, her eyes full of wonder.

"Not such a bad lover after all, am I?" I ask.

I meant it as a teasing remark, a continuation of our banter, but her face shuts down. "So that's what this was about? Proving you can make a woman come? Well, congratulations."

She pushes away from me and pulls up her stockings.

"I didn't mean it like that, Lucy," I say, a frantic feeling growing inside of me. She can't leave like this. She can't leave at all.

She gets to her feet, putting her hand on her luscious hip. "I'm pretty sure that's exactly how you meant it."

"This wasn't about proving anything," I say. "I want you." I gesture down to my dick straining against my pants. There's a crushed french fry stuck to my knee, and I fling it off. Jesus, what's become of me? "Obviously, I want you."

She studies me for a moment before her posture relaxes slightly. "It was a shitty remark."

"Yes. I'm an asshole who says dumb things, but I can do better. I want to do better."

She looks unconvinced, but then she shocks the hell out of me by reaching forward and running her fingers over the bulge in my pants.

I swear under my breath, the sensation of her hand on me unearthly, even with the layers of fabric separating us.

"You're so hard," she says, some of the wonder from earlier seeping into her voice. "I'm not totally inexperienced, you know. I've gotten to third base before a few times."

"I don't need to hear about the other men who've had the pleasure of touching you or putting their mouths on you."

She smiles, shaking her head, but continues to move her hand over me. "Do you have any condoms here?"

My mouth falls open. "Condoms?"

"Oh, what am I talking about? Three hot Italian men work here. Of course you have condoms hidden away somewhere."

"Lucia, I'm not going to take your virginity in the dining area of my family business."

Anger flashes through her eyes, and regrettably, she pulls her hand from my straining dick. "You said you wanted to be the one, and I'm agreeing. I don't need dinner and candlelight, Enzo. I know you don't want to romance me, and I don't want you to. We would *never* work out as a couple. I want to be with a nice guy, and you don't want to be with anyone. You just want sex. I thought that was the whole point."

It was. But this doesn't feel right. All that talking earlier made me feel connected to her. Besides, if I'm going to fuck her, I want to take my time and do it right. I want her to come multiple times, and not just on my face.

"We don't need candlelight and dinner, but I'd like to have a bed."

"And I wouldn't. I want to do it here. I want you to take me right here on this table."

My pulsing dick tells me to do as I'm told, but that nagging voice in my head insists I need to do better. She wants to get this over with, but I want to make it an experience that's good for her—one she'll remember fondly when she moves on to her nice guy.

Her fingers dance over my dick again, a hot, excruciating tease. It feels so good a groan seeps out of me, and I kiss the side of her face, her neck, luxuriating in her. Nothing The Haven offers could feel as good as this woman. Everything about her is soft and lush and delicious.

I want to take what she's offering. I'm desperate to. But I can't give Lucy what she wants, not like this.

Then her phone starts to vibrate on the floor.

Oh, fuck, I must have swept it off with the food.

She stoops to pick it up, inspecting the screen.

"Any cracks in your screen?" I ask.

She ignores me, though, and I peer over her shoulder to see the spiderweb cracks on her screen. Shit. I scarcely have a chance to notice the mess I made before I see the name flashing on it—Hudson Firehose.

Shit, shit, shit. My pulse starts hammering for a different and much more unpleasant reason as she answers the call. Is Hudson calling to tattle on me?

Sure enough, Lucy's face settles into an angry look, which gets madder the longer she listens. "He did, huh? Okay. Yeah, thanks for calling. I would *love* to get together again sometime. You're a good guy, Hudson."

She hangs up and tucks the damaged phone back into her purse before looking at me with hard eyes.

"Turns out your brother's the one who caused the fire emergency that pulled Hudson away from our date tonight. He left his popcorn in the microwave for too long. Are you *insane?*"

I lift my hands. "I know how to microwave popcorn. It's not my fault if Giovanni never learned."

Her expression turns fierce. "I didn't even say which brother."

Shit, she's got me there.

"What if he got hurt?" she asks tightly.

"I'd *never* do anything to hurt my brother. He set off his fire alarm manually. His neighbor calls the station every time an alarm goes off in the building."

"Right, you wouldn't mess with your brother because he's blood-related. But you'd do anything to destroy my date."

She's furious now, anger practically sparking off her.

"I don't understand why you're so upset about this," I say. "You didn't care about the power thing. Are you mad about your phone? Because that was my bad. I'm going to replace it."

"No. You're not. It'll be my reminder not to make terrible decisions."

"I figured the flyer with an X over my face would do the trick. Let me replace your phone."

She shakes her head as she picks up her coat, shaking off a couple of french fries. "This was a huge mistake. You're controlling and manipulative, and basically everything my mother ever warned me about."

"It's not a mistake," I say, suddenly frantic. Because she's going to leave angry—and not angry in the way she's been for the last week, but *actually* angry.

"Why do you even care?" she asks, her tone cold. "I'm sure you can find some tourist to sleep with. You don't need to fixate on me just because you know my secret."

She's waiting for an answer, her body a taut line now.

But I don't have one. All I know is that I *do* care. I'm interested in her, maybe even a little obsessed. It might have been her search for a man to sleep with that ratcheted up my interest, but it isn't the reason for it.

She wants a nice man, though, a man like Hudson. And I don't want anything else to hold me here in Hideaway.

Still, I say, "I don't want you to leave like this."

"But you don't get to control me, Enzo. I'm going."

"You'll let me walk you home. It's dark out."

"I won't. This town practically has a subzero crime rate, and it's lit up with thousands of Christmas lights."

"I don't like this," I say darkly. "I shouldn't have done that with Hudson. It was a step too far. But you were taunting me at dinner. I figured it was fair play, a part of our game."

"Goodbye, Enzo."

She makes it to the door before I grab my things and stop her with a light hand on her shoulder.

"Don't touch me right now," she says, turning to glare at me.

I hand her my scarf. "Please. It's windy."

She gives me a bewildered look but takes it, thank God, almost as if it's reflexive. She's not a woman to turn away a well-meant gesture. "Only if you promise not to follow me."

"Call me when you get home."

Her lips press into an unimpressed line. I'd like to kiss it, but she's made her disinterest in more kisses clear. "I don't have your number, and I don't want it."

"Call me," I insist. "I just need to know you got home okay."

She narrows her gaze. "I don't want you having my home phone number. I'll text you. The signal's been pretty good for me today."

She holds her hand out, and I grab my phone from my pants pocket and hand it over so she can plug her number in.

"Don't follow me," she sneers.

"I won't," I promise. "But if I don't hear from you, I'm going to have to call Eileen, and we both know that Eileen will have plenty to say if she knows we were together tonight."

"Everyone in town probably does since you insisted on walking in together, through the front entrance," she says, aggrieved.

"And you'll tell them you agreed to interview me for your project, angel that you are. And that I was just as much of an asshole as usual."

She gives me a look I can't read, then says, "Why were you on the Wishing Bridge last week?"

I'm not sure what answer she's looking for, but I stick with honesty. She already knows the truth, after all, might as well call it out. "I wanted to save Hidden Italy so I could leave."

"I thought this place was your family," she says sarcastically.

"You can love something and hate it at the same time," I reply.

She nods, her expression serious, then turns on her heel and leaves through the door, disappearing into the night.

If she didn't want people to wonder if we're together, she probably shouldn't have taken the scarf, which most Hidies would recognize as my mother's handiwork—made from two needles, not a hook. But that's not the main reason I gave it to her. I have a strange need to know that she's safe and warm. Protected.

It's only after the door shuts behind her that I look down at my phone screen. She's listed her number with the name "Your Worst Nightmare."

Fuck me, I can't help but laugh.

CHAPTER 16

LUCY

Oh, I hate him.

What a manipulative jerk.

What a talented tongue.

What lovely, perfectly-shaped fingers.

What a nice, hard dick.

What a good sense of humor.

I march away from Hidden Italy, determined to silence any appreciation of Enzo, but I don't go home. I find myself walking toward the Wishing Bridge, where it feels like all of this began.

I pick my way toward the bridge, greeting a couple of people I recognize as I wrap the scarf more tightly around my neck. It smells incredibly delicious, of course—spicy and manly and just like the side of Enzo's neck. He probably wears an expensive cologne. He's exactly the kind of man who would, and he'd take great pleasure in knowing it drives me crazy.

A pulse of remembered pleasure works through me, and I squeeze my legs together for a second before continuing onward.

He let me in tonight, telling me about his family. I felt a

moment of fierce connection with him then—we were just two caregivers who understood the toll and also the joy. I nearly told him why I'm taking the programming classes. But thank God I didn't, because now I have to wonder if it was all a ruse to get what he wanted.

But he didn't get what he wanted.

No, I left him with a rock-hard dick. Is he taking care of it now? Is he thinking of me while he does it?

I push down an image of Enzo with his hand wrapped around his dick, his other hand resting on the wall to prop himself up, his muscles rippling, because he wouldn't be easy on himself.

Okay, fine. I'm attracted to Lorenzo Cafiero. *Viciously* attracted to him. In the spirit of total honesty, I'll admit that I've been attracted to him from the first moment I saw him.

But sexual attraction means nothing. I'm attracted to dozens of famous actors, and they'll never know I exist. The important consideration is that I don't *like* Enzo, and I will continue to not like him. He's domineering and manipulative, and sure, he has a sharp, witty sense of humor, but I can watch a sitcom if I want to laugh. I'll just have to find someone else to be attracted to. Maybe even my sweet neighbor...if he's the rare *Golden Girls*-loving young guy.

I keep walking, my mind circling around and around but staying on an Enzo track. Enzo's lips. The brush of his fingers against mine as he reached for a french fry. The way he cleared that table with a single sweep of his arm in his desperation for me. Enzo on his knees in front of me...

He should have looked ridiculous with that red mustache, but if the marker couldn't make the photo of him less attractive, what hope did it have of marring the real thing?

Still, I take some pleasure from the thought that I used a real Sharpie, not a dry-erase marker. He'll still have traces of it on his face tomorrow, at work.

Something brushes against my hand, making me jerk to attention. I look down and see Skippy, who wags his tail. I smile at the jingle bell collar someone gifted him and give his head a rub. I'd love to have a pet, someone to keep me company and make the apartment feel less empty and alone, but my lease agreement insists I'm not allowed to have a cat or dog. At least there's Skippy, who has sweetness enough to share with all of us. I give him a kiss and another nuzzle before moving on. A few minutes later, I reach the bridge.

It's cold tonight, and the bridge is empty except for those locks lined up on its spokes.

I'm not sure why I'm here, other than that I need a moment to think. My mind wasn't working clearly—or at all—in Hidden Italy. It was so focused on Enzo, I couldn't see anything else.

I sit on the bridge, letting my legs dangle through the spokes and over the edge, and cautiously look down. No one's getting busy beneath it, thankfully.

Now that I'm here, ready to make a wish, I feel self-conscious, but I press a hand to my chest. I'm not even fully aware of what I'm doing, what I intend, until I say in a small voice, "I'm in over my head, Mom."

I rub a little more with my fingertips, feeling the cold press of the stone under my stockings. Feeling the grief surging against my rib cage.

"You *definitely* wouldn't approve of him, and you'd be right not to. Your advice was always good. *Great.* I've read your letter so many times, and I'm going to find a man just like the one you described to me. I'm not going to get hung up on some jerk."

That's why I'm here, I realize. That's the wish I should be whispering on the bridge tonight.

For a man my mother would approve of.

But I can't bring myself to say the words. Not when my lips

are swollen from him, and I can still feel the rasp of his stubble against my legs.

Enzo Cafiero is not a softhearted, biddable man.

He's definitely not easygoing.

But I can't deny that I want more of him.

I've been enjoying this push-pull between us, and it'll be hard to release it.

So I say the only thing I know is true. "I love you, Mom. And I miss you so much." Tears stream down my face, feeling instantly frozen by the chilly air. "I wish I knew you were okay. That somewhere you were okay."

At that exact moment, snow begins to fall in soft, powdery flakes.

I look up in shock, my heart expanding so much it feels like my entire chest is tight. Reaching out a hand, I catch a few flakes to assure myself they're real. *Of course* they're real.

I know it's probably just a coincidence, but pure happiness unleashes inside of me, and I don't want to reject it. I want to let myself live in this feeling. To accept this as a sign that my mother is somehow listening.

I want to believe in holiday magic.

Raising my head to the flakes, I stick out my tongue and catch them in my mouth. I laugh, even as a few final tears work down my cheeks, and then I leave the bridge to walk home.

And something even more astounding happens…

The flurries stop as abruptly as they started.

I stare back at the bridge with wide eyes, my entire being arrested.

"Mom?" I ask.

Of course there's no answer, but when I turn back toward the path, I'm a different person.

It feels like my mother just hugged me, in the only way she still can, and told me it's all going to be okay.

I'm in such a daze that I plow into someone else who's headed toward the bridge.

I trip and fall back onto my butt, startled.

"Oh my God, I'm so sorry," a familiar voice says.

Familiar not because I know her, but because I've heard recordings of her voice in dozens of movies.

It's Amanda Willis, her perfect honey-blonde hair framing her face beneath a dark beanie hat.

She reaches out to help me up, and I take her hand, struck dumb.

"Are you okay?" she asks.

"I'm…fine," I say at last, recovering the ability to speak, thank goodness. "And I'm the one who should be sorry. I bumped into you. I was distracted by the bridge."

I realize what that sounds like and laugh. "This is going to sound even crazier, but I made a wish, and it started snowing. Was it snowing over here?"

Her eyes widen. "No, not that I noticed, but I've been kind of lost in thought too." She glances past me at the bridge. "You look familiar. Do you work at Love at First Sip?"

I nod quickly. "Yes."

She smiles warmly at me. "Your boss is the one who told me about this place. Eileen's *lovely*. She came to see me this morning."

I know all about that, but I don't want to freak her out, so I just say, "Oh?"

"That's kind of why I'm here." She glances briefly at the bridge and laughs. "I feel like I'm at a literal crossroads. In my career. In my love life. Everything."

"So what better place to go than a bridge?" I ask with a smile. "Well, I'll leave you to it. You should be able to make your wish without anyone intruding."

"Actually," she says before I can walk away. "Can I ask you something?"

I pause, surprised. "Of course."

She shakes her head, her nose scrunching up. "I can't believe I'm about to say this. You're going to think I'm nuts."

"I think it just snowed on that bridge because I asked for a sign, so I probably am nuts. I'm the last person who'd judge you."

She gives me a grateful smile. "How do you know if someone really likes you, or if they only like the idea of you?"

I lift my eyebrows. I'd whistle if I could, but I've never had that talent. "That's a heavy one."

My mind shifts to Enzo.

Is that what he likes? The idea of me? Lucy, the twenty-eight-year-old virgin?

Am I one more challenge to be conquered?

Amanda looks around, ensuring we're alone, and then takes a half step closer. "You know who I am, don't you?"

I nod, because obviously I do. "And I'm Lucy."

"Nice to meet you, Lucy."

A sigh escapes her as she lifts her head the winter sky, eyes closed. I'm about to sneak off, leaving her to her Wishing Bridge moment, when she speaks.

"Everyone thinks they know me because they've seen my movies." She toes the snow with her boot, a humorless laugh escaping in a puff of hot air. "Or read the many tabloids about me." She meets my eyes. "But that's not really me, you know? And I've already been wrong about someone in the past, so I'm not sure I know how to tell if something's real."

I give this point the consideration it deserves, then say, "All you can do is be yourself." I smile. "I've never had a talent for being anyone else, and plenty of men have no patience for who I really am. But I've always been okay with that, because if we were right for each other, they'd like the real me. So be defiantly yourself. Maybe you'll scare some people away. But the ones who genuinely like you will stick around."

She smiles at me. "Defiantly myself, huh? I like that."

"Can I give you a hug?"

"As long as you don't ask me to sign your coat with a Sharpie."

"I think I'd rather be your friend," I say, and give her a quick hug. "Good luck with your wish. I'm starting to think the bridge really is magical."

"This whole place is magical," she says with a smile.

And it feels like that tonight, it really does.

"I'll see you around, Amanda," I say. Then I tighten the scarf around my neck and walk back toward my apartment, feeling a new conviction hardening in my chest.

This is what I'm fighting for. To be a part of this place. To make a home for myself. To be loved for who I am.

I want to believe all of that is possible.

I want to believe I can finally have a family that won't be torn away from me.

When I get home, I check my phone and find a text from Charlie:

> Call me immediately, or you're on my naughty list.

I'm about to do just that when I notice a text from another Hideaway number.

> I can still taste you. Hope my scarf kept you warm, Lucia.

I immediately respond to him:

> I'm home. Consider yourself blocked.

Then I save his number under "DO NOT ANSWER."

The signal really is good today, or at least at this particular moment, in this particular quadrant of the apartment, because a reply comes through straightaway.

I almost called the police, you know. Unless you live underwater, you should have been home half an hour ago.

So you actually listened and didn't follow me? Do you want a gold star?

There's something else I want more. A gold star wouldn't be much of a consolation prize.

I thought you were going to block me?

It's happening now.

3

2

Okay, there's one thing I wanted to tell you. I met Amanda Willis tonight. She's AMAZING. And I think she's into Portia.

I MIGHT have mentioned what you said to Eileen this morning. She already had plans in that regard, of course, and it seems like she's working her magic.

Do you have anyone else for Eileen to set up? She gets bored when she doesn't have a project, and I'm not quite ready for her to plan my wedding to Hudson.

He shouldn't have left your date.

Yeah, it's almost like he's a firefighter, and there was a boy who called fire.

I think you're getting your folktales mixed up. But my point is that I wouldn't have left.

So it's a very good thing for everyone that you're not a firefighter.

Probably. Although I'm excellent at most things I put my mind to.

And oh so humble.

False modesty is worse than arrogance.

I think your talents lie more toward starting fires, not putting them out.

Be careful. I might take that as a compliment.

You would.

Thanks for the semipermanent mustache, by the way. I think red's my color.

Speaking of which, what are you wearing?

I'm imagining something red and skimpy.

1. Blocked.

Unfortunately, ending the text conversation with Enzo doesn't calm my nerves as much as I'd hoped. I'm still worked up when I call Charlie on my landline and tell her nearly everything, from what happened at dinner, to Enzo getting down on his knees for me, to running into Amanda near the bridge.

As I spill my guts to my friend, I pack a bag, because I'm cat-sitting for the eccentric regular at the Sip who drew Charlie to Hideaway Harbor two years ago to paint her cat. She's insanely wealthy for undisclosed reasons but lives in an adorable one-bedroom cottage because she says too much empty space messes with her Chi.

Her calico cat is the cutest creature I've ever encountered, and I could really use some kitty snuggles.

I try not to speculate why I didn't *actually* block Enzo's number.

THE NEXT MORNING, I deface my No-Enzo flyer a little more, adding some flames around Enzo's head. He'll understand the reference when he sees it. Maybe I'll make a "fire starter" special too, to really drive the point home.

Charlie and I are both working this morning, because Eileen has some unspecified appointment, probably related to matchmaking. Two high school kids are covering the afternoon shift.

Whenever there's downtime, Charlie and I browse wedding dresses and google revenge schemes on Reddit.

At around eleven, I get a call from Lumi, the postmistress, who tells me I have a delivery to pick up from the post office.

"You mean Love at First Sip has a delivery?" I ask.

Truthfully, I don't know anyone outside of town who would send me a package. It's not that I didn't have any friends back in Asheville aside from Charlie, but those relationships never deepened. I was too busy. Too overwhelmed. Too sad.

"Oh, no, this one's for you," says Lumi.

Feeling a twinge of foreboding, I tell Charlie about it. She insists I should go immediately.

I hurry over to the post office, one of the most gorgeous historical buildings in Hideaway, and step inside, rubbing my hands from the cold.

There's a line of people waiting to send out packages, but when Lumi sees me she waves me over.

"Got it right here," she says with a grin, tapping the box. "Maybe you've got a secret admirer."

I take the box, feeling a sneaking suspicion I know who it's from, and sign for it on her tablet.

"I heard all about Santa Speed Dating," she says. "I'm glad I didn't let Eileen convince me to go. I appreciate a man with a good beard, but the head lice is a strong no."

"They weren't really head lice," I say defensively. "Just some poppy seeds and a guy who should get reading glasses."

"Even so." She sighs, eyeing the customers waiting for her, and says, "I've got my work cut out for me."

I give her a sympathetic nod and go, my box in hand. I'm itching to open it, but I wait until I'm back inside Love at First Sip, my coat and gloves removed.

"Come on," Charlie presses. "I'm dying of suspense."

"Better that than dying of old age," says a grizzled voice from the table closest to the counter.

Wayne, an older man just past retirement age, is our most loyal customer, but we can't decide why he spends so much time here, because he seems to find fault in everything. We're begrudgingly fond of him, and presumably he likes us at least a little, because he's almost always here until closing, reading a book, writing in one of his leather notebooks, or complaining about not getting a good signal on his phone.

"You'll outlive all of us," Charlie tells him.

"From your mouth to God's ears."

She laughs good-naturedly at his quip, then turns to me and nudges my arm. "Come on. Open it before someone else comes in."

"All right, all right," I say, laughing, and tear into the box… and find a brand-new iPhone.

"Holy crap," Charlie says, glancing over my shoulder. "Is that what I think it is?"

"I told him not to," I say, trying to decide if I'm pissed or pleased.

I give the boxed phone a once-over and realize that while it's clearly new, the seal on the carton has been cut. I pull the phone out of its packaging and turn it on. The wallpaper is a photo of Enzo pretending to twirl his red permanent marker mustache.

Definitely pissed. Even though I did smile before I gathered my wits.

"That man doesn't know how to listen," I complain.

Charlie lifts her brows. "In this particular case, I'd say he actually did the right thing."

"Nope. Not using it. Given his previous bad behavior, he probably has it set up so he can track me anywhere in Hideaway Harbor."

"So he can follow you around town and give you orgasms?" she says in a whisper. "Oh, the humanity."

I give her a censoring look. "This is serious. I can't give him the upper hand."

The bell on the door rings, sending the familiar first few bars of "Jingle Bells" reverberating through the café. Eileen found the bell at the Christmas pop-up shop on Lobstah Lane. It's run by Noelle, who's very sweet and very single, so of course Eileen pays her regular visits. This bell was acquired on her last shopping trip, and she's very proud of it. In theory, it's festive, but we get a lot of foot traffic during the holidays, and all day, it's been nothing but those first few bars of "Jingle Bells."

While Charlie and I and the other part-time employees have gotten very good at hustling in and out so fast it's not triggered, no one else has developed that skill, and honestly, it's enough to drive a person crazy.

"That dagnabbed thing," murmurs Wayne.

"He's right about that," Charlie says, wrinkling her nose in agreement. "Anyway, forget what I said about Enzo. He obviously has control issues and needs to learn his lesson. *Several* lessons. What are you going to do with the phone?"

"Give it back, but not before we have a photo shoot."

"*Excuse me*," says a firm, no-nonsense voice from the doorway. "I was told this is a coffee shop. Does no one work around here?"

Holy shit. It's Enzo's Nonna Francesca, in the flesh. She's wearing all black like she did the other day, her hair pulled back in a bun.

Did he send her over here? Is this another move from his playbook? Sweat instantly breaks out across my skin.

"Hello, Nonna Francesca," I say, before I can think better of it.

"Mrs. Cafiero," she corrects tersely. "Where is Eileen?"

"This is one of her days off," I say.

"Sloth is the gateway to the devil," she says, then makes the sign of the cross. "You'll take a minute to talk to me."

"Me?" I ask, flustered and hoping to buy some time.

"*You.*"

"Would you like a cinnamon cappuccino?" Charlie asks with a suspiciously innocent look on her face.

The older woman shoots her a glare so withering, I'm tempted to jump in front of it to deflect its force.

"Don't worry," Charlie tells me. "I've got the counter totally covered. Why don't you lovely ladies take a seat over there?" She points to an empty table, grinning, and suddenly I question my devotion to my best friend.

"It will do," Nonna Francesca says and marches over to it. I fall in behind her, the way I imagine people have been doing her entire life.

My whole body is tight with anxiety. Is it possible Mrs. Cafiero knows what happened last night? What if there's, like, a camera in their dining area and she saw me with my legs wrapped around Enzo's face?

Oh no, this isn't good.

My mom was a history buff. In her last year, when she couldn't do much, I played audiobooks for her. I wasn't sure how well she processed them anymore, but at least it made me feel like she was entertained. One of these books was about organized crime in Sicily.

I'll bet Nonna Francesca knows a guy.

"You told me you'd take down that flyer with my grandson's face on it," Nonna Francesa finally says, observing me with her dark eyes.

"Of course!" I say quickly, really hoping she doesn't look at the back wall of the café, where the blown-up, full-length photo of Enzo is taped to the wall with a dart in his...

Well, I really hope she doesn't look.

She hasn't been very nice to me, but after what Enzo told me last night, I have a grudging respect for her.

"I'm sorry I offended you," I gush. "It's a little game he and I are playing, and it got out of hand. It's no problem to take it down. Although, if I take mine down, I expect him to take down the one he made of me. It would only be fair. He drew that really awful hairy—"

"Enough," she says, lifting her hand, palm outward. "Enzo told me about this app you are making."

"Yes," I say, smiling, "I was happy to learn more about Hidden Italy. There's so much history."

She nods severely. "This is good. I'm glad you're including the shop. I want Enzo to stay in Hideaway Harbor."

Oh.

"Uh, he seemed pretty resolute about leaving."

Her lips purse. "This is what I must see Eileen about. You will tell her I came?"

I glance around, then lean in slightly. "You want her to set him up with someone?"

Her gaze settles on the scarf wrapped around my neck. Oh crap. It's Enzo's scarf. I wore it today as a victory flag—he made me borrow it, ergo, it is now mine. Is it possible she'll recognize it?

She looks up from it, thankfully, and meets my gaze. "Yes. I want Eileen to help me with this."

"But Enzo doesn't want to be in a relationship," I say, feeling a tightness in my chest.

She narrows her eyes. "He was in a relationship before you came along."

"Uhh…yeah. I'm sorry about that."

She waves her hand in dismissal. "I didn't like her. She was a rude girl with no respect for family. Always talking but saying nothing. Do *you* have respect for family?"

"Yes," I say honestly.

"Very well," she says. "Thank you for the cookies, although they made a mess."

"You're welcome," I say hastily. "I'll bring more over. And, look, I'm so sorry I brought up bad memories about Enzo's mom. I didn't know."

She surprises me by smiling. "When you get to be my age, your life is mostly memories, more behind you than before you. But my grandchildren give me purpose."

I sense she's about to get up, so before she can leave, I rush to say, "Nonna…I mean Mrs. Cafiero?"

"Yes?"

"Would you tell me some of those stories sometime?"

Maybe I'm being nuts, but I really want to know what this town used to be like. The story about how she and her husband acquired the property for Hidden Italy is insane. I'll bet she has dozens of other wild stories.

And maybe some ideas for my super-secret project.

I am *not* being nice to her for Enzo's sake.

She studies me for a long moment before nodding. "Yes, you will come see me sometime. I will show you how to make a real cappuccino, none of this nonsense you've been selling here."

Surprise lights me up inside. "Thank you. I'd enjoy that."

Then she gets up and leaves, every eye in the café on her as the door closes behind her.

I'm still sitting there, watching the door, when Charlie comes over and sits opposite me, setting a cinnamon stick cappuccino in front of me. "I'll bet hers isn't nearly as good."

"I wouldn't take those odds," I say, even though Charlie *does* make an excellent drink.

"So, did you make peace? Does this mean we don't get to do the photo shoot?"

I smile at her. "Oh, we're definitely doing the photo shoot. But I *did* promise to take down the flyer outside."

"Not this one?" She gestures to the full-length beauty attached to the wall.

"She didn't specify, but I'd like to keep it. I've become fond of it." I pause. "Charlie? I think Mrs. Cafiero is going to ask Eileen to set Enzo up with someone."

"How do we feel about that?" she asks, her tone sympathetic.

I still don't like it. Okay, fine, I like it even less than when I thought Eileen was going to set him up last week. I'm softening toward him, damn it. I'm like butter left in the microwave too long.

Sighing, I say, "Are we sure only an old dude would like *The Golden Girls*? Because my neighbor guy is really nice. He'd totally be the kind of guy Mom wanted me with."

"Yes, but here's a crazy thought…why don't you ask him?"

I groan. "I'll do it after I finish cat-sitting."

"Uh-huh. Sure."

I wonder if she knows why I'm hesitating.

If so, I wish she'd tell me.

CHAPTER 17

ENZO

When I come back to Hidden Italy from delivering a catering order with Nico, smelling like tomato sauce, Giovanni hands over an iPhone box with a grin on his face. "Lucy said she doesn't want it. But she went ahead and personalized it for you, whatever that means." He hesitates, waiting for an explanation I'm in no mood to give, then asks, "What are you doing buying her a phone?"

"I broke hers."

"On purpose?"

I pause, considering. "Sort of."

"Was it before or after she drew that mustache on your face."

"After."

His eyebrows wing upward, and he shakes his head slightly, the look of a man who knows sharing hour is over. "You've got a strange way of romancing women."

"I never said I was romancing her," I grumble, annoyed that she didn't accept the phone but also curious about what's on it. It's her next play, I'm sure of it.

I take a look around the room. "Where's Nonna?"

"She went home," he says. "But she was mighty interested in your red mustache too."

"It's a fashion statement," I say dryly.

"Yup, clearly," he scoffs. "I'm about to go home. Max and Dee are here." He signals toward the rear of the shop, where Max is manning the sandwich counter.

I nod, feeling the itch to look at the phone. But I don't want to do it in front of my brother. Or Max and Dee.

"I'm going home myself," I say. "Haven't been to the apartment for a couple of days." I spent the last two nights with Nonna, which was extremely fucking awkward last night, since I'd been so worked up after tasting Lucy. Still, no way was I going to jerk off at my grandmother's house. A man has his limits.

"Nico said he wants to meet us at Kippis later to toast my last night before Portia turns me into taffy. Have you seen those ridiculous flyers Eileen made for her?"

I snort. "I think everyone's seen them, man."

I might be distracted by Lucy, but that doesn't mean I'm blind. The poster has the same shirtless Santa on it as the one in the Santa Speed Dating poster, but Giovanni's head has been superimposed onto his, and he's throwing candy into the air, with the tagline: *Pull taffy with a shirtless Santa! Free candy tasting and fun.*

Portia's obviously trying to pack in as big of a crowd as possible.

"She loves to needle me. But I've got a little surprise for her."

"Yeah?"

"You gave me the idea with your marker mustache. I found a red Sharpie on the floor wedged beneath one of the shelves." He glances around, then lifts up his shirt, revealing his chest. Three words are written across his pecs in permanent marker: *Santa isn't real.*

I whistle, then laugh. "You really don't want to take your shirt off, huh? You been missing workouts?"

He rolls his eyes. "If I advertised what I look like without my shirt on, there'd be a stampede."

"Don't we want a stampede?" I ask, looking around the sleepy shop. A few people are browsing the shelves, but it's hardly a crowd.

"Yeah, maybe, but I don't want them taking a run at me. They can have all the sandwiches they want."

"Is this about Janine?" I ask. His high school girlfriend moved back to town last year. They recently tried dating again, but they broke up about a month ago.

I overheard him grumbling about her under his breath this morning, but never got the chance to ask him about it.

He glowers at me. "Janine's engaged. I just found out."

Shit. That was quick.

"Sorry, man."

"I'm not. This has nothing to do with her. It's about me not wanting to be treated like a piece of meat."

"Okay, fair enough." I'd be a hypocrite if I pressed for more. There's plenty I don't want to tell him either.

"You want to get that drink or what?"

"Nah, but I'll lift one up for you at the apartment."

"But you'll be at the taffy pulling tomorrow?"

"Of course. I already promised Aria I'd record it for her. The lobster trap tree lighting too."

"How joyful," he says wryly. "We can send her some of the taffy too. Maybe it can become a family tradition."

The idea tugs at something in my brain, but it's hard to think beyond getting home so I can look at the phone.

"You're dying to see what Lucy put on there, aren't you?" he asks with a knowing grin.

"Oh, fuck off," I say, then leave, letting the door shut behind me.

I climb the stairs to the ground level, and before I turn in the direction of home, I notice the flyers between the Sip and Hidden Italy are gone. Both of them. It makes me walk faster, fast enough that I slip on some black ice and nearly wipe out.

When I get home, a note is waiting outside Dancing Queen's apartment door, but I don't even pause to check it. I head straight inside to look at the phone.

The wallpaper is of the full-length photo of me that Giovanni took to the Sip the other day. Sure enough, it's been blown up and there's a dart lodged in the nuts.

I laugh, but to be honest, it's a disappointment.

I was hoping for some photos of her.

But then I click into the photos app, and there they are, like a wrapped gift waiting beneath the tree. There are snaps of Lucy wearing my mother's scarf all around town. In one of them, she's grimacing at the flyer of me; in another, she's wrapping the scarf around a dirty snowman. In a third, she and Charlie are playing tug of war with it. In a fourth, she's rubbing her face against it as if it's cat fur, her eyes closed, her full lips lifted in pleasure.

A smile spreads across my face. Lucy clearly thinks she stuck it to me with these photos, but she doesn't realize she's been gallivanting around town in a scarf everyone will no doubt recognize as mine—the one thing of my mother's I chose to keep.

It's not something that should make me happy, given I wanted to keep a low profile in town, but I feel a deep, thrumming satisfaction from it. So I decide I'm keeping the phone, too, until she agrees to take it back.

I take out my own cell and text her number:

> Nice photos. Now everyone in town knows
> who you've been out with. That's good. None
> of the other guys will bother you. ;-)

But why'd you return the phone? Something
wrong with it? Don't you like nice things?

She doesn't respond, but for all I know the text didn't go through. I feel like a caged animal waiting.

Hours later, she still hasn't responded. I spend half the night awake, checking my phone, carrying it around the apartment in the hope it'll get the only bar of reliable service in Hideaway Harbor. I'm acting like Aria did when she was a teenager, and I don't love it.

I take a long shower and jerk off, but it feels pathetic—a pale shadow of the sensation of Lucy running her fingers over me through my pants. She barely even touched me, and it's all I can think about. Damn it. Maybe she's ahead in the hate-off after all.

THE NEXT AFTERNOON, when Giovanni, Nico, and I get to The Sweetest Thing, it's already packed, but the crowd parts like the Red Sea to make room for us as we take off our coats. Okay, the Hidies part like the Red Sea. The tourists remain rooted to their spots, scattered throughout the store with their hands full of candy canes and treats. A few of them are wearing Larry the Lobstah hats, presumably in preparation for the tree lighting later.

Nico and I walk Giovanni through the entrance to Portia, who's waiting at the door leading to the candy kitchen, her colorful hair covered by a translucent hygiene cap. She's holding a box of sterile gloves and talking to Eileen. Lucy's standing with them, and from the scowl she gives me—and her bare neck—I'm guessing she definitely got my text message last night. I wave to her. She does not wave back.

Charlie and Lars are with their group; Lars gives me a quick nod, which I return.

The plate glass window in front of the candy kitchen has been completely cleared of displays and merchandise, allowing an unobstructed view of what goes on inside.

"There he is," Portia says with a grin as Giovanni comes to a stop next to her. "Well, let's get right to it. Take your shirt off and show us the goods."

He flashes her a victorious look. "You won't want me doing that."

She quirks her brow. "We advertised that it's happening shirtless. It needs to happen shirtless."

"Get on either side of me, guys," he tells us, and Nico and I fall in beside him, acting as human walls while he lifts the hem of his shirt and flashes the red-lettered message at Portia.

"Oh, for God's sake," she growls, "pull your shirt down. There are kids here."

"Exactly," he says in an undertone, "which is why it's better this way. I wore a festive shirt." He gestures to his red T-shirt. Its sleeves and hems are lined with puffy white paint to mimic Santa's coat. "Besides, wouldn't it be unhygienic for me to do it shirtless? What if my chest hair got into the candy?"

She gives him a murderous look. "They're expecting shirtless. It was part of our deal."

"It *is* a pity," Eileen says worriedly. "We wouldn't want to be accused of fraudulent advertising with the flyers."

Charlie laughs silently while Lars wraps an arm around her. But my gaze naturally settles on Lucy, who's looking at me with accusation in her eyes. "You did this."

"Me?" I scoff. "You think I wrote on my brother's chest? He's a big boy, Lucy. He did it all himself."

Giovanni nods.

"With *my* marker," she adds. "It was, wasn't it?"

He gives her a pointed look. "If it was your marker, what was it doing under one of the shelves at Hidden Italy?"

Her cheeks flush.

"You're a real dick, Giovanni," Portia says, shaking her head. "I can't believe you pulled this."

Lucy clears her throat, drawing everyone else's attention back to her—not mine, because mine never really left.

"It seems only fair if one of you"—her finger toggles between Nico and me—"takes his place. You said the person who bought a date with you could decide what the date would entail, and Portia asked for shirtless."

"I did," Portia says, grinning at Lucy. "*Thank you*, Lucy. You get it."

"It has to be Enzo," Charlie says.

Lars looks like someone just shoved a hot poker up his ass. Maybe he remembers the time I threatened to maim him if he ever hurt my sister. I sure remember. But I've already decided to give him a pass. My sister's happy. She wanted a break from Hideaway, and she got it. Then there's Lucy. She probably wouldn't appreciate it if I maimed her best friend's future husband.

So, yeah, Lars gets off scot-free as long as he keeps his mouth shut.

"It does," Lucy says, agreeing with Charlie. "Definitely Enzo."

"Why?" I ask calmly, meeting Lucy's gaze. Her eyes are shining with victory, and I'll be honest. I want to kiss her. I'm almost desperate for it. The way she's looking at me, like she's sure she's won, only makes me want it more.

"Because you had the easiest date. All you had to do was have dinner by yourself."

"I *am* good company," I say thoughtfully, while Nico laughs.

"What's wrong with my shirt?" Giovanni asks, his tone

sulky. "Can you really blame me for not wanting to be objectified?"

"No," Portia says, snorting. "But if you didn't want to be objectified, you probably shouldn't have auctioned yourself off. You backed yourself into this corner, and one of you Cafieros *will* be taking his shirt off."

My brothers both look at me, and Nico says, "Hey, man, I already have to pose for that ice thing, and it *was* your idea."

I hand my coat to him. Then I watch Lucy as I tug my long-sleeved red T-shirt over my head. The look on her face tells me that even though I lost this round, I might have won anyway.

I toss my shirt to her.

CHAPTER 18

LUCY

I'm still holding Enzo's shirt, gaping at his well-defined back and the small Trinacria tattoo on his shoulder blade, as he follows Portia into the kitchen. But I'm hardly the only one staring. Every woman in The Sweetest Thing is ogling him, along with some of the men. Who could blame us? Enzo's back looks positively pornographic. It's muscular and surprisingly tan given that it's December in Maine. And then there's his chest, which is sculpted and beautiful and...

And a couple of days ago he had his head between my legs, and I've been thinking about it almost every moment since.

Worse, I've been thinking about all the times he's made me laugh despite myself.

Enzo turns and waves out of the candy kitchen window, smirking at me. Like he knows exactly what's going through my head and why.

Like he's won.

No way. *I* won.

I wave the shirt at him like it's a victory flag, but it smells like his expensive cologne, and I have the horrible urge to lift it up to my nose for a sniff.

No, I will be strong.

Turning toward Enzo's brother Giovanni, who looks amused, I shove the shirt at him. "Here. You can hold his sweaty shirt for him."

"You don't want it?" he asks, cocking an eyebrow. "You ladies were desperate for him to strip, so I figured you'd want the shirt as a souvenir. You can add it to the scarf. Maybe you'll have enough to dress a whole snowman someday."

"Excuse me?" Charlie says, her arms crossed. "Are you implying my friend has an interest in stealing your rude brother's pants?"

He lifts his hands. "Just making a seasonal joke. No harm intended."

My cheeks are burning, but I straighten my back. "I didn't know it was his scarf," I lie. "It was in the Lost and Found at the Sip."

He barely suppresses a grin. "Ain't that a thing. I don't think he's been in there since that business with Rachelle."

"He blessed us with his presence for Santa Speed Dating," I say sweetly. "Must've left it then."

"I guess so," he says, running a hand across his chin.

"Yeah. I only put it on because it looked really old, and I figured no one wanted it. I didn't know it was his until someone identified it."

"It *is* old. My mother made that scarf."

My head whips over to peer at Enzo through the window. He's arguing with Portia about something in an undertone that can't be heard through the glass.

He kept his mother's scarf even though she left them.

He wrapped it around my neck, knowing people would see it.

Worst of all: his *grandmother* saw me wearing it.

She must know…

Honestly, I don't even know what there is to know other than that this thing between Enzo and me has gotten very confusing.

I'd hoped Lobster Stalker would answer my note this morning, giving me someone else to focus on—a man who's compassionate and capable of sharing his feelings—but when I left for the taffy pulling, the card I'd left for him was still sitting out there in the hallway. Ignored.

Maybe he's a senior citizen who just moved into assisted living.

Regardless, he can hardly compete with the very real, very aggravating, and impossibly beautiful man who's preparing to pull taffy across from me.

Giovanni is still studying me, I realize, waiting for some kind of response.

I clear my throat. "Then it's a good thing I didn't unravel the knitting after I found out the scarf was Enzo's."

I'd thought about it, to be honest. His texts had been so smug, and I could just imagine the look on his face, his brow raised, the corners of his lips turned up.

Giovanni laughs, shrugging. "I wouldn't have cared. It's Enzo who's sentimental about stuff like that."

"That doesn't sound like him at all."

He shrugs his shoulder. "Sure. Maybe you're right. I've only known him for over thirty years."

I look away, duly chastised.

"Our condolences," Charlie says, saving me from answering. She delivers the takedown with a teasing smile, though, and Enzo's brothers don't seem offended.

"Thank you," Giovanni says. "We gratefully accept them. He's only been home for a few weeks, and he already has us auctioning ourselves off. Changing the schedule at the shop. Switching suppliers. But I can't complain. He's been fixing my mistakes since I was too young to understand that I didn't have to wear the suspenders Nonna gave us."

My heart throbs as I push the shirt at Giovanni again, willing him to take it before I do something truly insane like pull it on.

"So he was always controlling," I say in a choked voice.

"Always," Nico says with a snort. "But he always stood up for us too. There's a reason we agreed to this insanity."

He motions to the kitchen window as Portia shoves a Santa hat at Enzo, who takes it with obvious reluctance and puts it on.

Giovanni still hasn't taken the shirt from me. I don't offer it again, my fingers squeezing the cloth without permission from my brain.

"Yes, Enzo's so protective of you three," Eileen says. I glance over to see she has her phone camera trained at Enzo, taking photos as if she's a paparazzo. "Ever since you were little."

That's right. Eileen was friendly with his mother, and I still haven't asked her about it. I'd like to ask her now—I have a whole baker's dozen of questions—but Enzo wouldn't like that much. For some reason, that matters.

Eileen gets on her toes and takes a photo from a different angle.

I haven't told her about Nonna Francesca's visit to the coffee shop to see her about making a match for Enzo, but it's possible someone else did.

What if she's not just photographing him for Portia? What if she plans on sharing those photos with single women around town?

The thought puts a sour twist in my stomach.

"Keep the shirt," Charlie says, nudging my arm. "We can auction it off."

"Yeah, I wouldn't recommend that," Nico interjects. "Auctions are a slippery slope, unless you're Giovanni. Then you get off scot-free."

Giovanni laughs. "So you say. Enzo's going to get lucky tonight. No doubt about it. All I'll have to show for this is some taffy with my brother's chest hair in it."

Everyone around us laughs with him, except for Lars, who still seems nervous to be surrounded by Cafieros. And me. I can't even force a smile. That sour feeling in my stomach is growing.

"All right, friends," Portia says, addressing us through the window. "The demonstration is about to begin. First, let's start with a round of applause for my helper here."

Everyone applauds, and someone wolf-whistles.

"His little brother Giovanni was supposed to help me, but he has a super gnarly rash. Really disgusting with lots of bumps and pustules and whatnot. We didn't want to subject all of you to that." She blows a kiss at Giovanni, who shakes his head, his mouth quirked in amusement. "We're pulling peppermint taffy today to celebrate the season, and we're giving away all of it to you lovely people, aren't we?"

Enzo lifts his hand in a wave. "Ho ho ho."

He says it so grumpily I can't help but laugh.

I don't want him to see me laughing, though, so I press my lips together as Portia pours hot taffy over the cold metal surface of a long table inside the kitchen. She guides us through what she's doing, and the majority of the people in the store stand rapt, their attention laser-focused on Portia and Enzo.

Portia has just finished spreading the taffy when a woman enters the store through the side entrance, her cap pulled low over her face. Eileen looks back, as if she were expecting this, and waves the woman over, beaming.

That's when I recognize Amanda—and realize she's heading straight for me.

I grin at her as she gets closer, then whisper, "How did your wish go the other night?"

She smiles back and says in an undertone, "I think it brought me here. Do you know Portia?"

"I do." I give her a meaningful look. "She's someone who's defiantly herself. I've always admired that about her."

"Me too," she says, peering through the window with that million-dollar smile of hers.

I'm giddy, the way Eileen must feel when she realizes she's played a part in something beautiful.

"Do I look incognito?" Amanda whispers, leaning into me.

"Absolutely not," I say. "But don't let that stop you."

She squeezes my hand. "I won't. Thanks, Lucy. I'll come by and see you soon."

She offers me a final smile before releasing me and edging in next to Eileen, who greets her with a warm hug and then whispers something in her ear.

Portia notices her, and although she doesn't wave, her whole face lights up as she talks about the importance of getting enough air bubbles in the taffy.

Enzo spots Amanda as well and smiles at me, his eyes twinkling. As if to say: *I did this.*

Of course he feels responsible.

He probably thinks he can get the whole world to march at his command.

Still, I can't deny my attention is hyperfocused on him as Portia lifts the ropes of taffy up and layers them over his arms, as if he's holding garland to decorate a tree.

"Now, this is where Santa's muscles are going to come in handy," she says with a smirk at the window. At Amanda. "He's going to stretch the taffy to get the right amount of air into it."

He starts, his muscles bunching with the movement.

"Harder," she says.

"Did every woman in here just ovulate?" Charlie whispers in my ear. "Other than me, of course."

Probably. I certainly did.

"Come on, Santa. Give it some muscle," Portia says.

And he does. Oh, how he does.

"Ho ho ho," I hear one woman murmur to her friend, who replies, "I have a renewed belief in Santa Claus."

I tighten my grip on the fabric of Enzo's shirt, still clutched to my chest, as I watch his arms rhythmically pull the taffy. A hot, needy longing steals over my body, changing me. Because I don't recognize this woman who wants a real man—not a fictional, perfect man straight out of the pages of a book or my mother's letter.

Portia grins as she inspects the candy. "That's good. That's how it should be looking. We'll give it another five minutes. Can someone set a timer?"

"I will," Giovanni offers.

Enzo gives him the scowl of a bear who's been pulled out of his den in the middle of winter.

"Nah," Portia says as she glances at Amanda. "'Last Christmas' is four and a half minutes long. That's close enough." So she pulls the song up on her phone and blasts it over the speaker it's connected to, all while Enzo works the taffy.

"I love this song," Charlie says, her enthusiasm bubbling up. Lars twirls her, and they start dancing in front of the glass window.

Then Eileen says, "Why not?" and she twirls Amanda Willis!

Suddenly, everyone in the store is dancing. Giovanni holds his hand out to me, and I don't even hesitate. I stuff Enzo's shirt into my bag and take his hand, and then we're dancing to the song along with everyone else. It's fun. Oh my goodness, it's fun, even though we're packed in here like sardines.

Portia starts dancing around Enzo and steals his hat,

putting it on her own head over her hairnet—something I see only in snatches as Giovanni whirls me around.

The song ends, and another starts, "Jingle Bell Rock." Someone hoots, and then a hand wraps around my waist from behind—

"May I cut in?"

I knew it was him before I heard his voice. I knew it from the way his hand wrapped around me.

"I don't have a death wish, so yeah," Giovanni says, laughing as he stops dancing.

I turn toward Enzo, whose hand is resting on my hip now. He's still only half clothed, his chest bared, and now he smells like peppermint candy.

"Why aren't your hands sticky?" I ask, struggling to stay composed. I focus on the faint remnants of his red-marker mustache to hold onto my sanity.

"Gloves," he says. "Would you like to see if the rest of me is sticky?"

Yes.

I make a face. "No, thanks. That's what showers are for."

He smiles as he waves Giovanni toward the kitchen. "Portia needs your help cutting the candy."

Giovanni steps away, and Enzo takes my hand, twirling me.

With several people still dancing, there's a party atmosphere in the shop, an intoxicating holiday feeling that's boosted by the scent of peppermint candy filling the air.

"You're still shirtless," I remark as Enzo draws me closer to his chest, his hand on the small of my back.

Eyes bright with amusement, he says, "You were so concerned about getting me shirtless, I figured you'd feel cheated if I put it on again so quickly."

"I have your shirt," I murmur as we sway together. It's a lively song, but he's holding me close, his hand still pressed to my back. The air between us seems to crackle.

"I know. You can keep it."

"Don't you want to put it on?"

"Not yet."

I give him an arch look. "You'd prefer to get my sweater sticky?"

"Yes, Lucia. You caught me in the act."

I'm smiling despite myself, and he's smiling too. My sweater is the only thing that separates us from being skin to skin as he keeps swaying me to the music, and every part of me is awake and full of need.

I've never felt like this with a man before.

Why does it have to be *him*?

"Have you finished with Hidden Italy on your app?" he asks. "I'd be curious to see what you said."

I take a beat before answering, giving myself time to adjust to the sudden change in topic. "I did. My project's due at the end of next week. I kept it purely factual."

"I'd expect nothing less." He gives me a wolfish grin. "If I'd hoped for more, that's between me and the Wishing Bridge."

I gape at him. Because it's almost like he knows I went there that night...

"Did you follow me there?" I ask in an undertone.

His surprise soothes my nerves. "No. You went back?"

I swallow down a surge of emotion, thinking of the snow falling down around me. Of meeting Amanda. Of feeling my mother's presence.

"I did."

"And did it give you what you wanted?"

I take him in—his glorious lack of a shirt, his thick arms, his hair slightly mussed when it's usually immaculately styled.

It feels like I got what I wanted that first night but didn't dare ask for. A beautiful man who wants me.

I'd figured it would be better to ask for less than I wanted than to ask for too much and end up disappointed.

The second night…the only thing I asked for was a sign from my mother, and it feels like I got that too.

"I don't know," I answer after a moment. "I guess we'll find out."

Mischief flashes in his eyes, and he says, "You had some fun with the phone, huh?"

It's easy to be annoyed by that, at least.

"You could have warned me about the scarf. Giovanni just explained its significance to me. You said you didn't want people in town to gossip about you. Isn't that exactly what they're going to do now?"

He shrugs, his eyes bright. "Probably, but it was worth it. I wish I'd been there to see the look on your face when you got my text messages."

I glower at him as he dips me, but it's hard to maintain it. "You're maddening."

"So are you," he says, dipping his head close to my ear. "I can hardly think of anything else. I'm gratified by how eager you were to get my shirt off."

"I wanted to preserve the innocence of children."

"Is that what we're doing here?" he asks, and truthfully, he has a point. Even though men walk around shirtless all the time, there's nothing innocent about Enzo without a shirt.

The song ends, changing over to "I'll be home for Christmas," which is considerably slower, but he doesn't release me—and I don't release him.

"What did you do with our flyers after you took them down?" he asks. "I noticed they weren't there when I went by earlier."

"I threw them away," I lie.

In fact, I'd intended to throw them away, but I couldn't bring myself to do it. I ended up tucking them into my purse instead and then a drawer.

"I'll draw you again," he says, his voice low and gravelly, and

I can't tell whether he's teasing me. Maybe he doesn't even know.

"I won't pose for you."

"You don't need to," he says. "I've memorized exactly what you look like."

The way he says it instantly makes me melt and want to murder him—a power uniquely his.

The song ends, and he pulls back slightly. I laugh, because my sweater sticks to his skin in patches. "So you *did* want to get me sticky."

He grins. "You tormented me with the taffy, so it seems just for you to share in it by being stuck to me."

But it doesn't seem like a torment at all. This moment is so magical it has made me temporarily forget that I don't like the way he does things.

I detach from him, then reach into my bag for his delicious-smelling shirt.

"You do the honors," he says, and leans over like he's about to be knighted. My hands shake slightly as I pull the shirt down over his head, my fingers brushing the hair they gripped just a couple of nights ago.

A few women groan theatrically as the shirt goes over his head, and I can't help laughing. Charlie's laughing too, with Lars's arms wrapped around her. Portia has left the candy kitchen and is having a whispered conversation with Eileen and Amanda.

The atmosphere in the shop is so heavenly I want to bottle it, so I can sip from it for the rest of the winter—the part of the season that's cold and gray but doesn't have Christmas.

Now fully clothed, more's the pity, Enzo leans down toward me, his cologne scent mingling with peppermint candy. "So… are you going to try my taffy?"

"I don't know. Giovanni pointed out that it might have chest hair in it."

"Oh, it definitely does. It's that special Cafiero touch. They're like extra flavor crystals."

I smile at him. "It would be fun if Portia did flavors for each of the shops in town. Ours could be our delicious cinnamon stick cappuccino. Yours could be chest hair."

His eyes widen, and he laughs, probably louder than the joke deserves. "That's it."

"That's what?" I ask, confused.

"You're a genius, Lucia."

He actually looks like he means it.

"For coming up with chest hair taffy? It's one of the worst ideas I've ever had. Feel free to steal it."

"For finding a beautiful solution to my problem. You'll be at the lobster trap tree lighting?"

"I'm told I can't miss it." By my possibly geriatric neighbor.

"Good. I'll find you there."

"Is that a threat?"

"Yes, wear that red coat."

He just guaranteed I'll be wearing something else. Then again, I suspect he'd be disappointed if I listened.

He leans in and kisses me on the cheek before finding his coat, which Giovanni ditched on the floor. He pulls it on and walks out into the cold.

The moment the door closes behind him, it feels like the magic that's been building in the shop shatters like old glass.

What on earth just happened?

<h1 style="text-align:center">CHAPTER 19</h1>

<h2 style="text-align:center">ENZO</h2>

TEXT CONVERSATION WITH GIOVANNI

Get over here. My place. We've got some planning to do. Bring Nico.

He's back behind the sandwich counter, man.

Then you come.

Giovanni?

Giovanni? Hello?

Fucking Wi-Fi.

Lucy is a beautiful genius.

This is what we've been missing.

This is the idea that's tried to bob into my head for days—finally brought to the surface in The Sweetest Thing. It wasn't just the comment Lucy had made; it was the whole atmosphere. The songs, the dancing, the sweetness.

It made me think differently about togetherness.

We need to work with the other businesses around us, the

way the Sip works with Making Whoopie. If we can develop specialty items with other shops specific to our brand, it'll help everyone. I'm thinking cannoli whoopie pies, limoncello candy canes, and chest hair taffy (okay, the name needs workshopping). Hell, we can even ask Chowder House Rules to make a special minestrone for us. Working together. Making the tourism seasons stronger for everyone. This is it..

This. Is. It.

I'm scribbling in my notebook, brainstorming, when a knock lands on my door.

I answer it, and Giovanni gives me a long look. "Did you even take a shower? You still smell like a can of air freshener."

No, my mind has been whirring too fast.

If other stores want to get in on the action, we could hand out bucket lists or scavenger hunts: *Try all the whoopie pies in Hideaway Harbor!* Or, *Find every place that carries The Sweetest Thing's candies!*

What could we stock at other shops?

"I think we need to get other shops to carry our mini panettones," I say, excitedly.

"Then you can be the one who tells Nico," he huffs. "And you'll have to help him."

He steps in, pushing an envelope at my chest.

I look down at it, frowning, as I close the door behind him. "What's this?"

"It's from the cabbage lady down the hall. I saw it outside her apartment."

"Right, yeah, thanks," I mumble, sticking the card in my pocket for later. I can't lose focus now. "I've got it, Giovanni. I've got a way to fix all of this for us."

He grins at me. "It's been a minute since you've thought you could conquer the world. Maybe it's Lucy who has kept you anchored to earth. She's good at chipping away at your ego."

Lucy.

Shit. I shouldn't have left her like that, but I'd needed to get this down on paper. I'd needed the ideas to flow out and give me peace. But I plan on making it up to her this evening at the trap tree lighting.

"How'd she seem when you left?"

"Are you ready to tell me what's going on between you two?" he asks, lifting his eyebrows. "This goes beyond that dumb hate-off game of yours. We all saw you together at The Sweetest Thing."

"The only reason I took my shirt off was to cover for you," I say. "And I threw it to her because she backed me into it. It's part of our…thing."

"Good, then you won't mind if I ask her out. She's very sexy, you know. Something about all of that curly hair. I can just imagine—"

I'm holding a fistful of his shirt before I'm even aware of having reached for it, growling, "You'll shut your mouth if you know what's good for you."

He grins, and I know I walked right into his trap.

"Yeah, fine," I admit, releasing his shirt. "Maybe I'm interested in her. This has all been kind of…" I search for the right word and land on, "fun. But she's looking for a nice guy like Hudson."

"Which is why you sabotaged her date with him," he says with amusement.

"Yeah, fine. I did that. I haven't been acting rationally with Lucy."

"No, which is why I know you genuinely like her."

Sighing, I pull the note out of my pocket and slump onto the couch with it. "I'm gonna read this."

"Yup. Changing the subject." He pauses, giving me a good, hard stare. "But you're not as smooth as you used to be, Enzo. She's got you rattled. Rachelle *never* had you rattled. Not even when she dumped you so she could spend the weekend getting massages and terrorizing the staff at The Haven. You were pissed off, but you weren't unsettled."

I rest the note card on my chest. "What do you want from me? Why do you suddenly care about my love life?"

"Nonna's not the only one who'd like you to stay, you know."

It feels like he just punched me in the chest, or maybe put a shackle around my wrist. The old longing to leave—to go just like our mother did—wraps around me.

"I'll stay as long as I'm needed."

"We don't *need* you," he says, which is another punch. "Whatever idea you have, I'm sure it's fucking genius, and I'm equally sure it'll work. But we don't *need* you. Nico and I aren't kids anymore, Enzo. We can take care of ourselves and the business. We would have figured it out if you hadn't come home."

"I never said I thought you needed me," I say. "It's not like I quit my job to come here. It wasn't some big sacrifice for the family. Like I said…I was ready to leave and the timing was right."

"Why were you suddenly ready to leave?"

I don't know why it's so hard to admit to my little brother that I fucked up. That I'm fallible. That I took a swing and missed. I was hoping my boss wouldn't call my bluff—that he'd say, yeah, Enzo, you're right, it *would* be fucked up to lay those people off right before Christmas, and I'm not going to lose you, so we won't do it.

Instead, I was the one who lost out.

Worse, I let my damned pride get in the way of collecting severance pay.

The one thing I am proud of is the thirty-five-page document I sent to *his* boss a couple of days ago, explaining how the situation could be addressed differently, without eliminating jobs right before the holidays. It'll probably be thrown away, but I'm proud of myself for going through with it. For listening to Dancing Queen's good advice.

I rub my forehead. "I had a disagreement with my boss."

He claps his hands. "Ah, we're getting closer to the truth. Finally! Honestly, getting personal information from you is harder than pulling taffy."

I blow out an annoyed breath. "As if you'd know."

"So you had a disagreement with the guy. What about? Did you call him a lazy piece of shit too?" I roll my eyes, because, yes, I did call my brother that last week. When he suggested calling in one of the kids to clean up after a tourist broke a huge glass bottle of lemonade and it spilled all over the floor.

"No. The work wasn't right for me anymore." I stop short of telling him that I didn't like letting people go, that I had no stomach for it anymore, because he'll think it's a sign of weakness. A sign, maybe, that I should settle down in Hideaway Harbor and have a family that I take boating every weekend. A little Lobster Scout of my own.

A voice in my mind wonders if that would really be so bad.

Living in New York City is exciting. Something's always happening, there are always deals being made, and you can walk around with the confidence that dozens of people you barely know aren't discussing your personal business in detail. But most of the people I know there are good time friends. They'll do you a favor, no problem, but only because they think you could return it in the future. The only friend I have in the city who isn't like that is my best friend Will, and he's from Hideaway Harbor too.

Still...the logical thing to do would be to finish my work here and return to New York City. I've actually had a couple of job offers since I left my old position, so I could take one of those jobs. Slip back into the life that's waiting for me.

The things is, those positions are basically carbon copies of the one I left. I'd be doing the same work—work I was fucking good at but maybe don't have the edge for anymore. I'd rather train people to do their jobs better than tear away their livelihoods.

As if he senses my weak resolve, my brother says, "You know, bud…you could come back home and not work at Hidden Italy, as crazy as that sounds. God knows, you've got the brains in this family. You could probably find a job you could do from anywhere."

"Nonna expects—"

"She expects someone to run the place, and Nico will never leave."

"And you?" I ask, surprised. I'd assumed he felt the same way as Nico. I'd assumed it, right up until this very minute.

"Me, I don't know. But I don't hate the business the way you do."

"I don't hate it either," I say automatically. "*Nonno* won it in—"

"A game of cards. Yup. Crazy. And good for him and Nonna, they made a good run of it. But it's been an anvil around your neck ever since you were ten years old. I know what that was like for you. All that responsibility. You never learned how to relax. How to have fun. But you've been having fun with Lucy."

"And with you," I say quietly.

Because it's true, damn it. It's been a while since we've spent this much time together, not just as brothers but friends.

My throat feels clogged with emotion, and I don't like it one bit.

"Ah, he admits it," Giovanni teases. "Maybe if you were nice to that girl she'd want to date you instead of publicly ridicule you."

"What would be the fun in that?" I joke, but then I nod, conceding the point. "I'll talk to her tonight. I told her I'd find her at the tree thing. Now, can I tell you my damn idea already?"

"Yes," he says, "but I need a beer."

"That makes two of us."

He gets us both a drink, and then we discuss my thoughts, Giovanni getting as excited as I am. "We should definitely stock the Six-Pack Santa taffy," he says. "It was a hit, so Portia's making more of it. She's even making them look like little six-packs."

"Six-Pack Santa?"

Eyes twinkling, he says, "Your girl came up with the name."

I smile at that. So Lucy liked what she saw, did she? I would hope so, because I can't seem to stop looking at her. Or at those damn photos she took on the phone she won't accept.

"You think she'd accept the cell phone as a Christmas present?" I ask.

"She didn't like you sending her the phone because she'd already told you no. She wants to know you're gonna listen, so no, you're not giving it to her again unless she asks for it."

"When did you get so wise?" I ask, kind of blown away. Giovanni's always been so carefree and easygoing. I didn't expect him to understand women like this.

"There you go," he says with a half-smile. "Learning to listen already. That's good, because I'll only have to tell you once: you've gotta get her something more thoughtful than a phone as a Christmas present."

"Like what?" I ask, surprised. "Jewelry?"

He snorts. "You ever seen her wear jewelry? She only wears earrings, and it's always the same pair."

"Maybe she wants a new pair."

His eyebrows go up. "Or maybe the ones she has are senti-mental, like that mangy stuffed animal Aria brings everywhere. Earrings would be the wrong move."

Well, shit. From my experience, women want expensive

presents. Women other than Nonna Francesca, that is. She'll only ever accept useful things—extension cords and salad bowls and help with household chores we would have done anyway. Still, Aria always gets away with getting her something special. Bottles of limoncello from the Amalfi Coast. A clay trivet with the Trinacria symbol of Sicily, like the tattoo on my back. *It's all in the delivery*, she always says. Then again, Aria's kind of a wizard with Nonna.

"We'll get Aria to help," he says, as if reading my mind.

I groan.

"What? You don't want our little sister to know you have a serious crush?"

"Jesus, no, especially not when you put it that way. Anyway, I'm not sure I *do* like her like that. It might just be…" I wave my hand suggestively because I don't want to discuss lust with my brother.

"Nah. But you'll figure that out eventually. You're a quick study when you pause to listen to what other people are saying. Now, go take a shower, peppermint boy."

CHAPTER 20

LUCY

𝓘'm standing by the docks with Charlie, Lars, and a few of Lars's friends, wrapped up in a long black overcoat that used to be my mother's. It's *freezing*, but it helps that we've been drinking hot buttered rum out in the street, along with half of Hideaway Harbor and dozens of tourists.

"This is delicious," I say for the fifth time. "So good. Like melted Werther's candies with booze in them." I lift up my third or maybe fourth drink, my hand a little unsteady. "I'm going to figure out how to make it into a latte. You think I can melt the candy and then mix it with the milk, or would that be a fire hazard?"

"Definitely a fire hazard," says a deep voice from behind me.

I turn, but I already know it's not Enzo.

I'm not waiting for him, obviously, but I'm not *not* waiting for him. I mean, he *did* say he was coming.

Hudson Locke beams down at me like he knows all about the hot buttered rum. Of course he does. He's a Hidie, and this is a yearly tradition. If I'd been here longer, I probably would have been familiar enough with the buttered rum to only indulge in one of them.

"You'd know," I say. "That's too bad, because I bet it would be really delicious."

"I'll bet," he agrees, his voice a low rumble. It seems like there's some insinuation buried inside of that statement, but I'm too tipsy to tell for sure, and suddenly I need to pee.

Shifting my weight from one foot to the other, I lean into Charlie and whisper, "I need to pee. It's a desperate need."

"The boat's coming," she says, pointing off the pier. Sure enough, the Hawthorne Fisheries boat is approaching slowly. Very slowly. I can see the mayor in his Santa costume waving from inside, next to a guy dressed like Larry the Lobstah.

"Is his claw supposed to be doing that?" I ask. It's flopping down like a broken breadstick, attached with nothing but a hope and a prayer.

There's a near roar of conversation as people take notice.

"Nope," Charlie says, laughing. "It's supposed to be fully erect."

"I can't bring you anywhere," Lars says fondly, leaning down to kiss the top of her head.

Gosh, they're adorable.

I shift my weight a little more, watching the boat as it moves toward us at the pace of a snail.

"I don't know if I can wait," I say, louder.

"You can't miss this," Charlie protests.

"Yeah, it's pretty fun," Hudson says, looking out at the water thoughtfully. "The lobster trap tree lighting was one of my favorite parts of Christmas when I was a kid."

"Really?" I ask. "My neighbor likes it a lot too. But he also likes *The Golden Girls*, so we think he might be an old person."

I can feel Hudson and Lars locking eyes, silently communicating, *This girl is wasted.*

"I'm not drunk," I insist. "I just really, really have to pee. It's getting worse."

I clap a hand over my mouth, because I hadn't intended to say that part out loud.

"Come on, Lucy, you can do this," Charlie says. "Hold it until the lobster traps get lit. You don't want to miss the big moment. You'll always regret it if you were stuffed into a smelly Porta Potty when something major happened."

"What could possibly happen? Do you think someone could get electrocuted? Mixing electricity and water does seem like a bad idea."

"He does it every year," Hudson comments, which reminds me that I'm casually discussing his dad's possible electrocution. Goodness. Can't take me anywhere.

I take a sip of my drink to buy a moment of silence, and Hudson says, "Isn't that going to make you need to pee more?"

The man has a point. But it's also really cold out here, so I take another half sip. Finally, I cave to nature's demands: "I'm going to the Porta Potties. I'll be right back."

"I'll go with you," Hudson offers, which is *horribly* embarrassing. There's no way I want him waiting outside while I hover over the Porta Potty seat after drinking three or four buttered rums.

"It's okay," I say, patting his arm. "I'm not going to fall through and go to Narnia. I'll go alone so you can see your dad flip the switch and shake the wobbly lobster claw."

"You're going to miss it," Charlie says, her eyes wide. "It only happens once a year."

"And then the tree's on for weeks," Lars says, smoothing her hair. "Let your friend pee."

There's been entirely too much discussion of my bladder, so I hand Charlie my half-finished drink and turn toward the Porta Potties, lined up by the pier. Okay, calling them Porta Potties, plural, makes it sound like there's a long line of them, but there's not. There are only two. At least no one's waiting— probably because everyone's excited to see the big moment.

As I approach them, I notice one of them has a sign across the front. "ENTER AT YOUR OWN PERIL."

Oh, that's certainly not promising.

The other says "occupied," so I stand waiting, toggling between one foot and the other. Finally, a guy wearing an antler headband comes out.

"Uh, sorry," he apologizes, and a cloud of stench follows him out.

Oh no. Suddenly the hot buttered rum in my stomach feels like it's sloshing around.

I hold my nose and step inside.

It's fine. All I have to do is lock the door, squat, and get out of here.

I lock the door, do my business, and use the hand sanitizer. But when I try to open the door, it won't budge.

I try again, my heart pounding, everything inside of me going into high alert. Will Hudson have to call the firehouse and get them to come save me with the Jaws of Life? Will he even realize I've been gone for too long? Maybe he'll assume I have explosive diarrhea and will be too polite to check.

Charlie's a little tipsy, too, and she's bound to be distracted by the lighting.

Oh no, oh no, oh no...

I start banging on the door, but at exactly the wrong time, because suddenly there's a roar of applause from outside.

Everyone will be at the docks now, talking and singing and carrying on. No one is going to hear me. Maybe not ever. I'll be in this stinky Porta Potty for the rest of my life.

I bang again, and again, and—

There's a cracking sound, and the door flies open, spilling me into someone's arms. I process his scent first, because I basically face-planted into his coat.

Enzo.

My first thought is relief. He saved me from the big, bad Porta Potty. But then I remember what it smells like in there.

"I didn't do that," I mumble into his coat.

He holds me out at arm's length and tucks some of the hair that escaped my crocheted hat back into it. He's wearing the same coat as earlier, and in addition to his delicious cologne scent, there's a hint of peppermint. There's a rock in his hand, which he must have used to bust the door open, and he sets it down.

"Didn't get stuck in a Porta Potty?" he asks, guiding me several feet away from it. "I'm afraid I don't believe you."

"I only peed," I say in an undertone, worried that Antlers will hear me being a narc. My face is burning with embarrassment now that the fear has passed. This is the absolute last place I wanted to run into Enzo.

"Good for you. I've heard a person should do that several times a day."

"You're making fun of me," I say, glowering at him.

Someone swears loudly. "Who broke the last Porta Potty?"

Enzo gives me a conspiratorial look before leading me another few feet away.

Which is when I glance over his shoulder and see it—the lobster trap tree, lit up in all its glory. "Oh, I really did miss it."

"But you're no longer locked in a Porta Potty, so your day has improved."

"How'd you know I was in there?" I ask. Then, because my mind isn't working on all cylinders, I add, "I'm not wearing the red coat."

He tucks more hair into my cap. "I know you too well to have expected it. I was looking for you, and I found your friends." He gestures toward them, and I glance in that direction. Hudson's talking to Giovanni, possibly about popcorn safety, and Charlie and Lars are embracing. "Someone should have come with you," he continues, recapturing my attention.

"Oh please, I can go to the bathroom alone."

He gives me an arch look. "Yes, I can see that. You know, you smell like—"

"Oh, my God," I say, stomping my foot. "I did not do that, Enzo. I told you I only peed."

He laughs. "I was going to say you smell like hot buttered rum."

My cheeks are burning despite the bitter cold. "Yeah…I like it," I say. "It tastes like these butterscotch candies my mom used to buy."

"It's disgusting," he says easily. "Have you been eating?"

"First I can't use the bathroom on my own, and now I don't know how to feed myself?"

"Have you?" he asks again. "Because I know the guy who makes that stuff, and you're going to have a hell of a hangover if you don't load up on carbs." He gives me a longer look, tipping his head in to match the angle of my unfortunately timed unintentional wobble. "You might be in for a hell of a hangover anyway."

"I ate some candy," I say. "And some of Lars's pretzel."

"They're selling lobster stew. Will you have some?"

I make a face.

"You don't like lobster," he says with a knowing smile. "I wondered the other night, at the restaurant."

"I love it," I lie. "It's stew that I hate."

"Okay, Lucia, have it your way."

"Why'd you rush off earlier?" I ask, hating the way my voice hitches slightly.

"You gave me an idea for Hidden Italy. I'd like to discuss it with you. Tomorrow, when you're sober."

"I'm not drunk," I complain.

"No, you're the picture of sobriety."

He leads me over to my friends, his hand firmly planted on the small of my back. He keeps it there as Hudson turns toward us. I know I should make a point of pulling away. I'm not Enzo's property, and he's made it clear he's not interested in any kind of real relationship with me, not that I'd want one anyway.

But I like the feel of his hand against my coat, steady and firm.

"Oh, good, you found her," Charlie says.

"I had to break the door of the only working Porta Potty to get to her."

Charlie fusses over me, and Hudson offers to buy everyone lobster stew.

"Uh, actually, we were just leaving," I say. "Enzo—" I hiccup and try again. "Enzo kindly offered to walk me home."

"Yeah, no," Charlie says. "I'll be doing that."

"On my grandfather's grave, I swear I would never touch her tonight," Enzo says severely.

Well, that's disappointing.

She looks him over and then nods after a moment. "Okay, but if anything happens to her, I'm going to kill you. Literally. I'm sorry, Lars, but you'll be in charge of disposing of his body."

"This is a strange reversal of fortunes," Lars says with an easy smile. "But I agree."

"So do I," Enzo says in a serious voice. "If anything happens to her, I accept my fate."

His brother pats him on the back. "It was nice knowing you."

"Come on, guys. I'm right here. You don't have to talk about me as if I'm on my deathbed. For God's sake. I can walk the fourth of a mile back to my bed just fine."

"Are you sure you don't want to stay and have some stew?" Hudson asks, not pushing, because he's not a pushy guy. He's not Enzo, whose hand is still pressed to my back.

Which might actually be a good thing, because I'm beginning to think I need the help. "No, I'm ready to go home. A bit too much exciting…uh…excitement."

"Says the woman who missed the main event," Charlie grouses.

"But got locked in a Porta Potty," I point out.

"Touché."

Enzo steers me away from the dock and back toward town with the gentle press of his palm, and I guide him to the tiny but immaculate turquoise cottage where I've been staying while cat-sitting.

"Do you have any food?" he asks.

"Oh, you and your obsession with food. There's some bread in the kitchen, I think."

"Bring me there," he says, as if he really is some gallant knight who's going to take care of me all night.

Smiling at the thought, I unlock the door—which only takes three tries!—and open it.

The adorable cat I'm sitting for slinks toward me, and starts doing figure eights around my legs. I get down to pet Bowie, and then fall back onto my butt.

"Be careful," I warn. "Gravity has changed."

The next thing I know, my face is being drawn into Enzo's strong chest, and his arm is sweeping under my legs.

"Uh-oh, gravity's changing again," I observe distantly as he lifts me into his arms.

"How many buttered rums did you have?" he asks. "Three or four?"

"I'm not sure, but I think maybe three and a half. Or two and a half. It was probably only two and a half, because three and a half seems like a lot."

"Three and a half, unless you're the biggest lightweight in Maine." He smiles down at me as he carries me over to the comfortable red velveteen couch, setting me on top of it. The decorated Christmas tree is right beside it, smelling of sweet pine.

"We'd better send a message to your friend. Who knows how long it'll take to go through."

"Oh, yes." I pull my phone out and stare at the screen, which seems to swim in front of my eyes as it unlocks. "There's something wrong with my phone. Can you text her?"

He nods seriously, grabbing the phone, and pecks off a text with one finger.

Why is it endearing that he texts like an old man?

"What'd you say?" I ask, curious.

"That you're safely home and very drunk, but it's nothing a good night's sleep won't cure. Now, I'm going to take off your boots."

"Take yours off first," I say. "Remember what they always tell you in airplanes. You can't undress other people until you've undressed yourself."

"Remind me to never fly on your favorite airline."

Still, he gets down and takes off his boots, then his coat, casting them aside in a careless way that doesn't seem at all like him. When I've imagined Enzo's apartment—and I have, obviously—it's always immaculately clean, with all of his nice things packed away in the closets. His shoe rack wouldn't dare to have a single speck of dust on it.

"What are you thinking about?" he asks.

"Your shoe rack."

He laughs to himself as he starts unlacing my boots, his touch surprisingly gentle. "I don't have one."

"I find that hard to believe."

"I don't. I'd swear to it on a stack of Bibles."

"Which would mean nothing to you, since clearly you worship the Anti-Christ."

"You've got me, Lucia," he says, his words making my heart race, even though he obviously doesn't mean them literally.

"I'll bet this isn't how you imagined undressing me," I remark as he switches from loosening one boot to working on the other.

"I've imagined at least a few dozen scenarios," he says thoughtfully.

"Me too," I admit with a sigh as he pulls off the first boot. "But this really wasn't one of them. I'm still wearing my coat, aren't I?"

The second boot thumps onto the floor, his warm hand caressing my stockinged foot before he turns back to face me. I reach out to run my fingers across his five-o'clock shadow before I can think better of it.

"Was that your subtle way of asking if I can help you get your coat off?" he asks with a slight smile.

"I don't know. My mind's not working so well right now, but I think I should probably take it off. It's nice and cozy in here, and there's a really fuzzy blanket on the back of the couch."

"Ah," he says, "maybe I should claim it for myself."

"You wouldn't. I think maybe you're more of a softy than you want anyone to know."

He arches his eyebrows defiantly, and then gets up, retrieves the fuzzy, multicolored blanket, and wraps it around his own shoulders.

I start laughing as he leans in and unzips my coat. But my laughter fades when his face is inches from mine. My gaze is hungry for the details of him. The curve of his mouth. The stubble on his cheeks, the slightest scar on his chin. Those thick eyelashes.

But then he finishes unzipping me, and his hand slips around to my back, holding me while he slides the sleeves off my arms.

Taking care of me.

Suddenly my emotions feel raw and turbulent. "You don't

need to do this," I say. "You can go home. I'll be fine in a few hours."

"You don't get to tell me what to do," he says, smiling as he sets my coat atop his and then pulls the fuzzy blanket from around his shoulders to engulf me in it.

Bowie, who's been watching us, must know it's his moment to shine, because he hops onto the couch and curls up next to me.

"There," Enzo says. "Now you can be comfortable."

And I am. I feel safe and comfortable and cared for, and it blows my mind that he's the one who made me feel that way.

It's not as if I actually believe Enzo's a devil worshipper, but I never expected him to be like this. To be sweet. To do something without expecting to get something in return.

So maybe he's doing it to get sex, a voice in my head whispers. *He's already told you he wants it.*

But that doesn't *feel* true.

I must fall asleep at some point, because the next thing I know, Enzo is sitting beside the couch with a peanut butter and jelly sandwich and a big glass of water. My stomach roils.

"I couldn't possibly," I say. "I think I could only eat cheese curls right now. Cheese curls are the best food on the planet. Don't let anyone tell you otherwise. And I'm not talking the pretty, organic ones. I'm talking about the gross orange ones covered in fake powdered cheese dust."

"You don't have any," he says, "but the sandwich might help. "The water definitely will."

I sit up, still feeling dizzy, and Bowie climbs out of the way.

"I didn't know you had a cat," Enzo comments, as if the two of us have exchanged buckets of personal information instead of just letting out the occasional snippet.

"I don't," I say, then take a small bite of the sandwich. Actually, he may be onto something, because suddenly I'm starving. I eat it quickly, chasing it with gulps of water.

"This isn't your cat?" he asks as Bowie rubs his head against my arm.

"No, I'm watching him for a friend, but I'd *really* like a cat. I keep looking at photos from the animal shelter. You know, when my phone works. I'm not supposed to have a pet, though. It's in the lease and everything. But Eileen told me to play with animals today."

He gives me a quizzical look, and I realize I'm probably not making much sense.

"Eileen. In her calendar."

"That doesn't help, Lucia."

I yawn and take a final sip of water before slumping onto the couch. "She made me an Advent calendar to help me feel better. There's a challenge every day. That's what you found at the bridge that day, one of my challenges."

"Ah, I see. Your boss told you to fuck someone? You know, they have whole HR departments to prevent that kind of thing."

I roll my eyes. "No. She told me to—"

"Make a wish," he finishes, tugging my hat off gently. He smooths his fingers through my hair, and I lean my head into his hand like I'm a cat. "Why were you feeling badly?"

"It wasn't because of you," I say pointedly. "You don't have that much power over me."

"I wouldn't want the power to make you feel badly," he says softly, running his fingers through my hair some more. "That's the only power I don't covet."

God that feels good. Why does that feel so good?

"My mom died last year," I say, the words tumbling out.

Some unreadable emotion flickers across his face.

"I'm sorry," I say, yawning.

"*You're* sorry? *I'm* sorry. Jesus, I had no idea you'd been through that. You mentioned you'd taken care of her, but I'd thought…hoped…she got better."

"It's not tattooed across my forehead or anything. Anyway, I know men find that kind of thing a turnoff. I mean, you should have seen the way guys closed down after they figured out my mom was sick and I was taking care of her. It was actually pretty funny. Between that and the virginity thing, I put off a lot of guys. And turned on all the wrong ones."

"Doesn't sound funny," he says in a harsh voice. "I'd like to teach them a lesson."

"Oh, aren't you so big and tough," I say, laughing. "And *always* a gentleman. Well, don't bother, Enzo. I didn't care. I wouldn't want to be with someone like that. I had more important things to do."

"Like taking care of your mom."

"Yeah," I say. "For years. She had Huntington's. That's why her husband left. He knew what was going to happen. There's no cure. If you have the gene, you have the disorder. She had it, and he decided he couldn't deal. It's like he only brought me into the family to make sure she wasn't alone when her health started to decline. So I guess at least he did one good thing for her."

I pause, then sigh discontentedly. "Two. They stayed legally married so she could be on his health insurance, but he never visited. Never called. He said it would be too painful for him. For him, can you imagine?"

"Like I said, a real man takes care of his family." He hesitates, a glimmer of dread in his eyes. "And you...do you have this gene?"

"I was adopted," I say. "But he's not my dad. Just her husband. He never wanted to be my dad."

"Oh." There's a world of meaning in that sound. "That stuff about blood being important." He rubs his nose. "I should keep my mouth shut more often."

"Yes, you *definitely* should," I agree. "But you didn't know about that."

"That's why you're taking classes now?"

"I finished college online a long time ago, but I had this idea for an app I wanted to make. For full-time caregivers like I was. I'd taught myself some programming, but I didn't have all the skills I needed." I yawn. "So I've been taking the classes, but Charlie doesn't think I need them. She says I just need more confidence in myself. Maybe she's right because the teachers really suck." I grimace. "That's not very Christmassy of me, but it's true. Also it's hard to do anything with the internet here, but I love this place so much."

"I know you do," he says softly, his voice like velvet.

"I think maybe I'm going to go to sleep now, and hopefully forget all of this happened. I really thought tonight was going to go differently, you know? I was hoping tonight would be *the* night."

His gaze sharpens. "You wanted…"

"The shirtless taffy making sealed it. I want you, Enzo. Like, really badly. I want to have sex with you."

He swears under his breath and runs a hand through his thick, dark hair, leaving it rumpled. "Lucia, you're destroying me right now."

"That's all it took?" I say, smiling at him.

"You're the hate-off victor, no question."

"Don't record this part, because I'm never going to say it again, but you were right. We don't have to like each other to have sex."

I expect him to laugh, but instead he shakes his head and says, "That's unfortunate, because I *do* like you."

My lips part, my brain trying to figure out how to process that. "When did you decide?"

"I've had a sinking suspicion for a while now," he says, his voice soft but unwavering. His hand curls behind my ear, tucking my hair back. "And I definitely liked having my mouth on you. I've thought of nothing else."

"I liked watching you pull that taffy," I admit. "I backed you into it, but you didn't hesitate. I admire you for that. And you looked incredibly sexy. Like a sexy candy god, and you're a good dancer. *Of course* you're a good dancer—" I yawn. "You'd probably even be able to dance to the 'Jingle Bells' doorbell.

"Ah, yes, the new atrocity at Love at First Sip."

"It's horrible, but Eileen's so proud of it. I can't bear to be the one to break the news. Charlie and I would worship anyone who saves us from it, though."

"Would you like me to carry you to bed?" he asks, running the pads of his fingers across my cheek.

"Will you stay for a while?"

"You really want me to?" He sounds shocked, but no more than I am by my answer.

"Yes."

CHAPTER 21

ENZO

*L*ucy is adorable drunk, which isn't a surprise, since she's adorable doing anything, first and foremost giving me shit.

When I carry her to her bedroom, she snuggles in close, and an odd sensation unleashes inside my chest.

I can practically hear Aria saying, *That's your heart growing two sizes, you dipshit.*

Nothing like a sibling to put you in your place—even if it's just as an imagined voice in your head.

But I tell myself the sentiment is bullshit. My heart has nothing to do with this situation. I'm just feeling protective of Lucy because of what she told me.

She delivered the information about her mother so matter-of-factly, but I know a brave front when I see one. Lucy would say I'm a pompous asshole for thinking in such aggrandizing metaphors, but I *created* the brave front.

I know enough about Huntington's to understand it wasn't easy, what she went through with her mother. At the end, she must have been doing everything for her mom. Practically living at the hospital.

Which means this woman in my arms is stronger than I realized. She's the kind of person who doesn't run from challenges but toward them.

Like you.

"Uh, Lucy," I say. "Where's your bedroom?"

She's out of it, but it would be impossible to get lost in a one-bedroom cottage, thankfully, so I find the bedroom and open the door. There's an enormous king-size bed inside with a bright pink, heart-shaped headboard.

It's a bit…tacky, and there's nothing about Lucy that strikes me as tacky, but then again, she and Eileen are obsessed with all this matchmaking business. Maybe I shouldn't be surprised.

I set her down on the mattress, and she surprises me again by tugging me down with her. "Lay with me," she mumbles. "Just for a little while."

Does she know she's tormenting me? Probably. If she's coherent enough, I'm guessing she's glad for it.

Smiling to myself, I adjust the blankets and then tug them over her, tucking her in the way I used to tuck in my little siblings.

It feels nothing like that. Lie to everyone else, but not yourself. She's unlocked something inside of you.

Then I lie down on top of the covers, facing her, and let myself wrap an arm around her.

"You're so warm, Enzo," she says, snuggling closer so her head is nestled against my chest, her hair tickling my nose.

"I'm glad I can be your space heater."

"Why are you so handsome?"

I laugh a little—but only a little, because even though I'd never touch her when she's like this, my body is reacting to her nearness. To the memory of what she tastes like and the throaty sounds she made when she came.

"It's a question for the gods, Lucia. You might also ask why they chose to give you such luscious, ticklish hair. I'll be waiting for their answer."

"You're very good at drawing," she says. "I kept the flyer you drew. I couldn't make myself throw it away. No one's ever drawn me like that. Only those people at fairs who give everyone big bobbleheads."

"A bobblehead of you would be a crime."

She laughs, her body shaking against mine, making my need for her more powerful. "You know what? I really, really want to see a bobblehead drawing of you. Do you think anyone does those here? Oh, why am I asking? It's probably your uncle's hairdresser's driver or something, and you know all about it because you're a Hidie."

"I don't believe my uncle has a hairdresser. He's as bald as a cue ball. But it's kind of you to ask."

She's quiet for several minutes, her body still and warm against me. Then suddenly she asks, "Did you love her, Enzo? Rachelle, I mean."

"No," I say, stroking her arm, her hair. "She didn't love me either. We weren't good together."

Rachelle had liked that my job involved firing people. Once, she'd asked me to talk about the people I'd let go that day as a kind of foreplay. It had made me sick.

"I shouldn't have said anything to her that day," she says softly. "She just seemed like she felt so left out. It's awful to feel that way. But it sounds like she wasn't very nice after all. I don't know why men are drawn to women like that."

"*You* haven't been very nice to me," I point out, despite the lump in my throat.

It's the thought of Lucy feeling left out that's affecting me.

Lucy, staying home to take care of her sick mother instead of acting like a twenty-year-old does.

"That's probably the only reason you want to sleep with me," she says dreamily.

"It's definitely not the only reason, but it doesn't hurt."

"Also because I'm a virgin."

"That doesn't make the list at all."

She snorts. "As if. You never would have given me a second thought if you hadn't seen that note."

"That's not true," I argue, because it's *not*. Sure, the note got my attention, but there's no way I wouldn't have noticed her. No man could work next door to her without being captivated, however reluctantly.

"That's your story, but it isn't mine."

"Okay, Lucia."

She nuzzles her head against my neck, and I thank God she doesn't have her back to me. If she did, there's no way she wouldn't feel—

"You're *very* hard. I can feel you. You know, I'm not really all that tipsy anymore. We could totally—"

"I'm getting up now," I say, pressing a kiss to her forehead.

"To take care of that?" she asks, interest flashing in her eyes as I climb out of the bed. Her gaze lingers on the bulge in my pants. "I mean, are you going to—"

"That's between me and my dick. Sleep well."

"You're leaving," she says, her mouth in a pout.

"You have your friend's cat to keep watch over you."

"You could sleep on the couch. It's late."

"Are you worried about me getting home safely?" I ask, amused by the thought. She's right about one thing when it comes to Hideaway Harbor. It's safe.

"I don't want to be alone tonight," she says, with a strain of sadness in her voice that guaran-fucking-tees I won't be leaving.

"I'll sleep on the couch," I assure her. "And I'll teach you to make a real cappuccino in the morning."

"Your grandmother already offered," she says sleepily.

That captures my attention. My dick deflates, my chin tips up. "When'd she offer to do that?"

More importantly: *why* did she offer to do that?

"I'm very tired," Lucy says, frowning. "But she came by yesterday. She wants Eileen to set you up with someone. I haven't told Eileen yet."

"Because you were jealous, Lucy?" I ask, needing to know. Maybe it's not fair, trying to get her to talk now, while she's still under the influence. But playing fair is for people who are okay with losing.

"Don't you wish," she says with a small smile. "No. I didn't want some innocent woman to suffer."

Ouch. But I did ask. I shouldn't expect her opinion of me to have changed that much, and I can't say she's wrong about me. I have been rude. Overbearing. Manipulative.

All the attributes that made me good at my old job seem to have made me bad at connecting with people.

She makes a sweet sound and turns over, tucking her legs in. And the cat appears out of nowhere, in the way only felines can, and jumps onto the bed, nestling into her body.

Lucky bastard.

I go to leave and she mumbles, "Enzo?"

"Yes?" I ask, turning, my heart rate speeding up.

"Don't draw a mustache on my face while I'm asleep."

I smile to myself, because I'd forgotten my threat to retaliate with the marker. Who could remember a thing like that after what happened between us in Hidden Italy?

"We'll see," I say ominously, and with that, I leave the room.

A MAN like Hudson would settle onto the couch, pull that fuzzy, colorful blanket over him, and call it a night.

But Lucy's held a monopoly over my mind for days, and

now that I'm here in her home, I want to learn about her. I'd like to know *everything*.

So after I take care of my big problem in the bathroom—something else Hudson wouldn't do—I give myself a tour of the cottage.

It's cute, cozy, and full of bright colors, all of which I was expecting, but there are a few things I couldn't have foreseen. Namely, a collection of vintage salt and pepper shakers in the kitchen—enough to furnish dozens of diners—fifty cans of tinned sardines in the cabinet, an enormous oil painting of the cat she says isn't hers, and in the living area, a wooden hutch housing a collection of taxidermied animals.

I scratch my head in stupefied disbelief as I study the squirrels, the walleyed rabbit that looks like it was scraped off the road, and a fox that resembles a chihuahua.

Did she…make these?

The thought doesn't cohere at all with the Lucy I've been getting to know. It's absolutely insane to think that she'd want to keep them, let alone make them herself, but here they are, sitting in a cupboard in her house.

Maybe she rents the place furnished?

Jesus Christ, I hope so. I mean, surely she must. She probably doesn't even know about this cabinet of curiosities.

Or…maybe the collections belonged to her mother? People can be sentimental about some strange shit—Nonna still has the chicken bone that nearly killed Nonno, and would have if my father, in a rare act of heroism, hadn't given him the hug of life.

I sit on the couch, my mind tripping over the closet of horrors, the sardines, and even that bed with the heart-shaped headboard. But my thoughts keep returning to Lucy, sleepy and pretty in her bed, telling me that she doesn't want to be alone. Lucy, revealing what happened to her mother.

Lucy, who's had as much fun with the hate-off as I have.

Presuming all this crap is hers, they're pretty harmless eccentricities. I mean, lots of people like sardines, right? My grandmother eats them several times a week. Maybe they can bond over their love of disgusting canned fish.

Oh, what the fuck am I thinking? I shouldn't *want* them to bond. The goal was and always has been to fix the problem with Hidden Italy, get my mojo back, and leave.

Sighing, I lean back on the velveteen couch, my gaze catching on a framed poster I hadn't noticed before. It's for *Cats*. Not the musical, but the CGI-packed live-action movie.

I don't know…maybe she only likes it because she has a thing for cats? Lots of people like cats. Truth be told, I myself like cats.

I fall into a fitful sleep—and wake up with a start to the cat licking my face with its sandpaper tongue. My heart hammers as I take a second to orient myself.

Judging from the light that's barely starting to seep through the windows, it's early morning.

I pet the cat, then get to my feet and stretch, my back feeling the strain of spending all night on a couch too small for me.

"Lucy?" I call out.

She doesn't answer, so I pour a glass of water for her in the kitchen—fuck, the glasses are *Cats*-themed too—and bring it to the bedroom to check on her.

The bed is empty, the covers rumpled. But the shower is running in the en suite bathroom. My gaze shoots to the door of the bathroom just as it opens and Lucy walks out…completely naked, her glorious hair gathered in a knot at the back of her neck.

She sees me and shrieks, her hands lifting to her breasts, hiding those pink nipples, then shifting down between her legs. But she does it with both of her arms, and it squeezes her breasts together, and oh God…

I force myself to look away.

"What are you doing here?" she asks. "You scared me."

So she doesn't remember. How much doesn't she remember?

"I took you home from the lobster trap tree lighting," I say, peering intently at the window shades, which thankfully don't have the logo for *Cats* painted onto them. "Don't you want a towel?"

"I didn't think you'd stay."

I detect no movement in my peripheral vision. She's still standing there, naked. Looking at me.

"You asked me to, so I did."

"I did?" she asks, sounding so surprised I almost laugh. I would if she weren't the greatest temptation of my life, standing almost within reach.

"You did."

"I sort of remember that, but you didn't stay *in here*," she points out. "I thought you were gone."

"I couldn't take the torment of feeling you pressed against me all night."

From the corner of my eye, I see her take a step toward me. Her voice husky, she says, "Would it be that miserable to be close to me?"

I risk a direct glance at her. God, she's beautiful. A few of her curls have sprung loose and are skimming over her breasts. Now, unclothed before me, she looks even more like one of the Italian masters' paintings—the kind of woman who makes you *want* to sink to your knees. I'd like to gather her hair in my fist, to run my hands and lips over her from head to toe. And I want, desperately, to sink into her.

"Yes," I say.

Amusement passes over her face. "For all your big talk, you're not very good at flirting."

"It was an absolute torment because of how much I wanted

to touch you. To kiss you. To explore every inch of you, Lucia. You make me crazy."

"I was about to take a shower," she says, her voice still low and breathy, the sound of it making my dick twitch. It's already rock hard—and has been from the second I saw her.

"Are you inviting me to join you?" I ask.

She's sober now, and if this *is* an invitation, there's no world in which I'd turn her down.

Her response is to reach for my hand. "Yes. But I'll write it on your forehead in Sharpie if you need me to."

"That won't be required."

"This is only about sex," she says. "We would never work."

"I understand."

I remind myself of the *Cats* memorabilia. The cabinet of horrors. Of my need to leave this place for good.

And I reach for her hand.

CHAPTER 22

LUCY

*H*is hand is warm and strong as it takes mine, his eyes fixed on me. He's staring at me as if I'm the most desirable woman in the universe.

My heart is beating so fast, I wouldn't be surprised if it escaped the cage of my chest.

Enzo's here. He stayed because I asked him. He wants me.

I remember most of last night, but the end is blurry. All I know is that Enzo forced me to eat a PB&J sandwich and then tucked me into bed as if I were a child. No, that's not quite true. I remember him lying beside me. Talking to me. Joking with me. I remember feeling really grateful he was there, and sad that he was going to leave. Surely, that was just the alcohol though. And hormones. Lots of hormones. An obscene amount of them are pulsing through me now.

A mild headache is pounding in my temples, but it's quickly forgotten when Enzo uses our linked hands to pull me toward him, almost as if we're still dancing the way we did in the candy shop. I'm mesmerized as he easily lifts me into his arms and stalks toward the bathroom, his head bowing to kiss my cheek, my lips. The feeling of him against my bare flesh is so overwhelming that I can't think beyond his hands, his lips, his—

"You're wearing too many clothes," I murmur against his mouth. He sets me down just inside the bathroom door, then pulls his shirt off and tosses it to me with the smirk of a man who knows exactly what he looks like shirtless.

I catch the shirt midair and let myself take a long sniff before dropping it.

"Did you just smell my shirt?" he asks, grinning.

"Yes, it smells terrible. You should invest in a new washer and dryer."

"Liar." He starts to unfasten his belt, and lust floods my body hard and fast, almost painful.

Oh, God. Is it a bad idea to do this with him?

Sex is different for women than it is for men. I've read enough dating books to know there's a consensus about that. If we do this, it's possible I'll continue to soften toward Enzo. I don't want to start making excuses for his behavior or expecting things he has no intention of giving me.

I remind myself that Enzo doesn't qualify as Mr. Perfect, the ideal man my mom talked about in her letter.

But he doesn't have to. I need practice with sex, and he'll give it to me. Simple as that.

It doesn't *feel* simple as I reach down to undo the button of his pants, then lower his zipper. He watches me with an inscrutable glint in his eyes.

"Were you afraid I would catch your dick in the zipper?" I ask.

"You're terrible at guessing my thoughts." He pushes his pants and boxer briefs down, and I gasp a little at the sight of him completely naked. Hard for me.

God, he's gorgeous.

"You like what you see?" he asks, ruining the effect.

Okay, only tarnishing it.

"Your arrogance needs no encouragement," I say, but I run my hands over his chest, feeling the ridges of muscle, and then stroke my fingers over his proudly jutting dick, tracing it from base to tip before playing with the head. It feels like there couldn't possibly be room for it inside of me.

Looking up into his hooded eyes, I say, "Uh...I don't think this is going to work."

He sucks in a sharp breath before leaning in to kiss my neck. He whispers into my ear, "By the time I sink into your sweet heat, you'll be so wet for me, it won't be a problem. If it is, I haven't done my job right, and I *always* do my job right. Let's get you into the shower, Lucia. I have plans for you there."

My knees feel weak as I walk into the oversized glass-walled shower stall. The warm water pounds down on my skin, awakening my nerve endings in a new way.

When Enzo follows me in, he fills up the space so utterly I nearly gasp. This man has such a presence. I've been feeling it all week, in the store beside mine. The knowledge that he's there has filled me with aggravation and, to be totally honest, desire. Unwanted, frustrating, smoking hot desire. I've never wanted someone so physically, so *viscerally*. I want him so much it feels like need.

It's not rational, but I almost hate him for making me feel so out of control.

He sinks to his knees in the shower, gazing up at me, and something in my chest catches.

"I feel like you're trying to make a point."

"It's not the first time I've gotten on my knees for you," he says, seeming not to notice the hot water pelting down on his thick hair, sticking it to his scalp. His face is dripping as he leans in to kiss my thigh. "Spread your legs for me."

I do, of course I do. Then, groaning, I bury a hand in his wet hair as he continues to kiss my thighs, his hands reaching up to caress my breasts.

He pushes me back into the wet tiles as he finally presses his mouth where I need it, sucking and licking and keeping up the pressure as pleasure radiates through me. My limbs are electrified, my nerves crazed, and the effect is only accentuated by the water pattering down on us and the sensation of his hair between my fingers as he continues to pleasure me. He seems to enjoy it. To revel in having this power to make me feel—oh, *of course* he does—but I won't deny him. Because the feeling of his mouth between my legs is revelatory.

My silicone toys get the job done, but it's not like this. It's not like having a beautiful man between my thighs, sucking on me as if I'm the only thing that can bring him life.

Maybe I should tell him to stop. This can't be as pleasurable for him as it is for me. But I can't bring myself to care. It feels too good. I've been dreaming about it too much...

Then he grazes his teeth over me lightly and sucks in hard, and it feels like my entire body explodes.

When he lifts his gaze, watching me, his expression self-satisfied, I tug on the hair I'm still clutching before releasing it.

He grins and climbs to his feet.

"Are you good and wet for me?" he asks.

"I'm dripping with water," I say, purposefully ignoring his meaning. Because yes. I can feel my body preparing itself for him, begging me to give it what it wants.

He presses me into the wall, his head bent over mine, and reaches down between my legs, feeling where I'm sopping for him. The smile on his face gets smugger as he lifts his finger up and sucks on it.

"It's from the shower."

"Little liar," he says, lifting my hands over my head and pinning them to the wall. The water continues to spray us as he lowers his head and kisses me hard. I kiss him back just as desperately, our tongues and teeth clashing, the energy between us chaotic and euphoric, heightened by his hardness pressed against me. My hips buck, wanting to get closer, to feel the pressure of his dick against my skin, but I also don't want to stop kissing him. I can't. His hands still have mine pinned to the wet shower wall as his mouth moves over mine.

Finally he pulls away slightly, panting. "Do you have a condom?"

I nod quickly. I bought some online the day I made my wish on the Wishing Bridge. I've been carrying them around in my purse as of yesterday.

"You tell me when you're ready," he says, tucking an escaped sodden curl behind my ear. His eyes are intense as they peer into mine, his thick eyelashes beaded with water, his hair dripping with it.

"I'm ready," I say.

He grunts and slams the shower stall door open before backing me out of it and into the room.

"Shouldn't we dry off?"

"No time," he says, guiding me onto the bed.

I fall back onto the soft comforter, and he splays my legs wide for him and leans in to kiss me between them, then kisses his way up my abdomen, stopping to suck each of my nipples before he feels between my legs and groans again.

"I told you you'd be ready for me."

"The condoms are in my purse," I say, nearly breathless. "In the living room."

I can tell it's hard for him to step away. But he gets up, a look of contrition crossing his face. Instead of going straight to the living room, he brings me a fluffy towel from the bathroom and uses it to dry my body, stopping to suck in my nipple and again to kiss the area beside my belly button.

I tear the towel from him, using it to wick some of the water out of my hair. "For the love of God, Enzo. Go get the condom."

His smile is a bit smug, and very much Enzo. "Your wish is

my command," he says, and I know we're both thinking of that pink slip of paper I dropped on the Wishing Bridge.

As he leaves the room, my gaze follows him with a thirst for details—the tattoo on his shoulder, the muscular flex of his butt—and I can't help but think that the bridge really did deliver.

It brought him to me.

His wish was to save his family store so he could leave, and he says that I helped him think of an idea that might accomplish that.

So maybe the bridge delivers on everyone's wishes.

My mind's fuzzy with dreams and wishes when he comes back in, holding the strip of condoms.

He breaks one off as he strides toward me, his dick so hard and ready.

I wondered if I'd be panicked at this moment. I know it might hurt. I've heard about it from other people, including Charlie, who said she bled so much it soaked through the sheets. But I'm not a teenager. I've been using tampons and vibrators for years. I'm more than ready.

"Put it on," I say, a hint of command in my voice.

He grins at me. "Getting impatient?"

"Yes."

A need matching mine flashes through his eyes, and he rips the wrapper and then rolls the condom onto his thick, hard length before edging between my legs again.

"Spread them wider."

I do, my heart beating hard as he lowers over me, his body so big and warm, his dick feeling huge as it presses between us. He kisses me again, a fierce, hungry kiss, as he reaches down to feel me one more time. What he finds must satisfy him—*gratify* him—because he reaches down to adjust himself, his mouth still pressed to mine. He thrusts in slightly, the pressure and feeling of him a delicious tease, then pulls back from our kiss.

Looking me in the eyes, he says, "I don't want to hurt you. Tell me if it hurts."

"It won't," I say.

Holding my gaze, he pushes in deeper. There's a slight resistance, and he hesitates, but I wrap my hand around his butt and push. So he lowers his forehead to mine and drives in deeper, moving slowly so my body can adjust to him. There's a quick burst of pain and a slightly uncomfortable and entirely foreign feeling of fullness. But it's accompanied by a dizzying pleasure, because he's really inside of me. All of him. He's *inside of me*.

And the guttural sound he makes feels delicious.

It's so different from using a toy—he's so big and thick, so warm, and his scent is all over me now. You'd think the shower would have washed it away, but it's stronger than ever, so maybe it's his pheromones I'm breathing in.

"Are you okay?" he asks, pressing a kiss beneath my ear. "Did it hurt?"

"Only a little."

"You feel so unbelievably good, Lucia," he says into my ear. "So tight and wet and—"

"Pin my hands over my head like you did in the shower," I say, my voice trembling. "I liked that."

He makes another almost pained sound as he captures my wrists with one hand, the other holding him up.

"Can I move?" he asks.

"If you don't, this will be a pretty disappointing experience for both of us."

He gives one of his *oh, Lucia* smiles and pulls out before thrusting in again, his hand tightening around my wrists. I feel a little sore, but I'm fascinated by the feeling of him inside of me, hot and pulsing. There's a dragging sensation as he pulls out, followed by the pleasure of him thrusting back in. The third time he does it, he nearly pulls all the way out, his tip teasing me, before he thrusts in harder.

A surprised gasp gusts from me, and a look of panic flashes in his eyes as he says, "Are you okay? Was that…?"

I kiss him to shut him up, and he moans into my mouth, losing some of his caution as he moves faster. Pulling his mouth from mine, he kisses down to my neck and then my breast. He sucks me in as he thrusts in again, and pleasure starts to build—a different kind of pleasure than before, because he's experiencing it with me.

He said he didn't kneel for anyone, but it doesn't escape me that Enzo has knelt for me twice, and now he's staring at me like I'm the most important woman in the world. His lips, his hands, and his cock are all attending to my needs. It's intoxicating, and it's dangerous, because I can't let myself believe this is about anything other than winning to him.

I shouldn't let it be about anything more than that for me either. I can't.

"*Sei belissima*," he says as he thrusts again, lowering his lips to my jaw while he holds my hands up high over my head. "*Bella ragazza*." I'm positive he only learned those phrases to impress women in the bedroom, but right now I don't care. I want all of him—his words, his clever hands, his lips, the brush of his stubble, and his beautiful, hard dick—making me feel things I didn't know my body was capable of feeling.

"Wrap your legs around me," he says.

He sucks in a ragged breath as I cinch my legs around him, taking him in deeper. The pressure is so profound, I feel it everywhere.

"You feel so good," I breathe out.

"You," he pants as he thrusts in faster, again and then again, "are a wonder."

I feel like one. I feel beautiful and desirable and *wanted*. I don't feel like Lucy, who's too serious, with her dying mother and her depressing job. Or Lucy, the oldest student in her classes because everyone else figured out what they wanted to do with their lives ages ago. None of that matters right now, with him. All that matters is that we want each other. Need each other.

He releases my hands and surprises me by rolling onto his back, bringing me with him. "Ride me, Lucy," he says, his fiery eyes meeting mine. "Take your pleasure from me."

It's on the tip of my tongue to say I don't know how, that I've never done this before. But he knows that, and I don't want to admit to any weakness with him, any more than he'd want to do so with me.

So I decide to embrace this for what it is—practice. Practice with a delicious man.

I rise up tentatively, and his hands grip my thighs, just this side of painful, as I sink down on him. I don't get the angle right the first time, but I still feel so full. So strange with him inside of me. Good but foreign. So I try again, and this time he lowers his hand down to just above where we're joined, rubbing me there as I move over him, and the combination of feelings makes pleasure spiral through me. I move faster, feeling myself clenching around him. He makes a sound deep in his throat as his hand keeps working me, his other hand reaching around to grip my butt as he thrusts upward, and then it happens—

The pleasure bursts, pushing me over the edge, and I cry out as it pulses through me, again and again.

I feel him tumble over the edge with me, whispering my name. Calling me Lucia.

I lie down on top of him, wanting to feel him against me for another few seconds, because it's done now. And maybe that means we're done with each other too.

We should be, anyway, because I can already feel it happening. My heart is starting to reach for this arrogant, funny, controlling jerk.

That means one thing: he has to go.

CHAPTER 23

ENZO

"Are you leaving?" Lucy asks as she pulls on her sweater.

I've only just tugged on my underwear and jeans.

She wants me to *leave*?

Right now, I'd like to stay forever. Hell, I'd buy some taxidermied birds and a couple of salt and pepper shakers to please her. Whatever it takes to bask in this feeling for a little while longer.

I haven't felt this kind of passion for anything in a long time. Not for a woman, not for my life, definitely not for my job.

But, as ridiculously humbling as it is to admit, maybe it wasn't as good for her. Having sex was one of her challenges for herself, a goal to be checked off.

The thought burns more than it should, given that's exactly what I'd hoped for just last week—hot, meaningless sex with someone who wasn't going to miss me when I left.

"How'd that feel for you?" I ask, my heart beating fast and hard as I pull on my shirt.

She laughs. "Do you want me to hold up a scorecard with a

perfect ten on it? Why am I not surprised? Should I write an anonymous letter to Lady Lovewatch and tell her you're a very good lover after all?"

I gather myself and give her the kind of answer she expects and probably wants: "Surely you can do better than *very good*, Lucia. There are millions of synonyms out there. I can think of at least a dozen for your pussy."

She throws a pillow at me, and I catch it, grinning. It's heart-shaped and covered in sequins.

"It *was* good," she says, holding my gaze. "Fantastic. Fun. Hot. Delicious." Then something earnest enters her gaze. "*Thank you*, Enzo."

"You're thanking me for sex?" I ask incredulously.

She laughs. "Yeah…no. I'm sure that happens to you all the time, but I was talking about last night. Thank you for taking care of me. You didn't have to do that."

"I did. You forgot how to work the door in the Porta Potty."

"You mean the lock didn't actually break?" she asks, aghast.

I grin. "I don't know, and neither do you, apparently. Someone had to step in."

I think of Hudson, standing there and laughing with her friends while she was trying to escape her plastic prison, and I clench my jaw. Nice guy and all, but nowhere near good enough for Lucy.

Which brings me to my next question…

"Lucy…I want to do this again."

Okay, not actually a question. More a statement of irrefutable fact. I need to do this again. My brother was right about one thing: I'm having more fun with Lucy than I've had in years.

A wicked smile crosses her face. She reaches into a tote bag on the floor and pulls out a red scarf. My mother's scarf, to be exact.

"You want to do what again, exactly?" she asks, advancing on me with the scarf.

I clear my throat. "Save you from every Porta Potty in coastal Maine."

"How gallant of you."

She steps closer and reaches up to wrap the scarf around my throat. Her warm hands slide from the scarf to my neck, and they linger there, although her body remains several inches away. Just a few minutes ago I was inside of her. I want to be inside of her again, preferably sooner rather than later. I'd like to spend the whole day inside of her.

"Are you going to strangle me?" I tease, holding her gaze as she plays with the ends of the scarf.

"What use would I have for you if you were dead?" she asks, her pupils dilated.

"Judging from the collection of taxidermied animals in the other room, you'd figure something out."

"*What?*" She steps back, her forehead creasing.

"Okay, fine. You caught me. I poked around a little last night. You would have done the same in my shoes. I know you would have."

"Yes, obviously I would have snooped, but I have no idea what you're talking about," she says, straight-faced, and I can tell she really doesn't.

Thank God.

"Lucy, there's a cupboard full of weird taxidermied animals in the living room."

Her gaze narrows. "You're messing with me. Again. Seriously, I thought we were beyond that."

I take her hand and lead her into the other room, my fingers linking naturally with hers, and come to a stop in front of the cabinet of curiosities.

"They're in there?" she asks, whispering even though we're alone in here except for Bowie.

"You can do the honors," I say, nodding toward it, and I drop her hand.

The last several months of my life have been so full of strange surprises that I half expect nothing will be in there. But she opens it tentatively, and there they are.

And the look on her face...

She turns to me. "Did you do this? Did you hide them all in there?"

I look at her deadpan. "You think I found half a dozen taxidermied animals last night, when everything was closed, and hid them in this cabinet while you were sleeping? I'm flattered you think so highly of my skills, but no. You really didn't know about them?"

She grimaces at the chihuahua fox. "No. I mean, the woman who owns this place is a little eccentric, but I wouldn't have expected this. I should have guessed there'd be more weird stuff. There must be fifty tins of sardines in the kitchen cabinet."

"This isn't your place," I say, my pulse racing. Puzzle pieces start rearranging themselves in my brain.

"You thought these were my taxidermied animals, and you slept with me anyway?" she asks, laughing. When she sees the look on my face, she laughs harder, bending over, her hair everywhere.

God, she's beautiful when she's laughing at me.

"I was trying to be nonjudgmental," I say with a smile. "I figured there was a risk I might end up in your cabinet of horrors, but it seemed like it was worth it."

"I'm flattered," she says, still laughing.

"You should be," I say. "So are we squatting in a serial killer's house?"

She's shaking with laughter as she gives my arm a light punch. "I'm cat-sitting for one of our regulars."

"Ah, so I don't have to add catnapping to your list of potential crimes."

"I won't say I'm not tempted," she says, her laughter finally dying down as she glances back toward the bedroom. "It's a bit lonely at my place. I lived with Charlie when I first moved to Hideaway Harbor, but she moved in with Lars a month ago. Well, you probably know all about that."

"Not really. I only met him a couple of times before he and Aria broke up."

"Long enough to threaten to kill him."

I smile at her. "I'd do anything for my sister. Would you like me to threaten to kill someone for you too? Turn me in their direction and set me loose. I have plenty of unprocessed anger to release."

"I guess I do too," she says, her expression becoming more serious. "I shouldn't have unleashed it on you. Even if you can be insufferable."

I reach up and run my fingers over her jaw, then cup my hand around her chin. "You can unleash your rage on me any time, Lucia. I can take it. Will you see me again?"

She pauses, her gaze unwavering. "Yes, but I meant what I said earlier. This can only be about sex."

Such words have never bothered me until this very moment.

Maybe it's that ego she keeps talking about, and I'd just like to believe she wants more from me.

Or maybe I have to concede Giovanni had a point after all.

I have feelings for this woman.

Still, this is what she's offering, and I won't say no. With my hand still cupped around her jaw, I lean in and kiss her hard.

I pull back, shifting my hand to cradle the side of her face. "Agreed. But while we're doing this, you're mine, Lucia. I don't share. No sweet little dinner dates with Hudson or any men dressed in Santa suits."

For a second, I think she's going to bite me—or maybe bite my head off.

Instead, she nods. "The same goes for you. If Eileen tries to set you up with anyone, you have to say no."

I snort, spearing my hand into her glorious curls. "I would have said no anyway."

"And no hookups with tourists or anyone else," she demands, scowling.

I make a sign over my chest. "Lobster Scout's honor."

"Is that really a thing here?" she asks, angling her head to study me, curiosity glinting in her eyes. "Someone else mentioned it to me."

"Really a thing." I grin, playing with one of her curls. "Everything in Hideaway Harbor has to be special and precious. No normal Boy Scouts for us."

"Did you always feel this way?"

"About Hideaway Harbor?" I shrug. "It was a place I needed to escape for my life to begin."

"And did it feel like your life began when you left?"

Her words wrench at something inside of me, carving into the bedrock of the stories I've told myself. The ones that have built me into the man I am.

Because, no, it still felt like something was missing. It has always felt like something was missing. First, my mother. Then, I felt like I could have my job but not my family, my family but not my freedom.

My hand drops from her hair.

"I'm sorry," she says quickly. "I shouldn't have asked you that. That's obviously not a frenemies-with-benefits question. But for a man who's so devoted to his family, you're surprisingly anxious to leave them."

The knife drives in deep, cutting through my armor and finding my heart. I rub a hand over my chest. "You know how to hit a man where it hurts, no question about that."

"I was curious, that's all. I just…home was always with my mom. Always. And after she died, all I could think about was finding a new home. And when I visited Charlie here, everyone was so kind to me. So welcoming."

I have to smile at that. "Was *I* welcoming?"

"There are exceptions to every rule," she says with an answering smile. "I guess I was wondering…what's home for you? Is it really in New York? Because I've been there a few times, and I mean, it's great and everything, but it always smells like pee and hot garbage, and everyone looks like they've been sucking on lemons. Hideaway Harbor smells like cinnamon sticks all the time, and everyone's always smiling. Maybe it's not actually Hideaway Harbor you don't like."

I shake my head slowly. "Who needs a therapist when they have a Lucia to analyze them?"

"You've become really fond of that nickname you've assigned to me."

"Yes," I say, wrapping a hand around her hip. "But listen, before I forget…I was going to tell you about my idea for Hidden Italy."

"The one I gave you," she says, shifting toward me, her scent wafting around me.

"Yes, you're generous like that. I'd prefer to tell you with you naked and bent over the back of the couch. It would be more in keeping with our…what did you call it?"

"Frenemies-with-benefits arrangement," she says, licking her lips. She does it purposefully, and the sight makes my dick rock hard in an instant.

"I'll bend you over so you can look at the tree while I fuck you. That seems like something you'd enjoy, don't you think?"

She angles her head and looks up at me through her lashes. "Yes. There's some extra garland in the closet you can tie my hands with."

Damn. *Damn.*

"You knew about the garland but not the dead animals?" I ask, already going for the button on her pants.

"I have my priorities straight," she says, and since she's reaching for the hem of my shirt, I'm not about to argue.

A few minutes later we're both undressed, the blinds are drawn, and her hands are captured behind her back with the glittery gold garland. I slide one hand between her legs and grip her hip with the other, holding her in place while I fuck her with my fingers.

And I explain my idea to her over the sound of her moaning.

"It sounds like an idea that only someone who loves Hideaway Harbor could come up with," she pants, her words poking at the raw place between my ribs.

"Which is why you're the one who came up with it," I quip. "It's entirely your idea, and I'm not at all sorry for stealing it."

"I really am brilliant, aren't I?" she says as my fingers find a spot that makes her writhe.

"Entirely. And beautiful, and so very hungry for my cock."

She kicks backward at me with one of her legs, and I laugh as I lean in to kiss her neck and the side of her face. "We should make a cappuccino together. A peace offering."

"So that's why you wanted to teach me," she says, suggesting she remembers more of last night than I thought earlier. "But I'll bet your grandmother makes a better cappuccino than you."

"Most assuredly." I curl my fingers and rub, and she releases a glorious moan into the upper couch cushion. "We'll visit her together."

"No..." she says through small throaty sounds that vibrate through me, settling somewhere in my chest. "That's definitely not a frenemies-with-benefits thing. I'll go...alone."

"As you wish," I say. "She'll be free on Wednesday evening. You can come over after closing. I'll make the arrangements."

It's the next time I'll be staying the night at Nonna's house, but no need to point that out. She might not show up if she knows.

"What if I don't want to make peace with you?" Lucy asks.

I've already put the condom on, and I run my tip between her legs, pushing in the slightest bit. "Then you have a funny way of showing it."

"This doesn't feel like peace," she groans. "You're teasing me."

"Always," I say as I thrust all the way in, feeling the tight heat of her as she engulfs me. Watching my hard length disappear inside her. Fuck, I'm not going to last long like this.

She moans as I slip my hand between her legs, helping her reach her climax as I move inside her. The Christmas lights twinkle across from us. The cabinet of horrors is behind us, and I have to be honest...

The holidays are suddenly feeling pretty merry and bright.

LATER, after Lucia kicks me out, I head back to my apartment for the first time in days.

It's only once I'm there that I remember the note Giovanni gave me, the one from my neighbor.

I take it out and settle onto the couch to read it.

Dear Lobster Stalker,

So, I'm just going to ask. You're into The Golden Girls, which is cool—I mean, who doesn't like Sophia?—but wondering minds want to know...does this mean you're on the older side? I know we promised not to do identifying details, but what about an age range?

Oh God, now I sound like a stalker too, but I guess I'd like a better idea of who I'm talking to. I'd be okay with exchanging letters with a grandfather. I never really had grandparents, and I always wondered what it would be like. When I was growing up, I felt a little left out because I didn't have them.

You inspired me to go see the lobster trap tree lighting tonight. I'll be thinking about you, wondering if you're there too.

Yours—

Dancer Stalker

So, either Giovanni was messing with me about the cabbage and the TV show, or someone else has moved into the apartment down the hall since Aria left. Doesn't matter which. What matters is that I've been corresponding with someone completely different than the kind, middle-aged woman I've been envisioning for the last several days. Someone younger. Someone who went to the lobster trap tree lighting last night.

A woman who lost her mother just before last Christmas.

A woman who struggles with her emotions, just like I struggle with mine.

I felt a glimmer of the truth earlier, when we were together, but now it hits me with the subtlety of hurled bricks.

She never did tell me where she lives, but I already know the answer in my heart.

I've been talking to my Lucia.

CHAPTER 24

LUCY

"Lucy, dear, let's chat for a minute, if you wouldn't mind," Eileen says, patting my hand as we finish cleaning up the Sip. It's just past noon, our closing time on Sundays. Wayne was here, as usual, and when we told him it was closing time, he left with a long-suffering sigh.

"Of course," I say, trying to act like I'm not deliciously sore in a way that makes me think of Enzo every time I move.

"You look just *beautiful* today," Eileen says, smiling widely at me as I wipe the counter for the fifth time. "I can't put my finger on what's changed. Did you do something different with your hair?"

I'm hit with a mental image of Enzo gripping my hair while he thrust into me from behind. Swallowing dryly, I say, "No, nothing different. I just stayed out late last night, so I left it a little wild."

"Oh, yes," she says as she starts making a latte that is hopefully meant for me. "I couldn't make it last night, but I heard *all* about the goings-on at the lobster trap tree lighting. That's partly what I wanted to talk to you about."

"Oh?" I ask innocently as she pours the latte into a huge white and red mug before starting in on another.

"Oh, yes. I heard the Larry's lobster claw wouldn't stay upright. Everyone's been tittering about it." She glances up at me, her eyes surprisingly shrewd. "Everyone's also been talking about our friend Enzo's performance at The Sweetest Thing. The dance party was divine! I took a turn with Amanda Willis, did you notice?"

"I did," I say with a grin. "Something tells me you're the one who invited her."

Her smile widens. "I did indeed."

I tell her about my talk with Amanda near the bridge, and she nods knowingly, as if she's not the least bit surprised.

"It's a special place," she says. "A place of wonders. I'm happy she and Portia have taken a shine to each other. They're a beautiful pairing. Grumpy and sunshine. Some people think like takes to like, but most of the time we do best with people who are unlike ourselves. What better way is there to learn and grow?"

"Were you and Murray like that?"

"Oh, yes," she says with a distant smile. "The first time I met him, I couldn't *stand* him."

"Really?" It's hard to imagine Eileen disliking anyone, let alone the man she's mourned for years.

"He made assumptions about me because I used to be a beauty queen. He was the accountant I went to for help with my taxes. But he quickly learned the error of his ways, and we had a beautiful relationship."

"I wish I could have known him."

She looks me in the eye and says, "In a way, you do. You know him because you know this place where he lived, because you know *me*, and he and I spent years helping shape each other. I'd like to think I know your mother in the same way."

Tears burn in my eyes. "Oh, Eileen," is all I can say. Leave it to her to find something so beautiful in grief.

She pats my hand. "Come. Let's sit and talk."

We each pick up a mug, and she leads the way to the cozy corner booth. I slide in next to her and sip the drink, letting its sweetness settle me. "Delicious, what is it?"

She beams at me. "A sugar cookie latte. It's one of the themed days on the town calendar, so I thought we might as well prepare for it."

She pauses, and I wonder if it's my turn to talk.

"So," I start. "I suppose you heard that I drank a little too much and Enzo helped me get back to my cat-sitting house."

"I did," she says with a grin, as if I'm a prized student who just earned an A+. "He's an honorable boy, so I knew you'd come to no harm. You know, the reason I didn't go to the lobster trap tree lighting last night was because I was having a delightful dinner with his grandmother."

Dread sits heavy in the pit of my stomach.

"Oh?"

"Yes, she invited me over to discuss some past business." Sighing, she adds, "I'm afraid this whole banning thing started because of me. Francesca has been holding a grudge over what happened with Enzo's mother. Daniela and I were friendly before she left town, and Francesca was certain I was the one who'd told her to leave."

My eyes widen. "You never would have told her to abandon her children."

"No, of course not," Eileen says, frowning. "And it's unthinkable that she did. Marco wouldn't have fought her for custody. But I *did* tell her to leave him. Enzo's parents weren't a love match, Lucy. It's so important to love the person you marry, because marriage isn't easy." She sips her drink. "Even with my Murray. We made a choice to love each other every day, and to let that love push us past everything else. Because there will always be arguments and grudges, and if you don't let love lead the way, you'll stumble over them."

I lean toward her, riveted. "But they didn't have that?"

Her expression turns sad. "They liked each other well enough in the beginning, but they didn't know each other. You can't truly love someone without knowing their flaws and your own. By the time she left, there was only resentment between them. Those children were so young. Thank goodness they had their grandparents here in town."

I think of little Enzo, left to take care of his siblings and the family business, and I feel a surge of empathy for him. I know as well as anyone what it's like to have to take on too much, too soon. The weight can be crushing.

No, Lucy. You're not supposed to fall for him!

Shoving the thought down as deep as it will go, I ask, "Did you and Daniela stay friends?"

She traces the rim of her mug, her gaze far off. "Murray and I tried to have children for a long time. I went to the Wishing Bridge hundreds of times and begged for them, but it never happened. Then we were told by a doctor that it never would. I couldn't forgive Daniela for leaving those beautiful children behind. Truthfully, I didn't want to forgive her."

"I'm so sorry," I say, reaching for her hand and squeezing it.

"Oh, that's all in the past." She pats my hand. "And I realized that the bridge *did* grant my wishes." She smiles at me, her eyes full of love. "I may not have children of my own, but I have you and Charlie and all the wonderful young people in this town who come to me for advice and some warmth and comfort. It's more than enough, my dear."

But I wonder, suddenly, if it is. Eileen spends so much time worrying about other people. *Loving* us. It seems unconscionable for her to be alone.

"I love you," I say honestly. "I don't know how I would have gotten through this past year without you and Charlie. And I definitely would be struggling more with this season if I didn't have your Advent calendar."

"What was today's challenge?" she asks, smiling slightly.

"To count the number of reindeer decorations I saw on the way to work. Forty-five." I smile back at her. "You always know how to make things fun. I've enjoyed all of my challenges."

"But I failed you with Santa Speed Dating," she says sadly. "I've been fretting about it for days. And I *was* hoping that something glorious would blossom between you and Hudson. It would be such a thing for one of my girls to marry Erica's son."

"I don't think he's my type," I say honestly.

"No, I expect not." She gives me a knowing look that makes me shrink into my seat. "I was really hoping to find you a nice man by Christmas."

I twist my mouth. "Maybe I'll go back to the Wishing Bridge to make another wish."

"The bridge always gives you what you need, Lucy," she says seriously, "especially if you go with an open heart, and most especially at this time of year. But what you need might not be what you think you want. Remember that."

Her words rattle me, but I can't fully process them. Not yet. So I change the subject. "Uh, so Francesca wants to bury the hatchet?"

"She told me all would be forgiven if I help her find life partners for her grandchildren."

Having just taken a sip of my latte, I almost spit it out at her. "All four?"

She smiles. "All four."

"Is there a time limit?"

She releases a sigh. "She'd prefer for it to happen before she leaves this mortal coil. Francesca is very dramatic."

"What did you say?"

"I said yes, of course." She smiles at me, every inch the beauty queen she once was. "There's nothing I enjoy more than a matchmaking challenge. If you want to know the truth, it feels like she gave me a beautiful Christmas present."

"Let me guess," I say, trying to act calm even though my pulse is racing. "You were already going to play matchmaker for all of them anyway?"

She tilts her head, gazing at me with a glint in her eyes. "Would you like to help?"

"I still don't think you should try to find someone for Enzo," I say, my mouth puckering. "He doesn't want to be in a relationship."

"Some people don't know what they want until they've had a taste of it," she says pointedly. "It's like the Wishing Bridge. It may grant you your wishes, but not necessarily in the way you thought it would."

The front door creaks open, and I glance over, half expecting it to be Enzo. But it's Charlie.

Of course it's Charlie. I'm honestly surprised she didn't show up sooner, but the hollows under her eyes suggests she's even more hungover than I am.

She gasps the second she sees me. "You've had sex," she accuses. "I knew it."

"Yes," Eileen says, unable to hide her amusement. "I rather think we were getting to that."

I bury my face in my hands. "I didn't want you to find out like this."

Charlie hurries over to us and pries one of my hands away from my face. "You didn't want us to find out at all."

"That too."

Eileen is beaming at me, and Charlie's watching me with sharp interest. I feel like a slide under a microscope.

"It happened this morning, not last night, right?" Charlie asks. "Because otherwise Enzo's a dead man."

"Definitely this morning. He was…" I sigh, hating the necessity of admitting this, "a perfect gentleman last night."

"Good," Charlie says. "So…tell us more. Tell us *everything*."

"Look, it's no big deal," I say, embarrassed, especially since Eileen is listening with interest. "It's only a physical connection."

Charlie lifts her eyebrows. "I beg to differ. It *is* a big deal. He's the first person you've ever slept with."

Damn it. I didn't think she knew that. I'd sidestepped the topic for years.

"Oh, *really*?" Eileen says with far too much interest.

"It doesn't mean anything," I insist, even though the wrenching feeling in my chest suggests otherwise. "I wanted to get it out of the way, and Enzo offered himself as tribute, and that's all there is to it."

"A lot of people would have offered," Charlie points out. "I suspect a lot of people *have* offered."

I shrug. "The timing was right. Like I said, Enzo isn't looking for anything, and he definitely doesn't tick all the boxes on my mom's checklist. Besides, we barely tolerate each other."

"Remember what I said about that," Eileen interjects, and I realize her pep talk about the beginning of her relationship with Murray was more pointed than I'd thought.

"Besides, it definitely didn't look like you hated each other yesterday," Charlie says. "You were dancing cheek to cheek at the candy shop, and he treated you like you were a ninety-year-old with brittle bones when he swooped in to take care of you last night."

"I don't want to be treated like a ninety-year-old with brittle bones. I want to be treated like a woman capable of making my own decisions."

"You weren't last night," Charlie says. "You were three sheets to the wind." She lifts a hand before I can protest. "So was I, so I'm in no position to judge. But, you know, he was actually pretty cool about everything."

"Because he liked being in control," I say, clutching the edge of the booth like it's a lifeline. That's partially true, but it doesn't feel fair, exactly. He has reasons for seeking out control.

"Remember the story of the Wishing Bridge," Eileen says again, tapping the side of the table.

"I know what you're implying," I say. "You're telling me Enzo might be exactly what I need, and I agree with you. He's exactly what I need *right now*. There's no future, and there shouldn't be. He's an egotistical jerk half the time, and he's desperate to leave Hideaway Harbor."

"Perhaps he simply hasn't realized that he'd like to stay," Eileen says with a sweet smile.

"Can we please talk about something else?" I ask. "I'm begging you. Let's go through your list of single people."

"I've got you covered," Charlie says, lifting up a finger. And she pulls up Eileen's Google doc, which she's shared with both of us, on her phone. "Ooh, I see you've got something cooking for Audrey today?"

I glance at the wall separating our business from Making Whoopie, wondering what Audrey has waiting for her. Audrey's a workaholic, but I can tell she's lonely, and both of us have groaned about the horrors of single life around here.

"Yes," Eileen says, her eyes glittering. "There's a very handsome lawyer in town—"

"Mark Parks?" I ask in horror.

"Oh, no, not him. This young man is a friend of Amanda's, as it happens. We sense some delicious tension between him and Audrey."

"What are they doing today?" I ask.

"A gingerbread house building competition."

"Why aren't we doing that?" Charlie asks. "It sounds fun."

"Have you ever tried to build a gingerbread house?" I ask. "It's not fun. You have to hold the pieces in place forever to get them to stick, and even then, they don't stick. I think those gorgeous houses people make must be made by wizardry."

"But Audrey will kill it," Charlie says, stealing my latte. "She's already a wizard."

I nod, stealing the phone from her to check out the rest of the list. Wren Wilde's on there, with the name Hawthorne next to hers, followed by a question mark. Fredrik, the bookstore owner is also on there. As well as Lumi, the postmistress, and half a dozen other people.

I scroll to the bottom of the list, smile at Eileen, and add three names: Giovanni Cafiero, Nico Cafiero, and Aria Cafiero.

But I don't add the fourth, and Eileen doesn't comment on it. She simply peers at me with a knowing smile.

WHEN I GET BACK to the little turquoise cottage with its weird collection of taxidermied animals, I gasp at the sight of a wrapped package sitting on the doorstep. Its wrapping paper is covered in little leaping cats.

I glance in every direction, as if it's a trap, then carry it inside. Bowie circles around me, demanding pets, which I give him as I examine the tag on the package.

For your cabinet of curiosities. Your landlord should have no problem with this one.

I open it and gape at the perfect, fuzzy little stuffed animal.
A calico cat.
I hug it, and breathe in its scent, because it smells just like him.

CHAPTER 25

ENZO

*I*t's finally Wednesday.

The last couple of days have been busy, full of "wheeling and dealing," as Aria would call it. Audrey at Making Whoopie loves the idea of the cannoli whoopie pie, and we've already come up with a name for it—Take the Gun, Leave the Cannoli. She has a remarkably in-depth menu for her shop, which provides a description for every item available. For the new cannoli, she wrote up a blurb that had my brothers and me laughing:

> *Take the Gun, Leave the Cannoli—criteria-zested vanilla whoopie pie cakes embrace a whipped ricotta-mascarpone filling flecked with mini dark chocolate chips and candied orange. Lightly dusted with powdered sugar and crowned with crushed pistachio.*
>
> *Subtle. Slightly dangerous. Just like your Nonna.*

Portia, who's my new best friend after the taffy pulling demonstration, is all in to provide the Six-Pack Santa taffy, as well as limoncello candy canes. I've been talking with the other shop owners too, doing what I do best.

But my nights have been full of Lucy. The words of her letters have been dancing through my head, along with the memory of her silhouette pirouetting around that Christmas tree.

I want to tell her that she's been writing to *me*.

Now that I know she's Dancing Queen, something has changed for me. I want to be with her, all the way. I want to know everything about her, and I want her to know me fully too.

But she insists she only wants me physically, and if she learns I'm Lobster Stalker, she might stop writing to him. She might also decide it would be best to stop sleeping with me.

So I haven't told her yet.

Instead, I'm determined to earn her good opinion before she learns I'm her anonymous pen pal. I want her to want me to be the man she's been writing to so openly. So I'm trying to think of ways to support her that she won't consider overreaching. Which is why I had a talk with Eileen, who agreed to disengage the "Jingle Bells" doorbell that Lucy finds so aggravating.

Then I texted Lucy yesterday asking if there are any fantasies she'd like help fulfilling.

She wrote back:

> Meet me at the Wishing Bridge at ten.

Honestly, I had plenty of substandard hookups at the Wishing Bridge when I was a teenager, and I'd prefer to have her somewhere comfortable, where I could take my time with her. But it was her fantasy, and I wasn't going to deny her. If sex was all she would take from me, I'd give her as much of it as she wanted.

Still, I didn't want her walking there by herself that late, so I replied:

> Are you still staying at the dead animal place?

> Until tomorrow.

> I'll meet you at the cottage at 9:45. I'd prefer to walk with you.

To my surprise, she didn't object and insist on meeting me at the bridge.

To my elation, she was waiting for me at the door in the skimpy red dress lined with fake white fur that she'd worn on the Santa Speed Dating night, and she had nothing on underneath it.

"Do you think I'm going to be on the naughty list this year?" she asked, her eyes glinting with mirth.

"You will be if I have anything to do with it," I said, guiding her inside.

We didn't make it very far. We had sex against the door, and then she admitted she'd had second thoughts about hooking up under the bridge.

"We'll still go," I said. "And we'll do what most people do out there."

So we made out for half an hour under the bridge, until the tips of our noses were frozen, and then I walked her back to the dead animal house—only to go home and write a letter for her to find when she returned to her apartment in the morning.

It's easier to be open when I know I won't have to look into her eyes and tell her what's in my heart, worrying that she'll decide she doesn't want it.

Dear Dancing Stalker,

Who doesn't like The Golden Girls? My grandmother used to watch it when it first aired, but I wasn't alive to watch it with her. Does that give you a better idea of how old I am?

I can imagine you pulling out your phone and doing the math, or maybe you're the kind of woman who can do that sort of equation in your head. I'll bet you are.

I'd like to know more about you, Dancing Stalker. About what you do and what your dreams are. I already know you love Hideaway Harbor in a way that makes me jealous. Because I don't see it like you do, not anymore, but I think I'd like to. I want to let go of the past and open my eyes to the present.

Here's something else I can tell you about me:

I played Santa Claus for my siblings when I was a kid, because my parents couldn't be bothered to. For years. I got help, but I stayed up late every Christmas Eve, wrapping gifts. I loved it, and I hated it too. Because I knew I shouldn't have to be the one who protected their innocence.

So this week, I'm going to buy presents for the people in my life just because I want to. Not because I have to or because they're expecting it. Although, to be honest, they will NOT be expecting it. I switched to giving gift cards years ago, which made it so easy, but not very much fun.

Your Lobster Stalker

I left the letter at her door last night, wondering if I'd given too much away. Maybe hoping that I had—and that the knowledge of who I am will open her eyes to possibilities, same as it's done for me.

The note's gone when I come back from a day of meetings to pack my bag for Nonna's—making sure to include the book I got my grandmother from the Hard to Find bookstore—but there's no reply waiting for me.

I'm on the way to the Chowder House Rules to pick up dinner for my grandmother and Lucy when my phone buzzes with a text, sent God only knows when, because everything's been coming through on a delay today.

I lift it up while I'm walking. The message is from Giovanni:

You made Lady Lovewatch again.

The text is accompanied by a photo of the article—

Everyone saw L and L together at the lobster trap tree lighting. It was gossiped about almost as much as poor Larry's floppy claw. This author looks forward to watching the holiday hate-off blossom into a holiday lovefest.

I'm not upset about it.
I still don't like people prodding into my business, but I

don't mind if people think there's something between Lucy and me. There *is* something between us, and I'd prefer it if the other men in town saw her as off-limits. As *mine*.

Maybe that's not fair, but that's where my head's at.

Do I know what the future holds?

I'm less certain every day.

I've enjoyed making changes at Hidden Italy, but once those changes have been made, I'll need a new professional challenge.

Still, I don't want to walk away from Lucy.

She and I fit.

I've suspected that for a while now, down deep, and the knowledge that she's Dancing Queen solidifies that. The fact that we've lived in the same building, down the hall from each other, all this time blows my mind.

Of course, I could be wrong about Dancing Queen's identity, but there are a limited number of newcomers to Hideaway Harbor every year, and it can't be a coincidence that she has the same backstory as Lucy. The same heart as Lucy. The same loneliness. The same love for Hideaway Harbor.

A love so profound that it makes me want to see my hometown through her eyes.

That's exactly what I'm trying to do as I wend through the streets, taking in the glowing lights. The cheerful displays. So earnest. *Too* earnest, I usually think. But maybe it's not just about showmanship and competition. Maybe some of it comes from a genuine place, from the joy of making people smile.

Don't get me wrong. I'm not about to put up twinkle lights in my window and invest in a Rudolph bust, but I'm willing to admit that my reaction to Hideaway Harbor looking like the inside of a snow globe every December is more about me than the town. It's about holding onto the past, and how it felt to see all of this and know it wasn't for me. Of knowing the only way my siblings could enjoy it was if I made myself one more person who lied to them.

My thoughts carry me all the way to the restaurant, where I pick up takeout, and then to my grandmother's doorstep. I knock once and then use my key to let myself in. Nonna's hearing has gone the way of her eyesight, not what it used to be.

No one is in the living room, but I hear murmuring from the kitchen.

I'm barely in the door, taking off my shoes and setting them on the rack near the entrance, when Lucy comes around the corner from the kitchen, her eyes narrowing on me.

She's wearing a red sweater that brings out the bright highlights in her riotous curls, and I'm gratified to see a mark on her neck that I put there.

I grin at her. "Lucia."

"I *knew* you had a shoe rack."

"My grandmother has a shoe rack."

She comes closer, a wooden spoon in her hand. Her expression stern, she says, "I told you it would be better if your grandmother and I did this alone."

"And you're welcome to," I say. "But this is where I'm sleeping for the next two nights. Would you turn me out in the cold?"

"You live here?" she asks, lowering the spoon.

"Has the threat of violence ended?" I retort, smiling at her.

"I wasn't going to—" She swallows, collecting herself, and glances back toward the kitchen. My grandmother has started singing lightly beneath her breath—some old Dean Martin song I can't identify. "I brought your grandmother some cookies to replace the ones that got messed up the other day. She offered to show me how she makes her famous thumbprint cookies in addition to the cappuccinos. That's why I'm still here." Her brow creases. "But we actually haven't made it to the cappuccinos yet either."

"You're making cookies with my grandmother, Lucia?" I ask, the thought pleasing me immensely.

"It's not a big deal," she says, looking away. "You weren't supposed to find out."

"Ah, yes," I say, removing my coat and hanging it on the hook by the door, "because you only want my—"

She puts her hand over my mouth forcefully, making me laugh through her splayed fingers. Especially since she looks so earnest, so worried my grandmother might hear me from the other room.

I capture her hand and kiss it, and the look in her eyes becomes warmer. Less worried.

I lower her hand but hold onto it. "I'm glad you're getting along with her."

"You tricked me," she accuses, but without any real heat.

"I wanted to see you," I admit. "And I'd like to make cookies and cappuccinos with you and my nonna. But if you don't want me around, I'll make myself scarce until you leave. You decide, Lucia."

"That doesn't sound like you," she says softly. "Who are you and what have you done with Enzo?"

I smile at her. "You're the one who's doing something to me, so you only have yourself to blame if you're not happy with the results. What'll it be?"

She holds my gaze, and I can feel my heart thumping in my chest. When was I ever this nervous with a woman? It feels like my future hinges on her decision—on something as small as making Christmas cookies, an activity I've never particularly enjoyed.

"You can stay if you help," she decides. "We can come up with a collaboration drink for the Sip and Hidden Italy." My grin must look victorious, because she rolls her eyes. "You didn't win anything, Enzo. Not everything's a competition."

"This one may not be a competition," I say, "but I disagree. I *did* win something." And because my self-control isn't limitless, I lean in to kiss her cheek, her soft skin warm and familiar beneath my lips.

She leans into me for a second, then pulls back and lifts the wooden spoon again. "But no funny business in the kitchen. I don't need your grandmother driving me to a church with a revolver pressed to my temple."

"You think she'd want you to make an honest man of me?" I ask, waggling my eyebrows. I resist the compulsion to grab her ass. Barely.

"Maybe," she says, looking a little embarrassed. I give in to the almost unbearable need to run my fingers down the length of one of her curls.

She shoves my arm, her fingers wrapping around it for a second, like she'd enjoy holding on for a while. She did last night.

"You didn't answer me before. You live here?" she asks again as her hand drops. There's a strange expression in her eyes, and I wonder if she's thinking about that letter I left at her doorstep earlier. Wondering if it was me.

"Only two or three days a week. Giovanni, Nico, and I keep a schedule."

Her gaze warms. "You take care of her."

"Just don't let her hear you saying that," I say with a grin. "But yes. She took care of us when we needed her, and we do the same. You take care of family." I give her a sidelong glance. "Whatever kind of family you have."

She nods. "Thank you for that."

We walk into the kitchen together, not holding hands, but our sides brushing slightly—and I like having her here, in this space that belongs to me and mine.

"About time," Nonna says as we walk in. Her brow furrows when she sees the takeout bag I'm carrying. "Nico cooks when he stays over."

"Nico can cook." I lean in to kiss her wrinkled cheek. "And the town calendar informs me it's Clam Chowder and Cornbread Day. We're Hidies. We couldn't possibly miss Clam Chowder Day."

"Oh, I don't want to interrupt your dinner," Lucy says, setting the wooden spoon down next to a mixing bowl full of dough that smells like butter and brown sugar.

"You won't be," I say as I set the bag down on the kitchen island. "I got you some vegetable chowder."

She throws me a mutinous look before murmuring a tight "thank you" for my grandmother's benefit, but I meant what I said earlier. If she'd told me to give them space, I would have. I'm trying to learn, like Giovanni advised me to do. That's also why I didn't tuck the cell phone I got her underneath the stuffed calico cat the way I'd wanted to.

"We eat before we finish baking," Nonna Francesca decrees. "And we'll make our cappuccino with dessert tonight."

"There's no use arguing," I say, smiling at Lucy. "The decree has been issued. Would you help me set the table?"

Nonna Francesca always uses her own plates, takeout or not—one of her eccentricities all of us are very accustomed to.

"Of course," Lucy says with a beatific smile.

I lead the way into the dining room, then to the old cabinet where Nonna keeps the ceramic bowls she bought in Tuscany on her last trip to the "old country" with my grandfather.

The silverware and napkins are in drawers beneath it.

"You planned this," Lucy complains, although she doesn't seem overly upset.

"Plan for the best, prepare for the worst."

Her eyebrows wing up as she accepts the silverware from me, her hand lingering over mine. "And what would the worst be?" she asks, looking up into my eyes. "If I sent you to your room like a bad boy?"

Blood immediately rushes south to my cock, not something

I'm comfortable with in my grandmother's house. Shaking my head, I say, "Oh, you like driving me crazy, don't you, Lucia?"

There's a teasing glint in her eyes as she pulls her hand away from mine. "I think that's what people call a shared interest."

"Ah, and everyone says shared interests are the bedrock of a good relationship," I say.

Her mouth parts with shock, and my grandmother enters the room, shaking her head. Her eyes are glittering, though, and I wonder how much she's picked up on. Maybe nothing; maybe everything. If she's trying to get Eileen to play match-maker for me, it's very possible the two of them are trading secrets.

Again, I'm surprised by how little this bothers me.

"You young people, always so slow," Nonna Francesca says, but it's a half-hearted complaint.

"Dinner is served," I tell her, making a grandiose gesture to the bag of takeout, probably tepid now.

CHAPTER 26

LUCY

He's *so* good to her. Why does he have to be so good to her?

Enzo listens to his grandmother while she tells stories he's probably heard countless times. Then he tells us about what he's been doing for Hidden Italy, giving credit for his plans to me—probably because he likes seeing a scowl on my face.

When we've finished eating the chowder and cornbread, he clears the dishes—all while she tells him it's unnecessary and she's still very capable of looking after herself.

"He's such a good boy," Mrs. Cafiero says with a note of pride once he's in the kitchen with the dirty dishes.

Enzo had insisted on personally attending to the dishes before we finish making dessert. The suspicious part of me wonders if he wanted his grandmother to sing his praises, the way any loving grandmother would. Maybe that's true, but there's no denying the love in her tired brown eyes.

"He's *always* been a good boy," she continues. "I counted on him too much when he was young. We all did." She shrugs. "You know about his mother leaving, of course."

I nod, feeling self-conscious and guilty. In the half hour I spent here before Enzo arrived with his duffel bag, she didn't once mention her daughter-in-law. I certainly didn't bring her up either. We discussed Hideaway Harbor, and she asked me about my family, tsk-tsking when I told her that I didn't have much of one anymore.

"Eileen's my family," I'd said, feeling defensive, the same way I would respond whenever anyone brought up arguments about blood or genetics. "And my friend Charlie."

To my surprise, she'd nodded staunchly. "Good. I am sorry about your mother, though. I will light a candle for her at church."

It's hard to reconcile this woman with the angry shop owner who put up that BANNED flyer months ago. But I remember what Enzo said about her hot temper and her struggle to stay in the present.

She's a tough woman. Difficult. But she's also devoted and loyal. Capable of kindness. The Cafiero family is full of people so complicated, a guidebook should be issued for each of them.

Mrs. Cafiero is watching me now, waiting for a response regarding Enzo's mother.

"I shouldn't have brought her up the other day," I say haltingly. "I wouldn't have said anything if I'd known it would upset you."

"*Madonne*, that's not what upset me. It was the thought of my boy leaving again. As if I could hope to forget that woman. Who could leave four young children like that? My son wasn't a good father or husband, anyone will tell you that, but at least he didn't leave."

I glance at the doorway leading into the kitchen. Is Enzo listening? Do I want him to be?

She follows my gaze to the kitchen and sighs. "He was always strong, my Enzo. But we relied on him too much. Now, he doesn't know how to turn it off. Always working. Always scheming." A surprisingly mischievous glint appears in her eyes. "You tell Eileen this. He needs a woman who'll remind him to have fun. A woman who will *challenge* him. Not like that Rachelle, always asking for this or that. Never satisfied. No. Not for my Lorenzo."

I clear my throat, feeling like a butterfly pinned in a box. "Uh. I'll tell her."

"You do that, *cara*," she says, her expression almost…smug. "Now, come. You'll learn the art of cappuccino, and we'll finish those cookies."

I help her out of her chair without asking, and we walk into the kitchen together.

Enzo's already taken out the ingredients for the cappuccinos. He watches us eagerly, his eyes taking in everything.

Confusion twists me up inside. What does he want? He made it very clear that he hates Hideaway Harbor, and he also said he was looking for no-strings sex. But he left me that adorable stuffed cat, and now we're making dessert with his grandmother. No part of this scenario feels stringless. I can practically feel a web of connectivity entangling us, pulling us closer together—and a big part of me wants to let it happen, even though I know Enzo isn't the sort of man I'm supposed to want.

Francesca Cafiero steps forward with purpose and stops in front of her espresso machine. "Watch very carefully," she says in her firm tone. "I only do this once, and then *you* do it."

"WHAT ABOUT THE Italian Stallion for a name?" I ask, sipping the almond cappuccino we settled on as the featured drink for Hidden Italy's collaboration with the Sip.

Enzo and I are sitting side by side in the swing on his grandmother's enclosed front porch, next to a space heater. It's peaceful out here, and Christmas lights twinkle from the houses surrounding hers.

His grandmother excused herself after teaching us the "art" of cappuccino. I was expecting some big secret that only Italian or Italian American people know, but honestly, it wasn't much different from what we do at the café. I'm beginning to think I got hosed by both of them, and that Mrs. Cafiero asked me to come over for an entirely different reason.

Like maybe she *wants* me to be with Enzo.

Again, it would have seemed impossible weeks ago, but she saw me in that scarf, and I know she's been talking to Eileen…

The possibility intrigues me, but I'm conflicted. As if someone cleaved me in half, and my heart is trying to choose a side.

"Yes," he says, rocking the swing with his heel. "There's nothing I love more than a stereotype."

Rolling my eyes, I nudge his arm. "So *you* come up with something. But it has to have a romantic name."

He raises his eyebrows. "Calling it the Italian Stallion is romantic?"

"That's what people used to call Sylvester Stallone. My mom had a huge crush on him back in the day."

He laughs. "Do you know why they called him that?"

"Because he's an attractive Italian guy. Isn't it obvious?"

His perfect eyebrows wing higher, and I trace the lines of them before I can stop myself.

The smile on his face says he's pretty pleased with himself, but I don't regret it. I don't regret last night either. Or Sunday morning.

But you might regret it, a voice in my head whispers. *You might regret all of it.*

"Would you like me to be the one who tells you?" he asks. "Or would you prefer to be embarrassed by your search engine?"

"What are you talking about?" I scoff.

"The name's from a porno he starred in."

"No, it's not. You're messing with me."

He shrugs. "If you want to name our cappuccino after a porno, I'm all for it. Then even the people who don't read Lady Lovewatch will know exactly how it is between us."

I give him another shove, and he wraps his arm around me.

I don't try to remove it, because I'm too busy laughing. "You're saying my mom watched a porno with Sylvester Stallone in it?"

"I'm guessing she did, yes. Don't shoot the messenger."

I sink back into his arm, wanting more of his warmth. "Actually, I'm kind of glad to hear that. I hope she had fun. I hope she had all the experiences she wanted to have while she could still have them."

He looks down at me, his eyes warm and appreciative, and I feel a pulse of such powerful longing in my heart that it almost makes me gasp.

"She was lucky to have you," he says, running his fingers across my cheekbone.

"We were lucky to have each other."

He nods. "Of course. I feel the same way about my grand-mother. I know I said this earlier, but I'm glad the two of you get along. It means a lot to me."

"She still terrifies me."

A smile crosses his face. "She terrifies me too."

We rock for a moment, his arm still wrapped around me, and the moment is so pleasant, so purely enjoyable it feels stolen.

"You lived in Asheville before," he says after a while. "I've been there. It's a beautiful little city."

I don't ask how he knows where I'm from. Probably the same way I found out about his mother.

"I couldn't stay," I say, my throat tight. "Everything back home reminded me of losing my mom."

"I remember what you said about her illness the other night," he says. "I'm sorry for your loss."

I nod. "Thank you. It's been tough. I'm sure it sounds stupid, but one of the hardest parts is living alone. I never have before. I keep waking up at night to check on her, only to remember that I'm by myself. There's no one to check on, no one to talk to. Just me. That's why I wanted a cat." I shrug, trying to act like it's no big deal. Like the cavernous emptiness of the apartment doesn't feel like it's swallowing me in every time I walk in. Those letters from my neighbor have helped. There was one waiting for me when I stopped by the apartment earlier, but I haven't opened it yet. A part of me didn't want to. I've been picking at that feeling for the last several hours, trying to understand it, but it's only now, sitting next to Enzo, that I really get it.

I'm not afraid my neighbor's a geriatric old man; I'm afraid he's not. I'm afraid he'll be everything my mother wanted for me in a man—because I'd rather see where this goes with Enzo than pursue Mr. Perfect.

Enzo shocks me by weaving his fingers through mine. "You're not alone, Lucia. Eileen would do anything for you, and so would your friend, Charlie. She threatened me with physical harm if anything happened to you the other night."

"There's been a lot of that going around," I mumble.

"You belong in this place. More than I do."

It's everything I wanted him to say a couple of weeks ago, but hearing it now, it feels wrong.

Because I want him to belong here too.

"Hideaway Harbor has room for anyone who wants to be here," I say.

"Realistically, no, it does not. But it's a nice sentiment," he says with a smile. Then, as if he'd like to move the conversation along, he says, "Can I see your app?"

"My project for class?"

"Yes, but I'd also like to see the other one. The reason you're taking the classes. You told me a little about it the other night."

"I said a lot of things," I tell him wryly, embarrassed. I've barely told anyone about my idea other than the professors I'm working with at the school and Charlie.

"This one made more of an impact than what you said about cheese curls. You told me it was for caregivers."

"Yeah," I say, feeling a swell of nerves. I don't know much about what Enzo used to do, other than that he's a successful businessman. So he'd probably know whether or not it's a stupid idea. Knowing him, he might very well tell me if it is. "It's just…I spent all those years with my mom, when she was sick, and it occurred to me that there should be one app that supports caregivers by reminding them about things like an exercise schedule and medicines, but also helps them take care of themselves. That's always the hardest part. Remembering to eat. To wash your hair. To read a book or do something else for yourself." I shrug self-consciously. "Anyway, there are probably a million different alternatives out there, but I have a unique idea for how to structure it, and I wanted to learn how to do it. I like teaching myself new things. It makes life more interesting."

"I'd like to see it," he says again, his forehead furrowing. "It's a good idea."

We rock a little more as I consider his offer. "CareWise is mostly at the idea stage. That's why I'm trying to develop my skills. But I built the app for the town shops in a similar way."

"You only really need for it to be at the idea stage," he says, raising his eyebrows. "If it's a good idea, you can hire other people to build it and oversee their work to make sure it's what you want. But you'll have to establish an office outside of Hideaway sooner rather than later. The internet's not consistent enough here."

"I've thought about that, but it wouldn't need to be far away. There are people who commute."

He nods. "You wouldn't have to go all the way to Bangor, just away from the mountains. Might be hard during the winter, but you could make it work."

I can only smile at him. "Already solving all my problems and setting up my fictional office. That's a very Enzo way of doing things."

"And insisting on doing everything yourself sounds like *your* way of doing things. You were your mother's caregiver for years, but you don't need to take care of everything yourself. You can delegate."

My smile stretches wide. "Is this your way of letting me know other people can do things for me?"

"Yes."

I give him a searching look, contemplating a nagging thought. "Are you responsible for taking care of the 'Jingle Bells' doorbell for me?"

"That depends. Do you consider it another instance of overreach?"

I give a theatrical shudder. "No. I'm too grateful."

"Then yes. Perhaps I sent it to sleep with the fishes. Or had a friendly adult conversation with Eileen about it." He hesitates before saying, "I'm interested in this app. It may be useful for my brothers and me, taking care of Nonna Francesca. I'll help you."

I turn toward him in disbelief. "You want to help me with CareWise?"

"Is that so hard to believe?"

"Yes, actually."

He clutches his chest dramatically. "You wound me, Lucia. But if you need it to be a bargain, we'll make one. Those

Advent calendar challenges you get from Eileen every day…I'd like to work on them with you. If you'll let me do that, I'll help with your app."

I narrow my gaze at him, searching for his angle, almost wanting to find it. Because I'm afraid to believe he might mean it. "Not a very good bargain for you. Both of those things would both benefit me."

"I'm glad to hear you enjoy my company so much," he says with a smile, but it falters slightly. "I want to see what you see when you look at Hideaway Harbor. I want to know if I still can."

This shakes me to my core.

I want to believe him. I want to think this strange relationship between us can grow and change—that we can too. But I'm so afraid to feel things for a man who already has one foot out the door.

"It's not really in keeping with the frenemies-with-benefits agreement," I say at last. I'm not sure which of us moved to face the other—maybe both—but only inches separate our mouths now. His face looks more intense, cast in shadow, and I feel my pulse pick up.

"Maybe I'm sick of following the rules," he says, his gaze lowering to my mouth.

He leans in slightly, and I feel myself doing the same, but I stop with a couple of inches still left between our lips. "You've never liked following rules. You make them your own."

"Yes," he says, the words practically whispered into my mouth. "And it just so happens I'd like to change your rule."

"Oh?" I say, my lips even nearer to his.

Anyone walking past could see us in here, nearly kissing, but the thought doesn't make me retreat.

"Yes. You called us frenemies with benefits. Lucia, I'm not sure whether you've realized this, but that implies we're friends *and* enemies. Friends spend time together. They don't just—"

I press my finger over his lips and glance through the front window, worried that Nonna Francesca didn't go upstairs like she said and is spying. Or maybe she has crazy sonar hearing.

He sucks my finger into his mouth, and I gasp at the unexpected sensation. "*Enzo.*"

"Although I have no problem fucking you whenever you want either."

"You're bad," I say.

He presses his forehead to mine. "Yes. But I still think the Italian Stallion is a terrible name. Let's call our cappuccino the Frenemy."

"Not romantic enough. It needs to be romantic."

"Feels pretty romantic to me," he says, edging close enough that I can feel him forming the words.

Then he leans in and kisses me there, on his grandmother's swing, on the front porch of her house, and I can feel the walls surrounding my heart crack for him.

We make out on his grandmother's porch like teenagers, pausing every now and then to talk, until she cracks open the door who-knows-how-long later.

"Stop this nonsense and come inside to fix my television. I need to watch my programs."

I'm mortified, but I don't miss the small, satisfied smile on her face.

After I return to my own place later that night, I pull out the letter from my neighbor. My plan was to open it when I got home, but I don't. I keep it in its envelope beside my bed.

CHAPTER 27

ENZO

I smile when I see the whiteboard sign outside Love at First Sip. "The Frenemy" is written on it with a green Sharpie, perhaps because I still have Lucia's red one—along with the promise that I can use it to write on her face at a time of my choosing.

Beneath it is scrawled,

You decide if you love it or hate it, and enter your vote!

Lucia has an eye for marketing, it seems. Now I'm even more interested in seeing her plans for the app.

I hadn't planned on going into the café until later, but I push through the door of the Sip as if gravity is indeed messed up and it's Lucy who changed the laws.

I escorted her home last night—to the door I've left all those notes at—and she told me she'd consider my offer. And also that we shouldn't sleep together again until we've renegotiated our rules.

I almost told her that I was Lobster Stalker. I wanted to tell her.

But I'm still worried she might be disappointed...or, worse, that she might shut me out entirely.

Eileen is behind the counter of the café, but there's no sign of Lucy.

"Oh, do come in," she says cheerfully, with a broad smile. "I'll make you a Frenemy."

There's only one other customer—the old-timer who's been here on every other occasion I've come in. I consider my options, then settle on staying and let the door shut behind me.

"Where's Lucy?" I let myself ask.

"At home working," Eileen says. "She has the next two days off to finish her online classes. But she sent me the recipe for your special drink, and I just had to put it on the menu today." She considers me shrewdly before she starts making my drink, humming under her breath.

"It's too sweet," the old-timer mutters.

Eileen gives him the kind of cross look I didn't think she had in her, then continues working with the machines. "I've heard all about your plans for cross-promotion, of course," she tells me. "Lovely Audrey next door told me about the whoopie pie, and I've spoken with Portia about the candy. It's an *inspired* idea. I hope this means you're considering staying in Hideaway Harbor, Enzo. It would mean so much to all of us."

I scratch the back of my neck. "That depends..."

Her gaze lifts to mine, piercing. "On my young friend?"

"Yes," I admit, figuring I might as well go for honesty. I love my family, but if I stay, it'll be because of Lucy. "But she doesn't seem inclined to take me seriously. I guess you can say I've gotten in my own way."

She pauses, a smile spreading across her face. I feel a trap closing around me, but if she wants to set me up with Lucy, we have complementary goals.

"Oh, Enzo, I'm so pleased. I knew you were much too honorable to trifle with her heart."

"I don't know about that," I say, rubbing my chest. Feeling like a bit of an asshole for the way I've pursued Lucy.

"I gave you an opening, you know," she says with a grin. "Erica and I did. When she texted me about your auction, I asked her to bid on you for Lucy."

"Lucy told me about that last night. She said Erica made a mistake," I say, my pulse speeding up.

"Erica and I never make mistakes. Now, I *will* admit we would have been equally happy had she fallen in love with Hudson, but that was never meant to be. There's no fire there."

"Maybe because his job is to put out fires," I say, still feeling a little salty about Hudson. Ridiculous, obviously, but there it is. I'm annoyed at any man who's ever held her hand.

"Oh, aren't you funny," she says, then finishes making the cappuccino. Two cappuccinos, I realize, when she pours them into two to-go cups. "Well, you'll bring her this cappuccino, of course, and perhaps you'll go next door to ask Audrey for one of the test whoopie pies she's been working on. But you'll need to do more than that to charm our girl. My dear Lucy will want to know you're earnest about exploring Hideaway Harbor's magic with her."

"She told you about that, did she?" I ask, embarrassed.

"Of course, she tells me everything."

Jesus, let's hope not.

"This weekend, you have the perfect opportunity to show her you mean business. I'll give her both days off, of course. There's the Santa Fun Run, caroling in the town square, and I heard a certain famous actor will be roaming around town."

"Amanda Willis."

"No, Brody King," she says, her eyes practically sparkling with expectation.

I'm guessing I don't give her the reaction she's looking for, but honestly, I have no idea who he is and care even less. Still, maybe Lucy would be into all the festivities, so I shrug. "Okay."

"And on Sunday, I know Lucy signed up to read stories to the children at the library. You can read with her."

The thought makes the back of my neck itch again. It reminds me a little too much of reading stories like that to my brothers and sister when I was younger. Trying to keep their excitement alive, though mine had died in the process.

"Maybe," I hedge.

"Then there's the woolen sock race that afternoon."

I nearly swear, but catch myself. "That's a lot of activities. Has anyone ever considered relaxing over the holidays?"

"Oh no," she says after handing the cups over. "We have the rest of the year to relax." She snaps her fingers just as I'm taking a sip of my drink. "Make sure you ask her about her vagina. Women love it when men take an interest in their hobbies."

I choke on the cappuccino.

"You've killed the boy," the old-timer remarks from his table.

"He's perfectly fine, Wayne," she grouses. "Maybe you can even come to our next Crochet Club meeting, Enzo. We don't only crochet vaginas."

"Yeah, no thanks," I say, relieved her advice was about yarn. Then I lift the cups. "Thank you for these, and for the advice. Can I pay you?"

"Don't you dare."

"Not a great way to run a business, Eileen," Wayne says.

The two of them start bickering as I head for the door, and I'm surprised to find myself smiling.

There's something about them that reminds me of Lucy and me.

But I pause on the threshold and turn back. Eileen and Wayne are in between verbal jabs, giving me an opening to ask something that's been on my mind lately. "Eileen, are you Lady Lovewatch?"

She laughs. "Why, of course not."

"You think she'd admit it if she were?" Wayne asks with a grunt.

"Well, no, I suppose I wouldn't," Eileen says, frowning, "but it isn't me, all the same. I'm no more her than I'm the Hideaway Elf."

I wouldn't be surprised if she were both, but I just nod and leave the Sip.

I head next door, where Audrey gives me a whole box of whoopie pies.

A sense of purpose pounds in my chest. I'm going to show Lucy I mean business. But as I'm passing the stairway leading down to Hidden Italy, I hear my brother calling my name.

It's Giovanni, standing in front of the door. "You got breakfast, and you're holding out on me?"

Giovanni and I have discussed the developments with Lucy —loosely, because there's no way I'd speak disrespectfully about her—and his advice has stayed consistent. Stop being a putz and show her you're interested.

I also told him more about the situation involving my job. Because he was right—he deserved for me to stop treating him like I was his problem solver and just be his brother.

"I'll be back," I say, feeling a powerful need to get to Lucy, as if a cord is tugging me back to the apartment building.

"Somebody called for you," he says, giving me a searching look. "Said they couldn't get through to your cell phone."

"Shocking," I say with a laugh. "I'll call them when I get back."

"They said it was urgent. Something about business, and it was a New York number, Enzo."

The hair on the back of my neck stands on end. New York. *Business.* Maybe it's nothing. Maybe I left a framed photo of my family in my office, and they're offering to give it back before they throw it in the bin. But I'm starting to trust my instincts again, and my instincts are telling me this call is significant in some way.

Still, I say, "Can't be too urgent if it's a call from New York. I've got more important things to do."

"Yeah, you do," he says with a cheesy smile. "Damn straight."

CHAPTER 28

LUCY

I turn Lobster Stalker's letter over in my hands. This one's in a sealed envelope, and I trace the seam with my fingers.

I should open it.

Even if I'm not interested in Lobster Stalker, he's become a friend. It would be cruel and shitty to not even read his letter, *especially* if he's a sweet, lonely old man living down the hall. There's also a possibility that I've barely allowed myself to consider...

Enzo mentioned the Lobster Scouts and went to the lobster trap tree lighting. It's possible it was his silhouette I saw on the street outside the building, his letters I've been reading...

So I have to open it for many reasons.

I'm definitely going to.

Just after I tweak my image carousels for each of the shops in my app.

There's a knock on my door, and I startle before getting to my feet. It must be Charlie. Eileen's at the Sip, but Charlie was commissioned to do an oil painting of a German shepherd chasing a running gingerbread cookie, and she has to finish before Christmas. Charlie has always procrastinated on deadlines, ever since we were teenagers, and I can easily imagine her visiting me as an excuse to avoid working.

But when I look through the peephole I gasp.

"Uh, just a second," I say, because it's Enzo, and I'm wearing a huge billowy T-shirt and exercise shorts. Worse, I have coffee breath.

Then I shake my head at my own nonsense and open the door. Because I won't change myself to try to impress him. If he genuinely wants to date me, he's going to realize sooner or later that when I get lost in my computer in the mornings, I look like this.

"*Bellissima,*" he says.

"Please." I cross my arms over my chest. "I'm perfectly aware of what I look like right now."

"Obviously not," he replies with a shrug.

Then I catch sight of the to-go cups and bakery box. "You brought breakfast?"

"I had to convince you to let me in somehow," he says, a twinkle in his eyes.

I step aside and allow him entry, marveling at having him here in my space. He left me at my door last night, but I didn't invite him in. I'd felt too raw at the idea of it.

He walks in, looking around curiously, and then sets the box and cups on the small table in the combined dining and living room.

"So this is where Lucia lives," he says as I close the door behind him.

I grin at him. "And now you're trapped inside. You may never be allowed to leave."

"Is that meant to scare me?"

"You should be scared. For all you know, I was lying, and I have a bathroom stuffed with taxidermied animals."

"That's a risk I'm willing to take," he says, taking a step

toward me. I take a step toward him too, pulled by a force I can't see and can only feel.

We stop inches from each other, close enough that I can feel the cold he brought in from outside.

"Are you going to take your coat off?"

"Are you going to take your shirt off?" he asks with a curl of his lips.

"For all you know, I'm very busy."

He watches me for another loaded second and then takes off his coat and hangs it on the back of one of the chairs at the table. "I know you're very busy. Eileen told me."

"Which explains the coffee cups, not your presence."

"So I thought I'd bring you some coffee and breakfast. It seemed only right for us to drink our Frenemies together."

My heart quakes at this bit of sweetness—and at the thought of him talking with Eileen. I don't mean to, but I reach up and trace the collar of his sweater. "Thank you for coming. I wanted to try one of them."

"They're awful," he says with a teasing grin. "Much sweeter than ours. Nonna Francesca will be pleased that her cappuccinos remain undefeated."

"And the box?" I ask, edging even closer, my shirt brushing off his sweater.

"The whoopie pies Audrey is making for Hidden Italy. I thought you'd want a taste."

"You say that like it's dirty talk," I tell him, my own voice lower and throatier than usual.

"It can be," he says, angling his head for a better look at me. "But that's not why I'm here. I came to bring you breakfast and to look at what you're working on, if you'll let me."

He surprises me by smiling sheepishly. "No, that's not entirely true. I came over because I wanted to see you."

"You're being disarmingly honest with me today," I say,

taking hold of the collar of his sweater and pulling him a little closer. "It's making me very suspicious."

"What was your challenge from Eileen today?"

I hesitate, knowing what he'll say. "*Do something unexpected.* It's very vague."

"Perfect," he says with a grin. "Do you want to do the Santa Fun Run with me on Saturday? And caroling? My brother Nico's getting immortalized in ice, too, so we won't want to miss seeing that."

I force a laugh. "You don't want to do all of that, Enzo, and you don't need to. You've already gotten into my pants, and you can get into them again right now if you play your cards right."

"I don't want to play cards this time," he says. "And no, I'd never, in a million years, go caroling by myself, but I think I'd like to do it with you. Something tells me you sing like an angel."

My heart thumps hard in my chest. "I'm extremely tone-deaf."

"Who says angels aren't?"

A smile tries to form on my mouth. "I also run very slowly."

"But I'll bet you do it with determination, don't you?"

"I do," I say, feeling heat in my eyes, which is ridiculous. I don't cry easily, especially not over someone offering to do holiday activities with me. But it feels like he's offering more than that.

"Then we'll run together, Lucia."

"You probably run like the wind."

He grins. "Thank you for the vote of confidence, and yes, I do. But I'd still prefer to run with you. We can go for broke and run in the woolen sock race on Sunday too. I hoped you might allow me to read to the kids at the library with you too. Eileen told me you'd signed up."

That's it. That's the moment I feel the last of those cracked walls falling away from my heart.

I lean in and kiss him, tasting the Frenemy cappuccino on his lips. He's delicious, but I'm conflicted. Because I'm doing exactly what I'd promised myself never to do. I'm letting him matter, and he's going to leave me...

Men like that always leave, Lucy.

I pull back, swallowing hard. "We can't do this. You're going back to New York."

"Is that a command?"

"It's a statement of reality. Besides, you wanted a no-strings arrangement that wouldn't land you in Lady Lovewatch, and we've already been in there twice."

"So you've seen the new one," he says. "I asked Eileen if she was the author, but she claims it isn't her. It's another mystery of Hideaway Harbor, I guess, just like our elf."

"You're not upset that we're in the column again?" I ask in disbelief.

"No, it turns out I like having my name linked to yours." He pauses, eyes on mine. "I don't know if I'm staying. I don't know if I have it in me to stay, after everything. But I want to explore the possibility. I *definitely* want to explore what's happening between us."

"Are we really doing the fun run?"

"Yes, unfortunately," he says, his brown eyes full of humor. "We're doing all of it. I won't feel like I've proven my sincerity to you until I've done every awful holiday activity Hideaway Harbor has to offer."

"Charlie and Lars are going," I say, watching him for a reaction. He'll need to spend time around Lars if we're going to try legitimately dating. He'll have to be kind.

"I promise not to make a single death threat." He grins, plenty of humor in his expression. "I have no problem with Lars. Aria is living in paradise. I'll buy him a drink, slap him on the back a little too hard, and we'll be good with each other, you watch."

"Okay," I say, my heart beating fast. "We're doing it."

"We're doing it," he confirms. "Together. Now, will you please show me what you're working on?"

"In a minute," I say, then take him by the hand and lead him to my bed. "I have other plans for you first."

CHAPTER 29

ENZO

I see the sealed letter on her windowsill, propped up.

She hasn't opened it. Why hasn't she opened it?

Even though her mouth is on me, her hand working at my belt buckle, I acknowledge to myself that it's time to tell her everything. If I keep the truth from her any longer, she might see it as another manipulation.

So I pull back and point to it. "It looks like you have a letter to read."

She gives me an incredulous look. "You seriously want me to stop taking your pants off so I can catch up on my correspondence?"

I swear under my breath, because I'm already straining to be inside her. That's what I need, but the next time we enjoy each other, I want it to be on an even playing field.

"Yes," I say, my voice almost sulky.

Her eyebrows wing up, and she regards me with wide eyes as she releases my belt. "Enzo…"

I nod to her. "Read the letter, Lucia."

She picks up the envelope and tears into it, eager enough

that it almost rips in half. My Lucia is no wilting flower. She tears into life like this. Into *me* like this.

A feeling of apprehension grips me as she starts reading. I want to take off my shoes but don't feel like I should until she finishes.

I stick my hand into my pocket, finding the red Sharpie I've been carrying around, just in case, and fiddle with the cap.

Finally, she sets the letter on her lap and looks at me, her eyes swimming with emotion. "It's you."

I take the Sharpie out of my pocket and step over to her, claim her trembling hand and draw a heart on it, with *DQ and LS* inside.

"I've only known for a few days," I say. "The first time I saw you through your apartment window, it filled me with joy. I wasn't happy to be back in Hideaway, Lucia. I felt like a failure. But I looked up and saw you dancing around that tree. I could only see your silhouette, but it changed my night."

Her lips part as she stares down at her hand. Then she looks up and meets my eyes. "You left your job because you wouldn't fire those people."

I smile at her. "You inspired me to send that brief to my boss's boss. I doubt it will do any good, but it made me feel less powerless. Thank you for that." I nod to the letter that's still on her lap. "And for writing to me. Sometimes it's hard for me to say what I'm feeling out loud. When I was younger, I was always told a man shouldn't share his feelings. My grandparents were wonderful, but they could be very old-school about such things. Writing is an easier way to share."

She stands, letting the letter drop to the floor. "You were Santa Claus for your brothers and sister."

"My grandparents helped," he says, "but yes. I did it until Giovanni and Nico found out. Then we kept it up for Aria for a few years."

Her eyes are brimming with tears, and my heart is pounding. She could still turn me out. She could decide I'm still not a man she could open her heart to.

She places her palms against my shirt, the heat of her searing me down to my soul. "Why didn't you tell me when you first figured it out?"

"You'd told me you only wanted this relationship to be physical. I was afraid you'd decide it crossed the boundaries of our agreement. I didn't want to stop writing to you."

"Don't," she says, getting up on her toes now, her lips near mine. "Keep writing to me, Enzo."

"Should I leave and write you a letter?" I say to her lips. "Should I prop it on your doorway?"

"What would it say?"

"It would say that I want you to be mine, and I don't care if Lady Lovewatch writes a book about us."

She closes the inches' worth of distance between us and kisses me, slow and deep, and I kiss her back the same way, pouring my feelings into it. My need for her. My fear. *Everything*.

Then I slowly undress her, kissing her body after I remove each item of clothing, glorying in the sight of her bare for me, her hair loose across her shoulders now—and then she surprises me by insisting it's her turn to undress me.

After I get my boots off, she very deliberately gets on her knees before me, as I've done with her a few times now, and unzips my pants. My cock instantly gets harder, which should be impossible, then even harder when she pushes down my pants and boxer briefs and runs her tongue around the tip, her eyes focused on mine. Teasing me.

Then she takes me in, grazing her teeth just the slightest bit over me—the sensation ungodly good. Groaning, I spear my hand through her hair, needing an anchor to her.

She pulls back and then reaches around and grips my ass as she bobs down again, taking me in deeper. Again and again. It nearly brings me to my knees. She looks up at me as she licks a line of pure pleasure down my dick before engulfing it with her mouth again. The small of my back is tingling with the need to come, because I have as much control as a teenager when I'm with her.

I tug slightly on her hair, pulling her back, because I'm not going to come in her mouth. No way. I have other needs.

"I want to be inside of you," I say. "I need to come inside you."

Caveman brain, maybe, but I want to claim her as mine.

"Good," she says, her eyes shining, "because I was really hoping you'd fuck me under the tree you saw me dance around that night."

I'm going to last maybe five minutes.

She smiles at me, her grin wicked. "And I have some extra garland in the closet. I think it's your turn to get tied up."

Usually, I don't like giving up control. Never have, never will, probably. But I press my wrists together and present them to her. "Do your worst."

She saunters over to the closet and pulls out a strand of bright gold garland, which she ties around my wrists, so loosely I could easily escape it even if I weren't a Lobster Scout.

"Surely you can do better than that," I challenge.

She does it again, putting some real muscle in it this time.

"That's my girl."

She disappears into her bedroom and returns with a condom, then leads me by my bound hands to the tree, holding the ends of the garland. I lie down on the plaid tree skirt, then reel her to me, using the garland still in her hands. She laughs as she tumbles onto me, the little lights twinkling above us, making the ornaments sparkle.

"You're at my mercy," she says, sitting up on top of me. Her hair hangs over her breasts, hiding them from me. I brush it to the side with my bound hands, revealing her beautiful pink budded nipples.

"Do you have any mercy for me?" I ask.

"As it happens, I do," she says, opening the foil packet and sliding the condom over me, her hand a delicious tease.

"Touch yourself for me," I tell her, overcome by her. "And be thorough about it."

"Your bossiness is finally taking a turn I appreciate," she says, her eyes bright as she reaches between us, her fingers rubbing and then sliding into her slick heat. I'm on the verge of losing my mind as I watch the motions of her hand and take in the little sounds she's making, the way her head tips back with pleasure. I need to be a part of her pleasure—if that's selfish, so be it—so I lift myself up enough to suck on one perfect nipple. My head collides with a lower branch on the tree, flooding my senses with pine, but it's worth it, and I immediately do it again.

She bucks against me, grinding her body against mine, and I do what's natural and beg.

"Please," I say. "I need to be inside you."

She smiles down at me. "I like hearing you say please."

She pushes my bound arms over my head, her small hands rendering me powerless even though I could so easily get up. And then she sinks down onto me, bringing me instantly to the edge of bliss.

She lowers her head and kisses me as she takes me in to the hilt. Her movements are a little uncertain at first—she's still getting used to this dance, to having control over me. But she likes it, because soon she's moving more quickly, her breath coming in pants. Mine is being expelled in groans. She feels so perfect, as if we were made to come together.

"I'm close, Enzo," she says in my ear, her hands still holding mine down. I could break free with no effort whatsoever, but who the hell would want to?

"Come for me, *bella* Lucia. Give me your passion."

And she clenches around me, taking me over the edge with her.

CHAPTER 30

LUCY

"You're dying, aren't you?" I ask, giving Enzo some serious side-eye. It's Saturday, and we're participating in the fun run. At my request, he's wearing a Santa hat and coat. To my disappointment, he doesn't seem the least bit self-conscious about it, but then again, why would he be?

I have a whole new understanding of the song "Santa Baby."

We came here with Lars and Charlie, but Lars runs like a wildebeest and still seems a bit wary of Enzo, so they were off like a shot as soon as the mayor said *go.*

Enzo and I, on the other hand, are running so slowly a seven-year-old child just sprinted past us, and I can practically feel Enzo's muscles urging him to speed ahead—to win. It's driving him *crazy,* and I can't deny that I'm enjoying it.

"No," he says, not even the slightest bit winded. "I love running at the speed of walking. You can see so much more this way."

I hold back the laughter bubbling up inside of me, grinning as another kid races past us, this one holding the leash for a golden retriever being "ridden" by a stuffed elf.

"Yes, it's pleasant, isn't it? You *did* want to see Hideaway Harbor through new eyes. You can't do that if you're racing past it."

He smiles at me as one of Eileen's elderly friends jogs past us. I think she usually uses a walker. "As always, you have a point."

I'm still stunned that he's Lobster Stalker. That we'd been sharing our deepest thoughts and feelings while we spent our days pecking at each other, each trying to pull ahead of the other. Maybe it's in our makeup to be stubborn and take charge —he, because he had to step up so early in life, and me, because you can't be a caregiver for a terminally ill person without learning how to be a pushy asshole.

I hadn't opened that letter because I'd feared what it would reveal, but as soon as Enzo told me to open it, I knew my secret hope had come to pass. And then I read his beautiful words, his heart. He tries so hard to hide it from the people around him, but his goodness has always been apparent in his Lobster Stalker letters. His fears. His love. His loyalty. He's complicated but a good man, and I'm falling hard. All the more so after he spent a couple of hours looking over my app and listening to my ideas about CareWise, building on them. He's obviously a brilliant businessman.

But when I couldn't sleep last night, I read my mother's letter again, the one advising me on what to look for in a man, and I'm still not sure how she would have felt about Enzo. I couldn't get back to sleep after that, so I kissed his forehead—he was still out cold—bundled up, and went for a walk he certainly wouldn't approve of. I found myself near the Wishing Bridge again, although I hadn't purposefully sought it out. The sight of it put a lump of emotion in my throat. Feelings of dread and anticipation danced inside of me.

I didn't go onto the bridge. Something held me back. I just

turned back toward home, and was surprised when I ran into Noelle from the Christmas shop.

"You can't sleep either?" I asked.

"I can never sleep," she said with a small smile. "But isn't this town gorgeous at night?"

It was, it is. Glowing lights reflected in the piles of snow. The cool breeze feeling and smelling like salt and winter and *cold*.

"We get to experience it in a way no one else does," she said.

I smiled at her, said goodnight, and returned home, climbing back into bed next to Enzo. He didn't wake up, not really, but he turned in his sleep and put his arms around me. I nestled into him, my heart aching, but it was a good ache.

Mostly.

Now we're here in public, running at the speed of a turtle with a toe ache, and even though it's very clearly driving him nuts, he also seems to be having fun. He really is checking out the scenery, pointing out the businesses he's met with over the past week to discuss collaborations.

Eileen being Eileen, when she learned of Enzo's idea about putting together scavenger hunts for the Hideaway Harbor specialties, she offered to make flyers for them. Even though I know what Enzo thinks of her graphics, he agreed good-naturedly. When I asked him about it later, he shrugged and insisted it was good for business. Locals love Eileen and her ridiculous flyers; tourists will appreciate the touch of whimsy. He was right—he's usually right about stuff like that—but that's not the full story. He wanted to please her, and me.

Just like he's running at this glacial pace to please me now.

"My knee is twinging," I say dramatically. "I think we'd better slow down so I don't injure myself."

His mouth twitches. "Ah, I see," he says as we jog along, passing an enormous inflatable snowman. "You're fucking with me."

"Oh, you'll know when I'm fucking with you," I say in an undertone after glancing back and forth to make sure no children are back here with us anymore.

Then I rocket ahead, showing him my six-minute mile.

I can hear him laughing behind me as he tries to catch up. Charlie's waiting at the finish line as I blast toward it, laughing and whooping. There's no sign of Lars. She, of course, knows all about my six-minute mile.

"He's right behind you," she hollers through gusts of laughter.

Sure enough, right after I cross the finish line, he catches me from behind in a sweaty Santa hug. "You've been a *very* naughty girl," he says, panting against my ear. "I'm proud of you, Lucia. You tricked me good."

Lars appears through the crowd with a tray of drinks. "Hot glögg," he says. "The drink of champions."

I grin at Enzo, buzzing with ridiculous, mischievous joy. "Then Enzo doesn't get one. He got lapped by several children and an old lady who uses a walker. Now, who wants to see another Cafiero get owned?"

It's time for the ice sculpture competition at the Locke Reserve, the protected estate at the edge of town, and for the youngest Cafiero boy's time in the spotlight. Giovanni's holding down the fort at Hidden Italy so Enzo can witness Nico's modeling debut.

"Oh, come on, Resa, that doesn't look a thing like me," Nico complains, frowning at the ice sculpture glinting in the sunlight. He's wearing a heavy overcoat Enzo brought him to put on right after she finished.

"I think it's a perfect likeness," she says primly as she sets down her tool kit to study her sculpture.

Charlie and I are both shaking with silent laughter. I can't tell whether the artist, Resa, is messing with him, the way I did with Enzo during that race, or if she actually thinks it's a good likeness. She gave him a nose like a swollen tomato and one eye significantly larger than the other, but it looks enough like him that everyone will know who it's supposed to be.

Some of the artists in this competition are professionals, and others are decidedly amateurs, like the man beside us, who carved what amounts to a smiley face in the ice. Resa, who's a teacher at the high school, is somewhere in between.

I know a few of the participants, including Lumi, who's with a very distinguished silver fox. Bearded, as she apparently likes them.

"It *is* really lifelike," Charlie says.

"You captured his eyes perfectly," I add, probably because of all the glögg we've been drinking. The post-race cup is long gone, but Lars has proven gifted at hunting down the glögg that's being passed around.

"My girl is an art aficionado," Enzo says, grinning at his brother, happy to give everyone he cares about shit, apparently. "Resa, would you mind if I take some photos?"

"Oh no, not at all," she says. "I want to submit it to the paper."

Nico grumbles; Enzo gets his phone out and starts snapping photos.

"Now let me take one of you standing next to it, Nico," Enzo says. "It's for Aria. You'll do it for Aria."

Apparently, Nico really *will* do it for Aria, which is incredibly sweet, because he sighs and drags his feet but poses for the photo.

"Put your Santa hat on Nico, Junior," Enzo says. "Share the wealth."

"I'm afraid not," Resa says, shaking her head adamantly. "We want the ice to last as long as possible. I checked the weather forecast, and it should last for a good long while."

"Let's get another drink," Nico mutters, rubbing his nose as if he's worried it might swell to the size of the ice sculpture's.

"Soon." Enzo eyes me, grinning. "I promised Lucia we'd go caroling. God forgive the man who upsets Lucia."

"Yes, let the fun continue," Charlie croons, hoisting up her latest cup of glögg. "Let it continue until the man in red gets stuck in a chimney."

"Maybe it should continue with less glögg," Lars jokes as he takes her gloved hand.

"I need all the glögg I can get," Nico mutters.

We head down to the town square, talking, and a warm glow forms in my chest, because everyone's getting along so well. There isn't even much awkwardness over the situation with Aria. Charlie told me that Enzo pulled Lars aside earlier, assured him that the threat of death had passed, and said he hoped they could be friends.

Enzo did it for me, obviously.

He's doing all of this for me, but he seems to be enjoying himself too.

It's given me the kind of happiness I'm not used to—simple, uncomplicated, and deep. I feel *joyful*.

When we get to the town square, we find positions as close to Love at First Sip as possible, because Eileen said she wanted to watch us through the front window—a sentiment that might have been creepy from anyone other than her.

Lola, the woman who runs the sex toy shop, leads a rendition of "Santa Baby" using a vibrator as her microphone, so we're presumably not the only ones who have been indulging in the glögg. I sing at the top of my lungs, my very off-pitch voice weaving with Enzo's equally off-pitch voice.

A human can only have so many gifts. I'm glad the universe

knew better than to give this perfect specimen of a man a perfect singing voice as well.

I glance at the Sip and see Eileen beaming at us through the plate glass window, singing along. I gesture for her to join us— the café must be empty, because half of the town is out here singing, filling the air like we're suddenly the Whos in *How the Grinch Stole Christmas!* But she shakes her head and points back at her sole customer: grumpy Wayne.

"Oh, come on, Wayne," I mutter.

"What's he doing this time?" Charlie asks.

"Eileen can't join us because he's in there."

"Maybe she wants to be in there too," Enzo says enigmatically, stroking my hair.

"Why?" I ask.

"Call it a hunch."

An older woman with thick white hair pulled back under a bright red hat marches up to Lola and wrestles the vibrator from her, causing a groan to rise up in the crowd. She wraps it up in a Santa hat someone discarded before handing it back to Lola with a sour expression and saying something under her breath.

"Fun's over!" Lola shouts. "The fun police have arrived."

But someone hands Lola a drink, and seconds later she's singing at the top of her lungs again.

The song shifts to "Jingle Bells," and we're halfway through it when Giovanni, in a thick coat and gloves, emerges from the staircase to Hidden Italy and approaches us.

"There's the man of the hour," he says, clapping Nico on the back. "Why's Aria the one sending me photos of you and your perfect likeness, man? It's gotta be the middle of the night in Greece, and you all couldn't bother to send them to me?"

"I did," Enzo says, his arms wrapped around me, holding me close enough that I can feel the rumble of his spoken words.

"That's Hideaway Harbor for you. It sends texts to Greece but not to Hidden Italy."

Giovanni grunts, then says, "Say, that guy from the city called back again today. I told him it was a Saturday, and he said he was aware of the day of the week, but he'd like to hear from you regardless. What do you think this is about, anyway?"

Cold runs down my spine, as if my body has suddenly remembered it's freezing outside—the kind of atmosphere more welcoming to an ice sculpture than a human body.

"Nothing important enough for me to respond on the weekend," Enzo says, but this isn't the Enzo who's been enjoying himself all day. His voice is tense, impatient.

"Seemed pretty important to the guy who keeps blowing up our phone," Giovanni says, sounding a bit annoyed by it, or maybe by being the one sober person in a sea of drunk people. "You think they're trying to get you back?"

"I'll call later," Enzo says. "Why don't you close early and join us? We can get dinner together."

"I'll cook for everyone at Nonna's house," Nico offers. "I've got an idea for a recipe I've been wanting to try."

"Well, we'll see you all later, then," Lars says politely, nodding.

Enzo laughs. "You think you're getting out of this so easily? We're friends now, we made a pact. You and Charlie need to come too. And Eileen."

I glance back at him, feeling a pulse of happiness again. Of hope. "Really?"

"I'm the one who's going to be cooking," Nico says with a sigh. "For nine people now."

But he doesn't really sound upset about it. Enzo isn't the only Cafiero who likes a challenge.

"If you'd like, we can invite Resa?" Enzo suggests, teasing in his voice. His brother cuffs him on the arm, and then someone starts a rendition of "It's Beginning to Look a Lot like Christmas."

It is. It really is. This is what I've been wanting, Christmas as it was before Mom's illness got bad, when we used to dance around and catch snowflakes on our tongues and eat hot chestnuts from street vendors.

I look up into the darkened sky, and I think, *I wish you were here.*

I wish I knew where you are, if you're anywhere.

I love you.

Enzo's arms tighten around me as if he knows exactly what I'm thinking.

But there's a little voice in my head, one that sounds unfortunately like my mother, that asks if he's already starting to say a long goodbye.

CHAPTER 31

ENZO

*D*inner tonight was loud, chaotic, and probably very stressful for Nico, who made us all lasagna. It was also a couple of the best hours of my life.

Lucy agreed to stay at my apartment, in my bed, and it feels like a victory. Not over her, but over myself. I was so reluctant to come home, so convinced Hideaway Harbor would feel like a cage. But I was wrong. I'm not usually grateful to be wrong, but I'm happy to make an exception.

It feels right to have her here, in my space, tucked in next to me in bed.

It also makes me realize how much I've held back—how little I've made this place mine. Maybe it's time to give up the apartment in New York and bring my things here. It doesn't have to be forever, even if a voice in my head whispers that it might be okay if it is. That this life I've been running from for years might be better than the one I had in New York.

I drift off to sleep, my arm around Lucy, and rouse to find her wide awake, her eyes full of sadness and worry.

"Is everything okay?" I ask, immediately on full alert. "Did something happen to Eileen?"

Or my grandmother? But I can't speak that fear to life.

"Oh, everything's fine," she says. "Sorry. I just… Did you call that guy in New York?"

"No." I settle back into my pillows. "God, you gave me the fright of my life."

"You should call him," she says.

"Right now? He might not thank me for it."

"*Tomorrow*."

"I'll call on Monday."

"What if it's important?"

"It can't possibly be. If it's my super and there's a leak in my apartment, he can let himself in to fix it."

Her lips try to form a smile but don't quite make it. "What if all your fancy suits got wet?"

"What use do I have for them here, anyway?"

"You know it's not your super. This is about your old job. They probably want you back."

She's clearly nervous about that possibility. I trace a finger over her lips, then say, "Usually you don't get invited back after you call your boss names."

"What'd you call him?" she asks, her mouth lifting at the corners.

"An asshole with poor vision."

She shrugs. "You could have done better."

"It wasn't my best work. I meant he had poor vision metaphorically, but he thought I was making fun of his glasses." I caress the side of her face. "I won't lie to you. I think it probably *is* him. Calling on the weekend and demanding an immediate response is just like him, even though he knows me too well to think he'll get what he wants. The thing is, I don't care if he wants to give me my old job back. I don't want it. I'm done doing things his way."

"Firing people."

"Sometimes people deserve to be fired. But just as often it's training that's at fault, or a person who should be doing job A is hired for job B. You don't always need to throw everything out to fix things."

She bites her bottom lip, her expression serious and thoughtful. "What if it's someone else who wants to hire you?"

"Then they can wait to make their pitch to me until after we've had our holiday fun." She still looks worried, so I smooth a finger between her brows. "You think I'm going to leave."

I understand that fear. I live with it in my bones. People who are supposed to love you can just leave. They can buy a plane ticket or a bus ticket or drive their car away.

But now that I'm older I realize some of the people who leave come back. Aria left, but she checks in nearly daily, and even though my father has always inhabited his own little world, he still calls one of us every week or so.

"I don't want you to regret staying."

"There are plenty of remote jobs I could get, or jobs with travel."

"You've been thinking about that?"

I tuck her hair behind her ear. "Yeah, I've been thinking about that. Everything is going well with the shop. Our new strategy seems like it's going to be a success. I'll need something to do."

"God forbid Enzo Cafiero gets bored," she says, but she's barely teasing.

"It would be hard to get bored with you around. You like to keep me on my toes."

I wrap my arm around her and pull her close, needing to feel her against me. To prove to both of us that we're here now, and that's what matters. I want to hold her. To soothe her.

"I've felt more alive this past month than I have in the past five years. I'd be a fool to walk away from you, and I'd like to believe I'm no fool."

Her only answer is to snuggle closer, although I know she's still thinking about it.

Truthfully, I'm grateful she cares. I'm definitely grateful she's decided she wants me here.

I have a surprise planned for Christmas. I told my sister about it, and she thinks I'm crazy for even considering the idea, but the truth is, I *am* crazy.

"Good night, Enzo."

I kiss the top of her head. "Good night, Lucia. Tomorrow we'll help shape minds and inspire children at the library."

"God help them," she whispers.

I laugh into her hair, feeling at peace, but then tug her closer. "You know, maybe I'm not so tired after all."

I ANSWER my landline phone in the living room while Lucy showers in the bathroom. It's Aria.

"You're honestly reading to kids this morning?" my sister asks. "I already like your new girlfriend. Rachelle would never read to kids."

"We don't need to talk about Rachelle," I say, feeling a strong inclination to never again hear her name and Lucy's in the same sentence. Even though I might never have talked to Lucy if not for my ex.

"Wow, you really do have it bad," Aria says, then murmurs something to someone on the other end of the phone. "I want to meet her. I want to buy her an insanely big bouquet of flowers. Or maybe chocolates. Does she like chocolate? Oh, what am I talking about, every sane person likes chocolate."

"I don't."

"My point stands." She pauses. "Giovanni tells me someone from New York is trying to get in touch with you, but you don't want to call them back. What game are you playing?"

I head into the kitchen and start the espresso machine. "No game. I think it's my ex-boss, and I don't mind making him sweat for a few days. I won't go back."

"You shouldn't. He sounds like an asshole. He's sounded like an asshole for years."

"He's probably been one for most of his life," I mutter. Switching gears, I ask, "So, what can I say to persuade you to come home for Christmas?"

She huffs into the phone. "Nothing. You're not nearly the dealmaker you think you are. Greece at this time of year is amazing. It's like thirty degrees warmer than at home, and there aren't many tourists. I'm basically on a paid vacation."

I pause, thinking of the honesty Lucy and I have been exchanging, first in letters, now in person. Then I admit: "I miss you. We all miss you. It won't seem like Christmas without you, and this year it really feels like Christmas, Aria."

I tell her a little bit about the taffy pulling and singing carols in the square last night. About how funny it was to watch Nico's expression when he saw his ice sculpture.

"You'd still be able to see it," I say, wheedling. "Resa seemed to think it would last a while."

"I love you, but no means no," she says.

"I love you too," I say, deflated, then try one more tactic. "I also really want you to meet Lucy."

"Soon," she promises. "I'm happy for you, Enzo. It's about time you got your head out of your ass."

Sisters.

She hangs up, and I finish making our cappuccinos—in to-go cups, because we need to head to the library.

"You made me a Frenemy," Lucy says when she sees it, her eyes lighting up.

"To prove my cappuccino supremacy," I joke. "Shall we?"

She studies me for a moment, looking for something, and

then takes her cappuccino from me. "Are you sure you want to do this?"

"I want to do it with you."

She gives me a doubtful look. "It occurred to me… I know you did a lot for your brothers and sister at Christmas when you were a kid. This won't bring back any hard memories?"

"No, Lucia. Reading a children's story isn't going to send me into hysterics."

Her skeptical look doesn't waver. "We don't have to go."

But we do. It's part of the plan I cooked up, and I'm *enjoying* the plan. Last night, laughing with my brothers, seeing my grandmother smile—several times, in fact—experiencing it all with my arm around Lucy, I found myself thinking, *I want more of this.*

"We're going," I say.

We walk to the library together, talking easily, and when we get there we ditch the coffee cups and enter. There's a crush of people, probably because the actor, Brody King, is doing the last reading. He's already there, surrounded by a large crowd, including Piper Locke and probably two dozen mothers in clothing more revealing than the weather calls for.

The book Lucy signed up to read is called *Stick Man*. She chose it because she found the name funny. What it has to do with Christmas is a mystery to me.

"Oh, Brody *is* really hot," Lucy says, but she's grinning at me, and it's obvious she's only giving me shit.

"Be careful. I've been known to attack circuit breakers in fits of jealousy."

She kisses me on the cheek, then whispers in my ear, "No one's as hot as the Italian Stallion."

One of the moms gives us a dirty look, as if cheek kissing is the gateway drug to pornography, but I just grin at her.

There's a magical feeling in the air, as if all of the season's miracles exist simply because the children surrounding us believe in them.

I'm reminded of when I was a kid, trying to make this time of year special for my brothers and sister. At the time, I'd felt so alone, but I remember being here at this library. I remember adults reading to us. I remember how my teacher gave me a bag of presents for all of us Cafieros, telling me that Santa had come to the wrong house, but they were meant for us.

They'd tried to help.

I hadn't been as alone as I'd felt.

Portia squeezes her way to us through the crowd and reaches out her hand for a fist bump. "There's my Peppermint Man."

Someone gives her a dramatic hush, so she adds in an undertone, "Amanda's reading too. I'm here for moral support."

I nod to Lucy. "We're reading together."

Amanda slips through the crowd to join us, plenty of people watching her.

"It's Defiantly Herself," she says, surprising me by giving Lucy a hug. There's a story there, obviously, and I'd like to hear it. But I'm not surprised she managed to befriend a famous actress. Honestly, I wouldn't be surprised if she'd charmed a dictator, won over a warlord, got offered a crown.

"We're up next," Amanda continues, "but good luck, you guys. We're going to stick around for a while to listen."

I'm feeling a little choked up by the time Lucy and I read our story, each doing a page at a time. It's a little existential book about a man who looks like a stick and almost gets burned alive, but I like it. It has a dark edge most Christmas books lack. An acknowledgement of the other side of life—the dark that makes the light glow brighter.

I'm in a strange mood by the time we step out into the sunlight, ready for the woolen sock race. And it's flurrying. Just a few flakes coming down, but the clouds look like they'll bring a white afternoon for us.

"It's beautiful," Lucy breathes out, stretching her hand to catch a snowflake.

"Can you catch one on your tongue?" I ask. Mostly because I want to see her with her head tipped back, tongue extended.

"You want me to look like an idiot," she accuses, but not hotly.

"You could never. Except maybe for that time you got caught in that Porta Potty."

I get the playful arm shove I was hoping for, and I wrap my arm around her. We've only taken a couple of steps toward the Locke Reserve, where the woolen sock race is being held, when I feel my cell phone vibrate in my pocket.

Thinking it might be my sister again, I slide it out.

There's a voice message, which is apparently only coming through now after having been left yesterday.

"There's a message," I say.

A dark look crosses her face, but she juts out her lower lip stubbornly. "Check it, Enzo."

So I do…

"Enzo, this is Martin Murphy. You're a hard man to reach. We got your brief the other day, and holy shit, man, it blew me away. Tom's gone. We don't need that kind of unilateral thinking in our company. We need innovation. We need *you*. I want to interview you for his job. Now, look, I know Christmas is coming up, but as you know, we're slammed, so we need you on board, like, yesterday. When can you be in New York for the interview?"

My heart rate picks up. My palms sweat.

Fuck. My boss's job. This is…

This is huge. Everything I thought I wanted, the life I've been working for since I left home.

"Enzo?" Lucy says, her voice fainter than usual. Full of trepidation. "Who was it?"

I can tell from the look on her face that she already knows.

"It was my ex-boss's boss," I say carefully. "They let him go. They want to interview me for his position."

"Of course they do," she says with a gratifying lack of surprise. "And you'll go."

"We can talk about that later. I believe we're supposed to do the woolen sock race. There's no way I'm missing that. What the fuck is a woolen sock race, anyway? Are we seriously going to be running in our socks in the snow? We may want to be bystanders for this one, Lucy. We can cheer on everyone else."

"We're racing," she says. "Because I also want to find out what the fuck a woolen sock race is, and I intend to win it."

I smile at her, but I feel an unfamiliar, uncomfortable tension between us that I'm not sure how to navigate. "You're not going to throw this one, Lucy?"

"No," she says. "I've already lost the element of surprise." She takes a brief pause, then says, "You have to take the interview, Enzo. You *have* to."

CHAPTER 32

LUCY

"*Y*ou have to take the interview," I tell Enzo for the fiftieth time. "This is a really big deal. Huge."

"Yeah," he says, shrugging. "But I don't *have* to take the interview. I don't have to do anything."

I can tell he wants to, though. I saw the ambition flash across his face when he listened to that message this morning.

He was so distracted at the woolen sock race that he barely seemed pissed off when Hudson won.

Afterward, we watched the fireworks with his brothers, Charlie, and a few other friends, but his mind was somewhere else. He was thinking about leaving…

Now, we're back in my apartment, drinking a final glass of wine at my small table, but he's still thinking about it.

"Don't be stubborn over this," I say. "It's a big opportunity. They want to do things your way. You could make a real difference."

The conflict is written all over his beautiful, sculpted face. He wants this, bad. But he also doesn't want to leave me.

I'm grateful for that, but at the same time…

He's going to take the job, ultimately.

He'd be a fool to say no, because Enzo is ambitious and talented, and he's right. If he stayed here without some other job to do, he'd be bored and unfulfilled. Eventually, he'd resent me.

I know this because…

I'm ashamed to admit it, even to myself, but even though I loved my mother with my whole being, even though I was grateful that I was able to be there for her…

I wanted to be like Charlie, able to travel anywhere at the drop of a hat. I wanted to date inappropriate men and make stupid decisions, and act my age.

But I didn't, and I resented my mom for it sometimes—and resented myself for feeling that way, because I knew it wasn't her fault. She hadn't chosen to be sick any more than anyone could choose their natural hair color. It had all been a game of genetics that she'd lost, badly.

I don't want him to resent me.

I don't want him to wake up every morning and wonder what his life would have been like if only he'd taken the opportunity presented to him.

"Please," I say, my voice faint. "You have to go."

"I'll call him in the morning," he insists. "I'm not sure I'm interested, though. I have some other ideas I want to pursue."

"*Enzo*, this is what you wanted. I remember what you wrote in your notes. I can't take you from your dream."

He reaches for my hand, and I give it to him, my heart lodged in my throat, choking me.

"Dreams change, *cara*. But maybe they'd let me work remotely part of the time. I have to go back to New York anyway to pack the rest of my things."

I nod, but it's hard to believe what he's saying. It already feels like he's being pulled up by the roots he's been regrowing here.

"Will you come with me?" he asks. "To New York?"

I consider the possibility, and I can almost see it. I wanted adventure, and everyone says New York City has a unique charm at this time of year. Everything's so big and bright. So… spectacular. But my heart aches at the thought of leaving, and besides, I've already taken the weekend off at the coffee shop.

I shake my head. "I can't. I can't leave right now."

I meant to say I can't leave Eileen in a lurch, but the last words didn't come out. Because the truth is I can't leave Hideaway Harbor.

I've always wanted it to be my home, ever since I first stepped foot here, and this past month, it's started to feel like it finally is.

He doesn't argue with me. Instead, he makes love to me with quiet intensity, as if he feels it too—the crux in the road we've been walking.

ENZO'S INTERVIEW is set for Wednesday.

He doesn't talk about it after making the arrangements, and neither do I, but it seems to hang over everything like ominous clouds. It hails on Tuesday morning, which feels like a bad omen.

I tell him as much when he stops in at the Sip before making the drive to New York City. It's eight hours, but he wants to have his car so he can bring some boxes back from his apartment. Or so he says.

Maybe he won't want to do that if they offer him the job.

Maybe he won't want to come back at all.

Eileen, who's covering the counter, gives me an encouraging smile and a thumbs-up.

I give her one back.

I'll need to return to work before too long. It's Whoopie Pie Appreciation Day today, and there's a line out the door at

Making Whoopie. Several people have come from there to here to grab a caffeinated drink, so we're busy too. Everyone's abuzz about Audrey's culinary genius.

It's been a successful day for her, although she didn't look all that happy when I popped in earlier. I'm not sure why, but I don't have the bandwidth to worry about it right now. Frankly, I'm not all that happy myself, given what's going on with Enzo.

"It's not a bad omen," Enzo insists, refusing to acknowledge the hail as anything but bad weather. "Now, if someone nabbed me in the balls again on that thing…" He nods to the dartboard I made of his photo, which is still hanging on the café wall. "That would be a bad omen. Try not to worry, all right? I'll call you when I get there, and again after the interview tomorrow."

"I'll be waiting," I say. "But I already know it's going to go great."

"Look on the bright side," he says with a huge grin. "Maybe I'll bomb it. Then we can get drunk at Kippis with my brothers and Charlie and Lars and talk about what assholes they all are."

"Oh, like you'd actually bomb it," I say, letting a trace of sourness leak into my tone. "You're going to charm the pants off them."

He smooths a hand over my hair. "I'd rather charm the pants off you. I'll see you on Thursday."

I kiss him once, then again, then again.

"I don't want you to leave," I admit. "I'm worried you won't come back."

"I'll come back," he insists. "You can't get rid of me so easily."

He kisses me again before he gets up and leaves, the door no longer chiming with that awful "Jingle Bells" song thanks to him.

I watch him through the window, so I see when he looks back. When he winks.

It makes my heart hurt.

The next thing I know, a pair of arms descends upon me from behind. I nearly jump out of my skin before I realize it's Eileen, and I lean my head back into her cloud of familiar light perfume.

"It's going to be okay, sweet girl," she says softly. "You'll see. There's magic at Christmastime in Hideaway Harbor."

But he's leaving Hideaway…

"Bad time to be traveling," Wayne says from two tables away. "Lots of snow at this time of year. There could be holdups on the road."

Eileen stiffens. "If we wanted your opinion, Wayne, we would have asked."

The door opens, capturing my attention and Eileen's. I'm surprised to see Nonna Francesca. The breach has officially been mended, but this is her first social visit to the café.

She shocks me all the more when she walks over and puts a hand on my shoulder. "We wait together," she says staunchly. "Now, make me one of those cappuccinos I taught you to make."

Tears fill my eyes, but I get up to make the drink, feeling a warmth in my chest even though the fear hasn't eased. Because I really do feel like a part of this place. Enzo is too, but I'm worried he hasn't realized it yet.

I tell Charlie as much later, at her house, and she gives me a long hug before saying, "This sounds ridiculous, but why don't you tell him what you're feeling in a letter? You don't need to send it. You can give it to him when he comes home."

"You're brilliant," I say.

"You won't think so after you see the German shepherd. It looks like that ice sculpture of Nico."

I smile, because the ice sculpture has melted slightly, making him look even more misshapen. Nico's been complaining about it to anyone who will listen.

"I'm sure you're exaggerating."

"She's not," Lars says conversationally. He's been sitting with us, good sport that he is, drinking some glögg. We all developed a fondness for it last weekend.

She nudges him with her shoulder, he kisses her head, and I *ache* inside.

I know this is my own doing. Enzo probably wouldn't have accepted the interview if I hadn't hounded him about it. But there's a chance they won't offer him the job, or he won't accept, or even that they'd allow him to work remotely.

Except…how likely is that? The internet is hardly reliable here, and—

Don't borrow trouble, I think to myself.

The next afternoon, Enzo calls my cell phone. The signal is patchy, so I call him back from the main line at the Sip.

"They want a follow-up interview tomorrow," he says. "I'll be home on Friday, Lucy. As soon as I can."

The day before Christmas Eve. That's cutting things close, especially since his grandmother already has big plans with Nico for the Feast of the Seven Fishes. We're all supposed to go. Even Charlie and Lars were invited, but Charlie's parents are flying in from Asheville to meet his family, so they can't come. Eileen will be there for part of the evening, but I know she has at least a dozen invitations.

"Okay," I say, hearing the choked sound of my voice. "Of course."

"This is only about seeing what they offer, if anything, Lucia," he says. "I'm coming home."

Hearing him call it that—*home*—makes me hopeful. I want him to see it that way again.

I want to believe it can be true.

CHAPTER 33

ENZO

It's Thursday afternoon, two days before Christmas Eve, and Martin just offered me a job.

The job.

I'd be the one calling the shots, controlling how things are done. I could do it all my way.

I study Martin. He's a big guy in a tailored suit, behind a ridiculously large mahogany desk that commands an expansive view of Midtown Manhattan. It's a power office that speaks of money and opportunity. He's just promised that if I play the hand he's given me, I can have my own share of money and power.

"Is there any way I can work remotely?" I ask. "At least part of the time."

He doesn't even consider this before shaking his head. "We need boots on the ground, Enzo. Your full devotion to the position."

Given what I know about Hideaway Harbor's spotty connectivity to the rest of the world, I know he's not wrong. But it's a hard pill to swallow.

"Can I think about it?"

He gives me a severe look, his brows knitting together across his forehead. "What's there to think about? This is the opportunity of a lifetime, and I don't mind telling you we wouldn't normally offer a job like this to someone so young. How old are you anyway, thirty-five?"

"Thirty-three." He knows exactly how old I am. This is his way of hammering home what a fantastic opportunity he's offering me. It's a manipulation—the backbone of what they do here at Murphy & Associates.

Doesn't sit right.

"Look at you, making my point for me," he says shrewdly. "But sure. You can have twenty-four hours."

"When would the position start?"

"Monday," he says significantly. "You'll be pulling long hours at the start, I don't mind telling you. You'll need to clean up after Tom. He didn't leave things nice and pretty."

I take a moment to think. Not about the job, but about Lucy and the life I've been living this past month. I'm proud of what I've done at Hidden Italy. Of having been there for my family and for Lucy. If I take this job, all of that's over.

A voice in my head suggests, *Maybe Lucy would be willing to move here or try long-distance.*

But how could I be in a long-distance relationship if I'm chained to my desk?

Then there's my grandmother to consider. I could hire someone to help her out since I'd be making bank, but there's a very good chance she wouldn't even allow them onto her porch, let alone into her house, and besides...

She's getting older. She told me herself that she's not sure how much time she has left. If I leave, I'll miss it.

"I'll take the twenty-four hours," I say.

He gives me a disapproving look but nods sharply. "Be sure to get an answer to me first thing tomorrow morning."

I can't help myself: "That wouldn't be a full twenty-four

hours, Martin." It's already late afternoon—I've spent the whole day here, talking with half a dozen different people, and I feel drained in a way I haven't in weeks.

Invigorated too. I can't deny that a part of me feels drawn to this opportunity. To the ability to shape things and make them my own. To be the man behind the curtain, like I always wanted to be when I was a kid, able to shape destiny rather than to be shaped by it.

He surprises me by laughing. "That's what I like about you, Enzo. No BS. All right. Tomorrow at 3 p.m. I'll be expecting your answer."

"And you'll have it," I say, shaking his hand again.

I leave the building and walk through the streets of Midtown, taking in the bustle. The smell. The busyness of everyone making their way somewhere, their bubbles barely brushing.

A part of me is drawn to the anonymity. No one here would care enough about my relationship with Lucy to gossip about it. It sure as fuck wouldn't make the paper.

In Hideaway Harbor, every local's life is subject to scrutiny, not just people like Amanda and Brody, who are interesting to the rest of the world too. (After the reading, Lucy insisted on googling Brody and learned he's apparently up for some huge movie role.)

Here, I can just be.

But I'd be alone.

Lucy won't want to live in New York. If she did agree to make the move, she'd lose the home she's longed for. The family.

I wouldn't ask her to make that sacrifice.

So if I take this job, I'll almost certainly lose Lucy.

Lucy, with her stubborn pride, her brilliant ideas, and her biting sense of humor.

Lucy, who cuts me down to the quick when I need it.

Lucy, who's waiting for me to call.

Lucy, who doesn't know about the holiday surprise I arranged for her.

And, just like that, I know I can't do it. I don't want to. I don't want to lose her, and to my surprise, I also don't want to lose the home she's been reintroducing me to. I've become closer to Giovanni and Nico over the last month. My grandmother too. And even though everything is moving in the right direction for Hidden Italy, I'd meant to see them through the transition—and also to convince Nonna that it wouldn't be the end of the world for her to have some kind of companion around to help her at home.

I don't need twenty-four hours to give Martin his answer. I'm ready to give it to him now.

Filled with determination, I whip around too fast and run into a man in a Santa suit. We both fall down, Santa tumbling onto his butt.

"That man hit Santa," a little kid cries out, pointing at me.

"It's okay," Santa Suit says from the ground. "Nothing to see here, man. It's all chill, chill, chill."

He reeks of marijuana and liquor.

The little boy's mother wraps an arm around his shoulders and hustles him away.

I frown, because we're in a city of 8.5 million people, and someone hired *this* guy to be Santa? His brown eyes are bloodshot, and he looks like he hasn't shaved in a week. Then again, who says anyone hired him? There's no law against random people running around in Santa suits. If there were, half of Hideaway Harbor would be arrested.

"Sorry," I say, reaching down to help him up as people stream around us. "I wasn't looking."

"Oh, that's okay, brother. I wasn't looking either. I was looking inward."

Fuck me, I have something in common with this clown.

"Say, you look like a helpful guy, and I could use some help," he continues.

Here goes, I think, half expecting him to tell me he dropped a bucket of quarters in the dark alley across from us, and he needs help picking them up so they can be donated to orphans. No doubt I look like a mark, walking around in a daze, wearing an expensive suit.

"What is it?" I ask stiffly.

"Never mind, never mind. It's probably a terrible idea."

"What is?" I ask, even though I'm inclined to agree with him.

He scratches his head. "It's just…my girlfriend broke up with me last night, and it was *brutal*. I mean, she said I lacked ambition. I went to acting school, and now I'm an actor, *Shannon*, how's that not ambitious? Anyway, I may have stayed out a little too late."

"It's almost 4 p.m."

"I may have stayed out all night," he says, waving a hand flippantly, "and I'm supposed to be Santa at this event, and man, I really don't want to disappoint those little fuckers. Those kids might ask some serious questions, if you know what I mean."

I pause, caught off guard, then point to myself. "Are you saying you want me to cover your shift as Santa Claus?"

"Uh, yeah. I mean, you could have my coat and beard and stuff, if you'll do it. I'm already going to be late, and I don't think I can stay awake for four more hours."

"No," I say, thinking of the Cheetos beard I took from Curtis the night of Santa Speed Dating. One borrowed fake beard is enough for a lifetime.

He scratches his head, which reminds me of lice, which in turn reminds me of Lucy. Because I guess everything does. God, she would love it if I play along and do this. She would also never let me live it down.

"So, is that a no to the whole thing?" Drunk Santa asks with another suspicious head scratch. "Or, like, just a no to the suit? They could maybe find you another suit if you were interested, I mean, I think they could. But it's probably too late for them to find another Santa."

"Give me a second," I say, stepping toward the side of the high-rise closest to us. He shrugs, then sits down on the sidewalk. People walk around him as if he's a new fire hydrant, although I see someone flick a few dollar bills at him. He shrugs and scoops them up as I pull out my cell phone and dial Lucy's cell number.

No ring. It goes directly to voicemail, suggesting today is one of those days in Hideaway Harbor.

I leave her a quick voicemail, saying I'll call her later—I don't want to spill my heart out with the brokenhearted Santa sitting in the middle of the sidewalk next to me and the smell of piss stinging my nostrils. Then I dial her home phone number—no answer—followed by the landline at the Sip. The phone is answered by an older man.

"Hello? Whatchu want?"

An interesting method of answering the phone at a place of business, but since he doesn't work there, I'm guessing he's not interested in tips on phone etiquette.

"Wayne?" I ask. "Why are you answering the phone?"

"Is this one of those sales calls?"

"No. I'm Lucy's boyfriend," I say, liking the sound of it. Wishing he weren't the first person I'd said it to.

"So you made it to New York. Good, that's good. Did you get that job?"

"I got the job offer, yeah, but I'm definitely not going to take it. Can you tell Lucy I'll call her later?"

"Okay, champ, I'll tell her all about it."

He hangs up, and I breathe a sigh of relief. At least Wayne will pass along the message. I think.

I walk over to the Santa on the sidewalk and find him fast asleep.

"Uh...Santa?" I shake his shoulder and he flails awake.

"Are you going to do it?" he asks as I come into focus for him.

"What do you know, I am," I say with a smile. "I've suddenly become flooded with the Christmas spirit."

"That's my man." He lifts himself to his feet and tries to wrap me in a liquor-scented hug that I immediately sidestep. "Oh, you're going to make those little tykes so happy, I can just tell. You've got that small-town, nice-guy vibe, you know? I can always tell when someone's a good person. I know it."

"Did you think Shannon was a good person?" I can't help but say.

He looks surprised for half a second, and then he starts guffawing loudly, clapping me on the back. "You're all right. Right this way, right this way."

I follow him, already half regretting the decision, and not just because of all the little children pointing at us and staring. But I'm still enjoying the novelty of doing something totally random and unplanned.

I figured he worked at some toy shop or bookstore, but he leads me to the winter village at Bryant Park, full of little glass stalls selling Christmassy wares. Everything is decorated with fairy lights and bows.

"This is it, my man. We're almost here."

"Uhh," I say, slowing to a stop near the park entrance. "This isn't what I was expecting."

I can't help but laugh a little. What the fuck am I even doing?

"Santa's here," says a little girl standing at a drink kiosk with her father. She tugs on his arm so hard he drops the hot chocolate he was just handed. Sighing, he holds out another ten-dollar bill. "Another, please."

Shannon's ex-boyfriend, whose name I still don't know, leads me to a festive red tent set up next to the Lodge, which serves food and beverages. A man in an elf costume is pacing the interior of the tent.

When we step inside, he stops and says, "Thank God you're here, Barry. I was getting—"

He must have just gotten a noseful of Barry, though, because his face twists into a grimace. "Not again. I warned you last time. We don't—"

"I got my best buddy here to be my replacement," Barry says eagerly, patting me on the back. "We're in acting school together."

"No, we're not," I say.

"I can't put just anyone out there with the kids," the elf hisses. "What the devil's gotten into you?"

"Shannon broke up with him," I say, figuring I might as well really lean into the whole situation. "You can run a quick background check if you want."

He watches me for a moment before nodding. "Okay, you can stay, if it comes back clean. Barry, you're fucking fired. Your last day is Saturday."

Barry scratches his head again. "My last day was Saturday anyway. That's Christmas Eve."

"Go," he says succinctly.

Barry shrugs and throws me a wave. "Bye, man, thanks for keeping those dreams alive."

I wave back, and the elf sighs and tells me, "It's too late for us to find anyone else, and they take advantage of it. Every year. You really down for this?"

"Sure, I guess so," I say. "As long as you'll take a photo for me. My girlfriend will go nuts for this."

"You've got yourself a deal, my friend," he says, shaking my hand.

He sets me up with a fresh Santa suit, thank Christ, and

takes the photo for Lucy, which I immediately text to Lucy. Then I stow my overcoat and suit jacket in Barry's cubby.

I spend the next four hours bombarded with child after child tugging on my fake beard and asking me if there are really sweatshops in the North Pole, why my magical reindeer can't be detected by radar, and why I don't have a belly like a bowlful of jelly. It's chaotic and quick and fun. Like last weekend, reading to those kids, I'm reminded of the role I played for my brothers and sister. And, what do you know, it feels good.

Right up until I get to the end of the shift and discover someone stole my overcoat, and my cell phone, wallet, and keys along with it.

Fuck. Fuckkkkk. Fuckity, fuck fuck fuck.

The officer I report the crime to doesn't seem particularly hopeful about recovering my stolen things. This comes as difficult news, especially since I have no idea how I'll even get into my apartment. I can't find a locksmith who takes Venmo, and I only know a few phone numbers by heart.

There *is* someone who has a copy of my key, however—Rachelle.

So I walk to her apartment building and press the call button.

"Who *is* it?" she croons, so maybe she's expecting company. Or Uber Eats.

"It's Enzo Cafiero," I say. "I need a favor."

She's quiet for so long I figure she stalked off, but finally she says, "Fifteen minutes."

I'm in no position to complain, so I pace outside for fifteen minutes, according to the clock I can see in the lobby. When I press the call button again, she buzzes me in without saying anything.

Her door's cracked open when I reach it, so I walk in without knocking—and find her splayed out dramatically on the sofa, wearing a black silk negligee.

So apparently she thought the favor was a pretense to see her.

When she gets a good look at me, she abruptly sits up.

"What the fuck happened to you?"

I'm still wearing the Santa coat, because the elf guy was mortified by the theft and didn't want to send me off with frostbite.

"A lot of things," I say, feeling it down to my bones. "I'm a changed man. I also got robbed, and someone stole my keys."

"Oh, you poor thing," she says. "You can stay here tonight."

"No," I say. "I can't. I need to get home to Hideaway Harbor as soon as possible."

She wrinkles her nose as if I'd just expressed enthusiasm for venereal diseases. "No offense, but that place is a dump, Enzo."

"It's my home," I say, and I'll be damned if I don't mean it. "Do you have my spare key?"

She makes a *hmf* sound, then gets up and retrieves the key from the junk drawer in her kitchen. She looks pissed off by my existence now that I haven't given her what she wants, and I marvel at myself. How could I have ever fooled myself into believing there were any real feelings between us?

Still, it is Christmas.

"Merry Christmas," I say, pausing in the doorframe on my way out.

She stalks over and shuts the door in my face, almost taking out my Cafiero nose.

I don't have my metro card or any cash, so I have to walk to my apartment. By the time I get there, it's past three in the morning. I'm so exhausted I collapse onto the couch.

At least I reached out to Lucy and sent her that photo. She'll know I'm okay, and I'll figure out the rest in the morning.

But I wake up to hammering on my door. I glance around, completely disoriented, and see the clock over the mantel. It's one o'clock. One *p.m.*

Fuck. I should be getting home right now, not just leaving here. But how can I leave? I don't have my car key, and I don't even have ID to show a locksmith to prove ownership. I don't even have a damn license.

My pulse is tripping over itself as I make my way to the door and open it, only then realizing no one even buzzed from the lobby.

I'm shocked to see Giovanni, Nico, and my grandmother gathered outside my door.

"What are you doing, you foolish boy?" my grandmother asks. "You can't take this job! You belong at home with us."

"And with Lucy," Giovanni says. "You love her."

Goddamn, it shouldn't have taken my little brother to point out something so obvious.

CHAPTER 34

LUCY

The beautiful, dreamy Christmas feeling that's hung over the last few weeks is gone. It's like I've woken up and found myself in some horrible dystopian landscape a masochist decided to decorate.

It's Friday afternoon, and there's no sign of Enzo. I haven't even talked to him since Wednesday.

All I know is this: He left a voice message on my phone yesterday afternoon saying he'd call me later, something that didn't happen. But he *did* call the café. He left a message with Wayne, who covered the phones so Eileen and I could go check on Audrey next door.

"Sounds like he got the job but wasn't planning on taking it," Wayne said. "I couldn't hear him properly, though. It's possible he said, 'I'm *definitely* taking it.'"

"That is very unhelpful, Wayne," Eileen said disapprovingly, to which he shrugged.

"Not one thing I can do about my hearing."

He said this while wearing a switched-off hearing aid in his ear, but I was too emotional to make a retort.

Thursday evening, a text came through from Enzo, and I

372

nearly dropped my phone and gave it another spiderweb crack when I saw it: a photo of Enzo wearing a Santa suit, with a text saying, *At my new job, Lucia.*

I waved my phone at Eileen almost hysterically. "Does this mean he took it?"

"And they made him dress up as Santa before sending him along to fire people?" Eileen asked. "I wouldn't put it past those New York types, but it would be *exceptionally* cruel, and I'm not convinced it makes sense."

"Maybe he's three sheets to the wind," Wayne suggested unhelpfully. "Or four." He shrugged. "Doesn't seem like the type who'd think it was fun to wander around looking like an idiot."

"Wait right here," Eileen told me, her expression firm. "I'm going to get to the bottom of this."

She returned minutes later with Giovanni. But he hadn't heard from Enzo either, and neither had Nico or Nonna Francesca.

Giovanni was sweet, and I spilled all my concerns about Enzo to him.

"We'll get to the bottom of this, Lucy," he said, patting my hand. "Don't you worry. But I'll tell you this. Enzo wouldn't take that job without talking to any of us. I know my brother. He'd ask them for time to think about it. And then he'd do the right thing and say *no*. He's crazy about you. I've never seen him happier than he is with you."

That had made me feel better, but I still finished my shift in a daze. Eileen asked me if I wanted to go home with her to crochet and make hot chocolate, but I said no.

Instead, I wandered to the Wishing Bridge.

This time I only wished for Enzo, with all my might, sitting at the edge of the bridge and throwing tiny stones over the side —until someone yelped.

Apparently the frigid weather hadn't made it less of a make-out spot.

My landline rang right after I walked through my front door. I lunged to answer it, certain the Wishing Bridge had worked its magic, but it was Charlie, calling because she was worried about me.

I lied and said I was fine, then called Enzo's number three times. Nothing. So I took a sleeping pill and fell into an uneasy sleep, only to wake up at three in the morning.

I instantly reached for my cell phone and found a message from his number:

> Men are better off without women. Period. Women lie and they cheat and they hold men back. They're all like Shannon, and he's better off without you. Sorry, but that's true.

I texted back multiple questions marks, but there was no response. The message obviously wasn't from Enzo. Even if he was drunk, he wouldn't say something like that and mean it.

So who had his phone?

Had something happened to him?

Or had he gone out drinking to celebrate his new job, and one of his friends had written me a kiss-off?

I didn't sleep any more that night, but I couldn't focus on anything, my mind skittering around like a wet spider.

❄

TODAY HAS PASSED in a horrible haze. Because there's a CLOSED sign in Hidden Italy's window, Nonna Francesca isn't at home, and Giovanni's cell phone isn't ringing.

"There must be a logical explanation," Charlie insisted after showing up at my apartment early this morning to check on me. But she didn't offer any other explanations.

The Bermuda Triangle might as well have swallowed the entire Cafiero family. It was weird, and we both knew it.

I sent several more texts to Enzo's phone before Charlie and I left my apartment for the Sip, but there was no answer.

"It's okay," Charlie said when she saw my furrowed brow. "Someone clearly stole his cell phone."

"The possibility that he was mugged does not make me feel better."

No, it just gave my fears more to chew on.

When we went into Love at First Sip, Eileen suggested I take the day off, but I refused. I needed something to do.

Enzo was gone. I didn't know what had happened to him or his phone or his *family*.

I might never see him again…

In the early afternoon, Amanda stopped in to get a couple of lattes. She took one look at my face and asked me what was wrong.

Ignoring the childish compulsion to say *everything*, I smiled and said, "It doesn't seem to be my day."

"Are you coming to the holiday dance later?" she asked.

I'd forgotten there was one. I just shook my head.

Concern creased her perfect face. "Go back to the Wishing Bridge, Lucy." She surprised me by pulling me in for a hug over the counter separating us. "I really feel like there's magic there."

"I will," I said, my mouth as dry as paper. All the water in my body seemed to be in the vicinity of my eyes. I wanted to cry but refused to. Because if I did, it would be like admitting that the worst had happened.

The hardest part was that I was worried about him *and* also worried he'd abandoned me. That he didn't care after all. That everything I'd dared to hope for had been a lie.

Now, it's two o'clock, and we're closing early by dictate of Eileen.

"We are going across the street to get some spiced cranberry cider," she says. "No arguments."

I don't try to argue. I can't. I don't know what I want—probably not cider, but I feel incapable of even voicing a protest. I feel a horrible powerlessness. I have no way of reaching Enzo, no way of knowing where he is or what he's doing.

No way of knowing if he still wants me...

All I know is that he told me he'd be home today, but New York City is at least eight hours away, so the earliest he could be back is three or maybe four o'clock this afternoon.

"All right, let's go," Wayne says.

"You're coming?" Eileen asks in disbelief.

"Yes," he replies simply.

And he does, sitting with us at a high-top table by the large front window in Kippis. The oversized Christmas tree in the town square is in full view, dressed in all of its splendor. It feels wrong for it to look like that. So beautiful. So cheerful.

The tears are close, but I still don't let them fall. Not when my friends are trying so hard to cheer me up.

"To Lucy," Charlie says, lifting her cider.

To my surprise, Wayne lifts his cup along with Eileen. "To Lucy."

"Who is nothing at all like Shannon," Charlie adds.

"Very funny," I grouse.

"Sorry," she says. "But you're not. And I think we can all agree that someone probably stole Enzo's cell phone. But he's a big, strong man, and I'm sure he's fine. In fact, I'll bet whoever took his phone is going to have some serious regrets about it. Enzo will be coming back anytime now."

"Tree's fallen across the road into town," the bartender calls out. "So any of you expecting out-of-town guests might want to call them."

Crap.

Abandoning my cider, I head up to the counter. "The road into town's really blocked?"

"Sure is," he says. "The mayor and his family are working with the crew to get it open before the town dance. Not a great time for us to get blocked off. Say, you heard from Enzo?"

"No," I say in a sour voice.

He lifts his hands defensively and turns to a different customer, not that I blame him. I wouldn't want to deal with me either.

I head back to the table.

Charlie purses her lips. "The messages seem to be on a delay today. I sent one to my parents earlier, and it still hasn't gone through."

Tears press at my eyes again, wanting to be released.

"I just need to know that he's okay," I say, finally letting some of them fall. "If he's changed his mind about me, that's fine. I understand."

"Give me your cell phone," Charlie says and presses her mouth into a tight line.

I do, and I watch as she types a message to Enzo's phone: *Did you hurt Enzo? If so, get ready to have your skin peeled from your cowardly hide.*

"You said the messages were on a delay," I say, tears streaming down my face.

"Oh, he'll get it eventually. And he'll respond. I promise. If the dude is this afraid of Shannon, he'll definitely answer a message like that. He'll squeal like a little pig."

"Let's talk of happier things," Eileen says. "Why don't we each share a lovely Christmas memory?"

Wayne rolls his eyes, but I notice he doesn't attempt to leave.

Later, Eileen encourages me to come to the dance and keep her company. "We'll drink cider and listen to music and think happy thoughts. Your man is coming home, my dear. I feel it."

I wish *I* felt it.

I go with her, because I might as well go with her. There's nowhere else I want to be, nowhere that will make me any less miserable with worry.

At the town dance, there's no sign of any Cafieros, even though the road is now open. So while the rec center is decorated beautifully and full of holiday cheer, I'm cold and numb inside.

My phone finally buzzes in my purse. I pull it out eagerly and discover a message from Enzo on the spiderwebbed screen:

> Oh, shit. I'm sorry. This is Barry. I'm on this epic bender, and I took your dude's coat by mistake because it was in my cubicle at work. And, yeah, I'm sorry. No need to get violent, man. A woman did me wrong, but it wasn't cool for me to speak for Lorenzo.

Some of my worry is soothed away. Enzo *was* robbed, but by an idiot. Still, I have no idea where he is or whether he's coming home, or anything.

> Do you know where he is?????

Surprisingly, the response comes quickly:

> Naw, man. But he's not at his place. I went there to try to give him his things back. Really, I did. His car is in the parking deck, though.

> Dude, I didn't try to steal it, so don't think that.

> But I tried the key fob just to see, you know?

I rub my forehead. The Christmas music spouting over the speakers in the rec center is giving me a headache suddenly.

Home. I'll go home and wait. If Enzo comes back, he'll find me there. But where can he be if he's not at his old apartment and he doesn't have his car?

I glance at the dance floor—Charlie is slow-dancing with Lars, and I won't interrupt them. I feel like I've already demanded enough from them. But I also don't want my friends to worry. So I tell the DJ that I'm leaving and ask him to give the message to Charlie.

I walk home quickly, my coat wrapped tightly around me. I planned on face-planting on my bed, hugging my stuffed cat, and disassociating for a while, but I find myself rummaging through my sock drawer until I find it: my mother's letter about the kind of man she wanted me to marry someday. *Mr. Perfect.*

Tears pressing at my eyes, I stuff it into my coat pocket, and then I'm out the door again, heading to the Wishing Bridge.

Halfway there, Skippy falls in beside me, wagging his tail, and a few of those tears drop, because it feels like he was waiting for me. Wanting to escort me. I bury my hand in his fur, petting him, and call him the good boy he is.

Finally, I reach the bridge, and I practically collapse onto it, Skippy lying down at my feet. I pull out the letter, unfold it, and read…

Lucy—

I love you too much to let you make the same mistakes I did.

Make sure you find a kind man—a man who thinks of others before himself. A man who will give the shirt off his back to a neighbor in need.

And, for the love of God, don't choose a man who's arrogant or ambitious.

If he's arrogant, he'll think his needs are more important than yours, and they're not. Mine weren't either, even though I've let you give up so much to take care of me.

Ambition poisons men. Your father left us because my sickness didn't fit into his plans, but a man should always leave room in his life for what's unplanned. So find a man who puts love before ambition, my dear. Money is well and good, and we all need it, but live with money, not for it.

Find a man who values community, because you, my dear, were not built for isolation. You deserve to be surrounded by people who love you just as much as you deserve a house that's truly a home.

I like imagining you with a big family, Lucy. A lovely big family.

I only wish I could see it, my dear girl.

And, finally, find a man who abhors games and speaks his emotions. You deserve plain speaking.

I love you so much.

Know that wherever I am, I miss you.

The most beautiful gift I had in this life was being your mother.

Enzo still doesn't fit her description of the perfect man. He's too ambitious. Too aware of his own talents and good looks. Too guarded. He's also very capable of playing games…

And yet, so am I. Is it so wrong for us to enjoy these games together?

"I love him, Mom," I whisper to the sky. "He may not be exactly the man you envisioned for me, but he *is* kind and bighearted and so loyal. He's the one I want, and I want him to come home. *Please* let him come home to me."

A sudden gust of wind captures the letter, and I watch, open-mouthed with horror as it rises up on the wind, stolen.

"That's mine," I say, rising to my feet, terrified it will fall into the burbling water and be gone forever. Skippy gets up beside me, panting, his gaze following the sheet of well-worn paper as another gust blows it out beyond the bridge, into the road.

I race after it, nearly face-planting in snow as I slip on a patch of ice. But I keep my feet and continue in pursuit of it.

I nearly smack right into Charlie—because she and Lars were hurrying up the path to the bridge.

I want to ask why they're here, but I need that letter. It's a piece of my mother I won't give away.

"Get that paper," I cry out.

Lars, who has much longer legs than I do, lunges for it. He *almost* catches it, but another breeze snatches it out of his hand at the last instant, whisking it down the road—past Eileen, who was following them.

"What are you guys doing here?" I ask, wheezing, as I rush after the paper.

"The DJ told us you were leaving, and someone saw you

walking toward the bridge. We wanted to make sure you didn't jump off," Charlie splutters as I scuttle past her.

"We wanted you to know you have a family here in Hideaway Harbor," Eileen proclaims, her breath coming quickly too as we all try to capture the paper. "And that we love you, Lucy. Everyone was worried about you tonight. Several people came by to ask about you."

Oh God, I want to hug her. To hug all of them. But I *need* that paper.

"It's my mom's letter," I gasp as Lars makes another grab for it—thwarted at the last moment, as if the paper's teasing him. "The wind ripped it away from me while I was on the bridge."

Something flashes in Eileen's eyes, and she shouts, "Stop, Lars! We have to follow the letter, not try to capture it."

"Eileen?" I blurt, whipping around to face her, hysteria bubbling inside me.

"It's taking us somewhere," she insists excitedly.

Enzo would think it's complete bullshit.

He'd probably be right, but my heart is so bruised and aching that I want to believe. I *need* to believe.

Lars darts a questioning glance at me. I nod, and the four of us continue our pursuit as the paper flits along the street, almost hovering in the air.

It's uncanny. A strange feeling comes over me, the same way it did on the bridge the night it snowed for me.

It's as if my mother is speaking to me.

And then, when my legs are tired and sore, and my heart wants nothing more than to return home and sleep…that's when it happens.

The letter gusts around a corner and slaps into someone, who reaches up to capture it with his hand.

It's him.

It's Enzo, wearing the Santa coat from that photo.

He came back to me.

And gathered behind him are the rest of the Cafieros.

I run to him, tears streaming down my face, and he captures me in his strong arms. And when he pulls me close, my face buried in his neck, I feel it.

I'm home.

"Oh, Lucia," he says, his voice husky. He kisses the side of my face, then my lips when I turn them toward him. "Thank God. Thank God you're here. I've had the craziest twenty-four hours. I've never needed anything like I needed to see you right now. We've been on the road for…I don't even know how long, but Giovanni and Nico broke every traffic law to get here as soon as possible."

"They still went too slow," Nonna Francesca murmurs. "I thought I teach you to drive better than that."

"Did you take the job?" I ask, needing him to tell me. To confirm what the flying letter has already seemed to say.

"No," he says, then pauses. "Well…I guess I forgot to tell Martin I didn't take it—I was too concerned about getting home to you—but I'm sure he got the message. This is my home, Lucia. Here with you."

"You're my home too," I say, staring up into his eyes. Marveling at how far we've come.

"I love you," he says as he stares into my eyes.

"I love you too," I say, lifting up a hand to cradle his face, seeping in the goodness of this moment. He came home to me. He loves me. And my mom…

I'm convinced she would approve of him. Everything feels so good, so sweet.

I kiss him again, then draw away and say, "Now, who's Barry, and why does he have your phone?"

"That little twerp's the one who took it?" He shakes his head, laughing a little. "He's Santa Claus."

CHAPTER 35

ENZO

"*Che botta al cuore*," my grandfather used to say when something big happened.

What a hit to the heart.

My family had thought I was making the worst mistake of my life—and even though they were wrong, they'd shown up at the exact moment I needed them most. They'd shown up for me the way I'd always shown up for them, and it had solidified something for me. I wasn't the rock expected to take care of his whole family. No, we were a family of people who took care of each other. A family we all wanted Lucy to be part of.

And ten hours—of insufferable bickering, traffic stops, and Nico's constant demands for piss breaks—later, we finally reached Hideaway Harbor.

But Lucy wasn't home at her apartment or in the rec center, where the dance was letting out. So I went to search the bridge, the place where we'd both gone looking for answers at the beginning of the month.

My family and I were only partway there when her mother's letter, flying in the wind, hit me in the chest like a homing pigeon.

A hit to the heart indeed.

When I finally wrapped my arms around her, it felt so deeply right there was a burning behind my eyes.

Still is. I can't seem to let her go. I'm not going to cry, obviously, but I've come much closer to tears than I'd like.

Lucia. My Lucy. My woman.

A mutual love for competition brought us together, and I'm determined nothing will ever tear us apart. She makes me want something more than professional success.

"I'm taking her home," I say, turning toward my family, Lucy still in my arms. "Thank you. God, thank you so much."

My grandmother smacks my arm. "Don't be late for dinner tomorrow. You both will stay at the house afterward. Nico and Giovanni too."

It's not a question. I glance at Lucy for her response—because if it's a no for her, I'll do battle with my grandmother.

But Lucy nods, her face glowing. "We will."

We walk hand in hand to her apartment, and once we're there, we take a shower together while I tell her all about Barry and Santa Claus and getting locked out.

"Rachelle tried to seduce you?" she asks with a degree of jealousy I appreciate as I glide the washcloth over her body.

"I don't think she put much effort into it."

She smiles at me and slides her hand over my cock. "Now, I'm even more insulted. I'd expect way better than a token effort for all of this."

"The things you do to me," I say.

"I can do more of them, if you'd like."

"Oh, absolutely, I would like."

Later, she lets me read the letter she wrote me when she was worried I wouldn't come home, and I feel a steely resolve form inside of me. I never want her to feel like that again, like I might have abandoned her.

I will *never* abandon her.

On Christmas Eve morning, I use Lucia's landline to call Barry and negotiate the return of my cell phone, wallet, and car keys.

I warn him not to go into my apartment, under any circumstances, and I learn he's already been in there.

Why am I not surprised?

Apparently, he found a self-help book my sister gave me for Christmas two years ago as a gag gift—*How to Unfuck Your Life*—and it's changed his life.

Afterward, I call Martin to inform him that I won't be taking the job.

"I figured as much when you ghosted us," he says gruffly, not at all amused. "I didn't take you for that sort, Enzo."

Maybe I should accept his criticism and move on with my life. But I'm not the sort. So I say, "I'm not."

I tell him about being robbed by a drunk Santa—and end by thanking him for the opportunity but insisting that I'm where I need to be, with my family. All of them. To my surprise, he says he'll be in touch about freelance opportunities.

I'll probably take a few jobs like that, but I've decided where my focus needs to be for the next several months—helping Lucy bring CareWise to life. With the two of us working together, it can hardly fail.

Is it arrogant of me to think so? Abso-fucking-lutely. But if there's one thing I disagree with Lucy's mom about, it's the dangers of arrogance. There's nothing wrong with having confidence in your abilities, so long as you have the balls to back it up.

After I'm done making calls, I have one more trick to pull off...

Lucy's present.

"Uh, no," Lucy says when I tell her I have an errand to run.

"You're not going anywhere without me right now. You will have a literal stalker everywhere you go."

"What if Giovanni comes with me?"

She considers this for a long moment before nodding. "Okay. But I swear to God, if you disappear for hours on end, I *will* come find you."

"Is that supposed to be a threat?" I ask, laughing as I pull her to me by the tantalizing little ribbon securing the collar of her sweater.

"It *is* a threat."

"You can always come find me. Except for now. Definitely don't try now. It would ruin everything."

She gives me a suspicious look. "You're being very mysterious."

"Thank God, I'm glad it's working. I'll be right back."

HALF AN HOUR LATER, I return with her present wrapped in a warm blanket.

I knock on the door, and Lucy opens it with a gasp. "What's this?"

"Your present is ready early," I tell her as I walk in, and shut the door behind me, "and I didn't want to give it to you in front of everyone."

I offer her the bundle, and she takes it from me—and gasps when the little calico kitten meows.

"He's yours," I say out loud.

Ours, I say in my head, because I'm a man who's all about efficiency, and there's nothing efficient about living down the hall from your girlfriend.

"But Enzo, we can't have pets in this building. I won't be able to keep him."

The way she says it, so sorrowful, makes me grin. Not

because I'm cruel, but because we've just gotten to my real present—

"You will," I say, my heart full as I watch her burrow her nose into the kitten's fur. "Did I not tell you I can convince anyone of anything, Lucia?"

She gapes at me, her surprise totally worth the price of talking to the landlord for several hours to negotiate the kitten's stay. One of the harder bargains I've made. I also tried to convince Bodhi Wilde to hand over the only kitten at his cat sanctuary, but he'd grown too fond of it, so I had to go elsewhere.

"You did this for me?" she asks, setting the kitten down.

"And I'd do so much more."

She wraps her arms around my neck. "I love you, Enzo."

I've never heard sweeter words.

"I love you too, Dancing Queen." I bend my head and kiss her before turning to the cat to rub his little head. "What are you going to name him?"

She grins at me, then at the kitten. "He looks an awful lot like a Lobster Stalker."

"A terrible name, Lucia."

"It's a perfect name. Incidentally, it's time for your present, but it's going to look lame in comparison now."

"Excellent," I say, tapping my fingers together. "I'm pleased to have won the gift-off."

She laughs and kisses my cheek before going to the hall closet to pull out a wrapped gift. "Do not, under pain of death, shake it, Enzo. You'll ruin everything."

I open it—and laugh my ass off when I see it's a framed poster for *Cats* the movie. "Do I have to put it up?"

"It's a joke," she says, nudging my shoulder with hers. "Open up the frame and take the poster out."

I painstakingly follow her directions, and what I find has me grinning stupidly at her. Beneath the poster is a big-headed sketch of us, like the bobblehead caricature drawings she talked about the night she was drunk off buttered rum. The sketch portrays her drawing a mustache on my face with a green marker.

"This is epic," I say, kissing her. "But it was red."

She laughs. "It looked like you a had a bloody lip, so we had to stretch reality."

"Did you get Charlie to do this?"

"She took a break from her oil painting of the German shepherd because she loves me."

"It's going over our mantel."

She raises her eyebrows, but there's a smile dancing on her lips. "Pretty presumptuous."

"Damn straight. It won't happen today, and it probably won't happen next week, but it's going to happen."

"Well, if Enzo Cafiero says it's going to happen…"

We walk to my grandmother's house, hand in hand, carrying Lobster Stalker in the pet carrier that's been hiding in my closet. My heart is full, and I have nothing but goodwill in my chest for everyone we pass. Even Hudson.

When we get to my grandmother's house, I knock on the door, and Aria answers. She has a deep tan, offset by her red sweater, and her dark hair is loose around her shoulders.

I nearly drop Lobster Stalker's carrier.

"You little fucking liar," I say, setting him on the doorstep. I squeeze Lucy's hand and then hug my sister, who's laughing maniacally.

"Finally. Finally, I got one over on you. It's only taken twenty-five years."

I give her a hug powerful enough to lift her off her feet. When I release her, she turns toward Lucy and immediately wraps her in a bear hug. "Oh my God. I'm Aria, and I can't wait to become friends with you. I've been trying to imagine the woman who could get through to Enzo, and I just know the reality is going to be better than my imagination could ever be. How did this asshole win you over, anyway?"

Lucy grins and looks at me affectionately. "He crashed my date and drew a poster of me with a hairy mole on my forehead. Then he lent me his scarf without telling me everyone in Hideaway Harbor would know it was his."

Aria laughs, delighted. "What a charmer! And you fell for him anyway. Good for you, Enzo. Too bad for you, Lucy, but I'm not sorry about it."

Lucy wraps her arms around my waist. "Neither am I."

"She left out the part where I saved her from a Porta Potty," I say, and Lucy tickles me. She *tickles* me. And I'll be damned if I don't laugh.

Christmas music starts playing inside the house—Nonna's choice, I'm guessing, because it's Dean Martin—and Giovanni dances into view with a nonexistent partner.

"Dance with Nonna, you goon," Aria yells, and we walk inside with Lobster Stalker.

"I warn you now, Lucia," I tell her, "we converse by yelling in this family."

"I knew I felt at home for a reason," she says, her eyes shining.

WE SPEND the rest of the day cooking for the Feast of the Seven Fishes, something Nonna insists we all do together, even though only she, Nico, Lucy, and Aria have any skill in the kitchen.

It's loud, it's chaotic. Nonna nearly throws a plate at Lobster Stalker when he tries to steal a shrimp.

I wouldn't prefer to be anywhere else in the world.

When we feast together, it feels like we earned it. Other friends stop by to enjoy some of the courses with us. Portia arrives first with Amanda, whom Aria is clearly starstruck over but tries not to be obvious about it. Eileen arrives shortly afterward.

She sits down at the empty place setting next to Lucy and says, "Giovanni's next, I think."

"Next for what?" I ask.

Lucy mimes a chopping block.

"Next to be murdered?" I guess, giving her a wry smile.

"Next to fall in love," Eileen says in a dreamy voice.

I feel like they're counting on me to make some kind of joke, but I don't have it in me. I'm too full of joy, of the feeling of family.

"You're right," I say. "He's actually been helping me screw my head on straight ever since I came home. And I get the sense he's a little heartbroken over his ex-girlfriend."

Eileen grimaces.

"Oh no, Eileen..." Lucy makes a face, glancing across the table at Giovanni, who's telling an animated story to Aria, who seems more interested in our conversation. "You're the one who set his ex up with someone else, aren't you?"

"All will be resolved," Eileen says enigmatically. "I'll find the perfect woman for him in no time." She sighs and says, "You know, I never thought I'd say this, but it's too bad Charlie's getting married."

"*Eileen*," Lucy says, while I laugh.

"Oh, I'm only kidding. She's much too similar to him anyway. A person needs their foil. I'll be giving this plenty of thought."

"Giovanni won't know what hit him," I say with a laugh.

Just then, my grandmother bangs on the table, hard enough that the baccalà jumps on its plate. "I have an announcement to make."

"Come on, Nonna, you don't need to scare us all to death," Aria says, rolling her eyes.

She gets the glare she knows she's earned. Then our grandmother turns to the table as a whole, wagging a finger at us, "You think I haven't noticed you children taking turns spending the night at my house?"

We exchange glances, because yeah, we figured we'd gotten away with it, or that she hadn't minded enough to question it.

"Well, I have noticed. I may be old, but I'm not stupid," she says. "There's no need to interrupt your lives to be here every night. If it becomes necessary for me to have someone every night, I'll hire a companion." She nods to Lucy. "Lucia has offered to help me find someone."

I gape at her, shocked by the easy use of my nickname for her as much as the offer. "What is it with the women in my life pulling one over on me lately?"

"You owe me at least that for the five heart attacks you gave me this week," Lucy murmurs.

"There will be no further discussion on this," Nonna says regally. Then she adds aggressively, "Why has no one tried the baccalà? You must all eat, *eat*."

We stuff ourselves and then watch Christmas movies in the family room before we walk to the church together for midnight mass—the one time of year all of us grandchildren go to church with Nonna.

Church lets out at midnight, and we spill out together, the whole city seeming to glow with twinkle lights.

"It's Christmas," Aria says with a glow. "Let's make snow angels."

Lucy grins up at me, and I don't even ask if she wants to do it. I know. So I grab her hand, and we run over to join Aria on the snow-covered lawn—all of us flopping down onto it to make angel impressions in the days-old snow with our arms and legs outstretched.

The snow is disgusting, but I feel brilliantly alive.

"Let's go put a hat and gloves on Nico's ice sculpture to see if it comes to life," Lucy suggests when we get up, panting from the freezing cold.

"Oh, come on, Lucy," Nico gripes. "I thought we were friends."

"I have enough nightmares," Giovanni tells her with a theatrical shudder. "But I'm all for putting a ski mask on it so we don't have to see his ugly mug every time we go to the Locke Reserve."

"Children," Nonna says regally. "You will all be going home and getting snug in your beds so Santa can come bring you some coal."

"I wouldn't want to miss my coal," Lucy said. "And I definitely don't want to upset Mrs. Cafiero, so I'm all for going home."

Nonna pats Lucy on the shoulder. "You're a good girl. You can call me Nonna."

Lucy is mine, and she's already been accepted as part of my family. It may only be just after midnight, but I swear to God, it's already the best Christmas a man could possibly have.

EPILOGUE

LUCY

I laugh with delight when I see Enzo's handwriting on the whiteboard sign outside of Love at First Sip. *Daily Special: Iced Frenemy Cappuccino! Half off!*

It's a Saturday in September, cool and breezy, and he asked me to meet him here after Charlie and I took a walk at the Locke Reserve.

"Weren't those cappuccinos incredibly gross?" Charlie asks.

"Incredibly," I say with my heart in my throat, because it's obvious from the whiteboard Enzo has something planned. Enzo always has something planned, and I'm the lucky recipient of all of his grand gestures. "He must want to celebrate CareWise."

We just launched our app—ours, because ultimately he's had as much of a hand in it as I have—and the interest it's generating has stunned me. Humbled me.

Nonna Francesca has already used it to pick out a home helper named Tess, who starts in two weeks. The Cafieros have had a range of different reactions to this news. Aria, still working in Greece, thinks it's a godsend. Enzo and Nico are relieved. And Giovanni, who's so easygoing about everything, is surprisingly displeased. He insists they don't need anyone else to help them take care of her, although that's increasingly untrue.

I've met Tess, and she's brisk and no-nonsense, exactly the sort of person most likely to survive as Nonna's helper.

"Because you're a bad bitch businesswoman," Charlie quips, nudging my shoulder, but I see something in her eyes—she knows what this is all about.

I pause before opening the door, even though I see Enzo waiting in front of the counter, Eileen behind it. "What did he do?"

"I've been sworn to silence on pain of death."

Laughing, I open the door.

"Are you here for a Frenemy?" Enzo says, his eyes dancing with mischief.

"I've been told I enjoy a good argument," I say, grinning at him. "You look like an idiot."

It's very untrue, but he does have a red marker mustache with curly ends on his face.

Someone laughs, and I glance over and am surprised to see Giovanni, Nico, Lars, and Nonna Francesca are sitting at the tables. Wayne, too, of course.

Giovanni lifts his hand. "I can't draw like you, Luce, but I did my best."

I peer at Enzo, my lips parting. "Is this some kind of party?"

"I hope so," he says, taking a to-go cup from Eileen, who's beaming.

My heart starts to beat faster as I take the cup from him. I glance inside of it, and see the shape of a diamond ring drawn into the top layer of the foam.

I set the drink down.

"You won't taste it?" he asks, even as he pulls a marker out of his pocket.

My heart beating fast, I say, "Isn't that my move?"

"It's my turn."

It is. We've taken to playing with our markers. Last week, I drew a blemish on his face with a red one after he made a dirty play in Strip Monopoly.

He takes my hand and writes onto the back of it: *Will you marry me, Lucia?*

Then he gets down on one knee and pulls out a little red box.

Tears press at my eyes as I open it and find an absurdly gorgeous diamond ring—a large central diamond surrounded by tiny red stones.

"Of course I'll marry you," I say, pulling him up, laughing even as the first tears fall. "You had to bring witnesses?"

He kisses the side of my face, my lips. "I thought you'd want to share this moment with our family."

This man knows me down to my bones, and he loves me, just as I am—the same way I love him.

"You *are* a smart man, and I don't care if it blows your ego to the stratosphere for me to say so."

"You agreeing to marry me has already done that," he says with a grin.

"Good," Nonna says with a stomp of her foot. "Now, we eat. Nico, where is the food? Giovanni, take more pictures. Someone has to take pictures for Aria."

Chaos breaks out, and it's good. Everything is exactly as it should be.

My gaze lifts and finds Eileen's, and I see she's watching Giovanni with a speculative glint in her eyes.

I laugh, and she gives a decisive nod. *He's next.*

READY FOR MORE HOLIDAY FUN IN Hideaway Harbor? Next up…
The Holiday Fakers by Evie Alexander

One fake boyfriend. One bed.

One very complicated Christmas ...

Piper

I promised my mom I'd bring a boyfriend home for the holidays.

I did not mean Brody King—Hollywood heartthrob, tabloid trainwreck, and the reason I have a folder of fantasy fan art I'll take to the grave.

He's also my brother's ex–best friend and the man who ghosted our small town (and me) twelve years ago.

Now we're sharing one bed, faking a relationship, and pretending he's changed.

The problem? I'm starting to believe it.

But Brody doesn't do forever.

And I don't do heartbreak twice.

Brody

The plan was simple: come home, look reformed, and don't fall for Piper Locke. Again.

Instead, I'm stuck in a snow-globe town with the girl I never stopped wanting.

Piper's smart, hilarious, way too sexy—and still completely off-limits.

She thinks I'll leave like last time.

And she's right. My next job's a world away from Hideaway Harbor.

But this fake relationship feels dangerously real, and Piper isn't just a PR fix.

She's the reason I want to stay.

Too bad I'm the last person who deserves her... and the one person who can't seem to walk away.

The Holiday Fakers is a laugh-out-loud, one-bed, fake-dating romcom with festive flair and serious steam. If you love small-town chaos, slow-burn tension, and a guaranteed happily ever after, this book is your perfect cozy escape.

CHECK out the whole Christmas at Hideaway Harbor series!
- The Holiday Hate-Off by Angela Casella
- The Holiday Fakers by Evie Alexander
- The Holiday Whoopie by Sara L. Hudson
- The Holiday Post by L.B. Dunbar
- The Holiday Clause by Lydia Michaels
- The Holiday Grump by Enni Amanda

ALL BOOKS ARE INTERCONNECTED standalones and can be read in any order.

ABOUT THE AUTHOR

ANGELA CASELLA is a romcom fanatic. Writing them, reading them, watching them—she's greedy, and she does it all. In addition to her solo releases, she was lucky enough to collaborate with Denise Grover Swank on three complete series.

She lives in Asheville, NC. Her hobbies include herding her daughter toward less dangerous activities, the aforementioned romcom addiction, and dreaming of having someone else clean her house.

Visit her website at www.angelacasella.com